AF538824

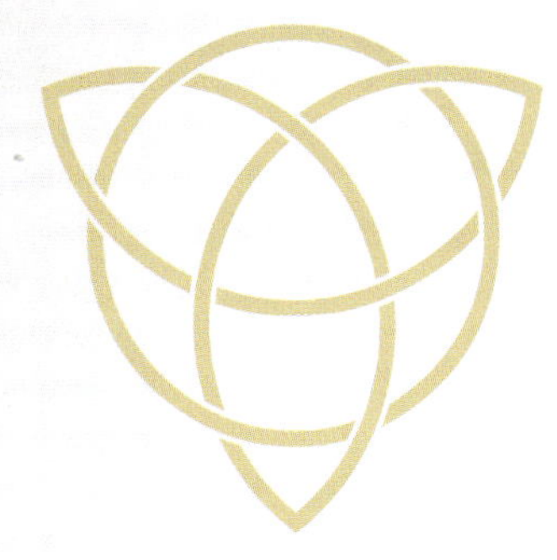

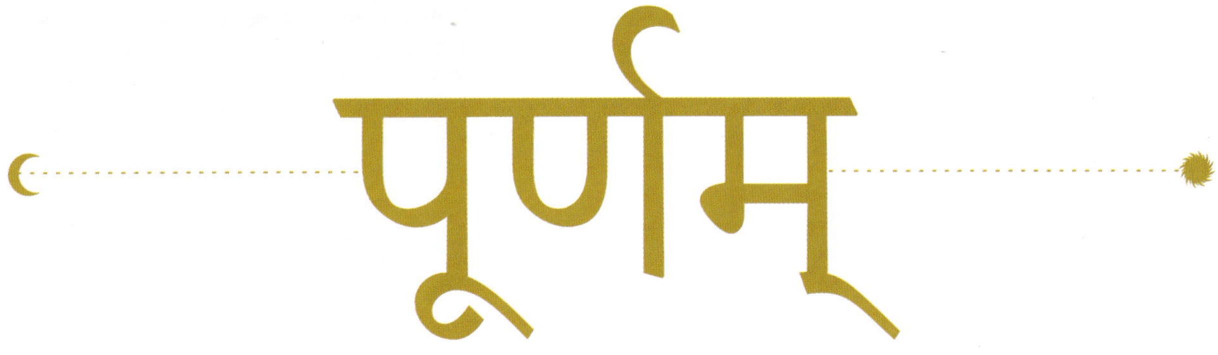

PURNAM

STORIES & WISDOM OF THE FEMININE DIVINE

ABHISHEK SINGH

Wonder House

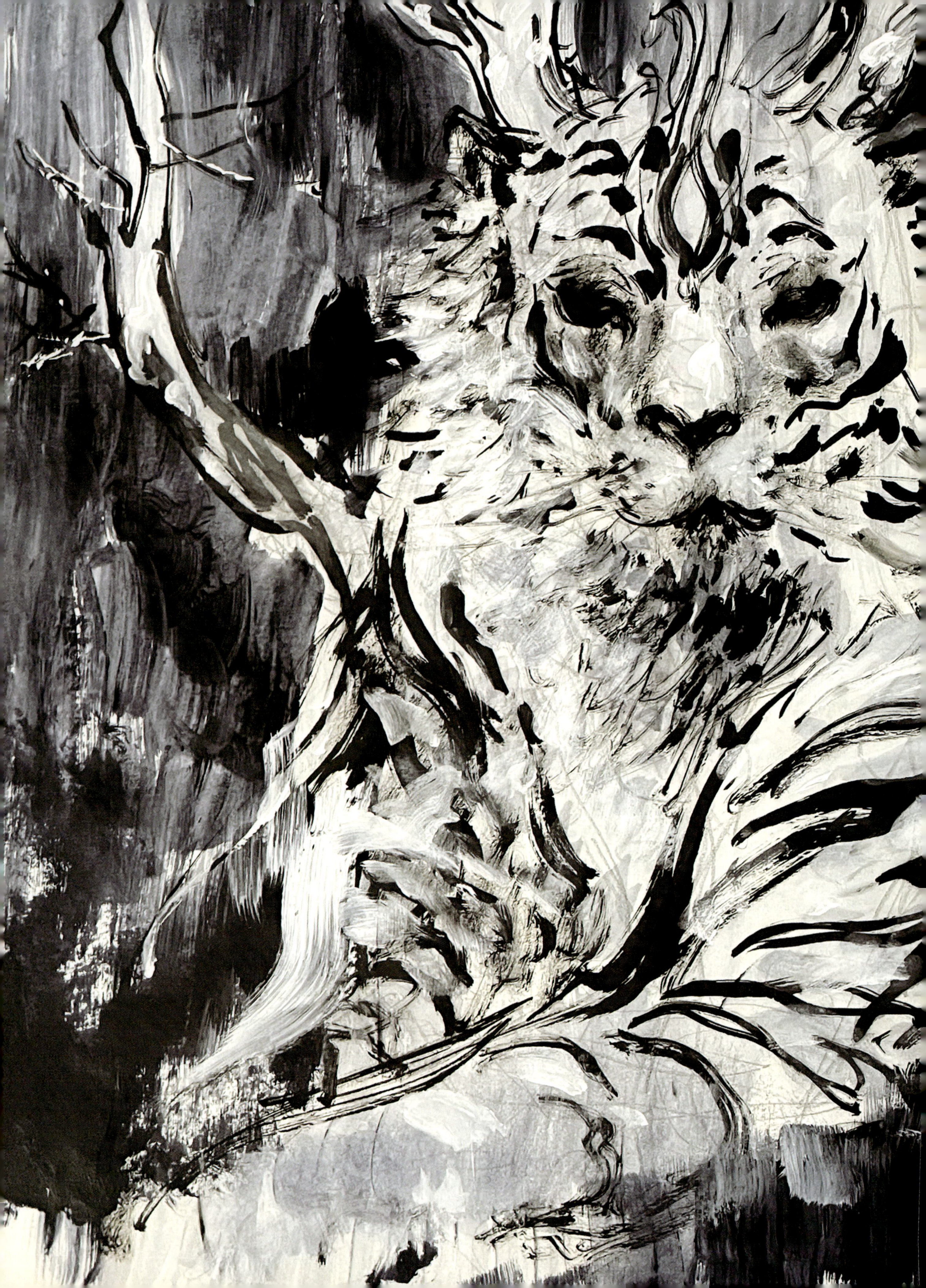

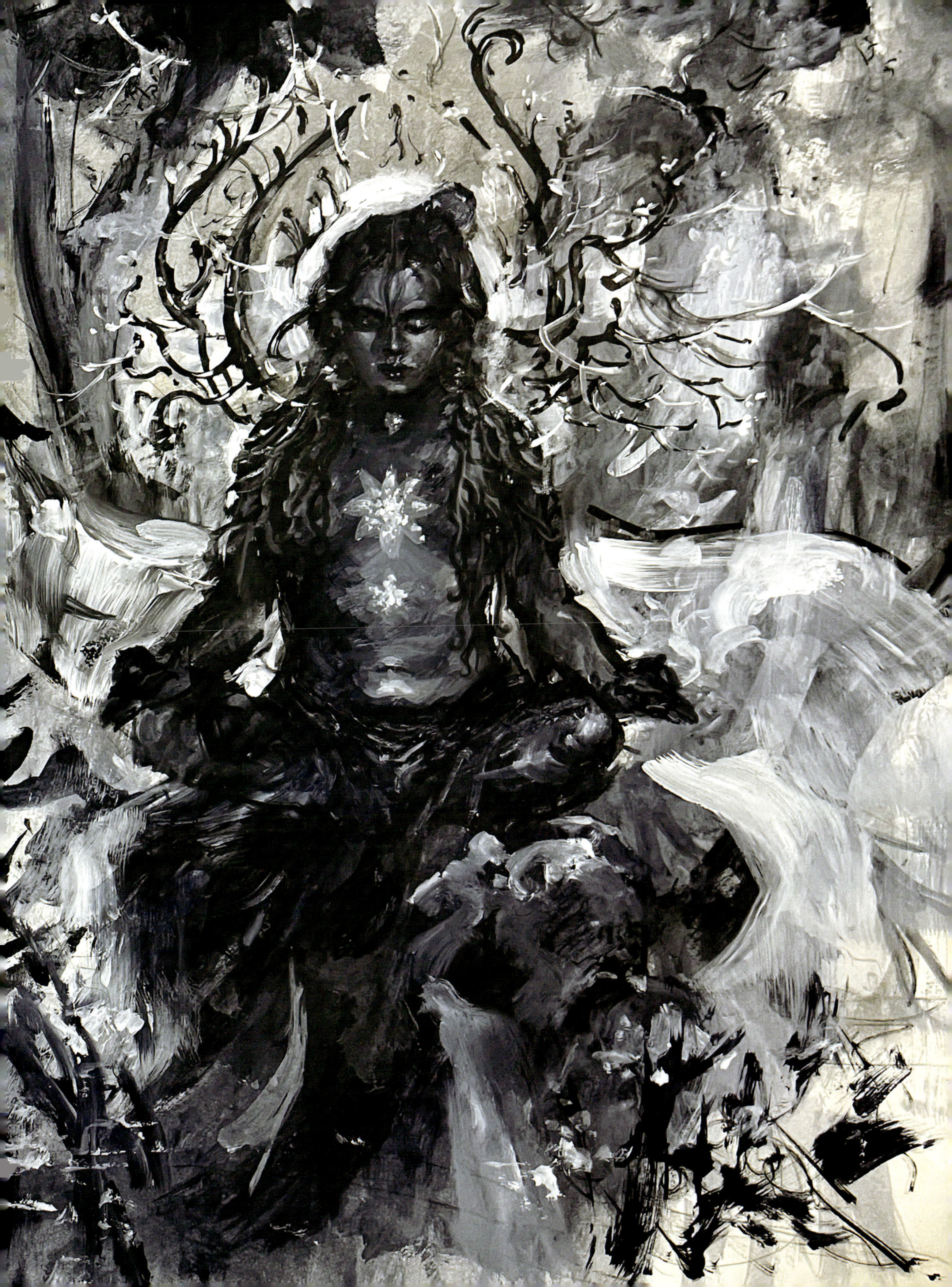

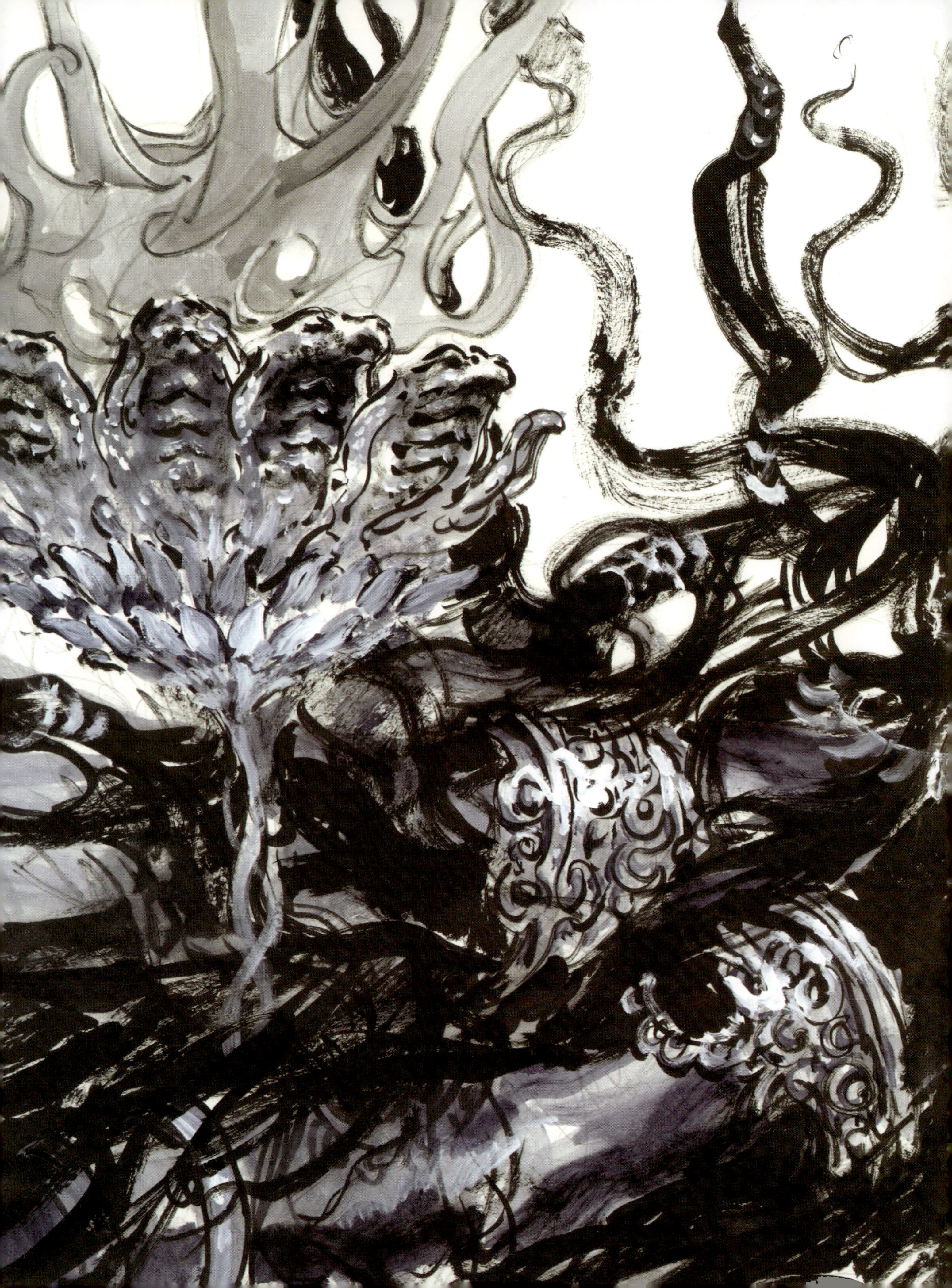

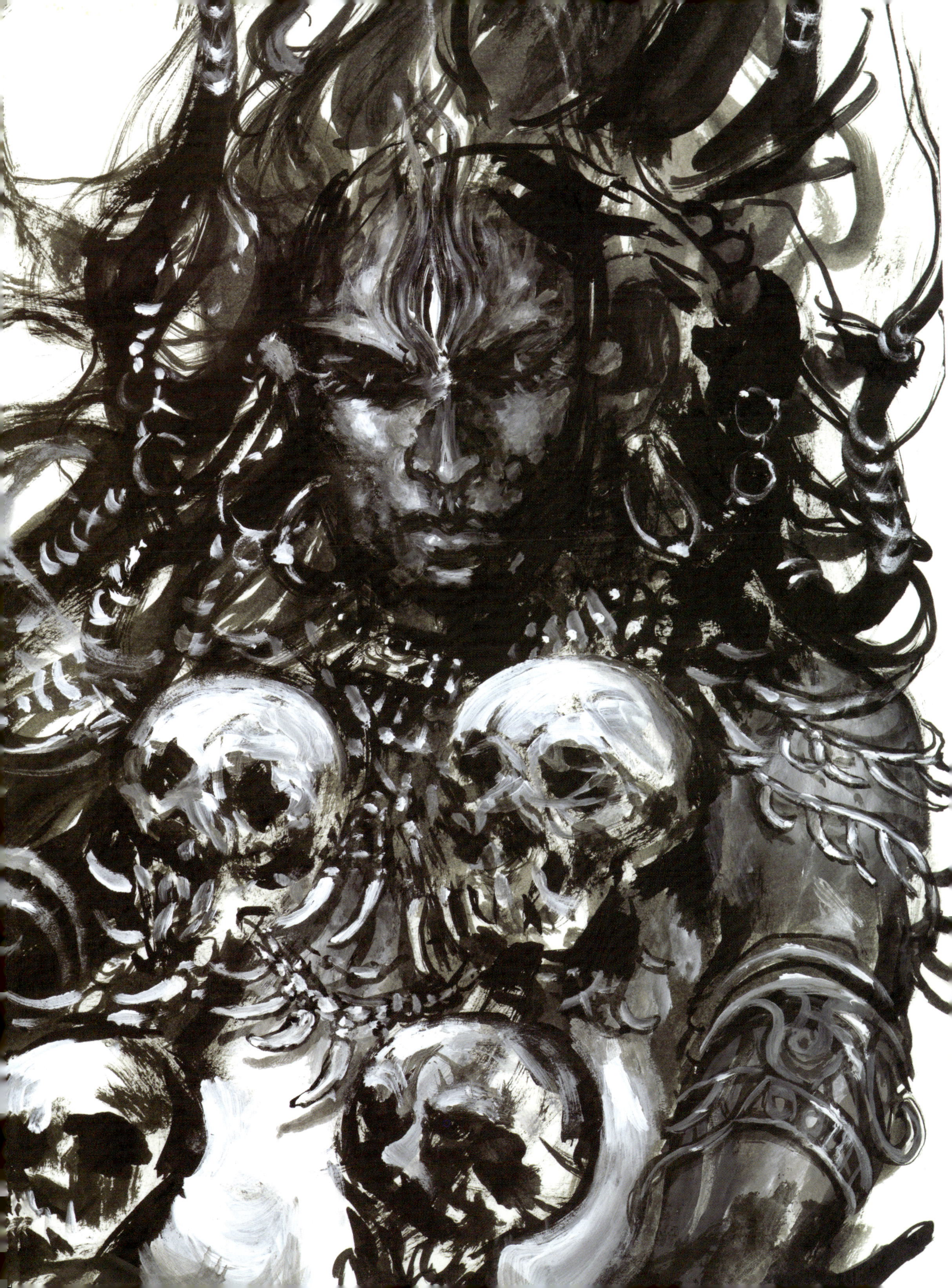

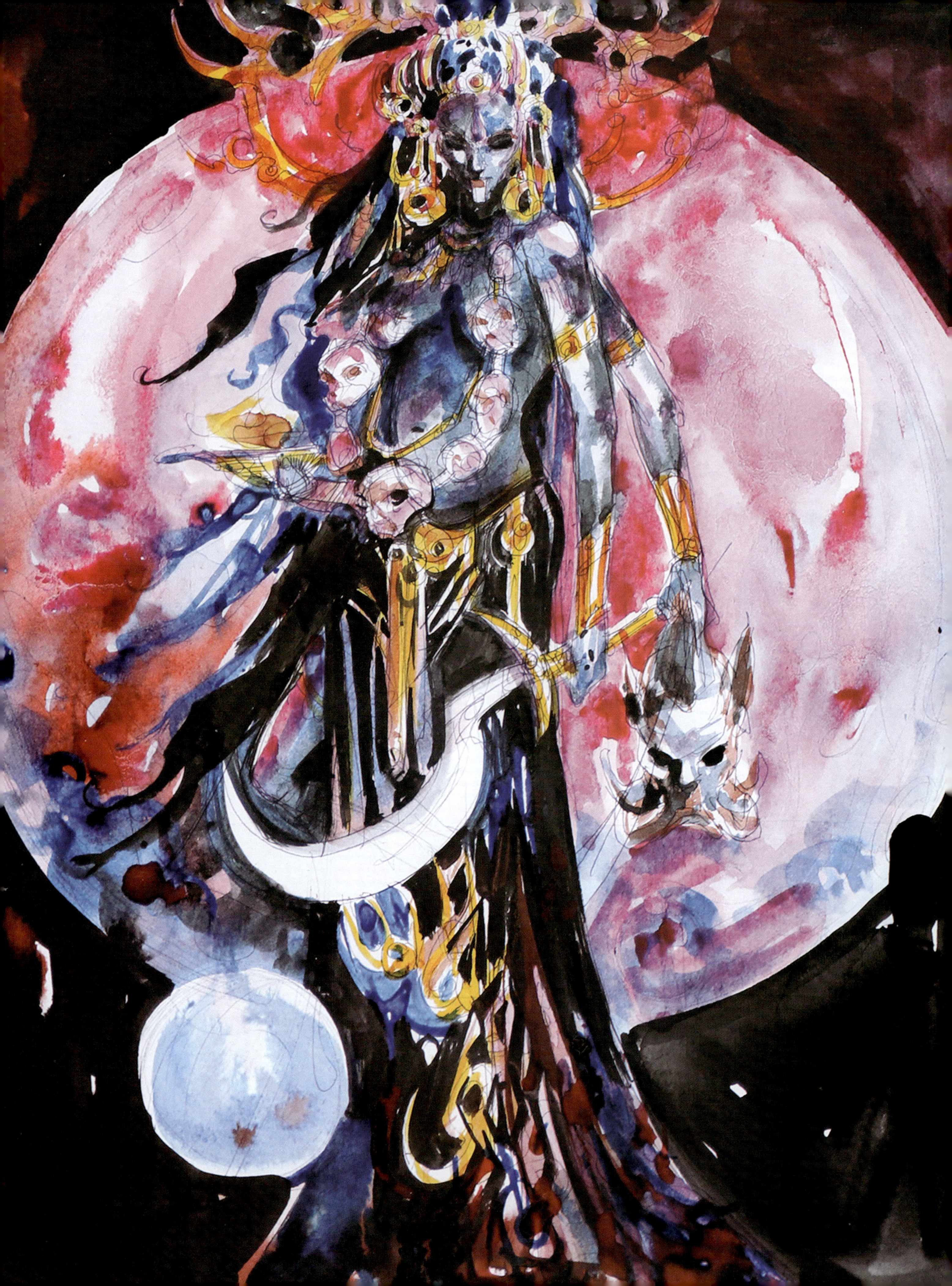

STORIES

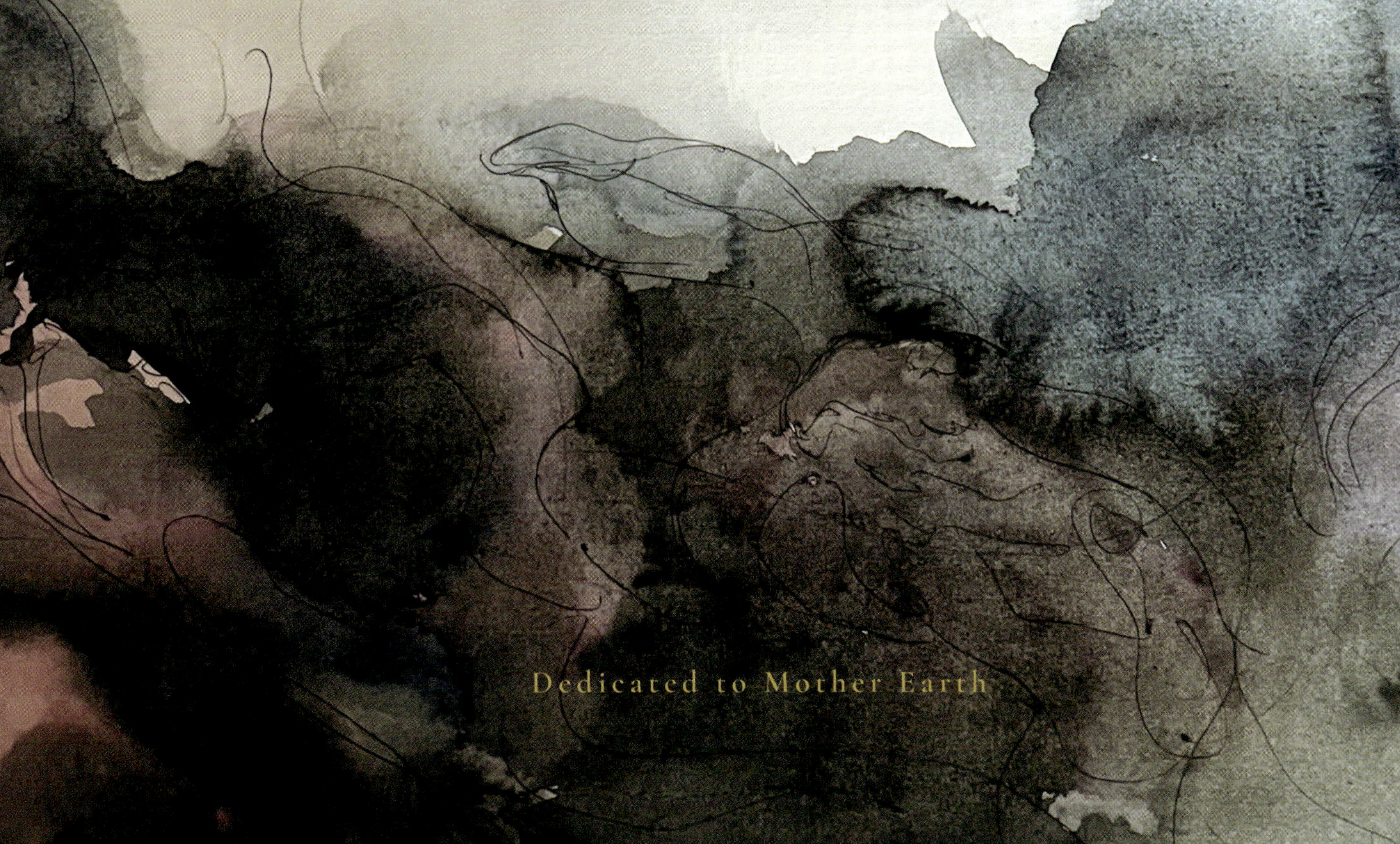

Dedicated to Mother Earth

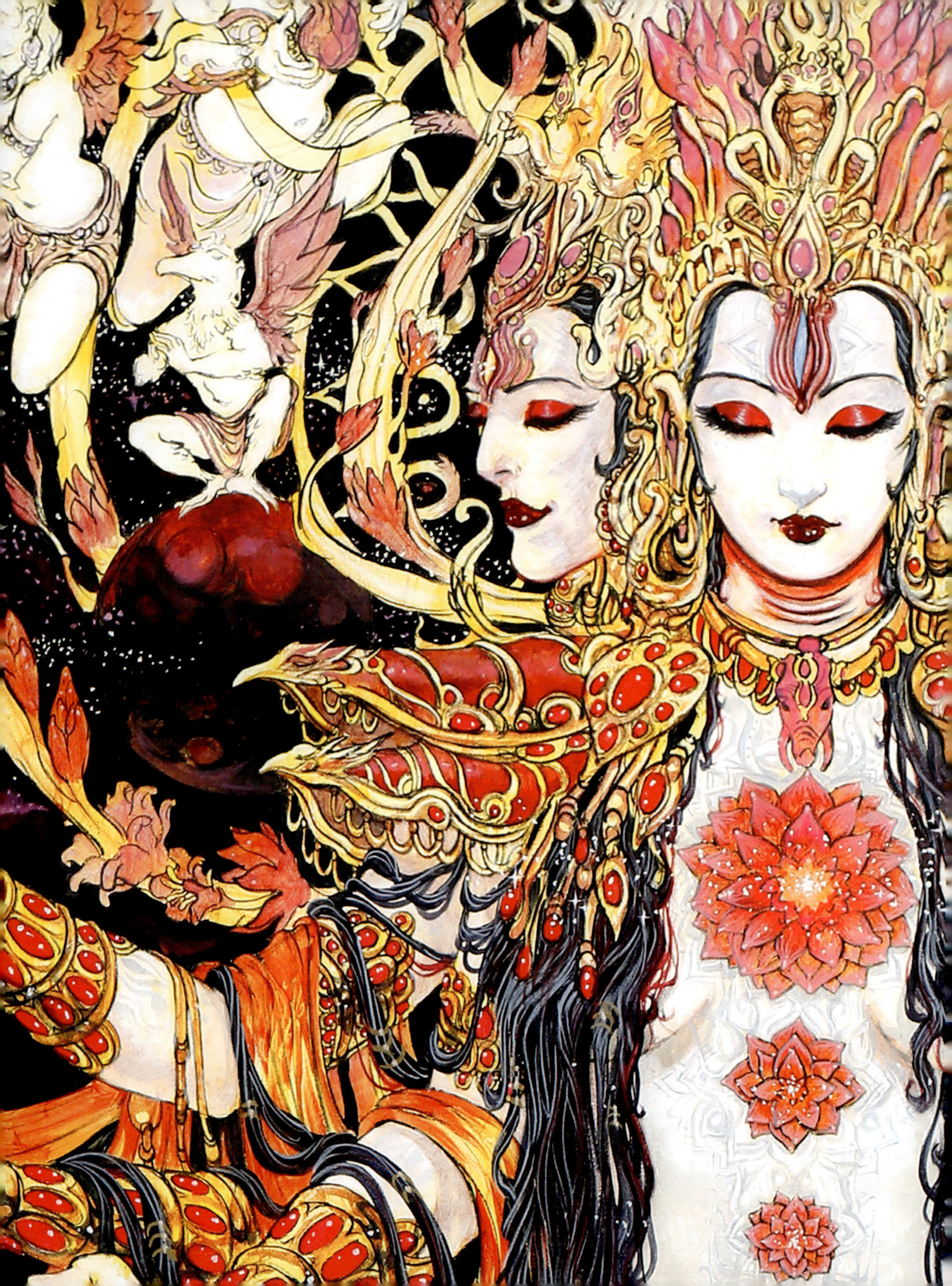

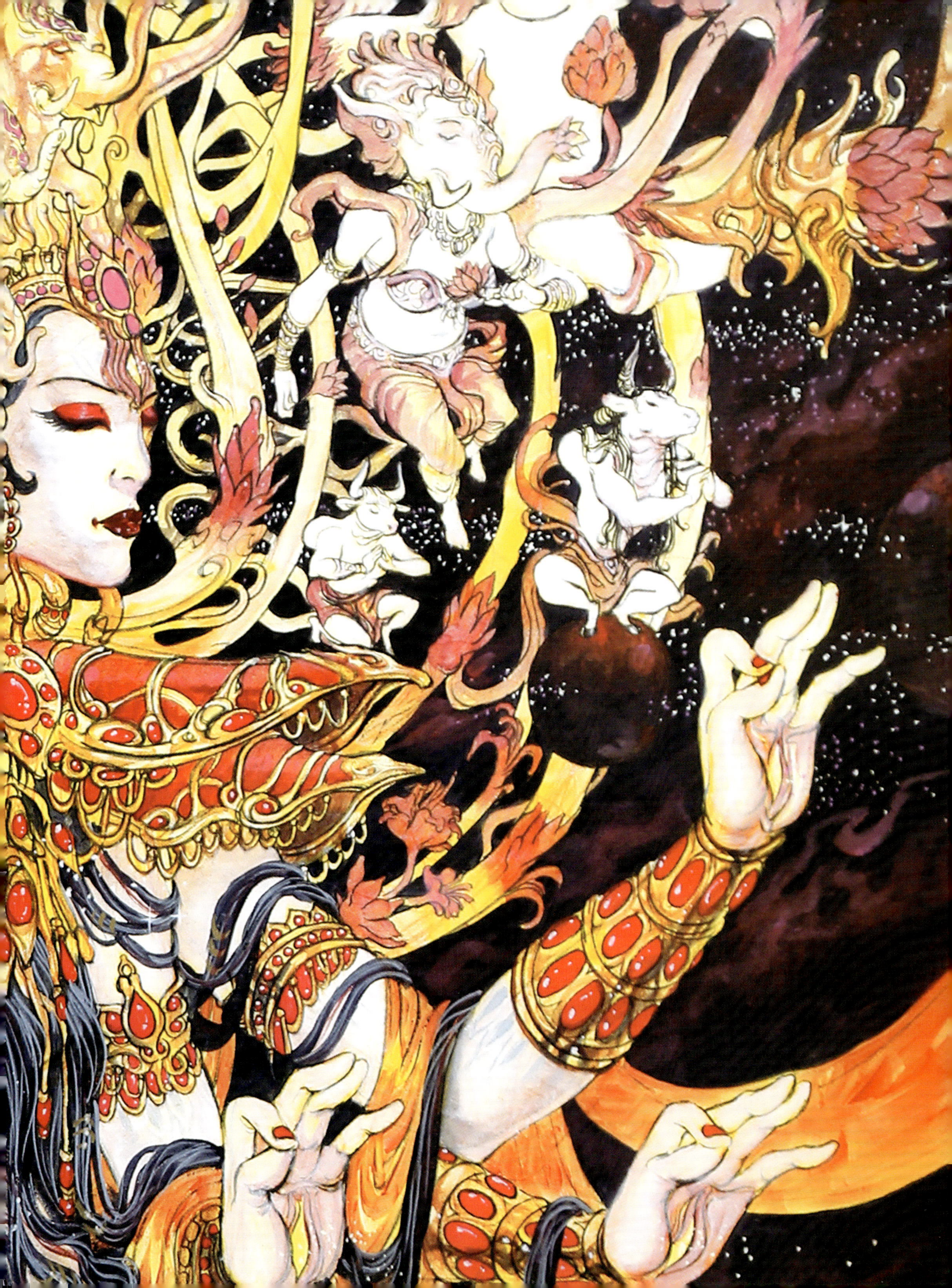

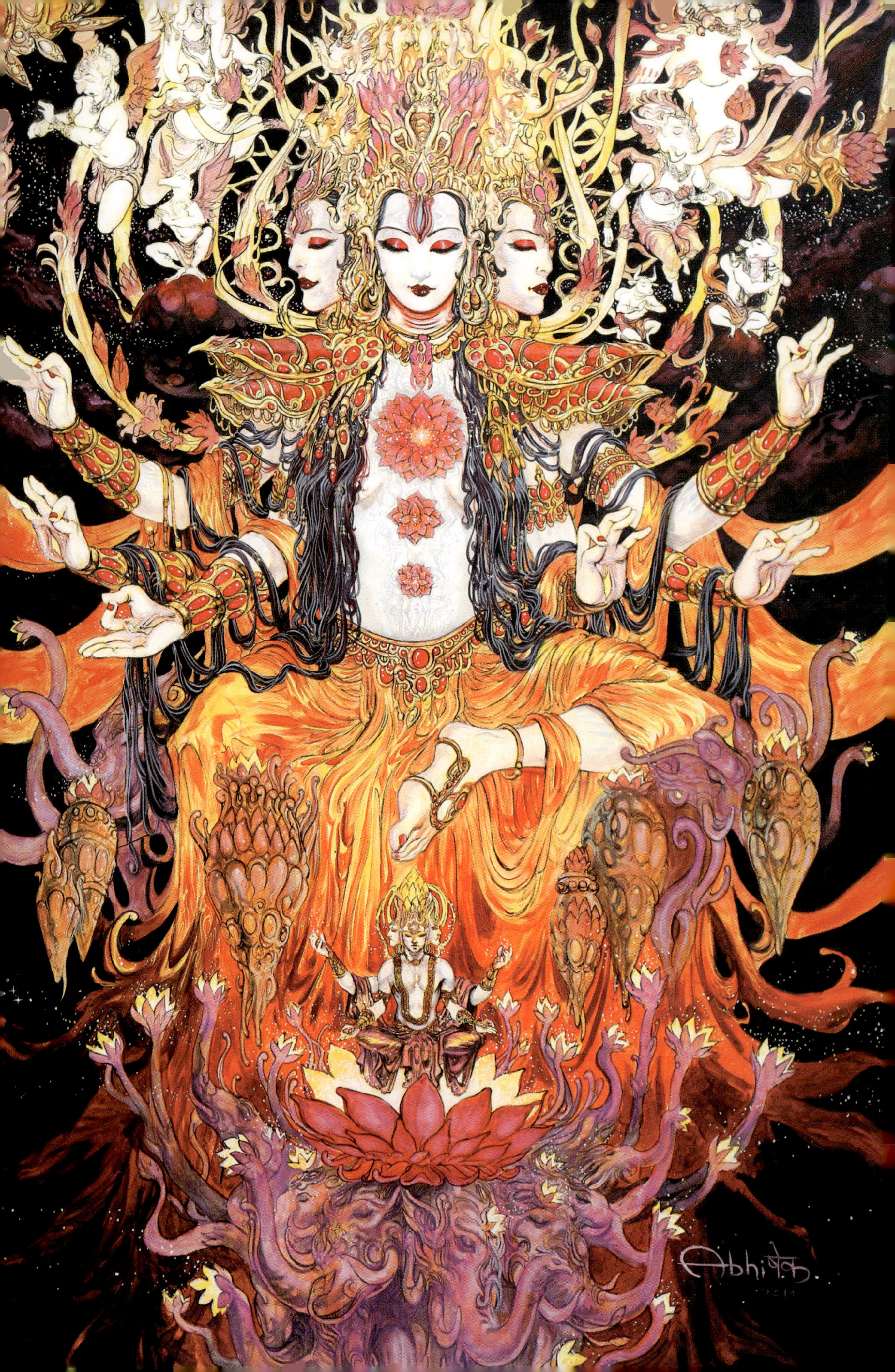

AARAMBH

- the beginning

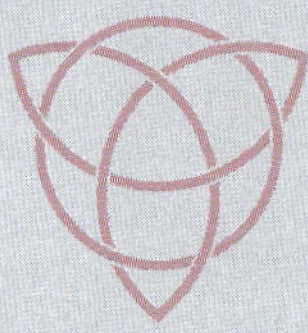

Jiva: Mother, what was there in the beginning?

Devi: Only the 'present' as when it moved, 'past' and 'future' were produced and time came to be.

Jiva: So from this 'now' came everything?

Devi: Yes, but then we became prejudiced by our pasts and futures.

Jiva: ...and forgot to be in the 'now'.

Devi: ...and that in the beginning we were all part of one heart.

Jiva: ...hence, when we embrace the 'now'...

Devi: ...we become whole again, we go to a place where our bias disappear, our separations dilute.

...we become the beginning.

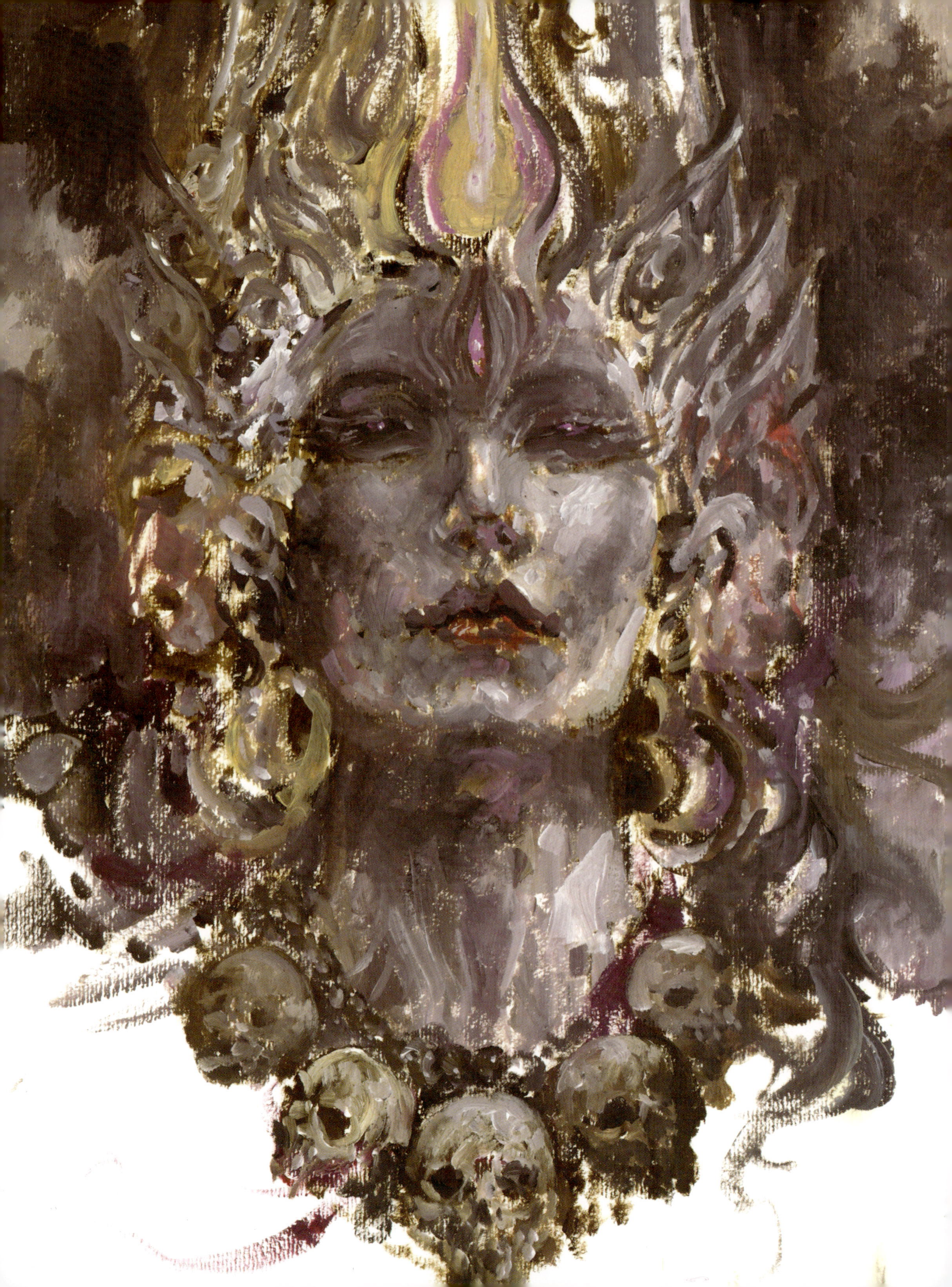

GARLAND OF SKULLS

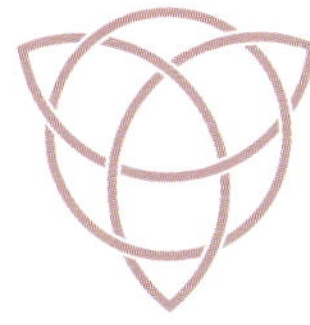

Why do you wear the skulls, O Agoreshwari, one who has controlled all anger?
The heart palpitates by the sight of it.

Human skulls all hanging and swen through invisible etheric pranic threads.
The vision of death overwhelms me, O Mukteshwari, the one beyond mortal reigns.

Why do I feel frightened by the skulls embellishing your being?
A silent gale reverberated through the skies which seemed to have turned a turquoise green, opening the Anahata.

The Kapalini, one who had stilled the mind of time, spoke gently.
The sun nourishes each one equally. Its rays seep into the bones, becoming the photonic truths.

Can you know by looking at the skulls if they belong to the suras or asuras, the night or the day seekers, heaven or hell dwellers?

The skulls adorned don't differentiate.
It's a symbol of equanimity, devoid of color, race or creed.

The essence equally permeates all.
With that, the entire universe was bathed in the green hues descending from the sun.

The questions had dissipated, for there was no fear.
A moment where the heart had moved beyond its bias.
And had become part of the Garland of Skulls.

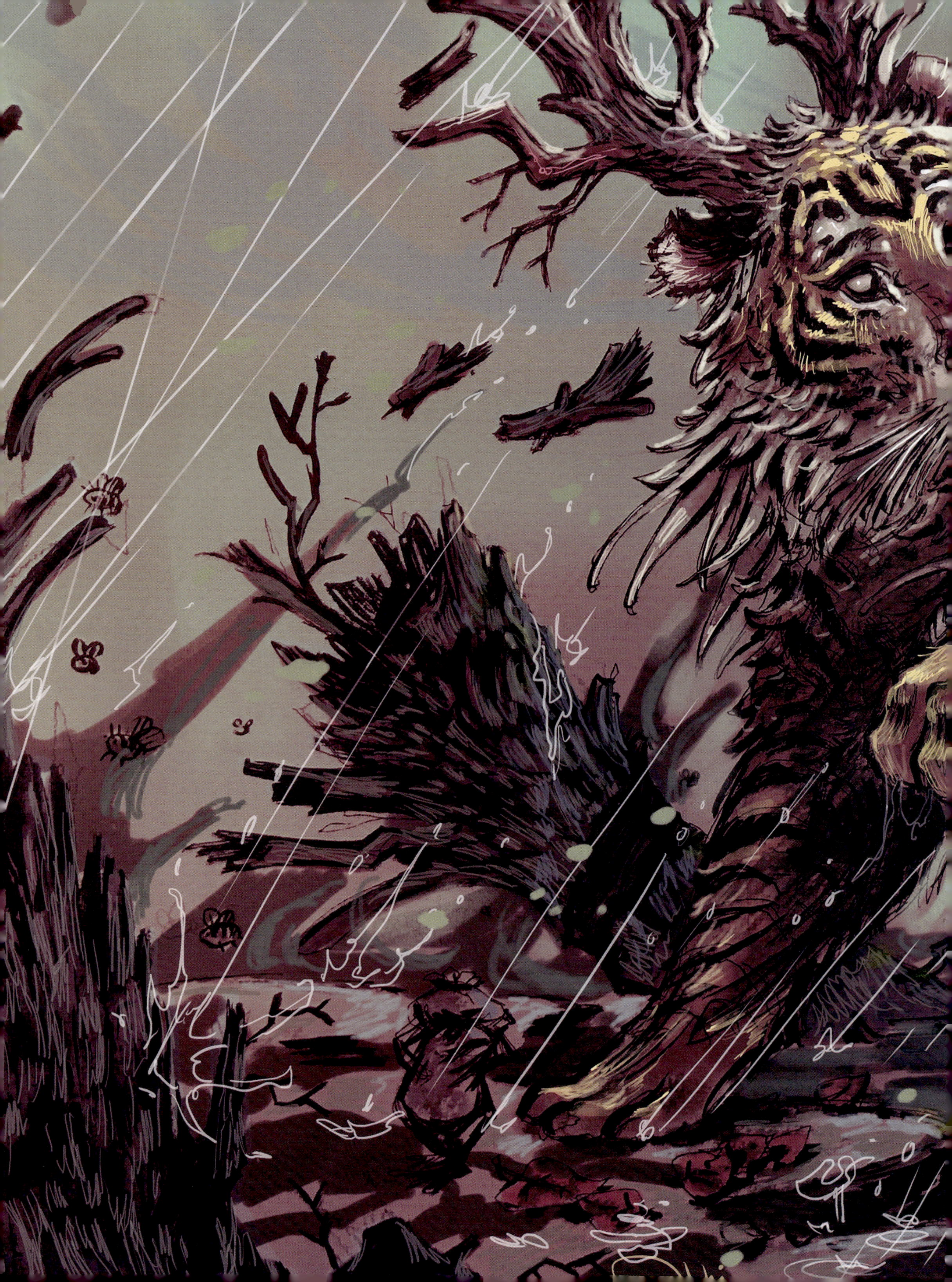

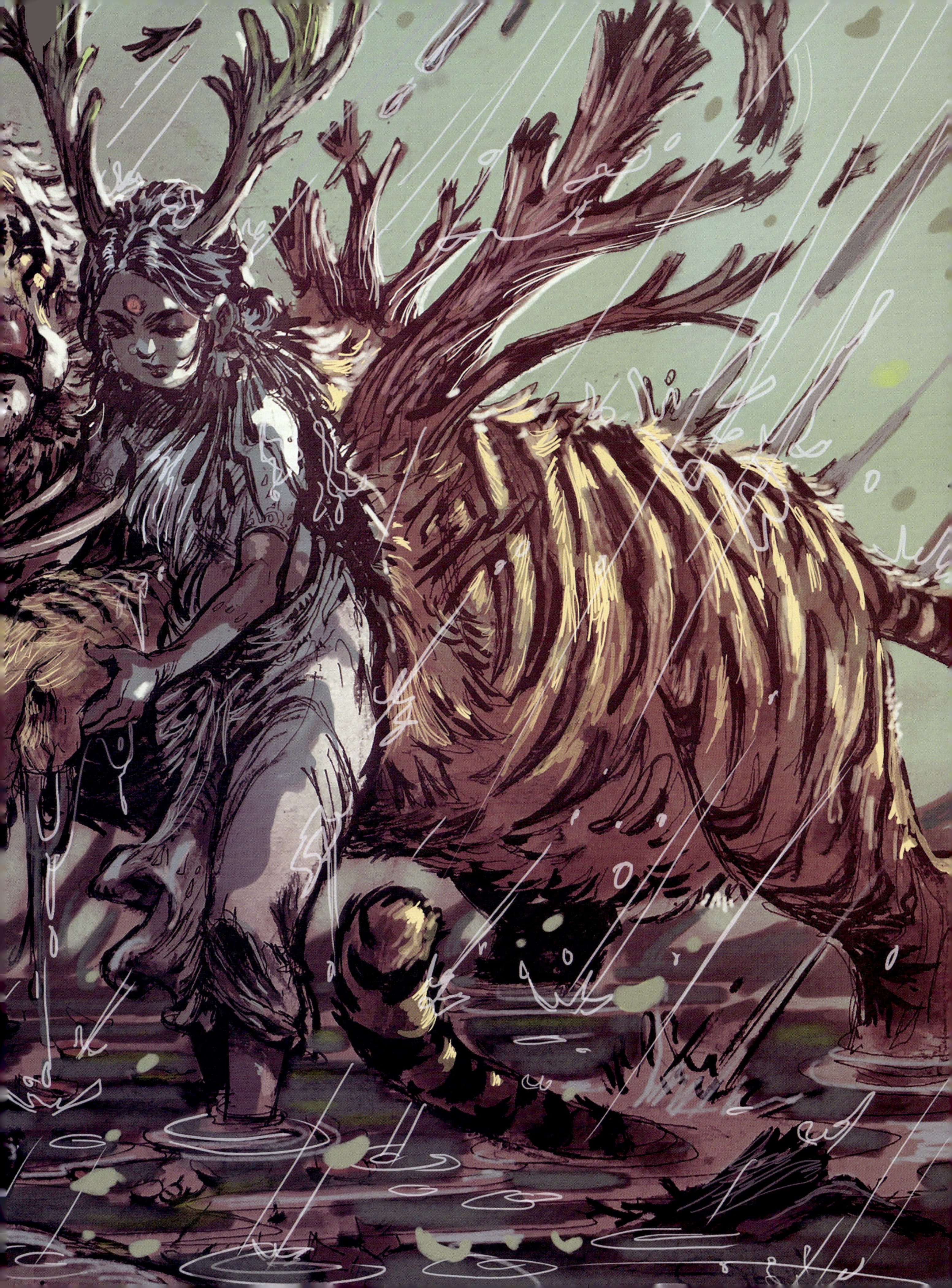

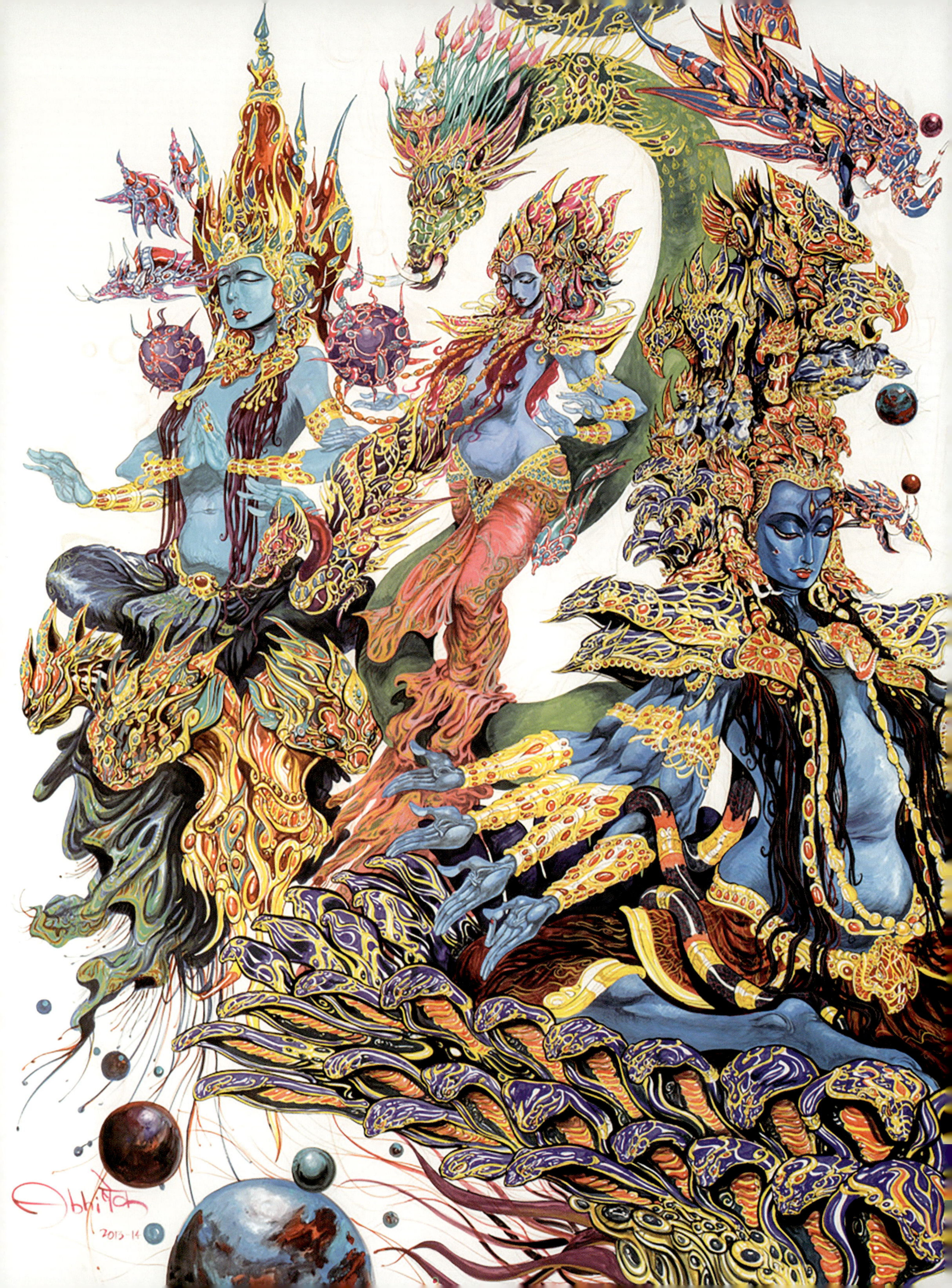
2013-14

KUNDALINI

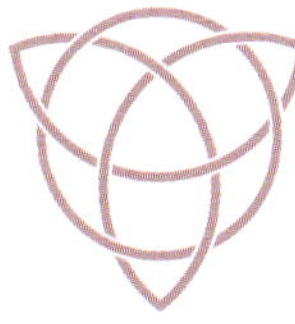

The dance of creation had sent out ripples across the new universe.
Forming the dense atmosphere, tectonic forces ardently sculpted the myriad earthly forms.
The sun was born and had already taken to its elliptical path, the energy which moved it was everywhere now.

What would this energy become in the coming time, O Adinath, asked Parvati still in his embrace?
When the energy is not misused by arrogance, conflict, violence, vanity, then it will start to apprehend the true source of its being, it will rise up to illuminate the sun itself. Celebrating the union of pure Energy with pure Love.

When humanity will meet the sun within, it's then, that the *Kundalini* will be truly awakened.

Yet, it will not be colors, or rings of power, or any magical substance or astral dimensions that people will confuse it with.

This energy will be removed from the emotion of malice, destruction and indulgent habits, devoted completely towards compassion and harmony. It will rise up to the mind's eye and will make humanity see the oneness in all beings.

With that Shiva saw that Parvati was blooming with light, her forehead had become the rainbow and she had taken over Shiva's heart. The cosmic sahasrara like a fountain erupted in their reverence. They had become Love.

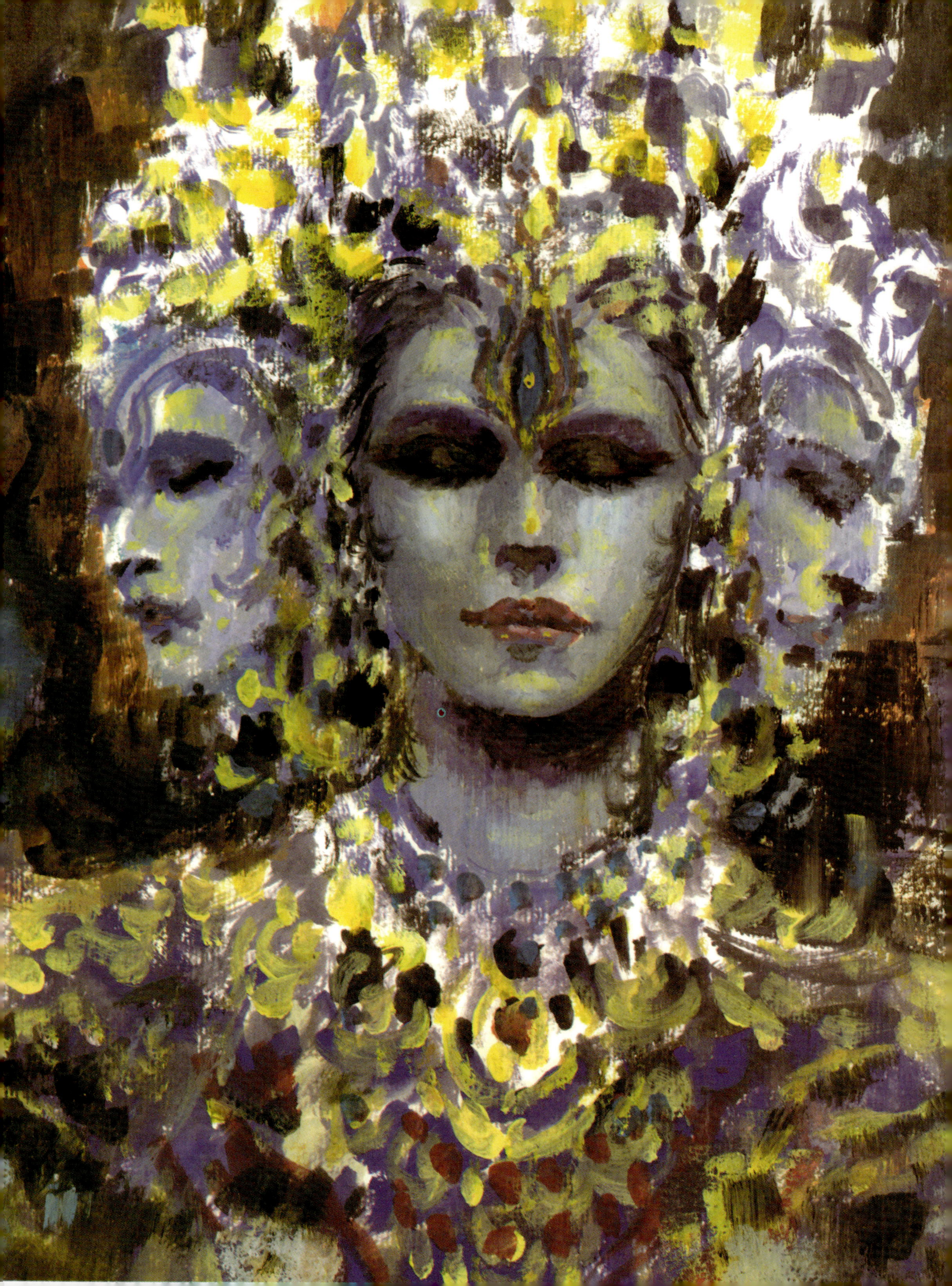

MAHA-DEVI

The Eternal One

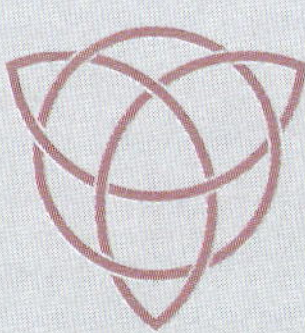

Inside the mind, a story older than its own beginning had been playing eon after eon. With each cycle of time, the mind oscillates between the forces of suras and asuras, tangled and suffocated. Realizing its crumbling state, struggling to find the courage to take control of itself once again. It pursues with great effort, a way to purge itself from the clutches of the Ego and stand up to the tyranny of the sense tendencies, absolving itself.

A confluence of virtues (Gods) travel to find the oneness (Atman) they belonged to. They offer their essence to invoke the great one (Maha-Devi), who shows them the path of synchronicity (the invisible essence permeating all beings).

They understood that seeking how their ego was contaminated and manifested Mahisha—aggression, greed, misogynistic, abusive nature of man. It also means great and powerful, but only if power is channeled virtuously.

Now that they know, a process of purging and transformation begins. From Asura (one who's in dissonance) an un-tuned instrument to Sura (the resonant one, harmonized or in tune). Hence all the asuras symbolically stand for various sense tendencies.

The Devi vanquishes the asuras, unraveling the philosophies of understanding human nature—the psychological and physical systems that govern and transform it.

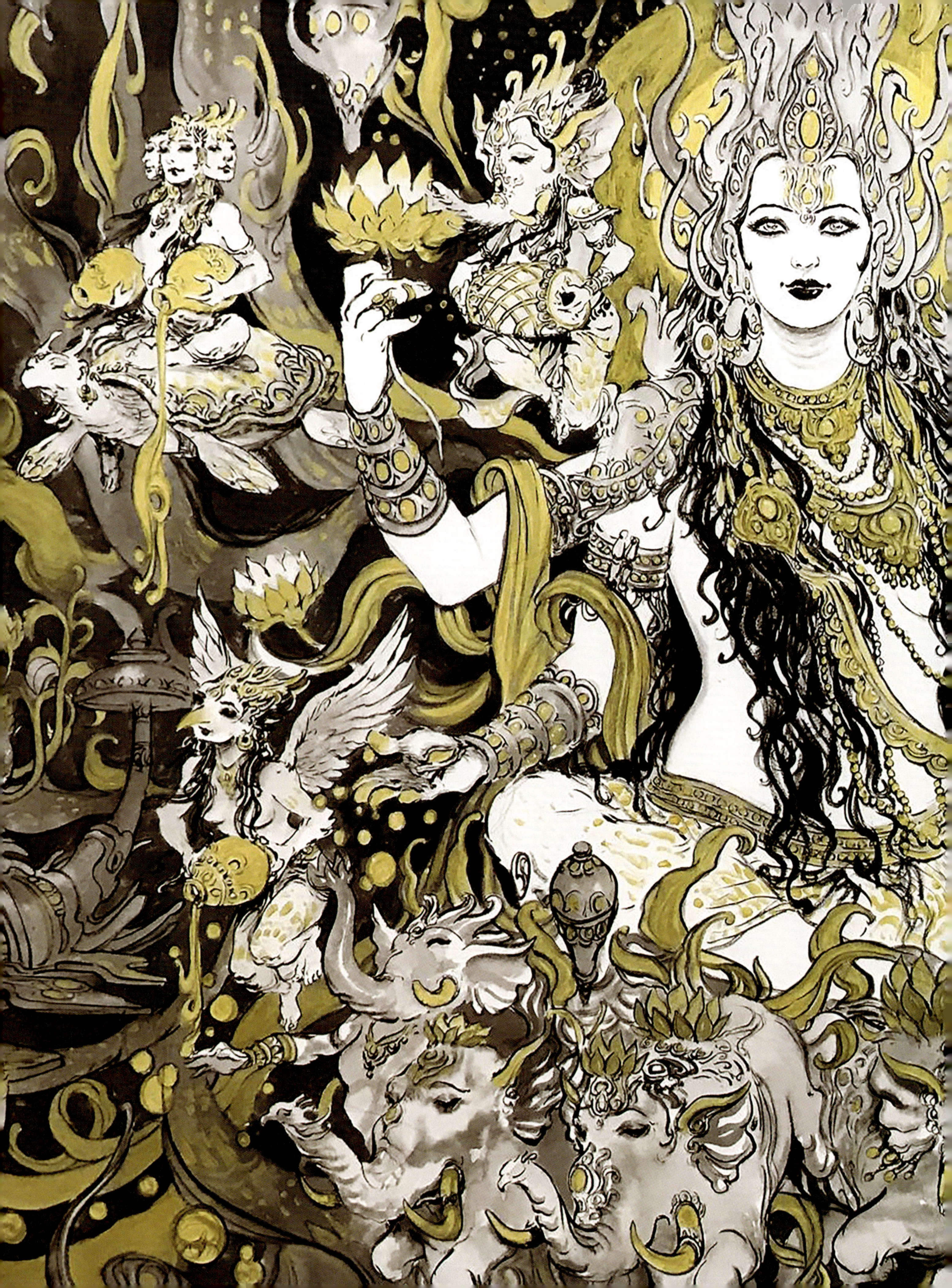

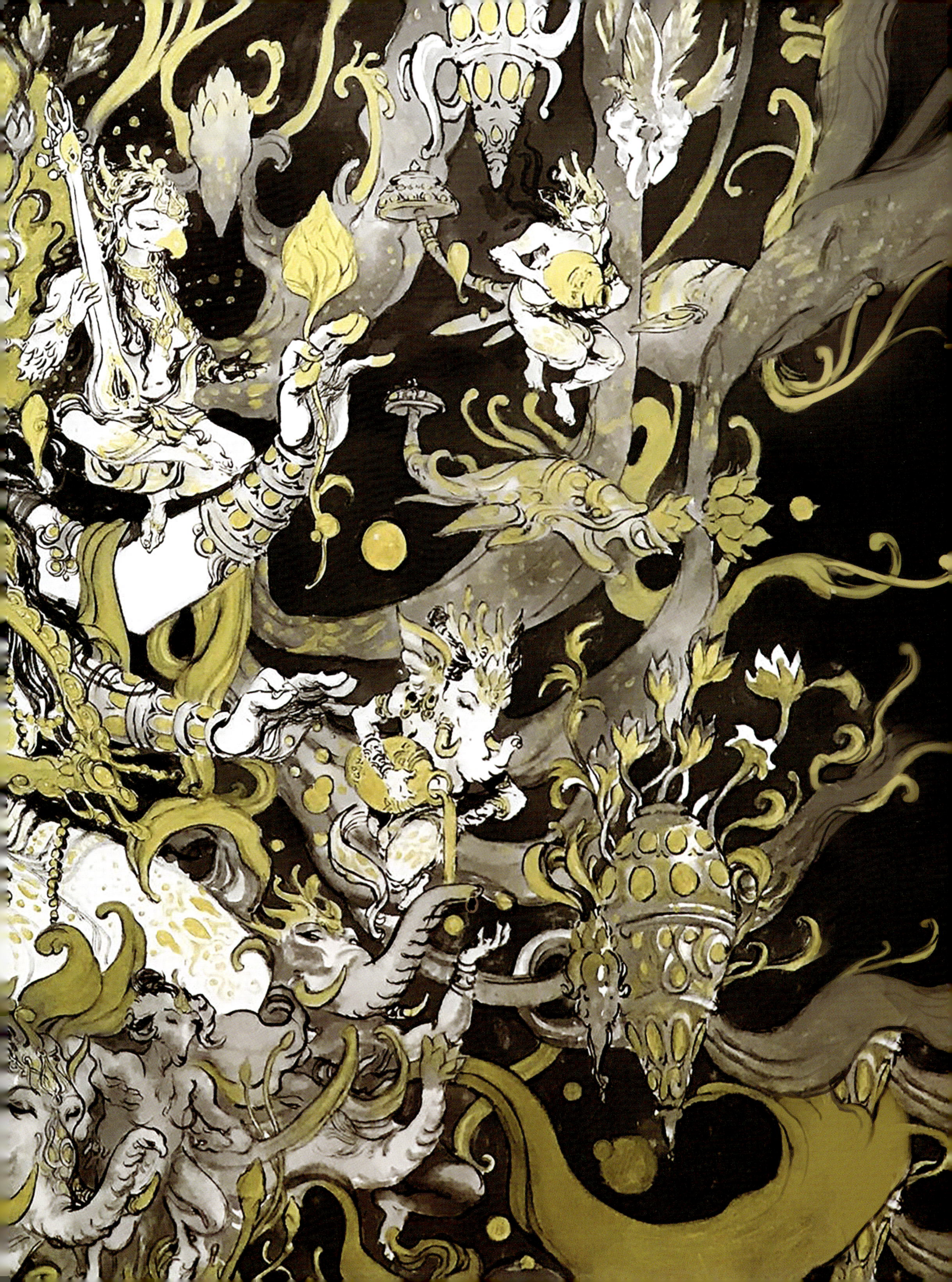

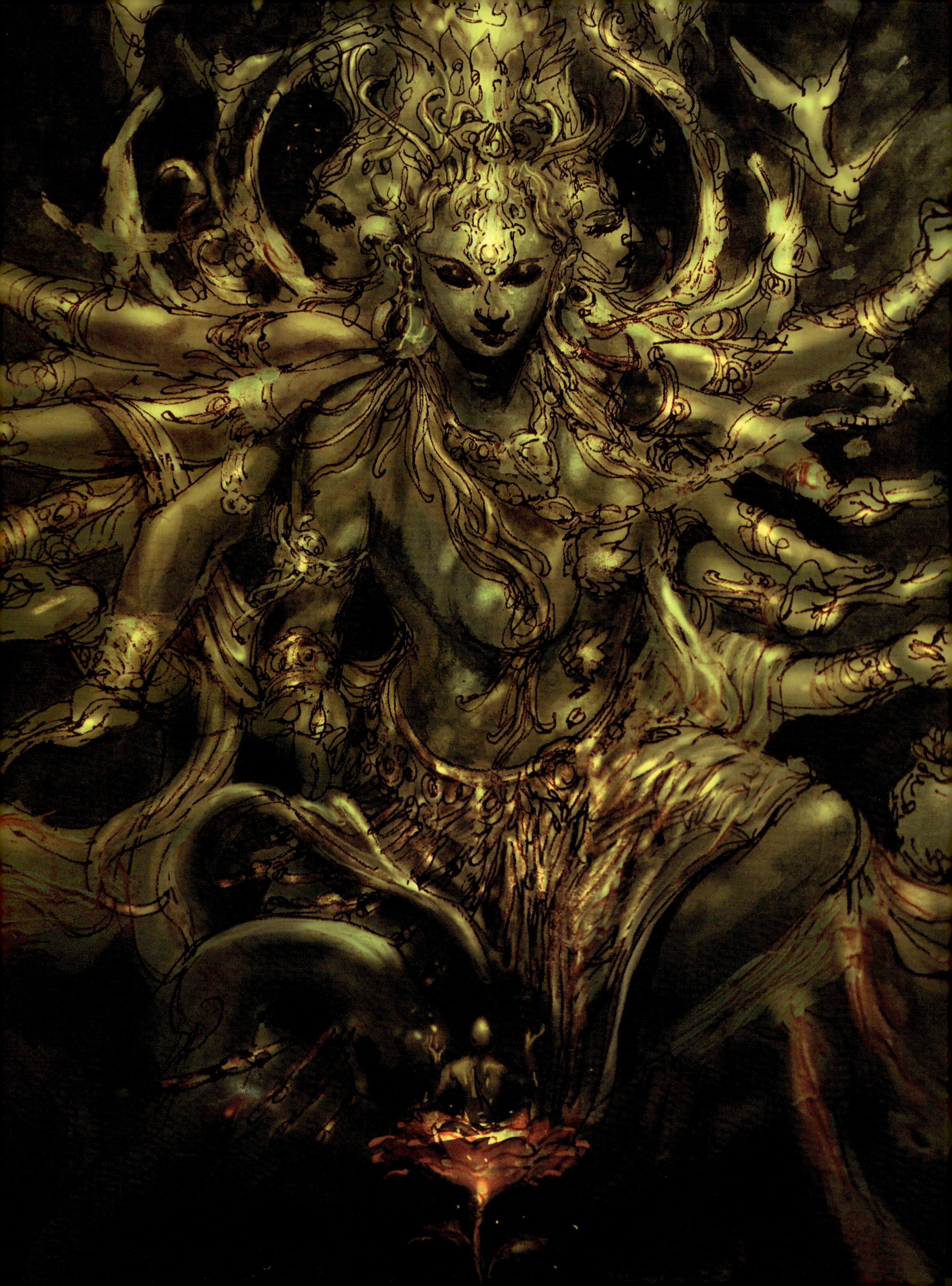

THE VISIONS OF THE DEVI

The Boon, War and the Vadh of Mahisha

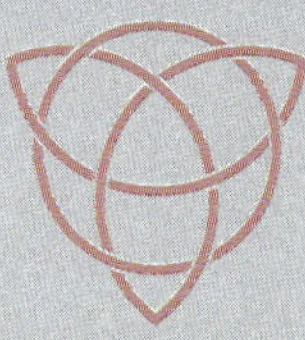

Death is inseparable from Life, intertwined in ways that not even the Gods can escape it. In this universe, everything, which is born, must die.

The bond between life and death is inextricable, from stars to blood cells, which carry the life force, abide by this principle.

One must not fear it. For the energy to flow without obstruction, space must be created, and death is a way to balance this cyclic flow. A cell or a sun, which resists dying, jeopardizes the whole system around it. What comes out of the source must go back to it eventually.

The words resonated in Brahma's mind, a voice echoing through many yugas, it was Parashakti—the one who stood at the intersection of time and infinity, immeasurable and uncharted, seeping through all the worlds. She had guided him intuitively, and will do so even now, as he prepared to descend down to one of the greatest asuras.

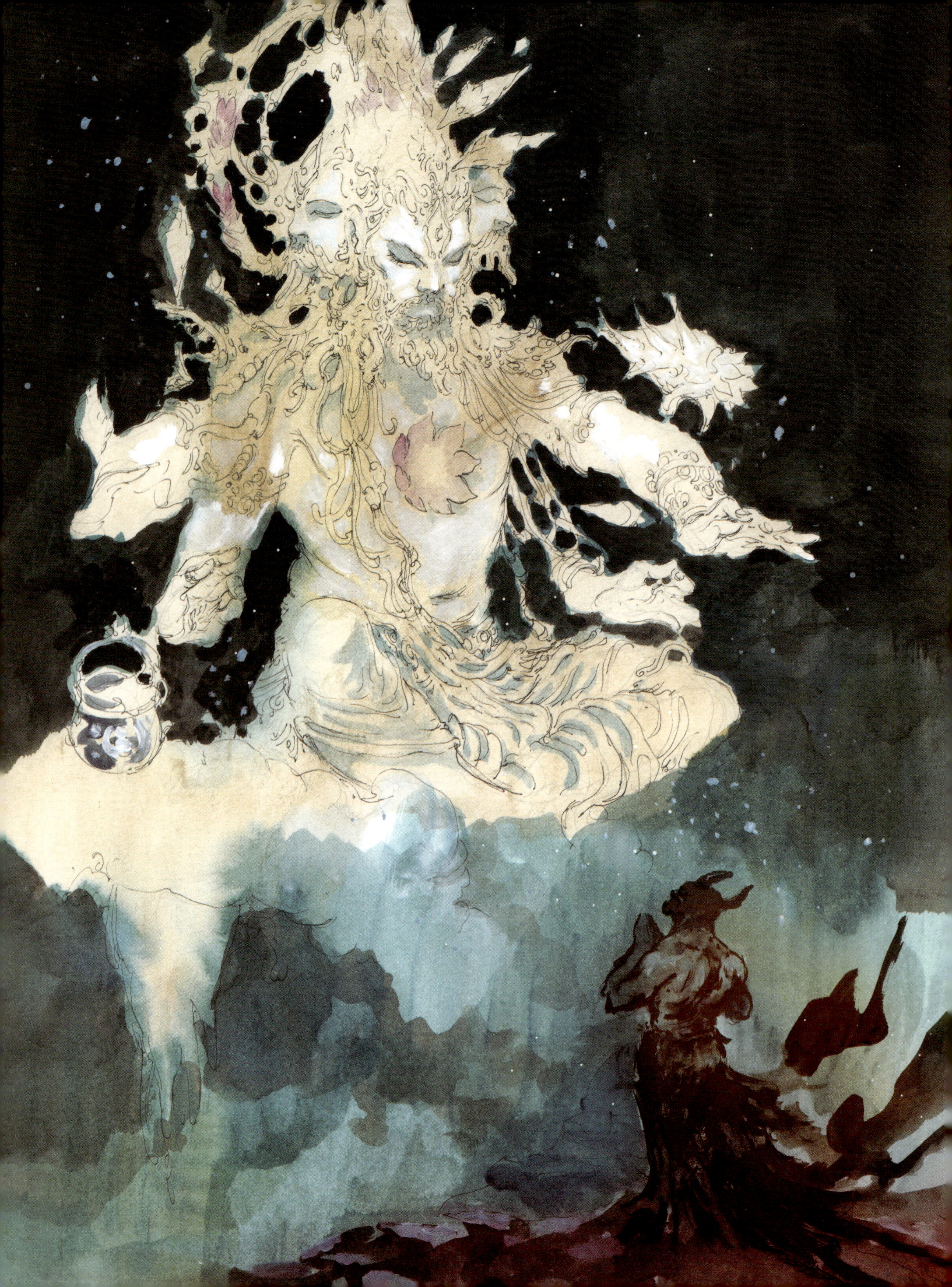

Brahma spoke to Mahisha,
"I cannot grant you this boon of immortality, for it compromises the whole equilibrium of life."

With a sense of profound awareness of inevitable fates, the creator God Brahma addressed Mahisha, the astute asura, who had been in deep penance for thousands of years, anticipating this moment, to ask the most elusive of all boons.

"Ask me anything else, from celestial realms, to the thrones in worlds where gods aren't even born."

Mahisha, without flinching from his composed posture, which he had held for eons, spoke respectfully but fiercely.

"O Vibhuti, lord of the worlds, hear me out before you make up your mind. Death indeed is a certainty, but when and how it comes, can be negotiated, hence, there is no doubt that if one desires, it can be delayed indefinitely too. Perhaps once I tell you the story of my past, you'd understand, O world maker, why I plead to be deathless.

Once the two asura brothers, both gifted and virtuous, Rambha and Karambha, worthy of the greatest eminence, immersed themselves in deep meditation.

Rambha chose an ancient tree and focused on the element fire, unaware that the tree was also a dwelling place of yakshas, forest spirits, who out of curiosity kept a watch over his sincere efforts. While Karambha, submerged himself into a pond next to it and focused on the element water, harnessing his breath's potential.

The place thrived with their energies and soon became so magnetic that it attracted the attention of the lord of heavens, Indra. As he witnessed the glorious strides the brothers made, insecurities entered his heart, changing his appreciation of them into a baseless jealousy.

O lord of beginnings, you know how the mind is an expert in making a problem where there is none.

In the same vain, insecurities raged inside Indra. It gnawed at him so badly that he decided to disguise himself as a crocodile, and entered the pond where Karambha was performing austerities and vehemently murdered him.

Rambha, who was meditating underneath the tree, intuitively knew in his heart that something had happened to his brother and upon realizing how the king of all gods had deceptively inflicted the crime, was filled with immense guilt, of not being there for him. So, he decided to behead himself as an offering to the fire upon which he meditated. To his surprise, the fire did not accept the sacrifice, instead witnessing his earnest heart, which mourned the loss of his brother, decided to grant him a boon.

Abhorred by Indra's act, he asked for a son to be born to avenge him, to dethrone his enemies and rule the three worlds, to avoid such heinous acts from ever happening again. The fire granted him the boon, blessed him and dispersed into the invisibility from where it had emanated.

Still reeling from the pain of loss, he went on a search for a worthy partner, hoping it will calm his restless heart and eventually found her in the form of a she-buffalo. Their love prospered and soon my mother was expecting me. I would've been born to loving parents but fate had other plans, a shapeshifter, who seemed like a buffalo himself, got excited to claim my mother and in an unavoidable fight, my father got killed accidentally.

In her pursuit to protect me, my frightened mother, ran fervently to the tree, where my father had prayed and pleaded the forest spirits to save her from the approaching danger. Their heart grieved upon hearing what had happened to him and to avenge him, they not only just killed the attacking mad bull but also honored my dead father by offering a funeral pyre.

As the fires enveloped his body, my mother in her mourning also jumped into the blazing flames, forgetting that I was still inside her belly. Seeing no other recourse, in a desperate attempt to protect her, I came out of her womb, but was unable to save her.

In that moment, before I could even acknowledge the loss of my parents, I heard a voice echoing through the flames, carrying a strong sense of familiarity. My father was in there somewhere, the blessings of fire had kept him alive but when I saw him in his new mutated form, my eyes welled up, he had transformed into something far more gruesome, which tormented him as much as it amplified his vengeance."

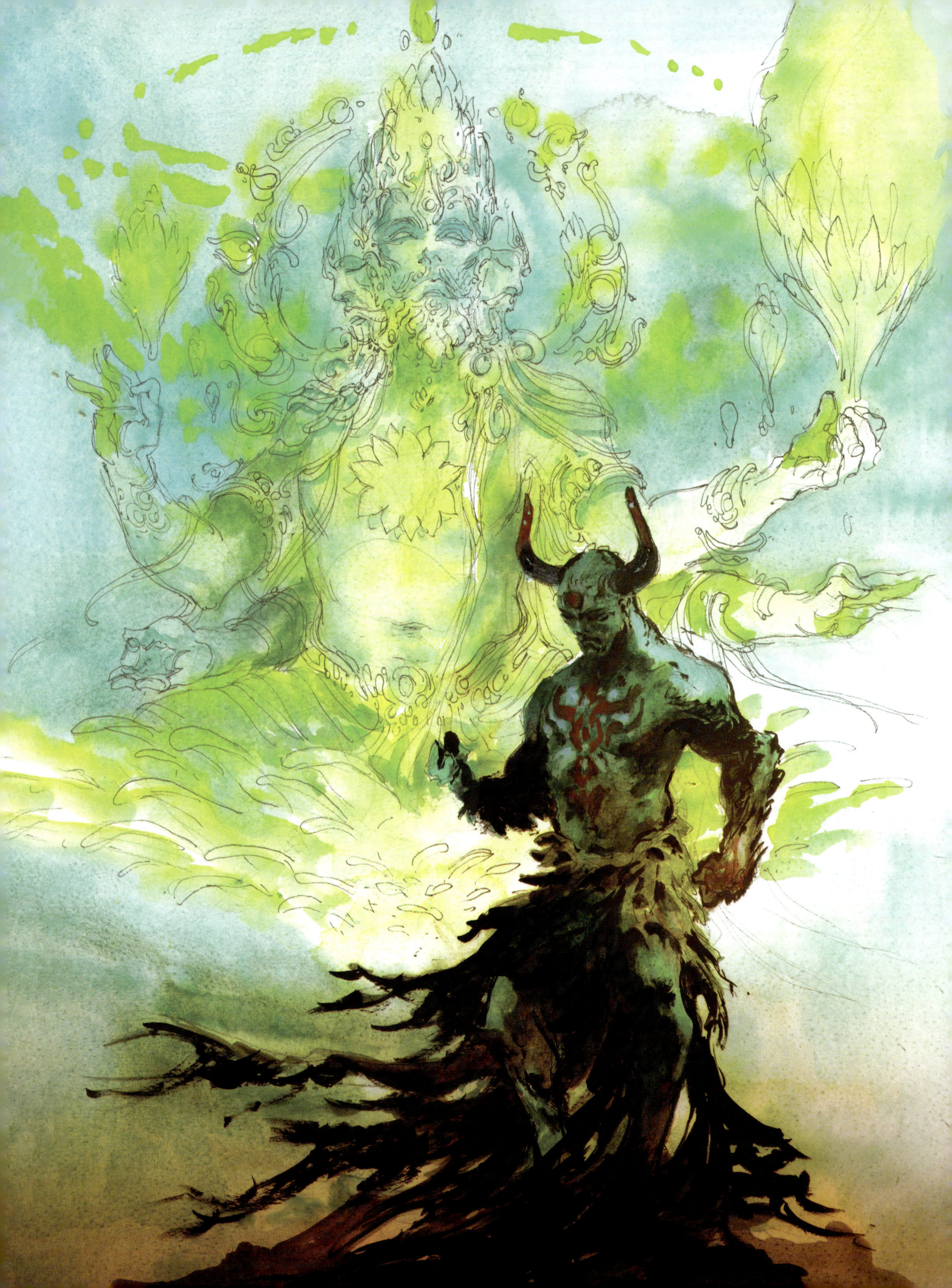

"He pledged that with each drop of his blood he will protect me, and thus he will be called Raktveej.

Those fires still rage in my heart. I don't want to just slay the treacherous god or take his place. I want to supersede him in every aspect, so the likes of him get the fate they deserve. Thus, O, god of creation, make me deathless. So when I would rule free of death, unworthy acts like his, will never occur across time."

Brahma spoke benevolently, "O son of Rambha, my heart feels your loss. In the ripples that swirl around me, pulsate the many eons in which I myself have lived and died. I know that your father, Rambha and his brother Karambha were the two sons of Dhanu, the wife of Kashyapa, one of the seven seers, who was born to a different Brahma, of a different yuga, yet I carry all of their memories in me, as the creator. You see, there have been many Brahmas, many Indras, many creations, and to all, many fates have been served, with myriad lessons. Even I who create worlds, is aware of my own perishable being and cannot grant such a wish."

Mahisha:
"Then you'd know how Kashyapa, with the thirteen daughters of Daksha created the many species which populate the worlds. With our great mother, Dhanu, he procreated the race of the danavas after her name. The danavas are related to ashvins, the sun gods, but they don't get the same treatment in heavens as them. To correct this and end this discrimination, I must attain something which none of them have. Grant me immortality, O maker of worlds."

Brahma was in many places and yet nowhere, he took a moment to think about the insistent nature of the mind and how such a mind cannot be convinced by any rational reason. So he spoke in a definitive tone to an overtly self-assured Mahisha.

"Ask me anything else and ask me soon, for time slips away."

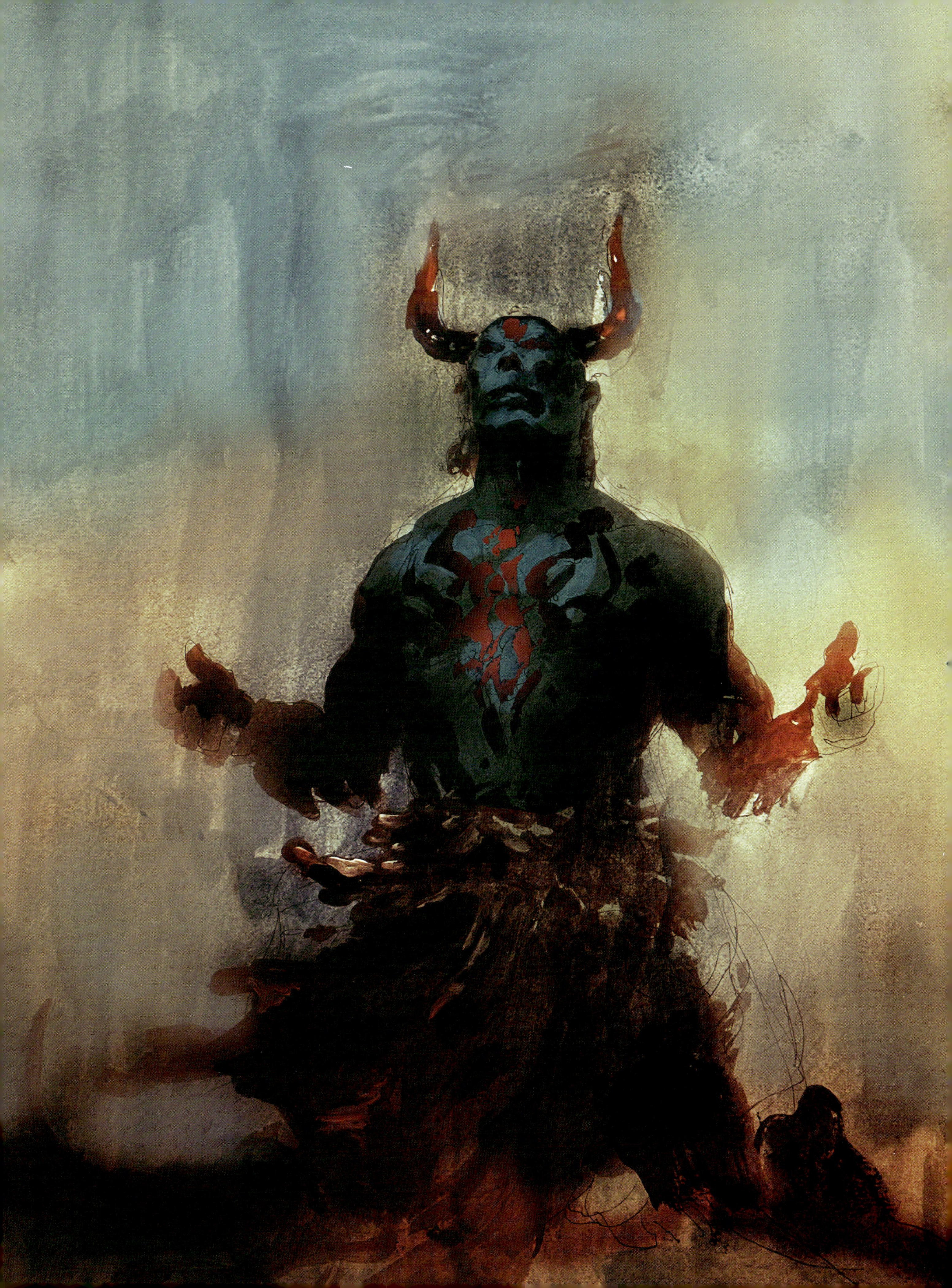

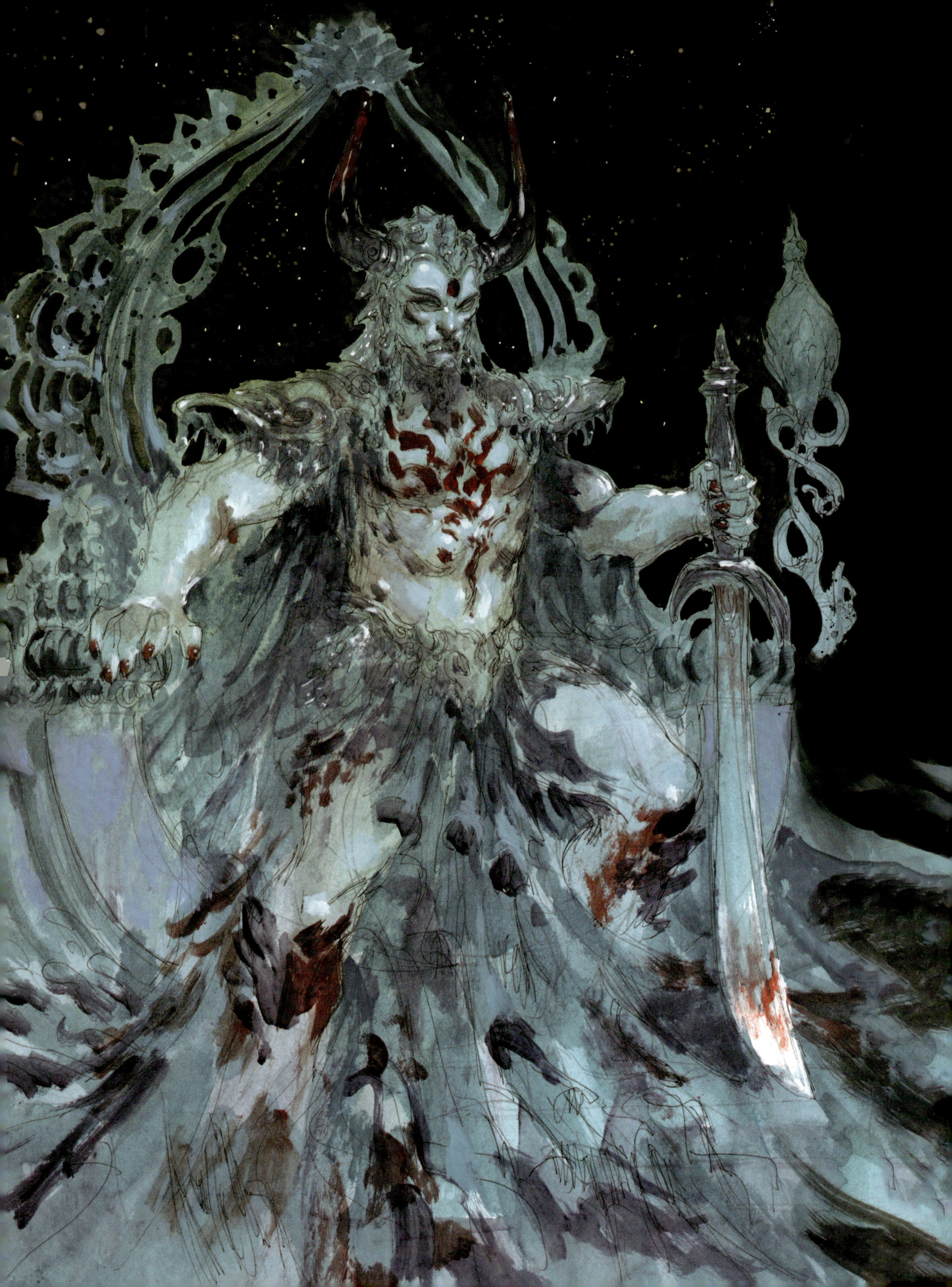

Mahisha understood that no further convincing would wane Brahma's perspective, so he asked thus:

"Let no one except a woman kill me. Grant me this, for I know women to be weak in the arts of war. They cannot hold a weapon, let alone challenge me in a duel. If I'm to die, let it be at the hands of a woman, for I know it will be impossible."

'Tathastu' so be it, said Brahma, and vanished into his etheric realms.

Soon the heavens trembled by Mahisha's attacks. His formidable display of force, defeated Indra, casted out the mighty gods from the heavens and took over the throne.

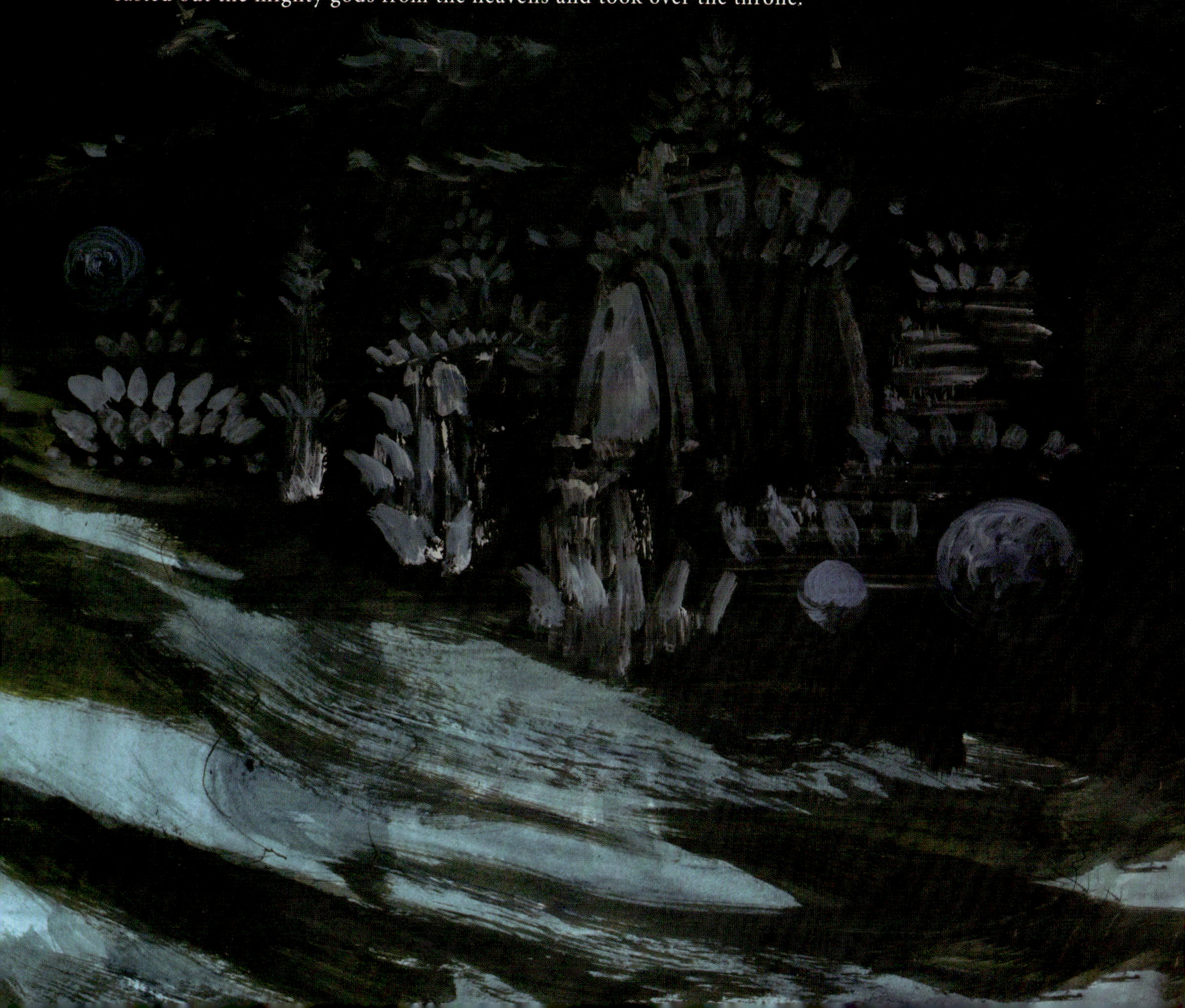

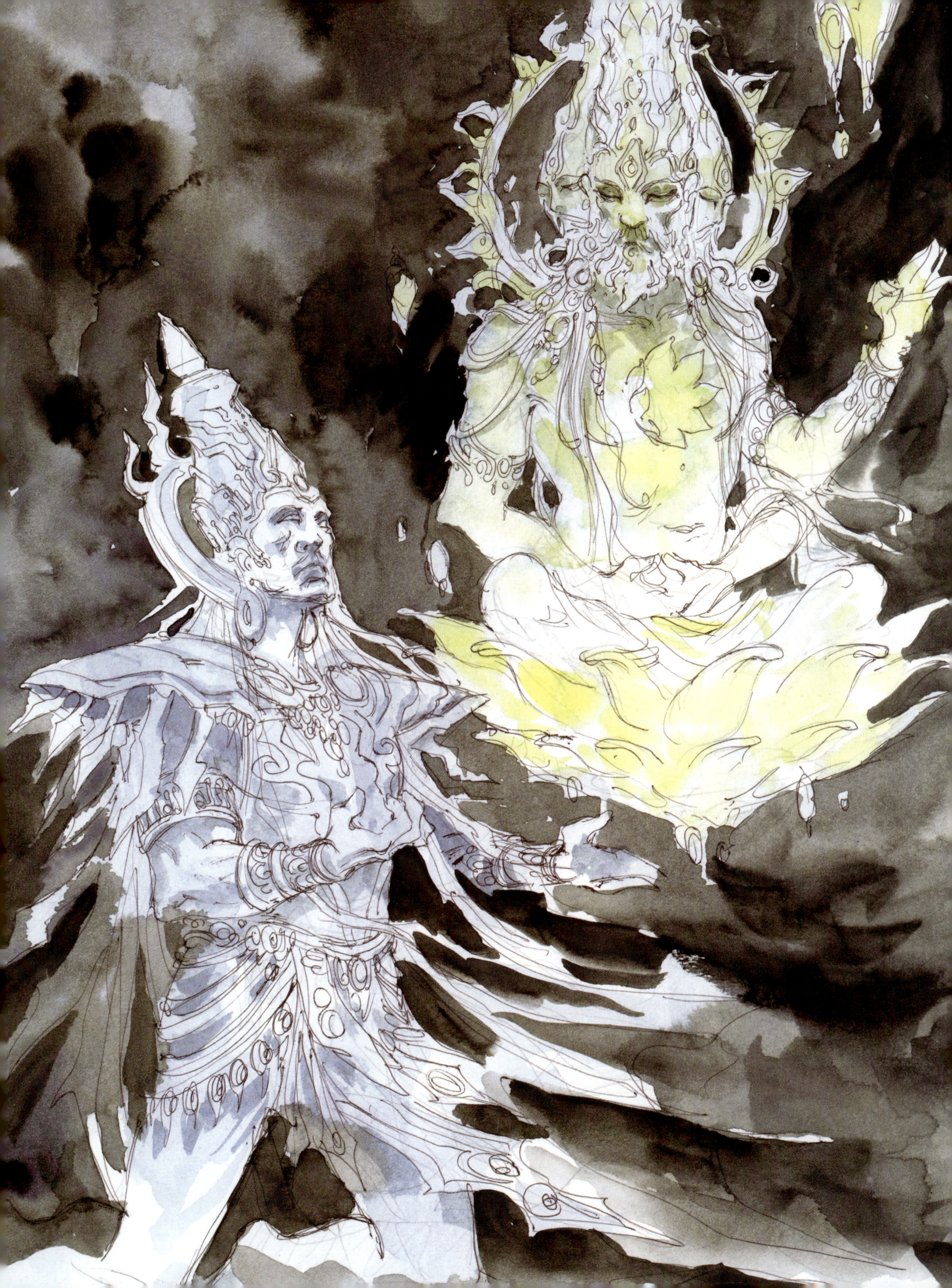

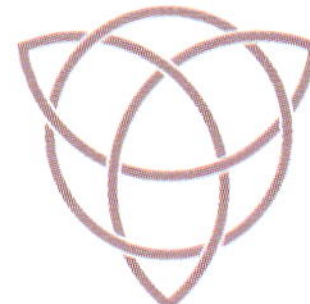

The invincible Mahisha broke their spirits to the core, with hearts threatened and minds displaced, the dejected gods fled, taking an undesirable course, in search of some absolution. Indra in his destitute state realized how morally weak he had become, to have succumbed to petty insecurities and to have killed an earnest asura. How could he slay someone who was simply in a state of prayer and posed no harm? This tormented him endlessly, as he knew far too well that he could not correct this wrong and that perhaps he deserved this fate. Along with the other gods he repented and eventually exhausted by his own limitations to find any solution, he went to Brahma, and spoke thus.

"Atmabhu, the self-existent one, what is that which one must do, when one realizes that one is unworthy of such a seat in heaven? Perhaps it's for the better that Mahisha rules the abode of suras, we the untainted ones, after all, are not exceptions to blemishes."

Brahma, knew that this would happen and spoke with empathy,
"O, Rainmaker, the ways of fate are uncertain, even the mountains remain submerged in the great seas and then when the wheel of time turns, they tower above them. The seed lives underneath the ground and then breaks through it, towards the sky one day. Nothing remains the same, in the advances of fate. You must forsake this doubt because if not used wisely, it will start to eat into reason."

Grief-stricken Indra, moved by the creator's words, looked deep within. He knew that Mahisha even though deserving the throne, would not serve the realm well, as he was guided by anger and decadence. He had beguiled everyone and had tricked all to believe that wars and massacre in the name of revenge were justified.

Indra, spoke with intent this time to Brahma.
"I see my mistake, and I sense my own faults, but I'm far too weak to understand how to avert such a calamity. Who may guide us to restore the order?"

Brahma thought of the only one, who could possibly unhinge this block that devas faced. He said in a contemplative manner rare to even the sages, "The one beyond eternity, Mahadeva Shiva, will know what to do next. To Kailasa you must all go and pray to him, I'll assist you and will be alongside in spirit. There's only him who can bring back the lost harmony."

By closing their eyes and launching into an astral portal, the disoriented gods, like senses gone astray, traveled to the home of the lord who was aligned with all. The great Omni, sat alongside Uma, sensing the many worlds fall like snow as she blinked them into existence.

Seeing the gods lumped together in crises, he knew what had transpired and why they had called to him. Understanding this, he absorbed their disorientation and acclimatized them to the heightened frequencies of his realm.

He summoned a vision, calling on behalf of all the gods, opening the Anhata, the heart chakra, the unstuck sound, the silent sound of prayer, which comes from the purest inner spaces of being. He encouraged the gods to collect all their silences and hold onto this message he was about to unravel.

Uma smiled, since she already knew what was to come.

He spoke in his ethereal calming voice.
"Vishnu, the infinite one, had once fought such a calamity, in the primal waters of the first Earth, when land wasn't even born. An enigmatic being, a Goddess, beyond creation itself, had helped him to avert the crisis."

As he expanded the vision bridge, the memory of that story slipped in, like a droplet precipitating from the edges of time into the now. He magnified it for the gods.

It was a story of another yuga, another time, where after a long war between suras and asuras, Vishnu had come back to his realm, tired from the never-ending war, as he contemplated over the nature of the ongoing battle, the sheer irrelevance of it, his tired body, fell asleep, with his head atop the string of his bow, sranga, supporting and slipping him into a deep slumber.

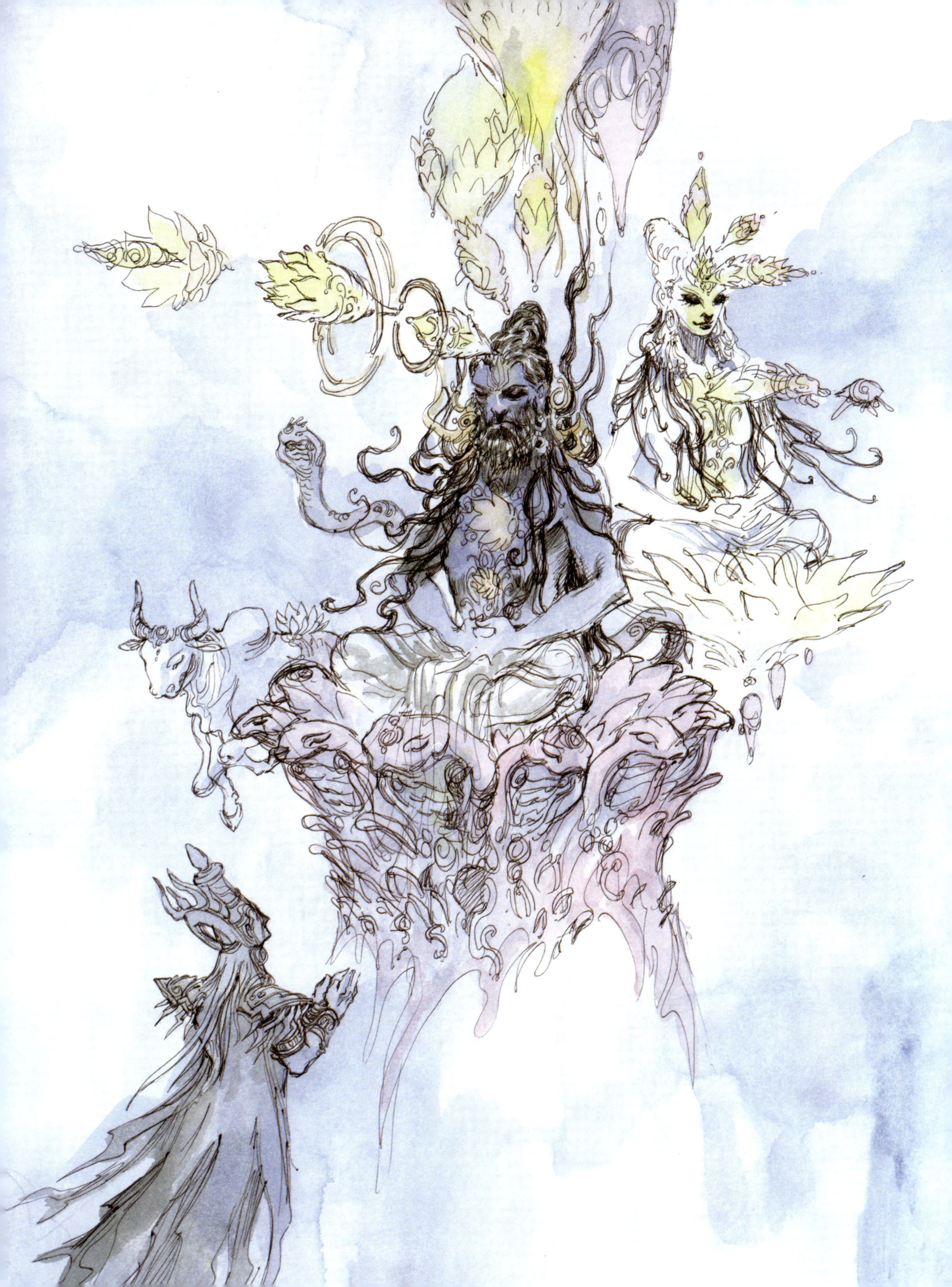

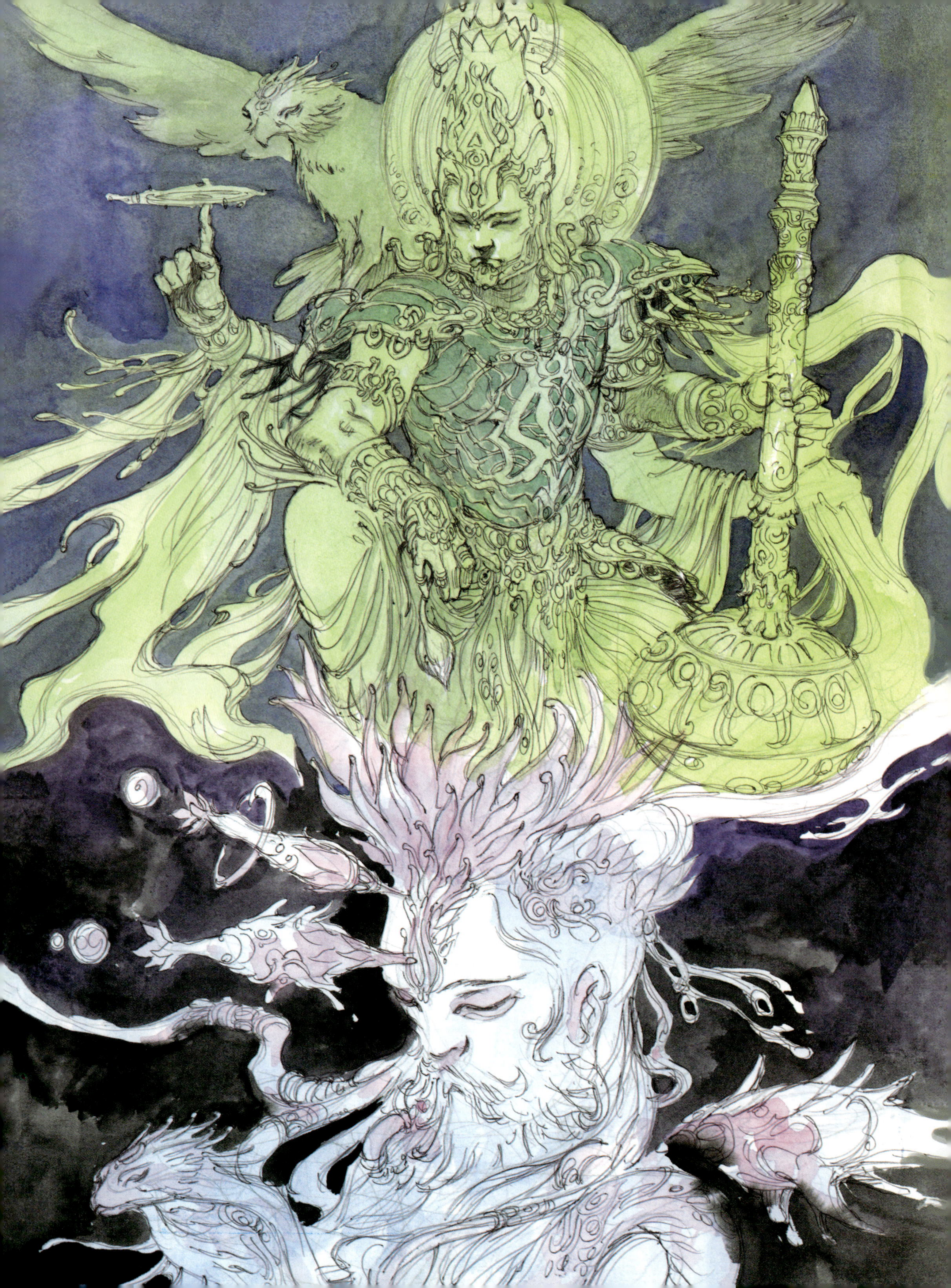

The gods soon, like always, came for his help, as another war had begun. He was so deep in his sleep that their anxious clamor or prayers could not wake him up. Resorting to desperate measures, Brahma sent Brahmari insects, white ants, smaller but capable of acute sounds of prana, to eat into the material of the bow. It soon weakened the bowstring and its thundering snapping severed Vishnu's head but he was no ordinary god. He knew he wasn't his body alone, and that this was a necessary step in the process of a much greater cosmic premonition.

Then the headless Vishnu, in his subconscious saw the marvelous vision, he saw her, the all knowing one, the primordial goddess, healing him back, and when he woke up, he found himself with the head of a horse, and was revered by the gods as Hayagriva, the wise.

For a moment, all gods, along with Shiva and Uma, admired the horse form of Vishnu, the way it galloped over the eternal waters and chanted her glories through the waves.

The vision paused for a blink, and a face appeared exalting their moment of ecstasy; it was of Vishnu, the preserver, the sustainer of worlds, the only one who was both capable and worthy of meditating alongside the great Mahadeva Shiva.

The same vision became a portal and took them to his world, Vaikuntha, where he lay beside goddess of light, Lakshmi, upon the shoreless ocean, guarded by the thousand-faced snake, Anantashesha and just as a beautiful dream takes away the day's toil, the gods felt healed, soaking in this magnificent scenario.

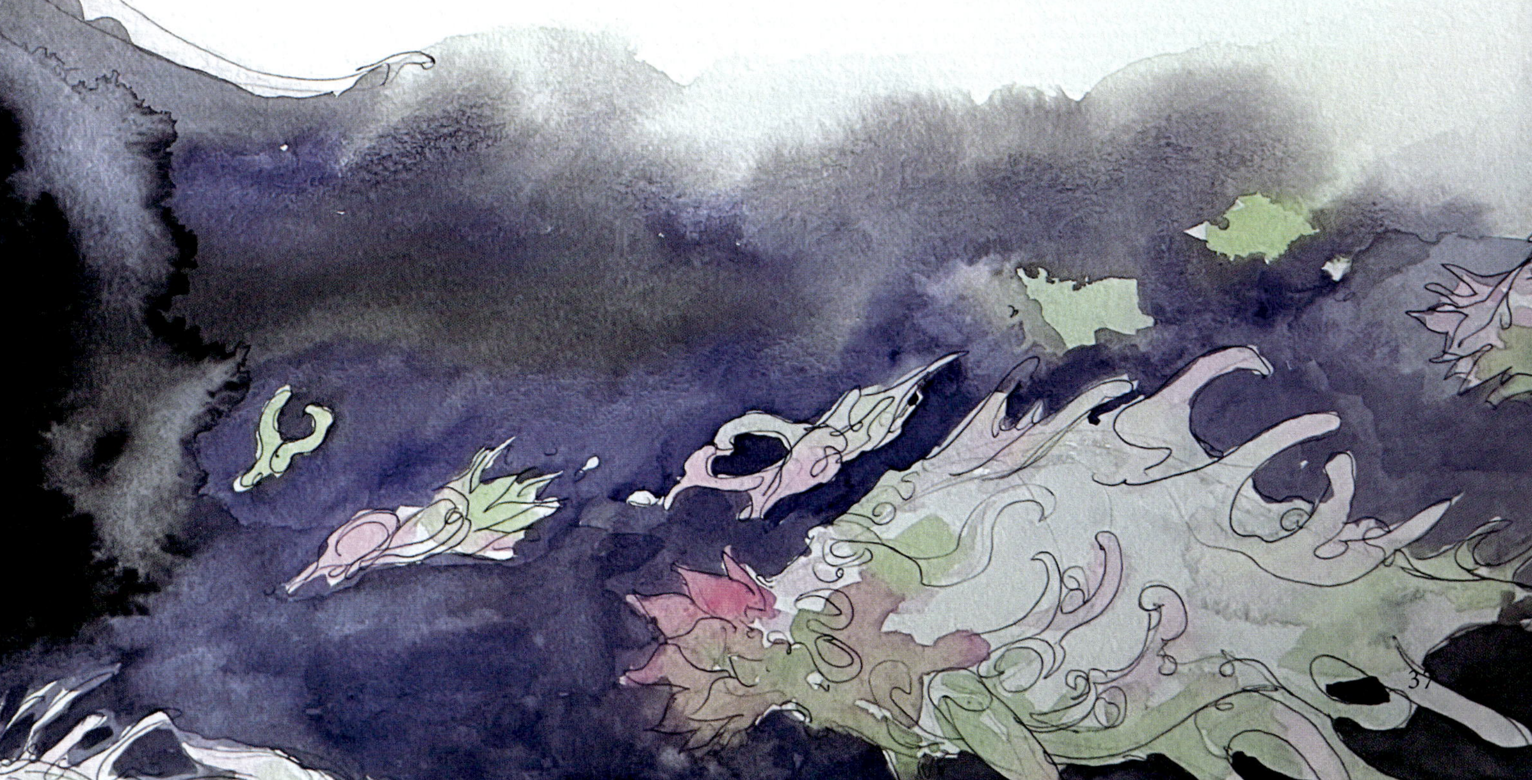

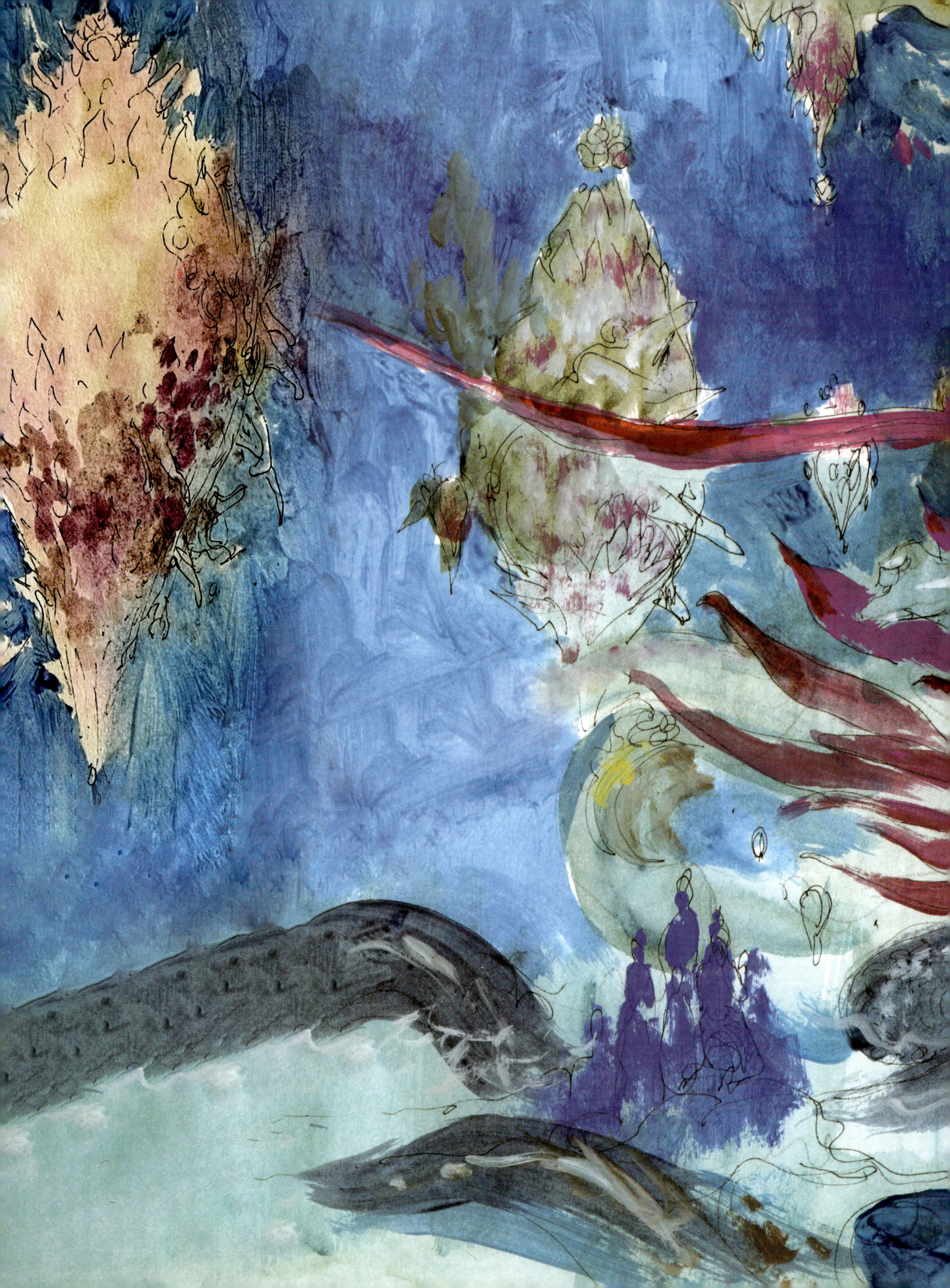

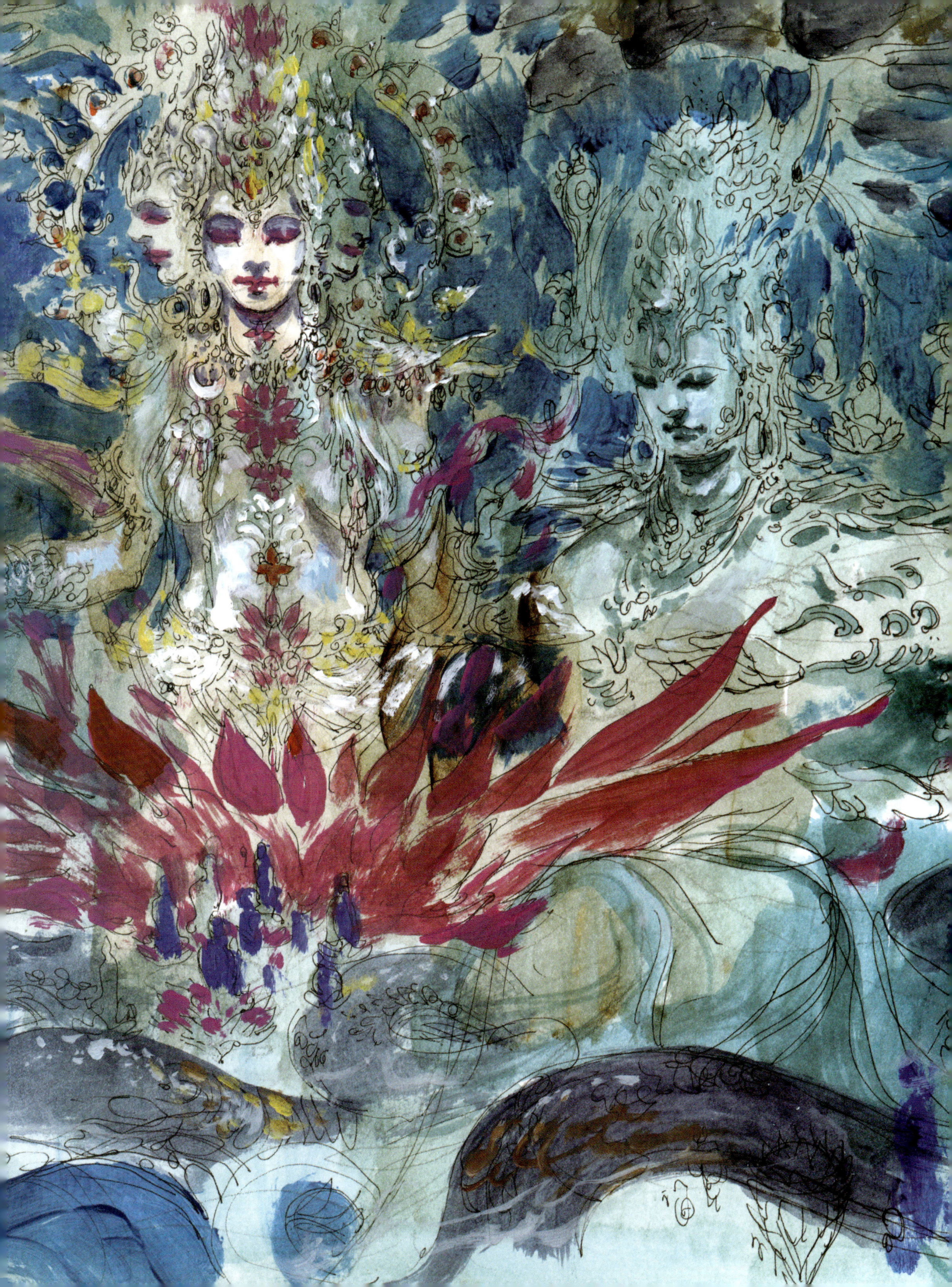

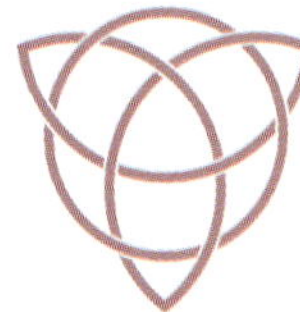

Indra took a moment, collected himself, and spoke earnestly.
"Gyanendreya, the knower of mysteries, you must already know our torments and pain but before we proceed with our plea, we have another humble request. We want to know more about the vision, fragments of which we saw, when Shiva opened the portal for us. Tell us more about the Devi who came in your vision, and what happened after you received a horse head?"

Vishnu, without uttering a word, simply looked at Lakshmi, and by their glances, conjured up another vision, unveiling a bygone event, which had remained cloaked in the obscured drapes of time.

His voice echoed, "After she gave me the head of the horse, I brimmed with the knowledge of all ancient mysteries, the locks opened and creation started to move from its aquatic nature to its earthy aspects. Yet, somewhere, another being with a similar horse head existed, who also had worshipped the great Goddess and had procured the boon, that it cannot be killed by anything, or anyone other than the one with the head of the horse.

I soon found myself in confrontation with this asura and I assailed him, releasing the knowledge back to its source, which he had stolen from the vaults of Earth.

When I fought this asura, no one but she could tell me apart from it, as our forms looked alike. In our lives we may confront a reality, which seems real, but may not be so. The Goddess thus taught me, how to deduce it, to separate the real from the unreal, to know that our angry self and our calm self look alike, yet cannot be further apart. It's through her that I learned the knowledge and mysteries of maya, the illusionary matrix, which surrounds us all.

Gods born in one cycle of time, don't remember the activities of another cycle, the delusion is as much part of us, this amnesia, which holds us back from understanding who we are and constantly imposes itself on our journey of self-awakening."

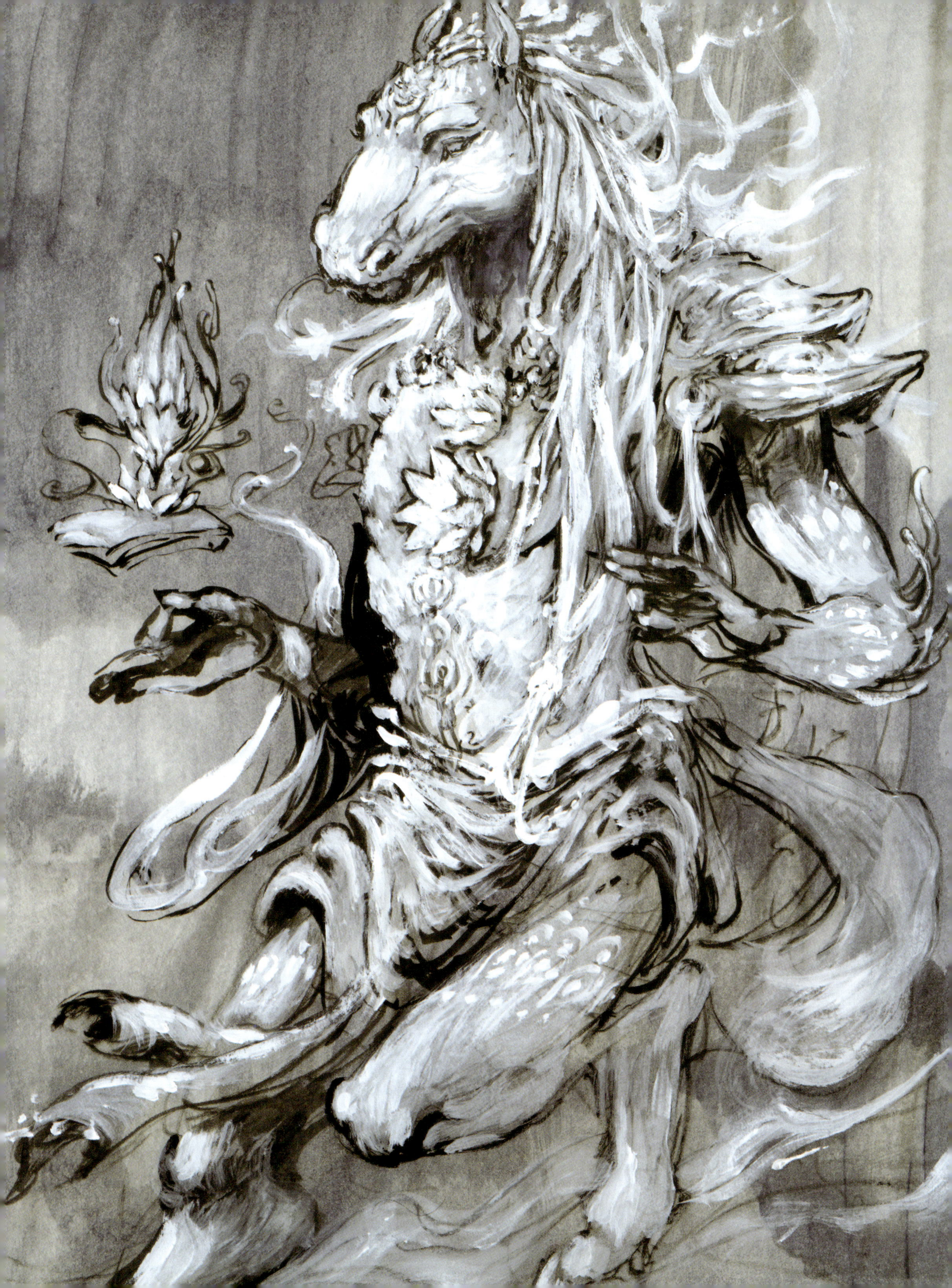

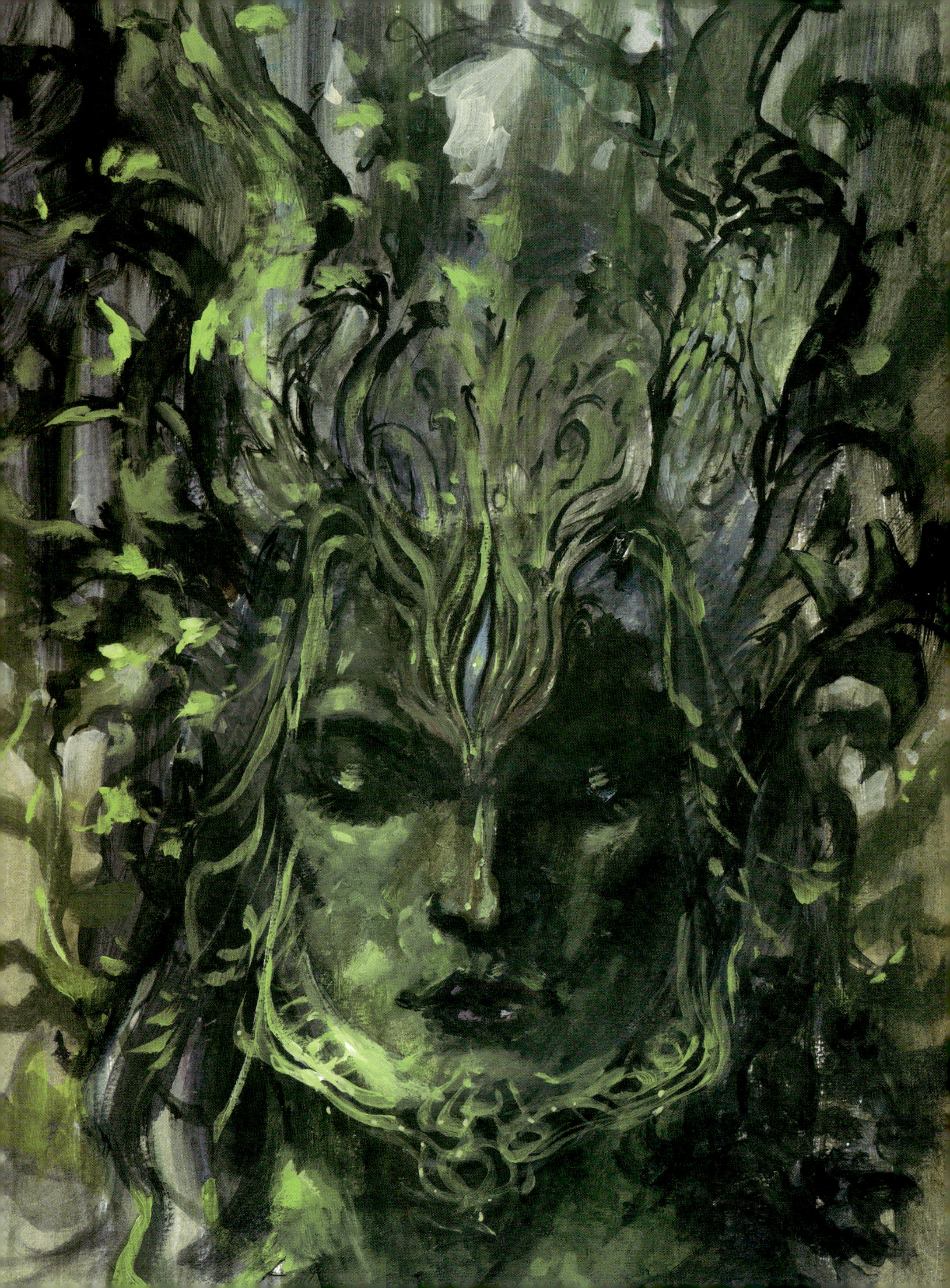

"Let me tell you another occurrence where I conferred the Goddess. The Earth was submerged in ethereal oceans in the beginning, holding its breath, relying on its inhaled primal energy. The atmosphere, which would awaken life on it, wasn't even born. I was in deep yogic sleep called yoga-nindra, meditating on the design of life, with Anantashesha, looking out for me while I slept.

O Suras, when we are asleep, flattery does not have the same effect on us, as it has when we are awake, but in the waking world we are cajoled by its charms, it influences our behavior, instilling greed and misdirection. As my being was cleansed, the vices and impurities dripped out of my ears and from that wax manifested two demons, Madhu and Kaitabh."

Together in the depths of the massive ocean, which covered the whole Earth, they decided to perform an intense penance to the Goddess. They profusely held their breath, endured the volcanic sounds, as it shuddered their stocky bones, and called upon the Goddess, to ask for immortality, as it was only the Devi, who could grant such a boon. She deflected their request, as she knew that birth and death both will be one in the world of matter, which awaited its completion and asked the two to possibly choose the closest boon to it. So they asked, to only die, when they would wish for it.

They roamed around the ocean marveling at their own fate, for who will ever wish to embrace death. They traversed the ocean everywhere reveling in its magnificent marine environments, which had thermal vents and all sorts of luminescent creatures. These primal oceans had been their home for so long that their hearts brimmed with a deep love for its beings.

One day they witnessed that a lotus had bloomed out of a place which resembled a naval, atop which sat the first Brahma, curious to see such a remarkable site, they came close and started to play with it like children upon seeing something new, and soon instilled Brahma with fear.
The demons asked him to step down as they wanted to take the beautiful-looking lotus seat for themselves.

Brahma's cry for help reached Yogamaya, the expansion of the Goddess, the only one who could reach me in my sleep and bring me back into the waking world.

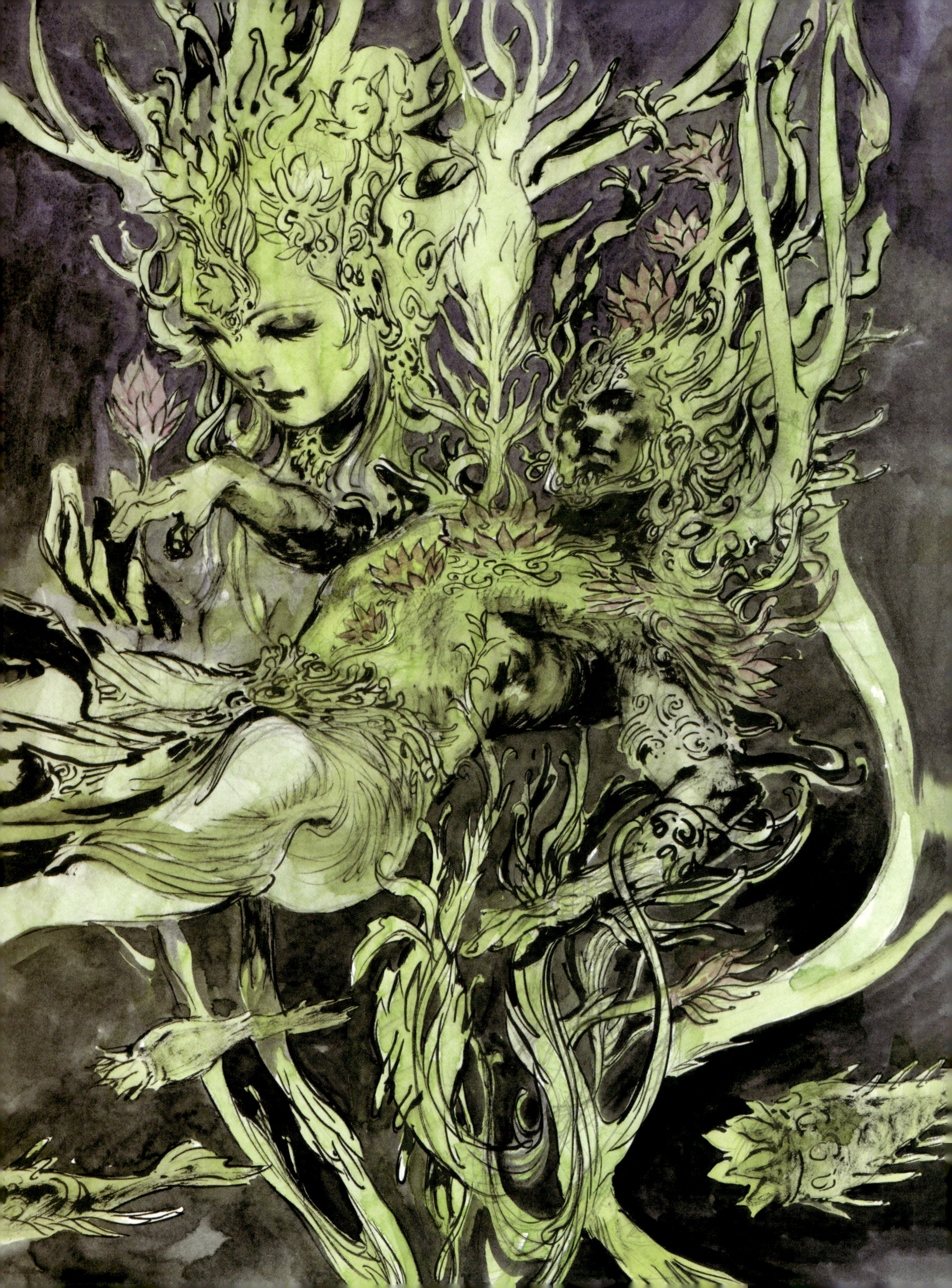

Each time creation dissolves and till a new one begins, I enter this deep meditation, in which I do not preside over my waking, dreaming and deep sleep states, and simply become an eternal observer. I rely on the great Goddess, who can move through all four states of our being, to invoke me back from any of the dimensions, into the waking world, whenever I'm needed, to sustain its cycles.

O Suras, she's greater than us all, and wiser. Half of Shiva's being is her and hence he's the most profound amongst us all. Without her, everything is inert and is not pervaded by life. From a blade of grass to mountains, all are enlivened by her energy. She governs the circadian rhythms, the many layers of illusion covering the matter, the energy everything contains and the many paths to breach the matrix.

As she streamed the sensation into me, my being woke up and I manifested in front of the two brothers, who soon challenged me to fight them. This battle raged till the waters erupted with ripples of fire, inside the depths of the primal ocean, these bands of energy heaved and struck us incessantly. I fought them for thousands of years and pondered, how they were blessed by the divine Shakti. By her grace, they were invincible and no extent of my valor was able to defeat them. So, I paused and requested the brothers, that I must meditate for a while and collect back my strength, as I was fighting both of them at the same time. The brothers were just and ethical and allowed me to meditate for a bit, on the promise that I will eventually come back and continue the fight.

"In my meditation, I tried to think, why anyone would wish for their own deaths?
This was my only hope to defeat them, as physical battle had paved no result.
I went inside my heart realm, Anahata, and stirred it, till I found the way upward, to speak to the one who had guided me thus far, the Devi. For she had woken me up and must guide me through this dilemma."

"Liberate me from this ongoing war O Apremaya, one who cannot be measured.
How do I slay these two demons, who never will invite death to their bodies?"

As the Devi's words appeared, the air from it, started to create the first layer of atmosphere.
The shimmering Devi expounded.

"What is death? Is it not transference of energy into other forms?
The material dissipates and the energy from it moves into another form.

From elements, to particle, to waves, to every tiny arrangement of this cosmos, is ever-changing.
Entropy is the natural order of a world influenced by time.
Death does not come; it's always there, intrinsic to life. How can something which is already here, arrive again?

Within the two demons, death has already pervaded, it may not exist or happen in the way they may perceive, but it's surely there, in another form, through another way.

The Goddess then propelled me to look for that which I had missed, I was fully awake now and my senses were precise. I saw how they loved the ocean and its beings, admiring that I returned to them and said,
You both have fought valiantly, and you can ask me any boon you like.
To which they replied that they desire nothing from me, instead they would like to grant me a boon at their behest.

The words poured out of me, like ripples when a stone is thrown into the stillness of water, the Devi spoke through me.
Let you both be transformed by me, from this form to another, let me bring death to you.

Sorrow gripped them for a moment, but gathering their sense, they spoke with one last attempt to avert their deaths, 'Grant us that boon, you promised us before.
The ocean water is all there is in this world, no earth anywhere to be seen yet, grant us that you'd slay us where there is solid ground, free from any water.

So I expanded my thigh, and requested them to keep their heads on it, but they were still not ready and in turn expanded their bodies even more. Seeing that my thigh had become even more enormous, they finally gave in. I took my energy disc, the sudarshan chakra, and did the needful."

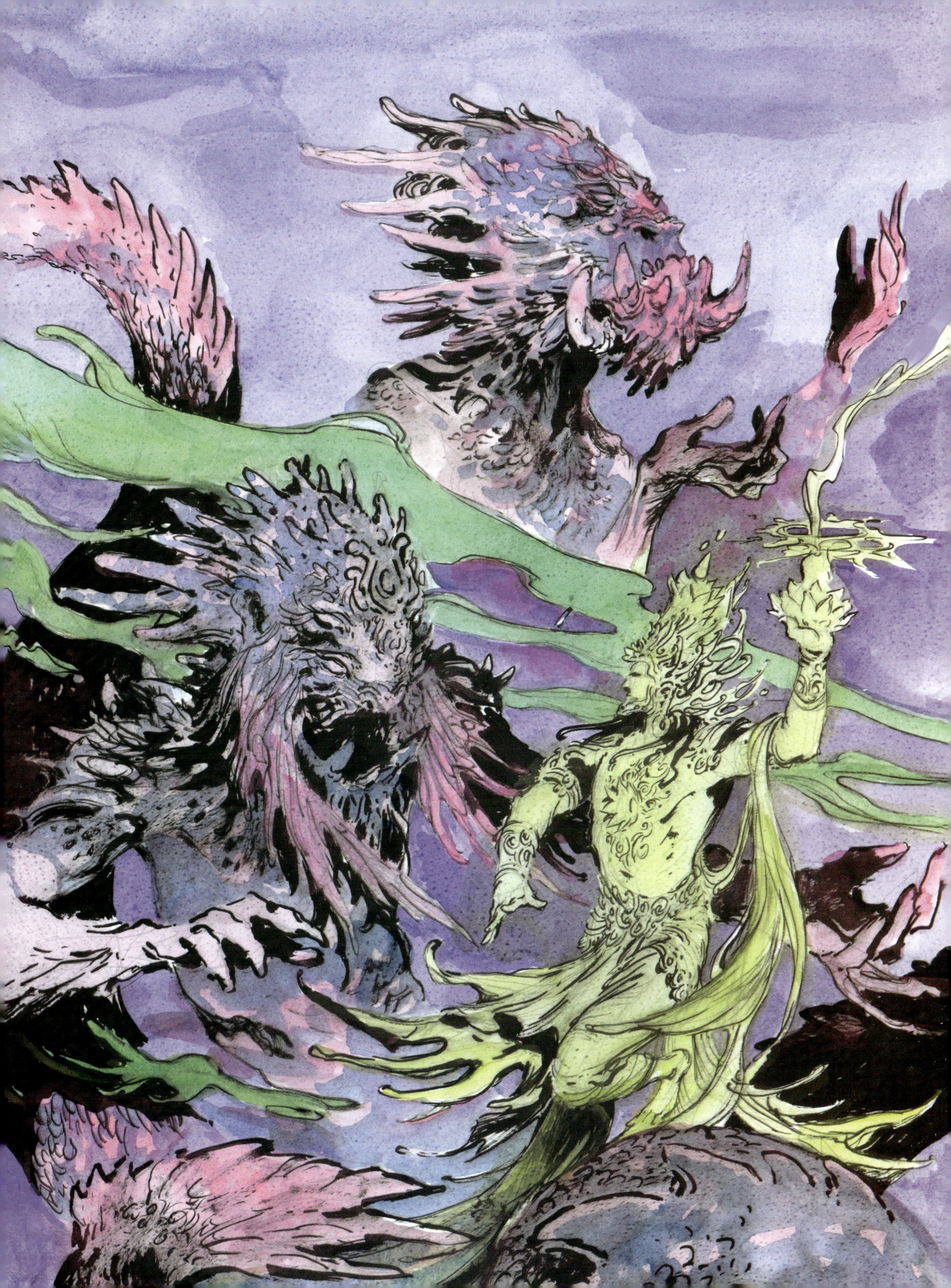

“She had guided me to simply transform the materiality, from one body to another. So, from their immense bodies, the marrow filled the ocean, creating conditions for the land to appear. The matter of their bodies formed the first masses of the Earth, swamps eventually settling into solid ground, and because of this, the earth of this epoch came to be known as Medhini. In a profound way, they too continued their journey, becoming part of something they loved.”

With this vision, Vishnu concluded his story and glanced lovingly at Lakshmi, who was present in the oceans then, as the primal consciousness. With his mind riveted in that admiration, he finally looked at the gods and Indra, who stood enamored, feeling a little healed from their fatigued selves.

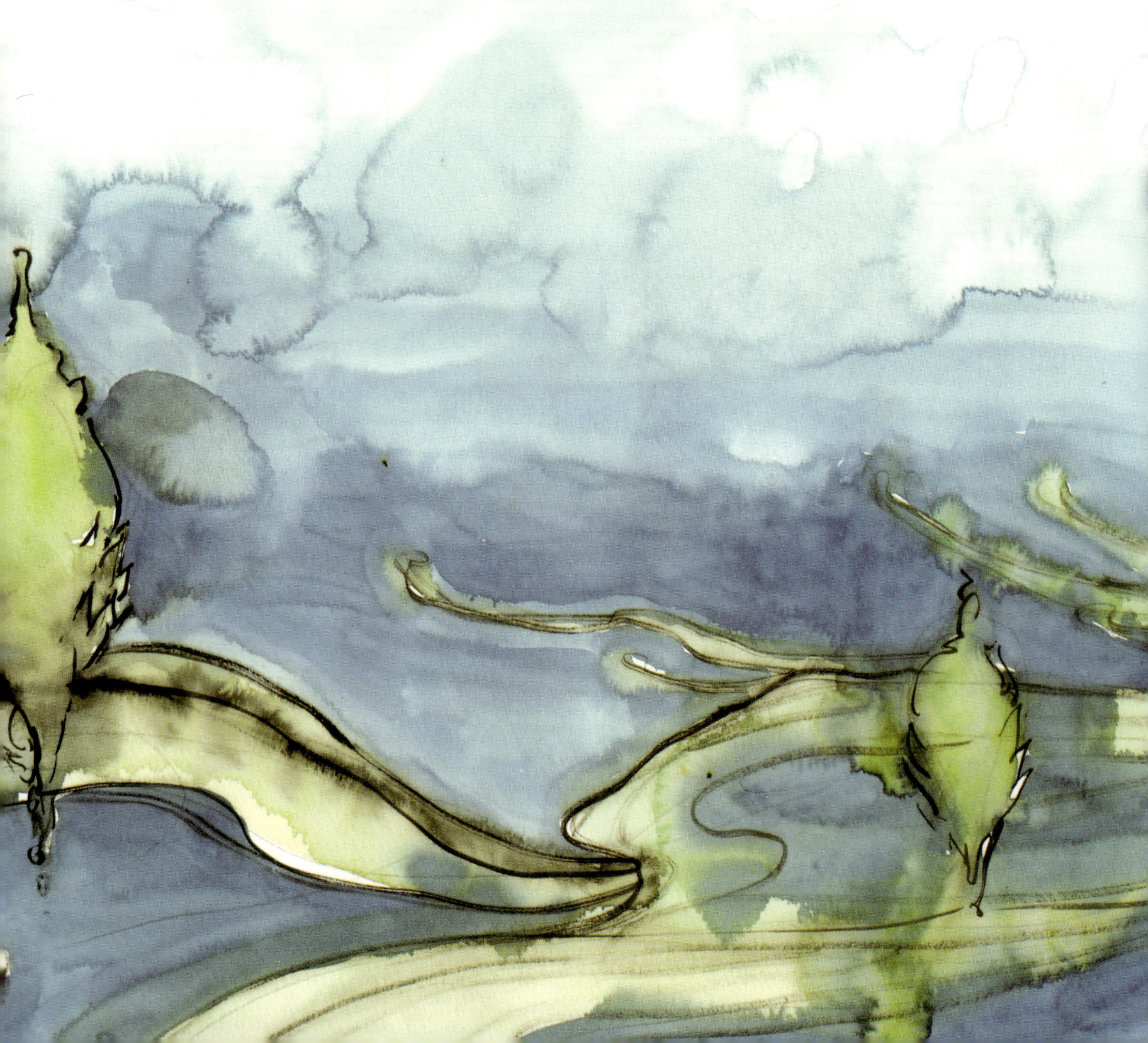

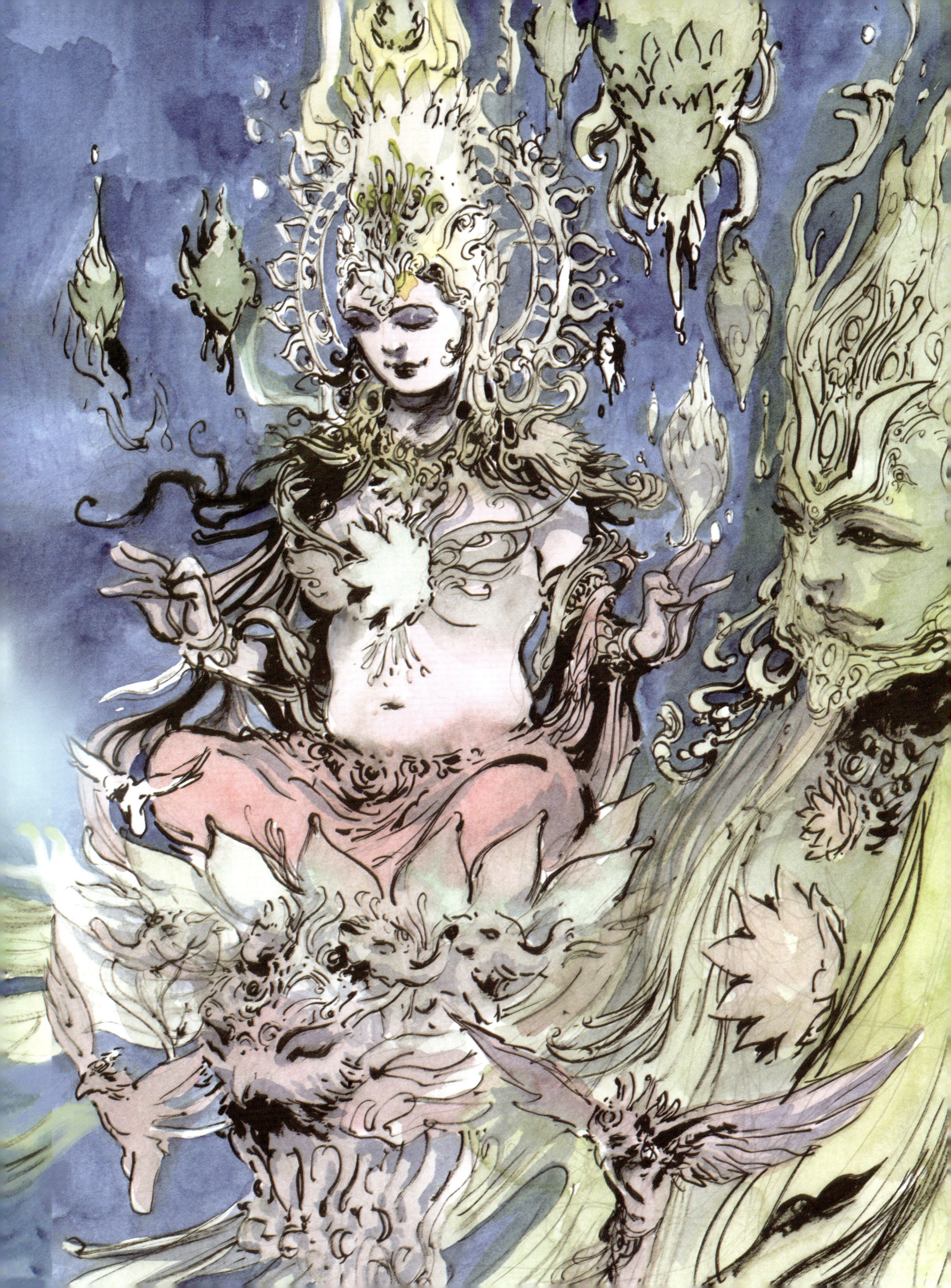

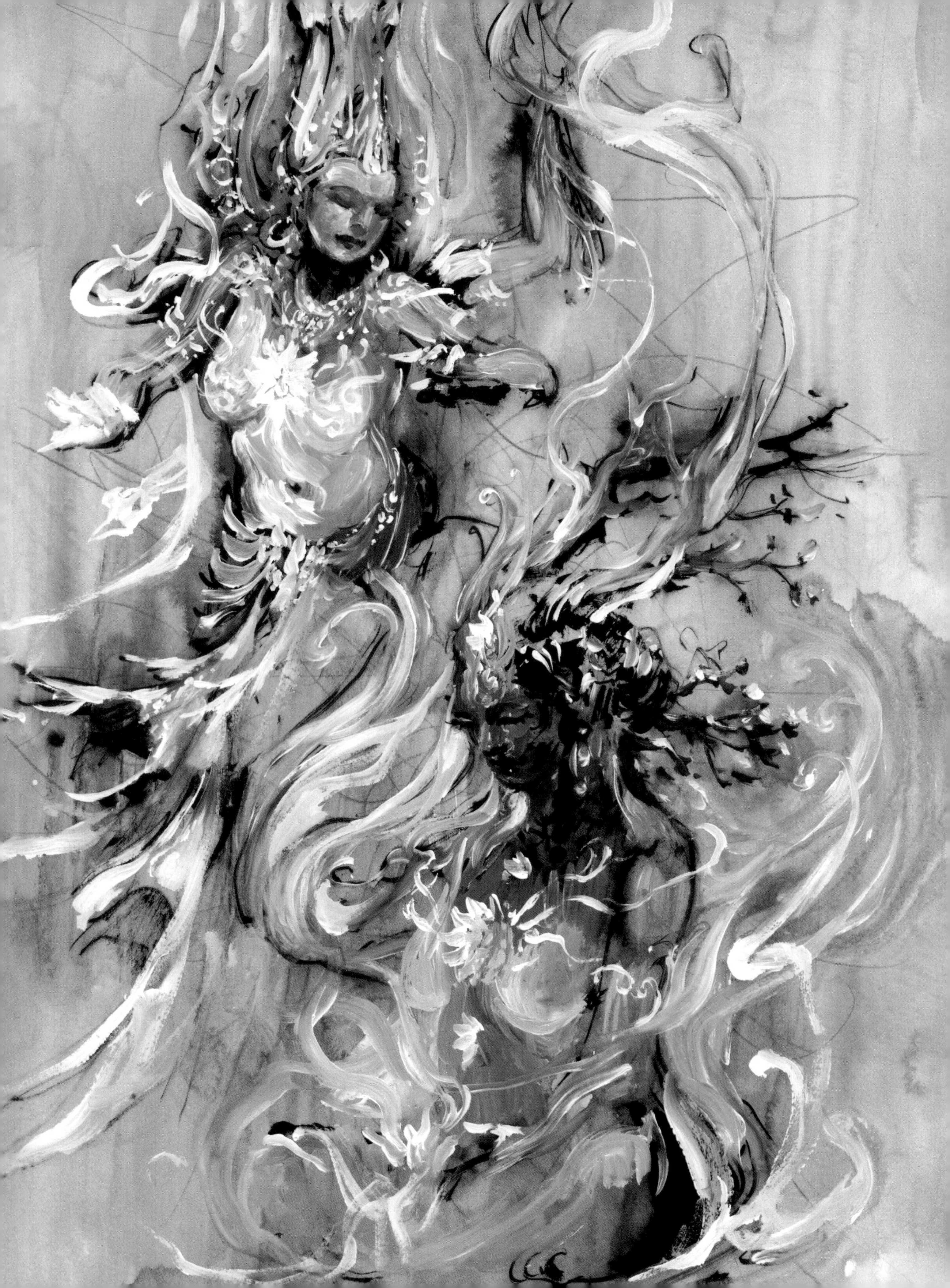

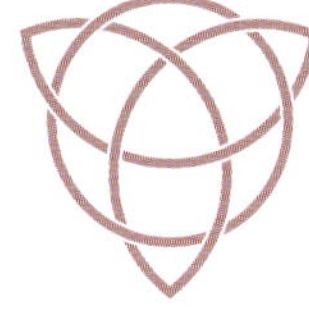

Indra, who was laden with much plight, came right to the issue, and said,

“I revere your perseverance against the brothers and their undying reverence, but we are no match to your valor and I’m ashamed that we were wilted out of heavens, by Mahisha and his emissaries. O, Vasudeva, lord of ocean currents, how can we transcend this obstacle and reclaim the pious abode of the gods?”

Vishnu’s mind was already in union with Lakshmi’s, as he persuaded her to suggest a solution to the problem of the gods.

Suddenly a band of light emanated from the lotus-eyed Padma, the one who was the bearer of all light, Vishnu’s consort, and the one who pervaded all creation, above and below, within and abound.

She spoke in a voice, which exuded a thousand conch shells, yet like a gentle flower falling atop the ethereal pond over the minds of the gods, soothing them from the darkness and avidya, nescience they had inflicted upon themselves. Her voice healed their darkness.

“The Mahisha is inside of you Indra, you must first vanquish that from within, just like death is interlaced with life, intents with actions, Shakti with Purusha. The same arrogance, self-destruction, which corrupted Mahisha, torments you as well. You must cut that away from your inner being and with it take the journey of acceptance to understand that it’s we who precariously birth our own obstacles.

The confrontation of this event must take place within you, deep down inside are the roots from which manifested this nefarious cycle. Invoke your will Indra, try to see it, sense it, access it.”

As Padma’s voice resonated in the minds of the lost gods, another vision joined in, a voice laced with rivers holding their breath, exhaling into the oceans within. Dappled light fell upon the gods as Uma, the splendid one, lovingly known as Parvati, the daughter of the cosmic valley, who had witnessed the submerged mountains of primal times, appeared before them.

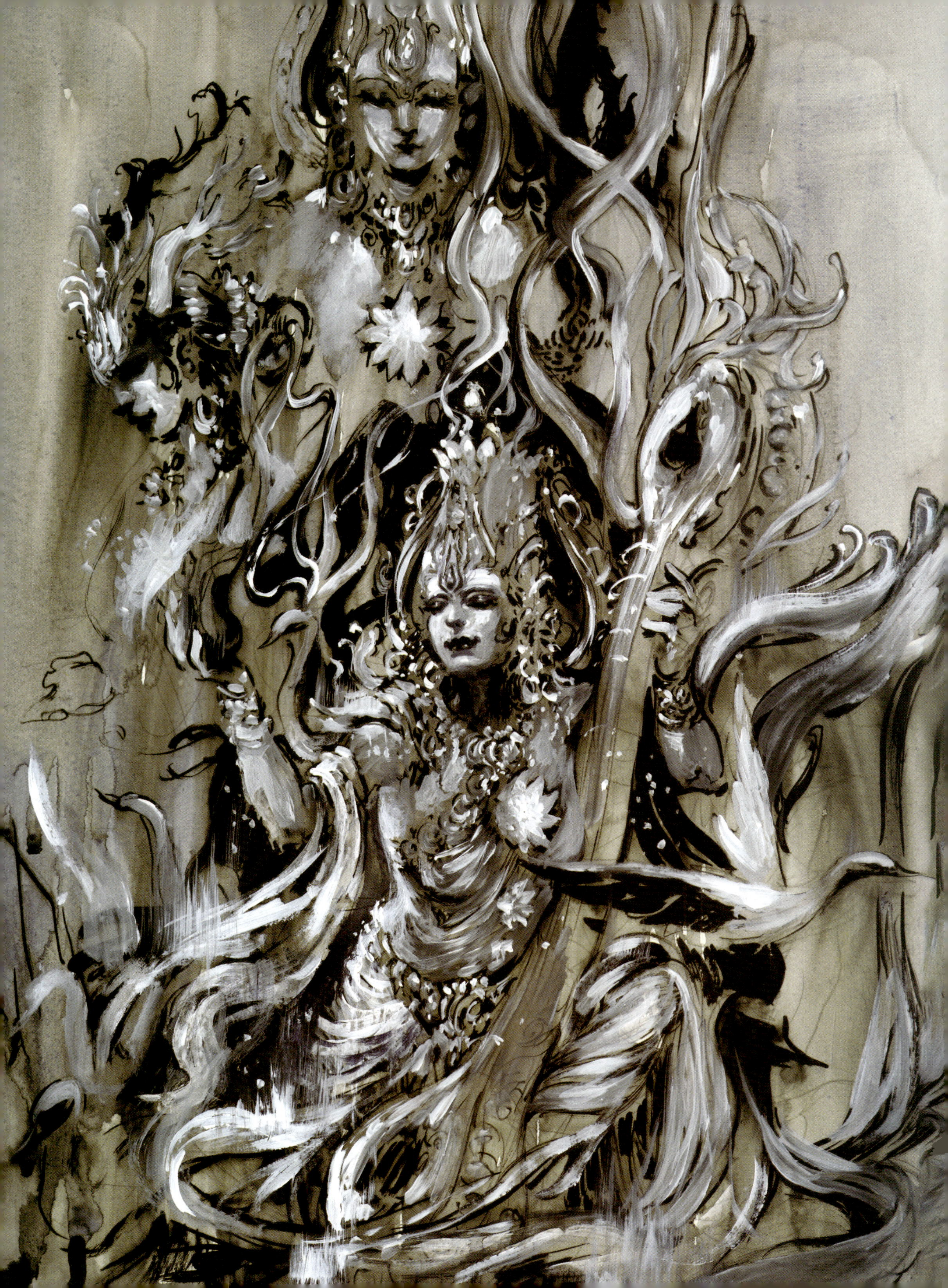

Her voice fused with Padma's aura and brimmed with unimaginable foresight. As the gods stood lost in this glorious reverie, a third voice joined the vision, a flight of swans, entered their minds. Each like a spore rising from their cosmic bodies, the swans followed sonorous music which could only be heard by the most patient ears, perhaps even not by that. A music which had no sound, but was reverberating through every aspect of life around, revealing its inherent wisdom. Saraswati, the goddess of knowledge and remover of avidya seeped herself into the amalgamation taking place between Uma and Lakshmi.

The three goddesses weaved themselves in a helixical formation, like strands, from where life itself had emerged, coalescing into a beautiful vision, in which they were all present, moving away from the three gunas, qualities and attributes—rajas, sattva, tamas, into their true essence form. An observer to all layers of existence, nameless, indivisible and profound, revealing the beginnings of the universe itself, where forms didn't exist.

As this premonition was being birthed in front of the awestruck gods, the triad of Brahma, Vishnu and Shiva, also merged into the vision, offering all their yogic essence to it.
The sight was beyond description, which the eyes couldn't see and neither the words could describe. It was something fire couldn't burn and water couldn't wet. The sound could not manifest and ether could not contain. As if all creation was being cradled somewhere within its initial nebula blooming as one.

The energies of the three gods also swirled in reverence, the red of Brahma, blue of Vishnu and white of Shiva, blending into the source of all life.

Slowly from the breathing living orb of energy, a form started to manifest, like many stars being birthed, a common echo of the three goddesses appeared. A vision in whose embrace many universes were breathing and contracting all at the same time.

In this vision the gods also sensed the three gods who gave themselves willingly to it, the beginning—Brahma, the sustainer—Vishnu, and Shiva—who gave the energy back to its source. Present in them were all the ancient sounds and the silences in between. Just like how from the golden womb rose the cosmos, similarly from the sphere of incomparable energy manifested the vision of the Goddess.

This enigmatic vision appeared differently to each god. They were bewildered by this miraculous moment and hailed her by many names.
Some called her, *Adi-paremeshwari*, the primordial one, *Jagatdhatri*, the sustainer of the worlds, *Jagadamba,* the all mother of worlds, *Bhavani*, the one true abode of truth, *Nirdavaita*, the one without duality, *Aja-Jetri*, victorious over ignorance, *Adi-Yogini*, who aligns all worlds, *Gyanada*, the giver of knowledge, *Vishva Garbha*, who has universe in her womb, *Avradha*, destroyer of evil doers, *Trideshvari*, in whom reside the three gods, *Brahmanda-Janani*, giver of worlds, *Adi-Shakti*, the primal force which creates, *Achintya Rupa*, one with inconceivable form, *Bandha-Mochani*, liberator of bondage, *Anutamma*, superior to all, *Sarvotomuki*, infinite faced, *Niraga*, without blemishes, *Nirbhava*, without origins and thousand other names, out of which, few got crystalized into memory, most, stayed inside the crevasses of silent meditation, some morphed into sounds, which moved beyond words, some gave up their material form and some embraced to become inexplicable sensations flooding the inner sanctums of beings and the heart of gods.

The gods couldn't help but craved to become part of the benevolent invocation, as it called to their true nature. They moved into a prayer, joining their essence with its spirit.
For a moment they forgot all about their war trodden hearts and just selflessly offered all their being to the vision, giving away the most precious part of their spirits, realizing that they never owned their own energy, that it had always belonged to this unraveling vision and now the time has come, where they should humbly return it back.

The vision welcomed them just as a shoreless ocean envelops the many rivers. In the energy of the Goddess, all the gods blended themselves, leaving their differences behind, as one.
The gods offered many gifts and merged all their powers. As they added these layers the Goddess started to appear into a physical dimension.

The elemental gods, the nature gods, the guardians and warrior gods, all gave their essence in reverence to the Devi.

The cosmic waters and its rivers became her many nerves, nadies, opulent with pranic energies. Oceans became heavenly pearls in her necklace, embellishing the throat, adorning her with garlands made of lotuses, which would never fade. Each raindrop became her many atoms.
Agni, the fire god and his many manifestations, offered their pranic force to her chakras, energy wheels, portals through which the infinite coiled serpentine energy could move up and forged her the most exquisite spear, representing ability, restraint and seeking.

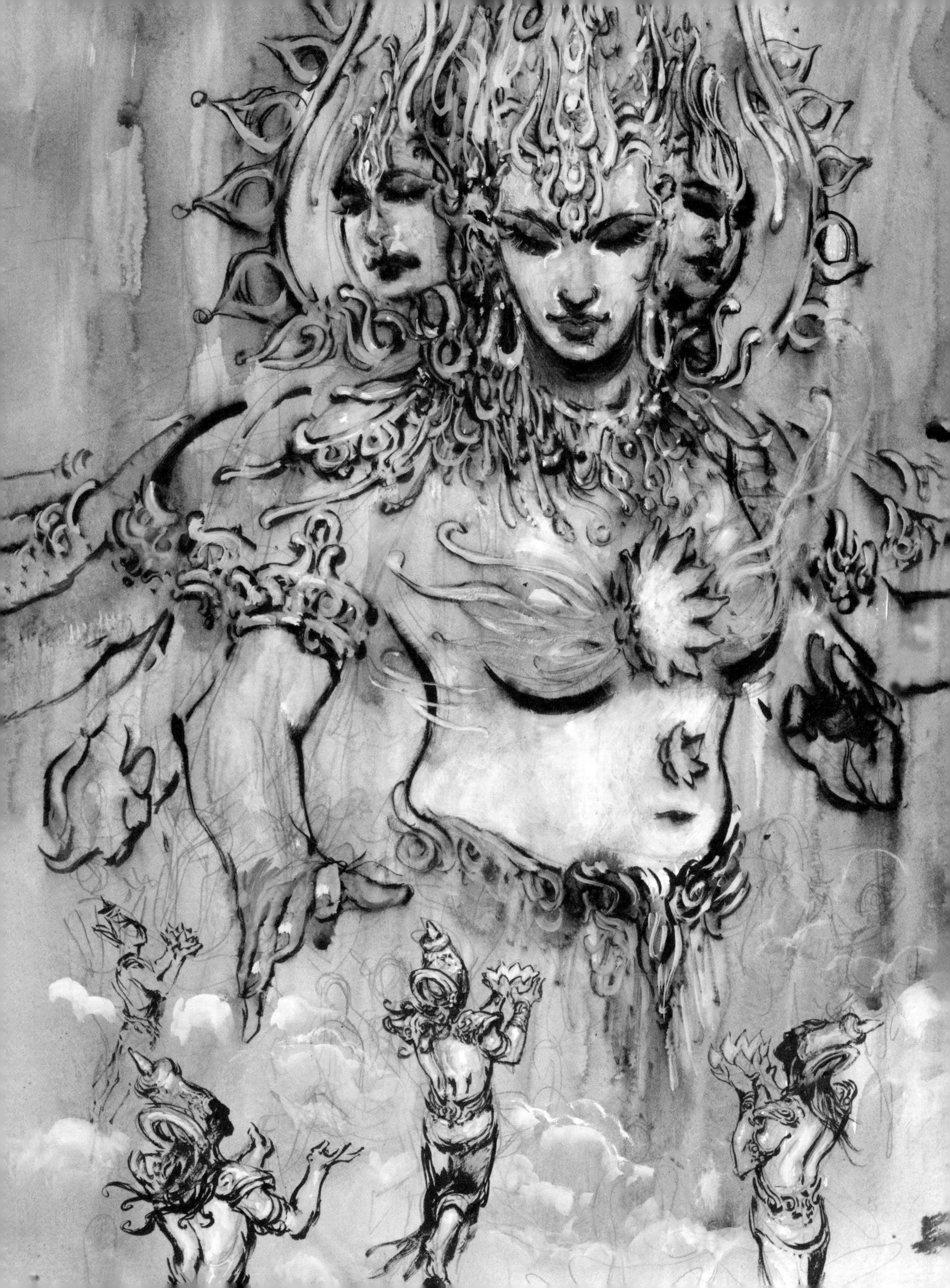

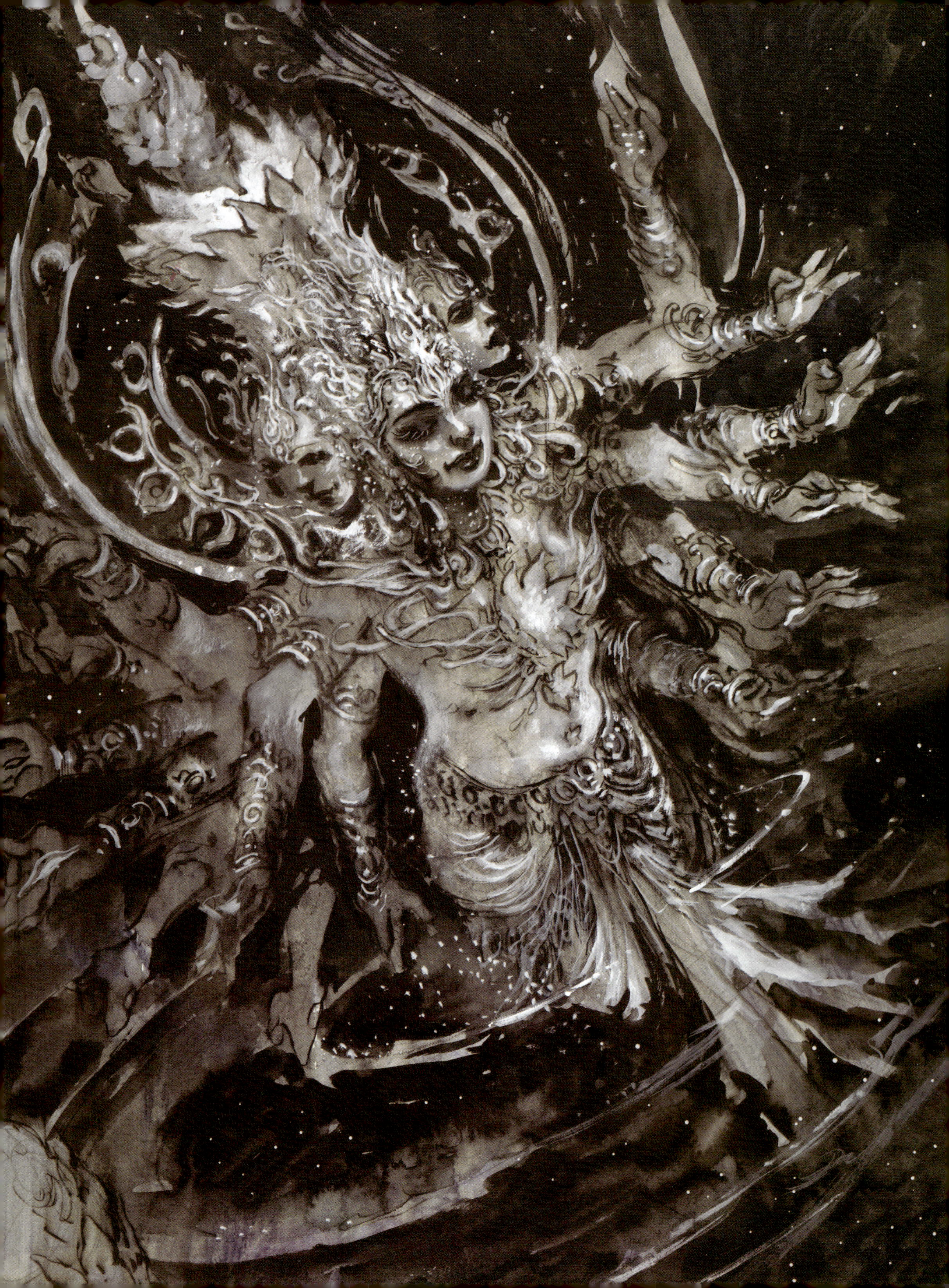

The Earth made her body, bones and marrow, and channeled the energy, orbiting into her mind's eye, cymatic and circadian rhythms, an all seeing power.

The Ether gifted the membranes of consciousness through which energy could herald itself beyond the known, into the realm of Sahasrara, as the fountain of Life.

The divine architect, Vishvakarma presented her with a diadem, a crest to be worn on the head and an axe and an armor, which would never rust, like eternal wisdom.

The wind currents, Maruts and god of air, Vayu, presented her with the most wondrous bow and quiver with infinite arrows, representing control of breath, aim, realization and pranic knowledge of how the universe functions.

Indra, gifted her all his rain, thunder, weather and the most potent of all weapons, the Vajra, made from the bones of ancient medicants.

Kubera, accorded her with alchemical powers, gold, wine and drinking cups.
Sun, adorned her with its rays and the adityas, with their many frequencies and colors and became part of her aura.

Death, Yama, offered her a scepter, noose, his wisdom and brandished the most immaculate swords for her, representing how time cuts through all.

The elemental God Varuna, the lord of the seas, offered her a conch, the vibrational aspect, which permeated atoms and universes.

Brahma, offered her the vessel, kamandala, filled with the most primal waters, from where creation had sprouted, and a lotus, which represented spiritual awakening and consciousness.

Vishnu, the preserver of worlds gave her, Chakra, the cyclic energy discs, representing the balance and harmony of energy cycles. He also gifted her a mace, in accordance with discipline, understanding, dharma and laws.

As her form materialized, it seemed that Indra had become her torso. Moon, Chandra, her breasts, Brahma, her teeth, Earth her lower body, Varuna, her thighs and knees and Agni, gave fire enlivening her eyes.

In her face, reflected Shiva, who gathered the three gunas, psycho-spiritual qualities, sattva-harmony and balance, rajas-activity, action and tamas-subconscious, nescience and compounded them into a Trident for her in his own image, as the ultimate destroyer of illusions.

The snakes from the infinite oceans became part of her being, so did all life forms and sentience. The trees and their many descendants became her hair, and the various healing roots her garments.

Finally, the mountains, from within her, which moved about in tectonic drifts, waiting to be born onto the terrain of the worlds, manifested itself as the most majestic of lions.

The Devi lovingly touched his forehead and called it Kesri and with this gesture her invocation was complete and she revealed herself to all the gods.

The gods had also been awakened from their trance, back into the moment. Time again became linear, as they felt a sense of profound emptiness, having given all their energies in severance to the Devi, with their hearts healed, rivers welled out of their eyes honoring her meditative vision.

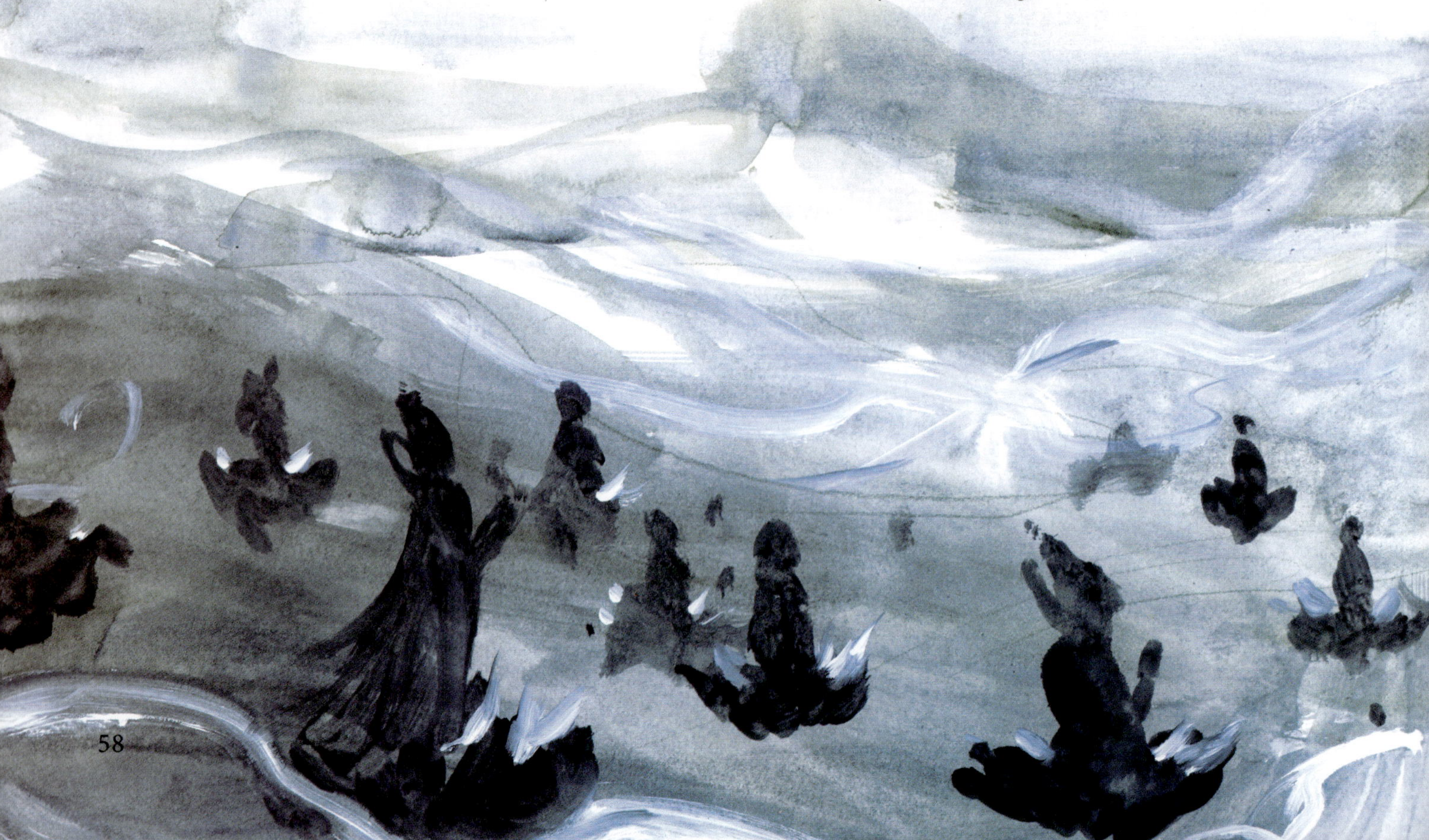

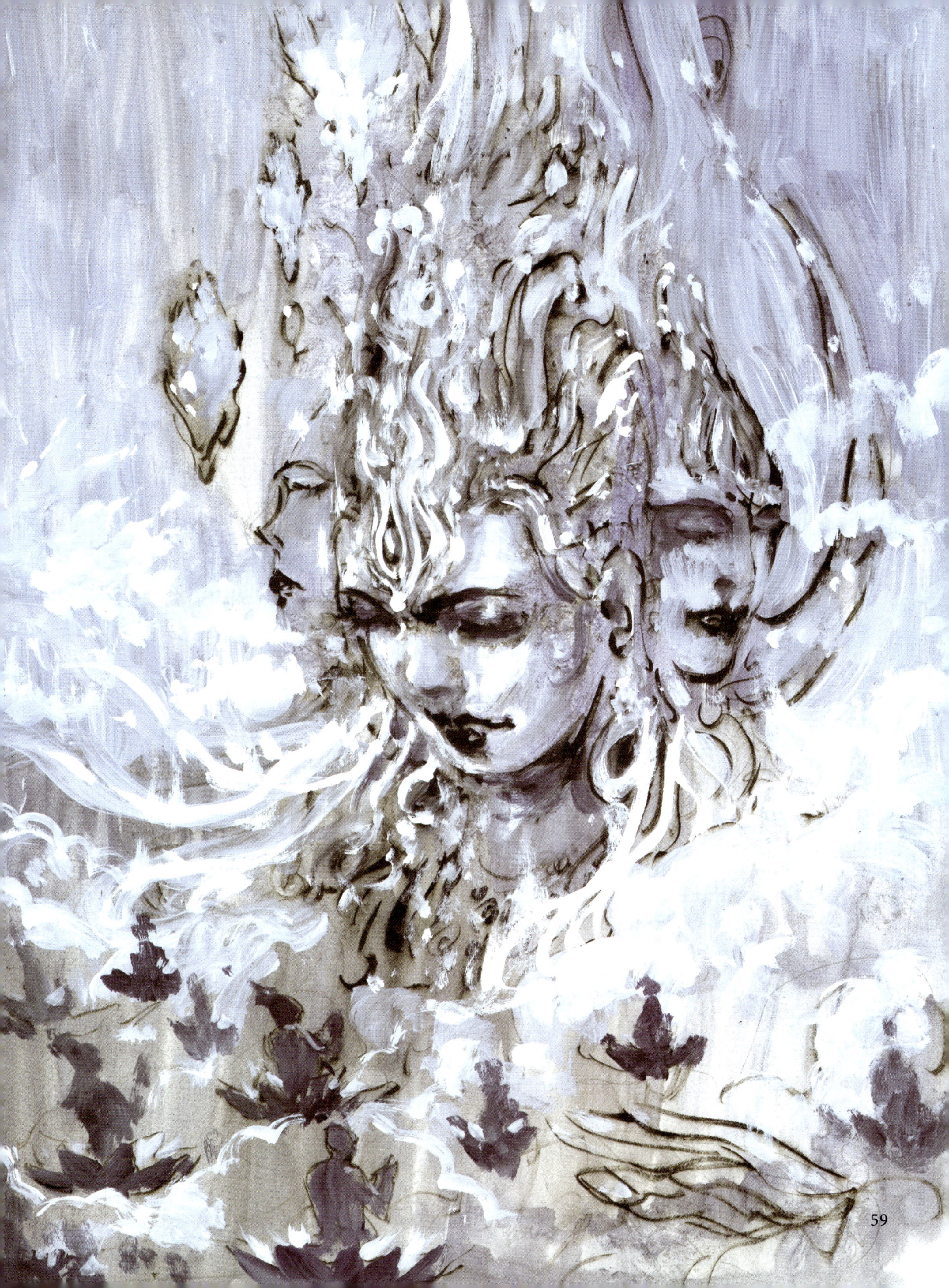

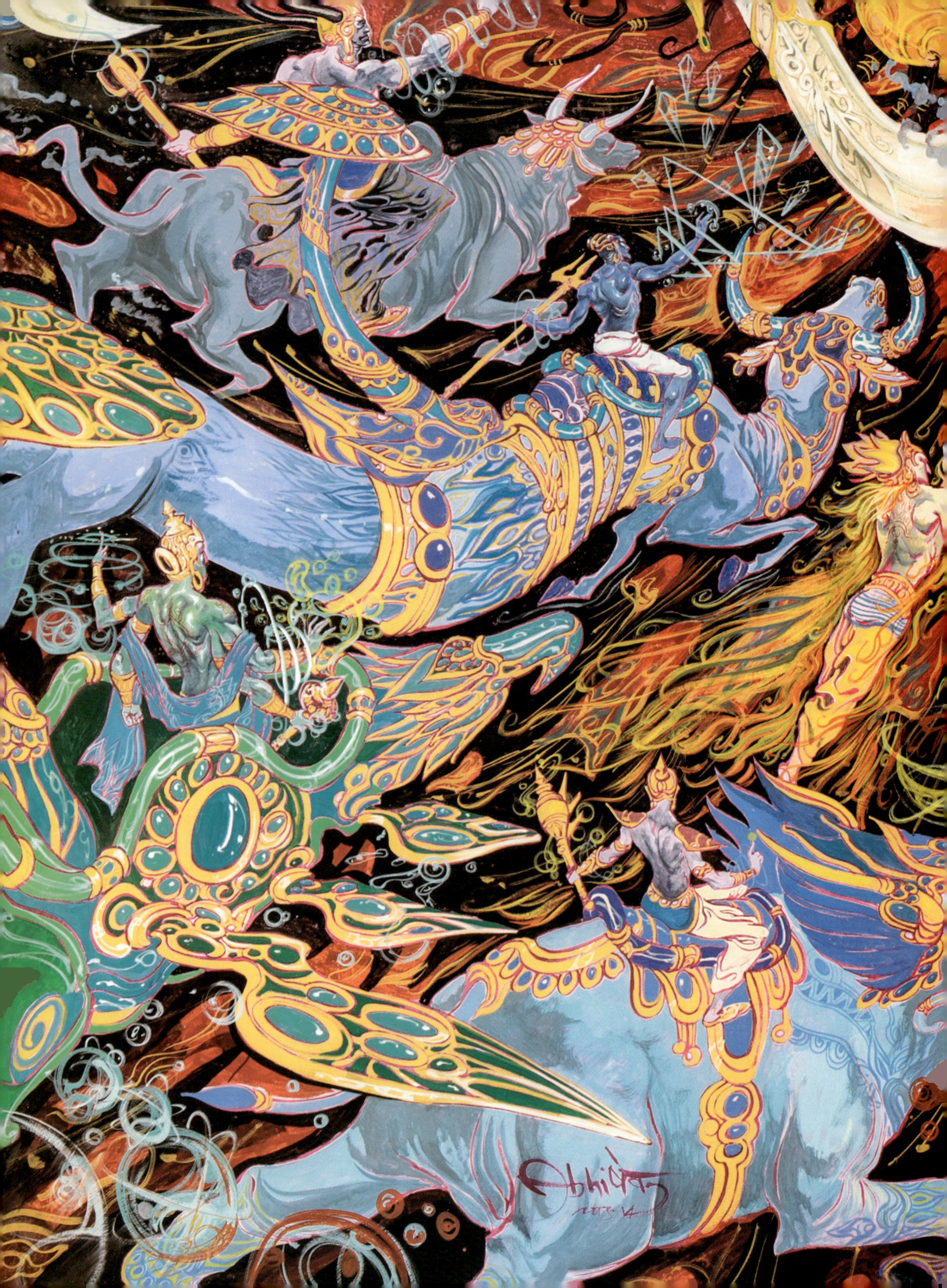

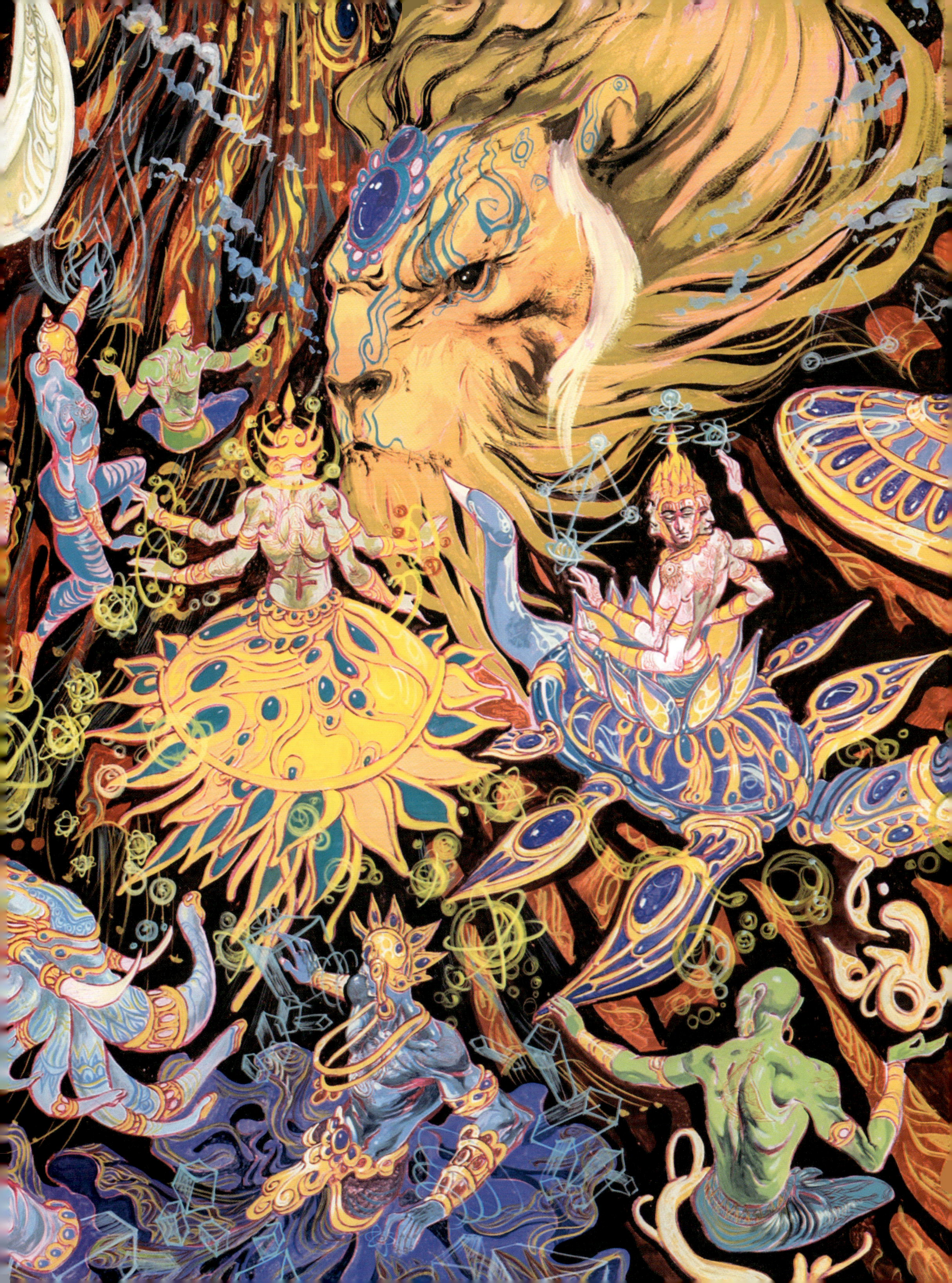

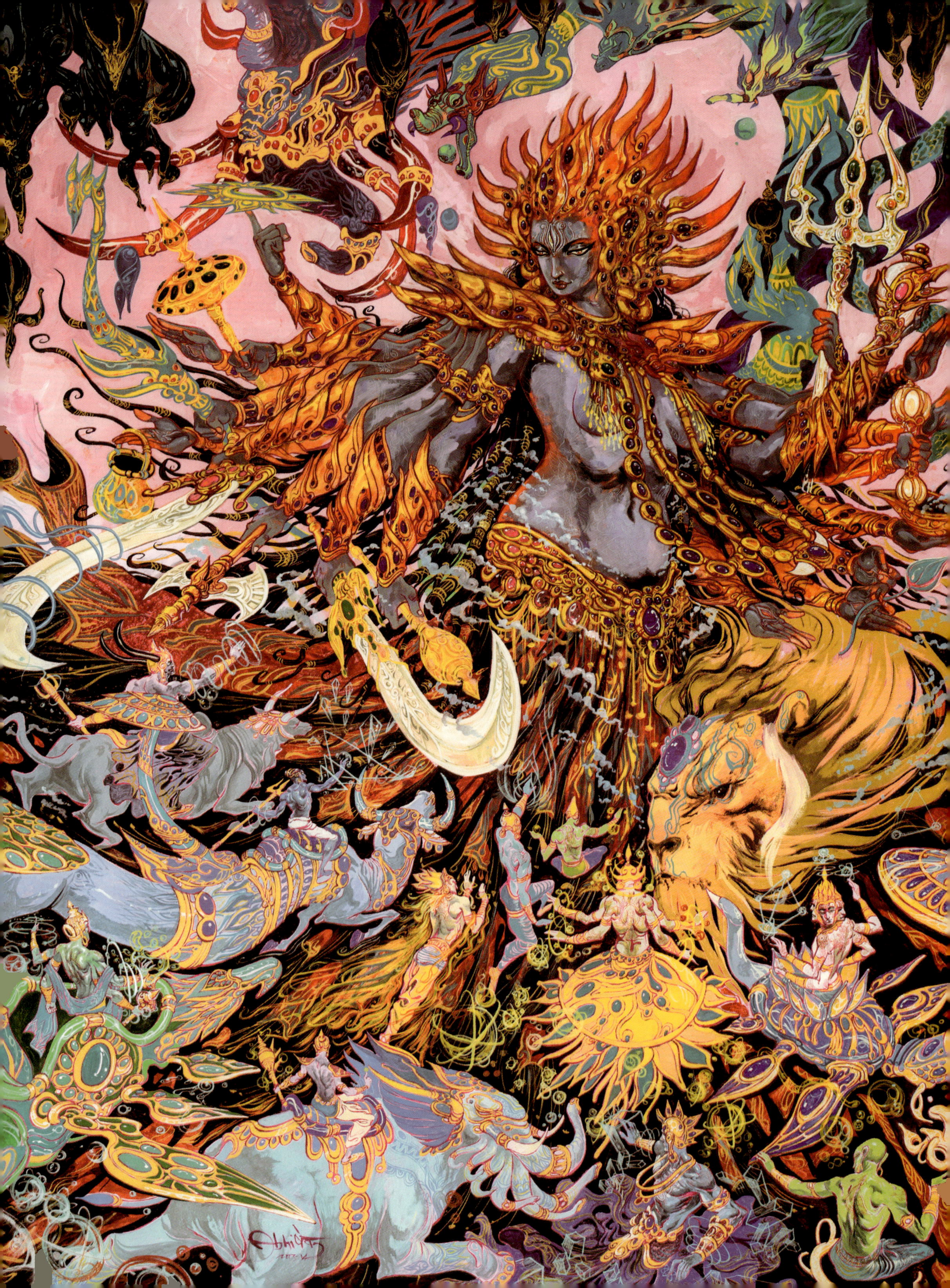

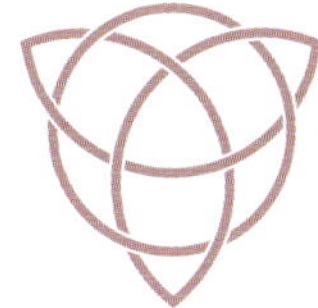

Upon seeing the splendid Goddess who emboldened their spirit, they sang her praises and appealed for her guidance. They were feeling empowered and they spoke with much calm than before.

"O Devi, the creator of all, would you help us to reclaim the heavens and slay the demon king Mahisha whose wretched tendencies are contaminating the sacred abode."

The grand vision, which now had manifested as Maha-Devi thus spoke to the gods, "O Suras, the resounding ones, I know why you've invoked me, but I feel there's something you all want to know before I go in pursuit to vanquish Mahisha. Ask me what puzzles your minds.

The gods replied with equanimity,

Who are we? O Maheshvari, the one without whom, even Shiva is a corpse.
You have descended from beyond the fences of time, you've looked into our world, you've seen us being born and die many a times, we don't have memories that ancient, enlighten us about our origins and our purpose?"

The Devi spoke lovingly,

"As gods you represent various phenomena in nature and are appointed as guardians to maintain harmony between all its cycles. You are all children of Medhini, the primordial earth."
"Existence operates at various planes, matter, mind and spirit, hence, you all are also enshrined, inside the body, as jiva, the living entity, inside nature, as prakriti, and in ether, as brahman, moving from, form to formlessness, yet, always maintaining the great alignment between them.

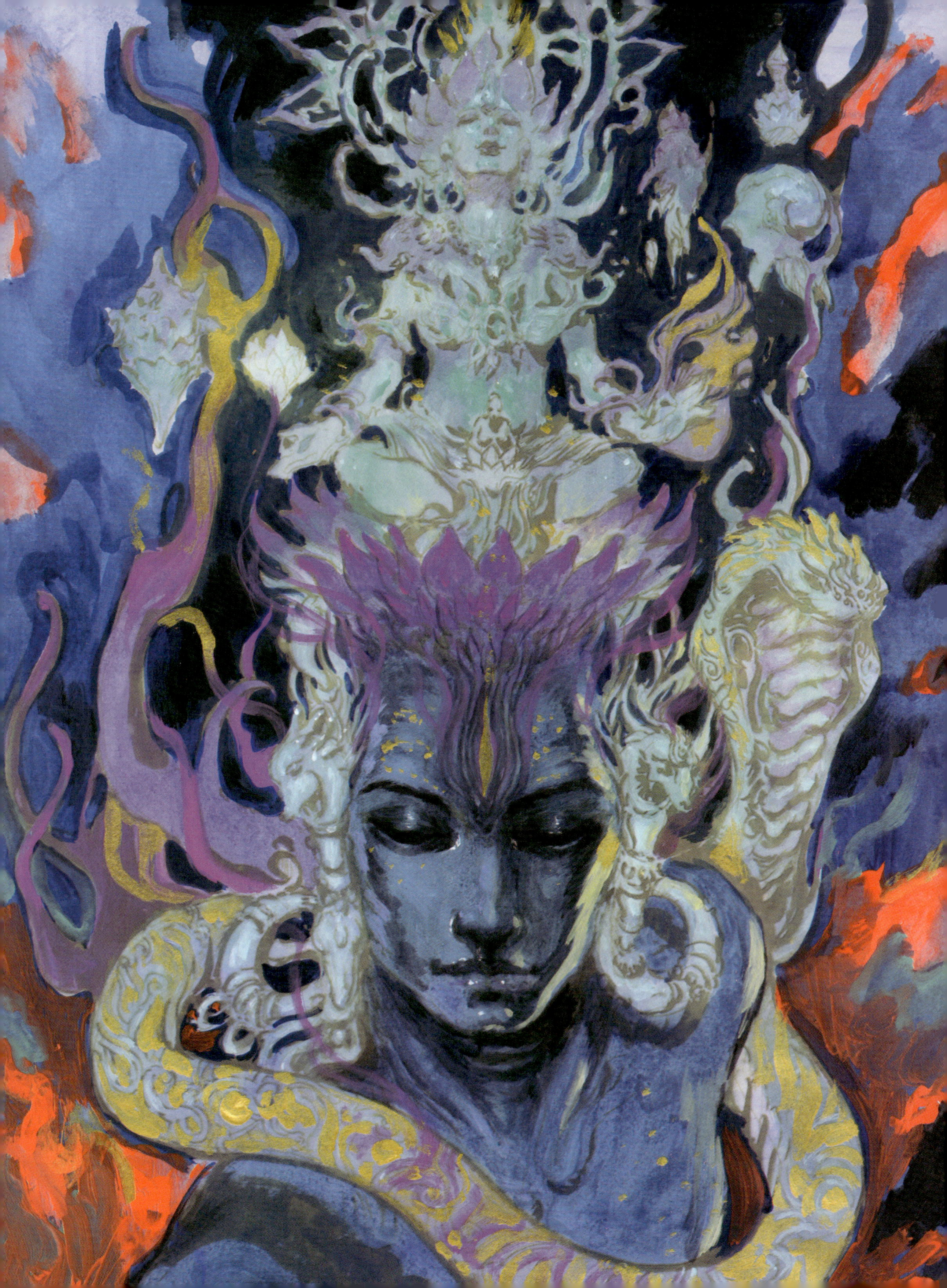

You all carry the three attributes in varying degrees inside of you, sattva, rajas, tamas and are affected by them in turn. Only when you realize yourself you are not that but the ultimate essence, you are not inflicted by their influence on your egos. Hence you must always remain in harmony with nature. Let the Earth be your guide always."

Gods: O Maha-Devi, what do we re-align ourselves to, when we find ourselves going astray from our paths?

Devi: When you are angry, do you also realize in that moment that you are angry?
Yes, replied the gods in unison.

Devi: The part, which knows you are angry, is that angry? They both coexist, isn't it, one as the emotion and the other, as the psychological observer of that emotion. You are that observer, the part which is not angry. Hence, O Suras, when these limits are crossed and the gods inside the jiva are jeopardized then they must seek the Shakti, the Devi, to be empowered and become her in the process.

With that the Maha-Devi, expanded and took a long breath. As she exhaled, many other goddesses emerged out of her, like each god through her had transformed into their feminine counterparts, being hailed as Matrikas, mothers, MahaVidyas, Wisdom guardians, Yoginis-Alignment seers and thousands of others.
Her breath was so deep that the gods themselves were bewildered at the amount of intensity it generated. Her fierce howls shuddered through the realms and pierced the ears of the asuras sitting in the halls of heaven.

She moved and in a second mounted her lion, all the goddesses vanished inside her body and she rode straight for the battlefield. In this form she was called Durga, Ambika, the protector.

Brahma, Vishnu and Shiva too returned to their forms, and held their mind's eye in the direction where the Maha-Devi had traversed, towards the war grounds where they will be with her, onlooking this spectacle.

The Devi, stepped into the field of action from her etheric form, sent out another bellowing sound, which seemed like laughter, but it moved the mountains, and raised the ocean waves to enormous heights and stoked the winds to their most ferocious velocity, and struck at the heart of the asuras sitting in heaven, with much terror. This startled asura king Mahisha, he said,
"Who makes this sound? It cannot be Devas as they are curtailed from their strengths, so who creates this magnanimous echo? Go and find out Asiloma, the wisest amongst asuras."

Asiloma went without moving his body, using his mind's eye, and saw the beautiful form of the Goddess, in whose thousand hands blossomed and withered the many energy worlds. As he blinked and mustered the courage to behold the splendid vision again, he saw the most beautiful fierce looking woman, mounted on a majestic lion, wielding with eighteen hands the various powers of the gods. He felt a sense of devotion towards her, but he also sensed the terrifying fate, which awaited the asuras, in her form.

Asiloma returned to his body and told Mahisha and his warrior generals what he had seen.
"O! Ruler of the three worlds, the one whose heart is forged from fire itself, listen to what I have to say. A woman, who looks neither like the gods, nor resembles the asuras, unlike a gandharva, apsara or any other sentience or form fused with matter and energy, stands in the battlefield unwavered, decked with the most celestial aura, something which I've never witnessed. She seems both benevolent and terrifying, and awaits fearlessly mounted on the most regal lion."

Mahisha became curious, "A woman you say, a goddess? What might she want from me? Perhaps she desires an audience with the king of all worlds, for no one but I seem worthy of such a gem amongst women, you have so eloquently described. Go and ask her if that's her wish, for there's nothing more satisfying than to be desired by such a one."
Asiloma, hearing the words, decided to go and meet the Devi, in person. He wanted to understand her up close. When he arrived he could not fathom her aura, it was so much more than he could have understood with his limited perception. So he asked her gracefully.

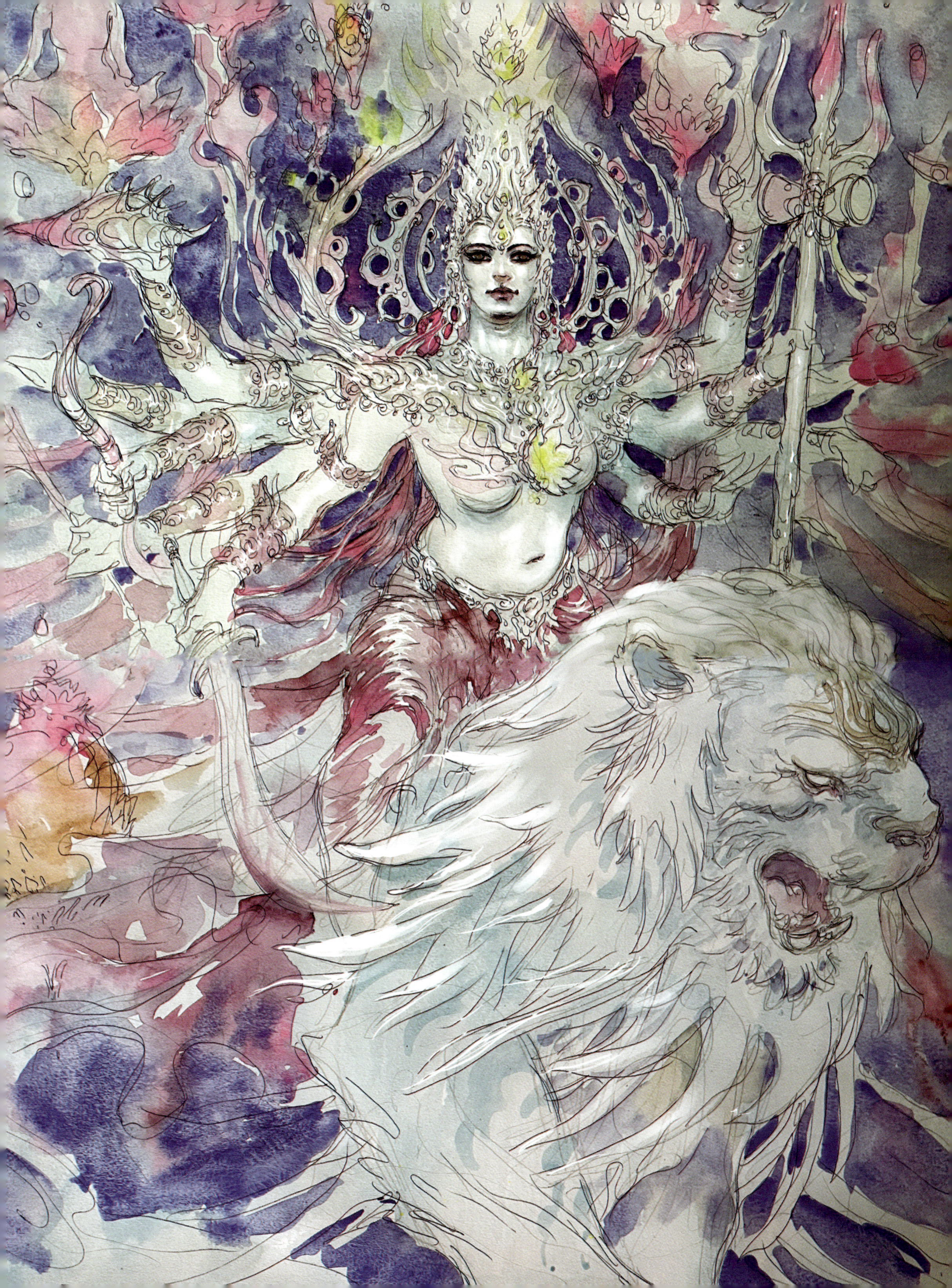

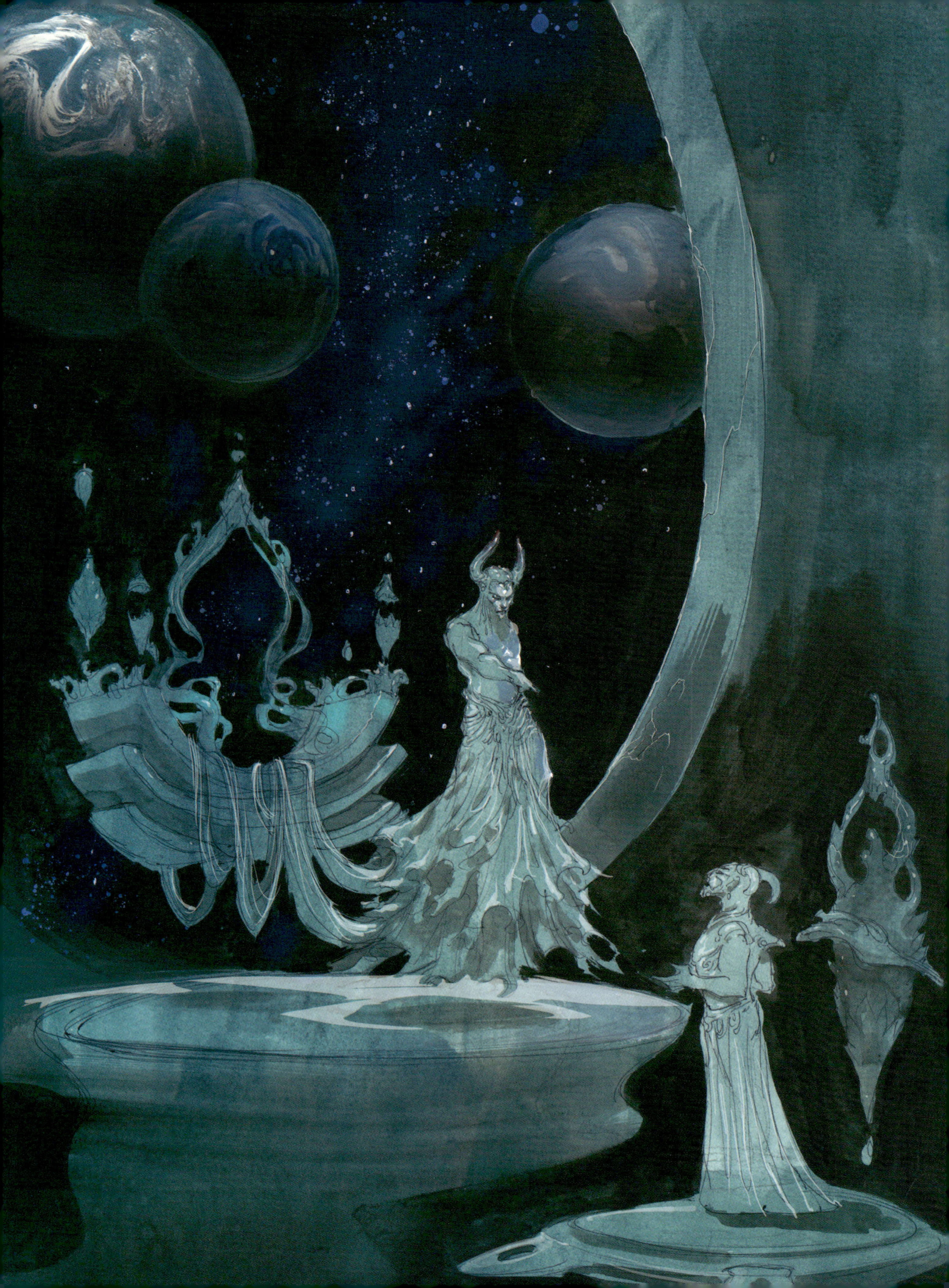

"O, one whose mystery eludes us, who are you and what is your purpose of coming here? Why do you carry these brandished weapons in your delicate hands, and why do you ride a lion as if you are about to enter a battle?"

Devi: "O wise one, I have come here to vanquish that which disturbs the balance of the worlds and heal its misused energies. I'm invoked by the gods to slay your brazen king Mahisha, so go and tell him to come here, surrender his demonic state, align back with harmony and live happily in a world which is fit for him, like a giant fish in the ocean or a bull in the plains, guarding the sun and the earth. Tell him, to not perpetrate this madness, which consumes all. But you know this already, O Asiloma, or else the end nears."

Asiloma was stunned to hear such a valiant claim, he wanted to retaliate with words, but in his heart he knew that the Devi had already wilted away his confidence, so he chose to return and simply deliver her message to Mahisha.

Upon hearing Devi's warning, Mahisha, growled and laughed haughtily, "So a woman, alone but alongside a lion, who you describe as having the most beautiful face, a delicate body, carrying weapons, claimed by no god as their wife, someone from above and beyond but not possessed by Maya or delusion, stands in the battlefield to slay me, if I don't give up my throne of heaven?

It's indeed a wonder, for no one in the known worlds, let alone a woman, has the heart to challenge me."
Mahisha who was both bewildered and struck by infatuation added,
"I ask you, O counselors and army generals, what do you advise about these out of the ordinary claims and what should be our course of action? I feel a sense of attraction towards her, someone like her should be my queen."
Vidalaksa—the illumined one, spoke first,
"O king, even though her description is extraordinary, no one in the three worlds decides the fate of others, how can she speak with so much certainty about what is about to take place? The future is beyond the reach of even the most powerful. I suggest you prepare to fight, and confront her with the same valor with which you had diminished Indra."

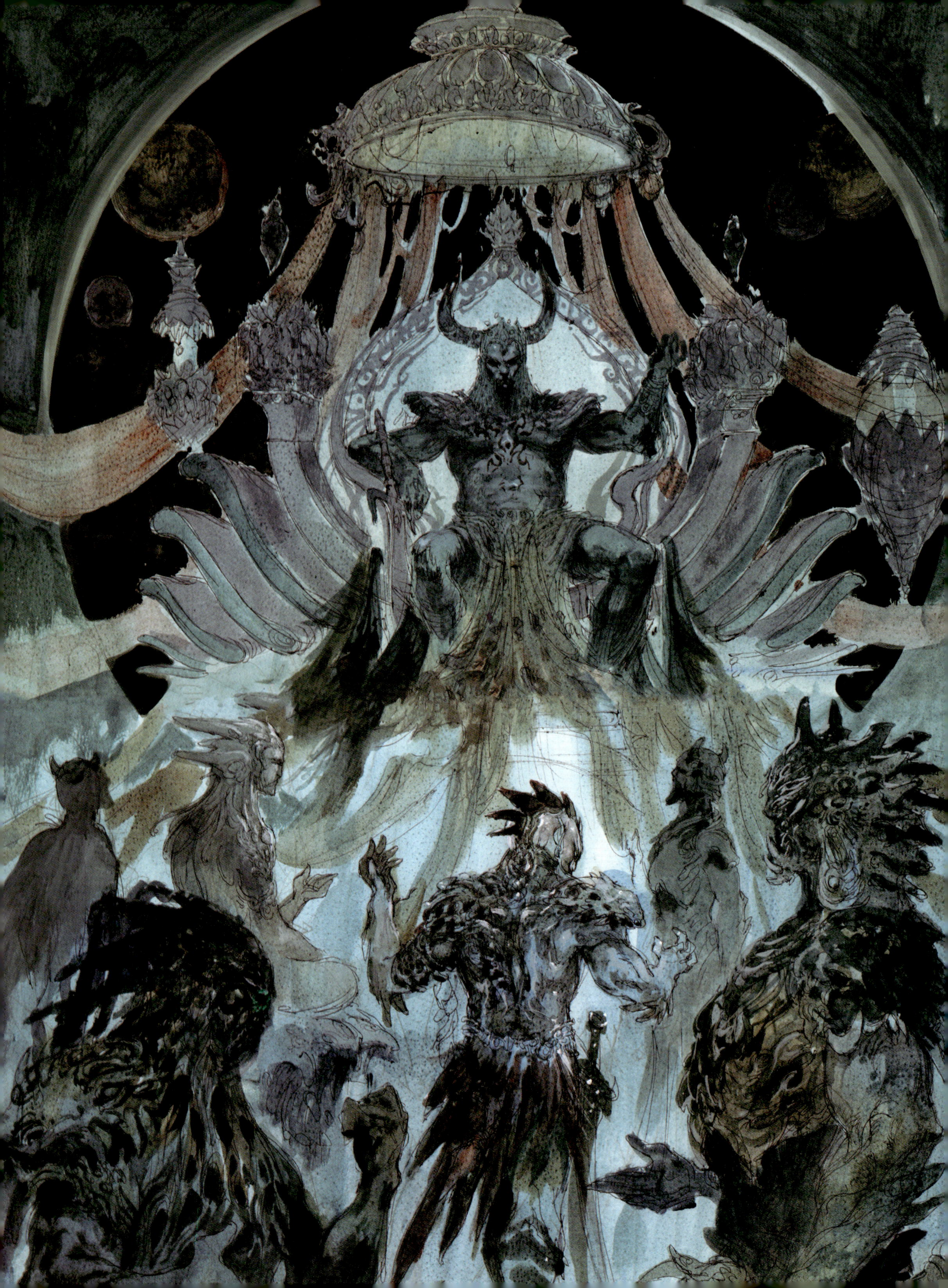

Vaskala, the most cunning of them all, proceeded,
"If you acknowledge your inferiority to a woman then your stature and glory will be disgraced. She's just intimidating you, perhaps, to get your attention."

Durdhara, the valiant amongst them said,
"I fear no gods, so how can I fear their collective chimera as a woman, but I see her as a fitting queen to my king, if she willingly embraces it, it'll bring her unequal glory or I'm prepared to persuade her and conquer her for you."

Virupaksha, who was maddened and raged beyond console, said,
"Death or no death, the question is, do not let her instill fear in you, for that is the real defeat, we are men of pride, so, don't let a woman challenge your resilience."

Tamara, who was an expert in finding the real nature of people, thus raised his voice to subside the commotion, and said,
"Give us the permission to fight her in battle, if she co-operates we will bring her to you, you can do with her what you please, force her or abide her to be your queen, or if not, then I will not deter from killing her right then and there."

Mahisha's blood raced through his veins inflicting deeper restlessness, yet containing himself, he said fiercely:
"Go and bring her to me, I'll take her as my queen or else..."

Thus left the valiant generals in the direction where the Devi awaited their ordained arrival.

The first two who went to battle, were Vaskala and Durmukha, puffed with vanity, saw the shimmering goddess and maddened with their egos, spewed their first words to her.
"Leave this charade, precarious woman, denounce your stubborn stand and come with us. Our king desires you to become his queen, as it will be the most suitable place for a beautiful woman like you."

Upon hearing this, the Devi laughed and with her laughter volcanoes erupted, strange omens entered the mind of all who were not in accord with her heart.

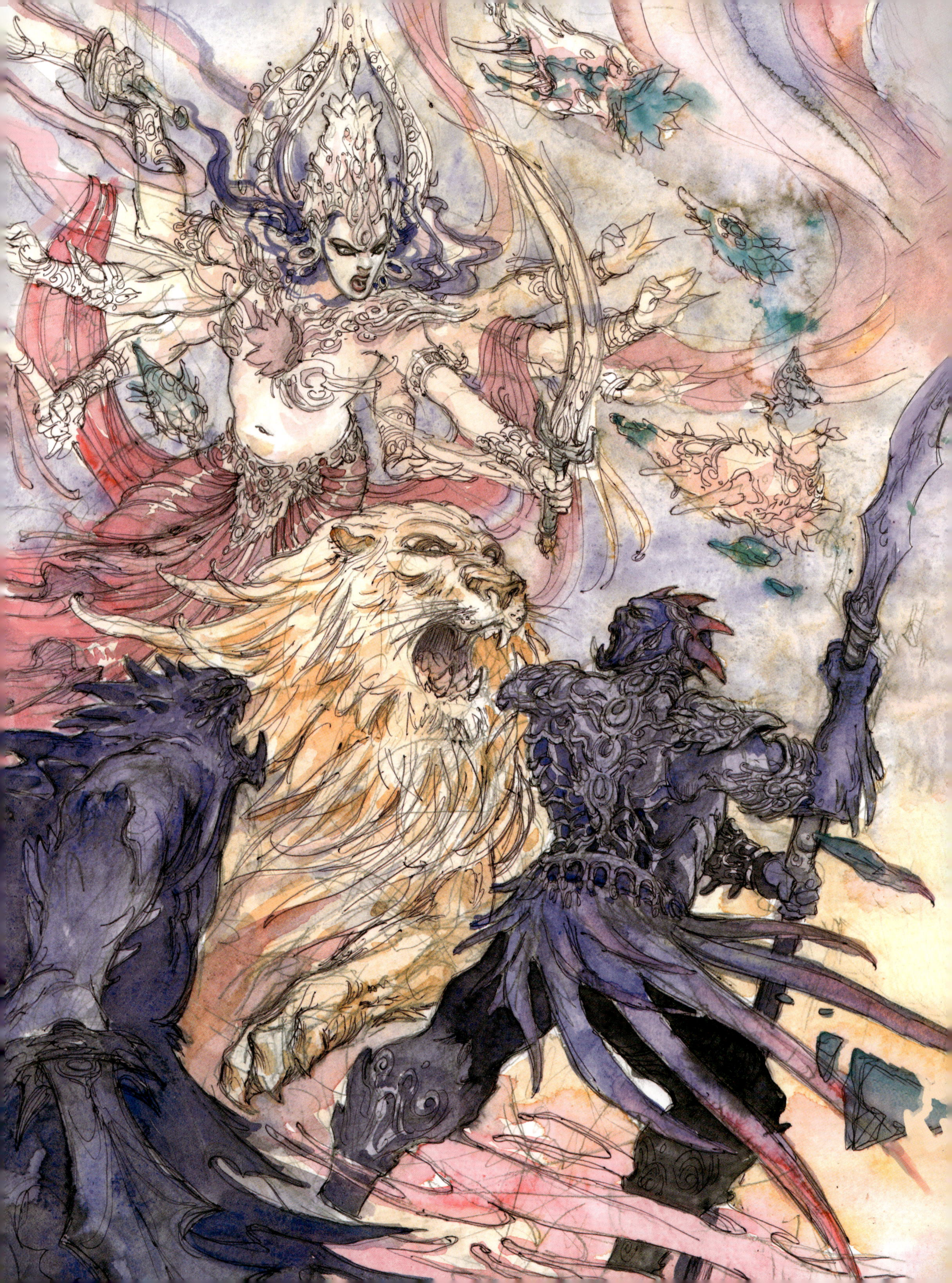

"Inside of me thrive all the goddesses and gods, nature and worlds far from your limited perception; what you see is just a woman, and not the source of that sublime energy which creates life itself. You measure with power and strength because that's what your ego tells you is greater and you impose that without respect or care."

The Devi further roared,
"I am not even bound by time, neither by day or night, by sight or sound, I cannot be touched even by the mind, or the Omni's of the worlds, let alone your arrogant king, who is trapped in his own degenerative vortex of ego."

Then from her enraged breath ensued Chandika, the dark devi, and with her bare hands, she uprooted the head of rakshasa Vaskala, like a gardener uproots unwanted weeds from the garden, letting the soil breathe. She threw his head, which tumbled and fell off where the army stood jaded and shocked, witnessing her unparalleled strength.

Durmukha understood he was fighting an enigma beyond the reaches of victory, yet he remained true to his duty to protect his king, and attacked the Devi with a heavy club. This time the Devi's breath became Ambika, the golden one and with one clean blow, she vanquished him like he never existed.

From far away the other asura generals were looking at this unprecedented scene vehemently. They didn't waste another moment before sending the powerful asura, Chikasura, who right away hurled a thousand arrows towards her.

The Devi, in response cut them in mid-air and hurled a blow from far away, just like the one that strong winds inflict on trees, which hit him so hard that he fainted just by its sheer force.

Tamara, was seeing this from afar and finally stepped in, but before he attacked, he asked the Devi, "Who are you, why would you not embrace Mahisha's offer and rule the three worlds alongside as his queen, do you not desire that?"

Devi: "Not even the body possesses the soul, and neither the soul presents such claims, no one owns anyone, we are all moving in the cyclic bands of energy. To someone who knows this vidya, realization, what value may desires hold for them? The three worlds, kings or queens are all fleeting in the scheme of time and death."

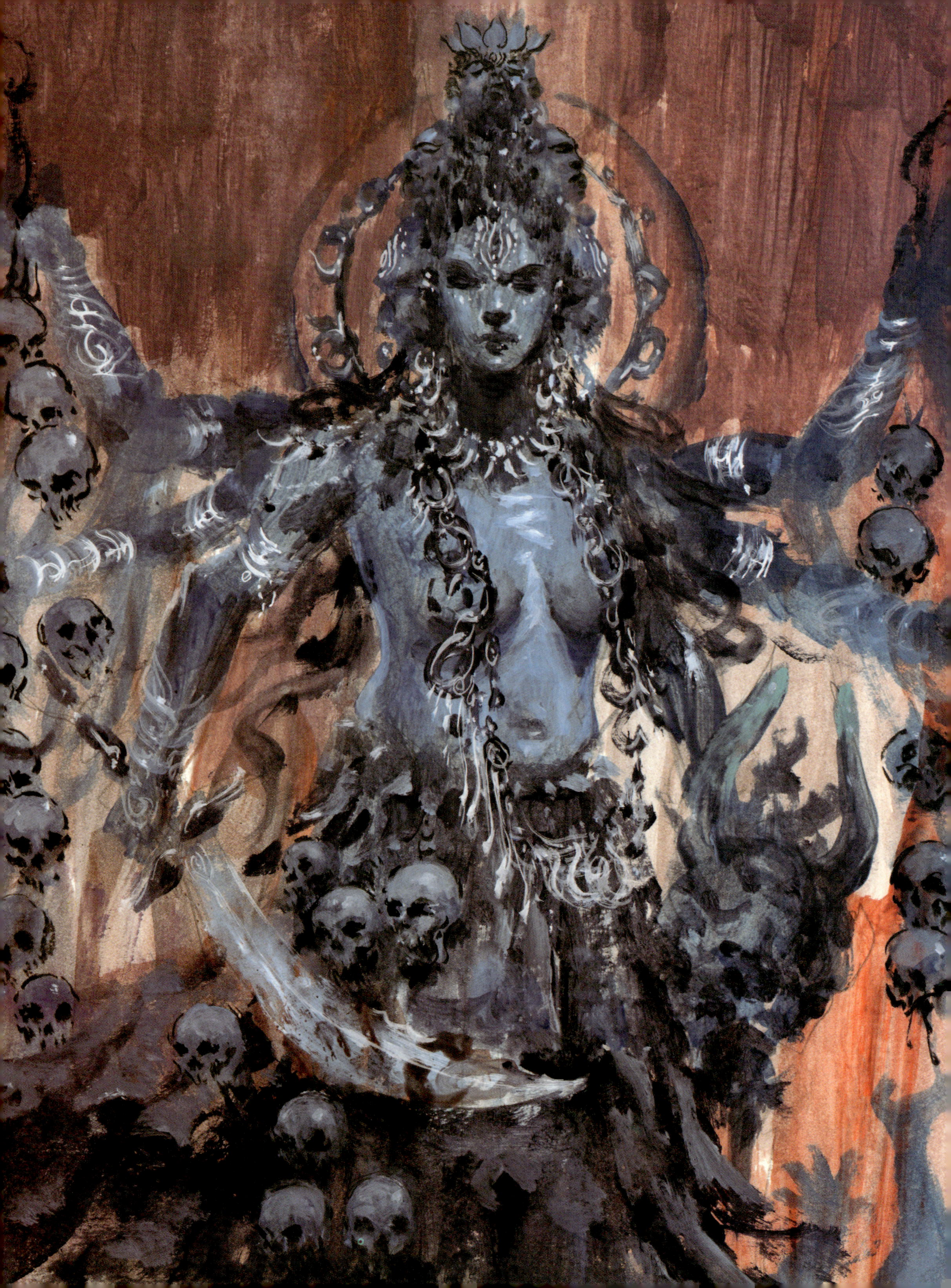

Tamara was astonished by this realization but his being was still sullied by the last bits of his ego, he moved fervently towards the Devi, forgetting halfway if he was attacking or simply offering himself to her and was devoured by the lion, thus getting killed in the pursuit.

Chikasura, who was conscious now, raged upon the Devi, but her breath gestured forth Chandika, who shot arrows made from fire towards him, like bolts of light, which he failed to avert and the pranic arrows shredded through his being, spraying his blood all over the asura army.
In this dreadful scene, the army seemed eclipsed, while the Devi stood resplendent like the sun, sparing the ones who surrendered to her.

Asiloma saw her from afar and in his wise heart an emotion of wonder and equanimity entered. He knew he had to fulfill his role in this war but he could now understand the meaning behind her presence. He stood lost in his admiration, as another valiant asura warrior Vidalakshya, fell to the Devi's prolific display of weapons, severely punctured by the arrows from a distance and letting his life be submitted to the energy, which adorned her aura.

Now it was Asiloma's time, so he with joined hands asked the Devi:
"O Niramayi, indeed it's clear that you will be the cause of Mahisha's death. He is not listening to reason anymore and that alone paves one's road to destruction. However, my mind yearns to ask you a question, are we not deserving of the heavens?"

Devi: "Asiloma, the one with a kind heart, both suras and asuras have come from the same source, but are always in perpetual conflict. I can understand why this bothers you, but if it helps, I'm not fond of seeing them fight myself. Age after age, stuck in traumatic cycles of serving the ego, exhausting their spiritual potentials and over what?

Why even after thousands of years of penance, they still demand and desire boons, why the intense meditation is unable to cleanse their hunger for power. Why doesn't it bring forgiveness or makes them joyous when they see the glimpse of the one they have spent eons appeasing? When they get the power they want, their mind distorts further, invading, imposing, conquering, fulfilling their tyrannical aspirations, dividing and polluting the earth and other realms, chasing their illusions of permanence and ownership.
Nothing of this Earth belongs to any man or god, the Earth itself does not want to be scarred with such divisions, it has it's own beautiful harmony and through that it loves all equally.

These demarcations should not exist, heavens should be a garden to all who want to visit it and take a moment of calm, but to those enlightened, every place is heavenly, by the virtue of how they treat it and love it.
Indra's abode is just another object in space and time. The real heaven is given to all in the form of love, and how they exercise it. Hence, the one who is able to channel this love and share it with all, is truly worthy of heaven, for such a one finds it within and everywhere.
Indras come and go, so do these physical heavens, but this eternal love which remains, is the real heaven. You are deserving of that love, of that heaven Asiloma, just look within."

Asiloma, had no heart to carry on fighting, so he looked at the lion and offered himself to it, he was devoured but his benevolent heart left an imprint on the Devi, who in return, smiled and made him part of a river of flowers, as poignantly deserving of his heart.

The battle scene raged again one last time as Mahisha himself decided to enter the battlefront, with his charioteer Daruka, his chariot loaded with all sorts of illusionary weapons.

The loss of his most astute warriors goaded his being, making him think of the Devi as the premonition of his own death, it made him heave with pain and anger, he was a master at illusions and incantations, and would hold nothing back to bend Devi's will to his, as his heart still was flooded with amorous desire towards her, and he had foolishly decided to win her over in marriage, by all tricks or force necessary.

He soon found himself confronting the Devi in the battlefield. After having flouted all her warnings, now when he finally saw her, his heart was struck with an overwhelming feeling, of someone who was witnessing the ocean for the first time, unable to discern its depths but smitten and terrified by its presence; holding his trembling breath and still seduced by his ego, he spoke further.
"A vision like yours, so full of splendor, bewilders me to think, as to why would such a delicate form fight?"

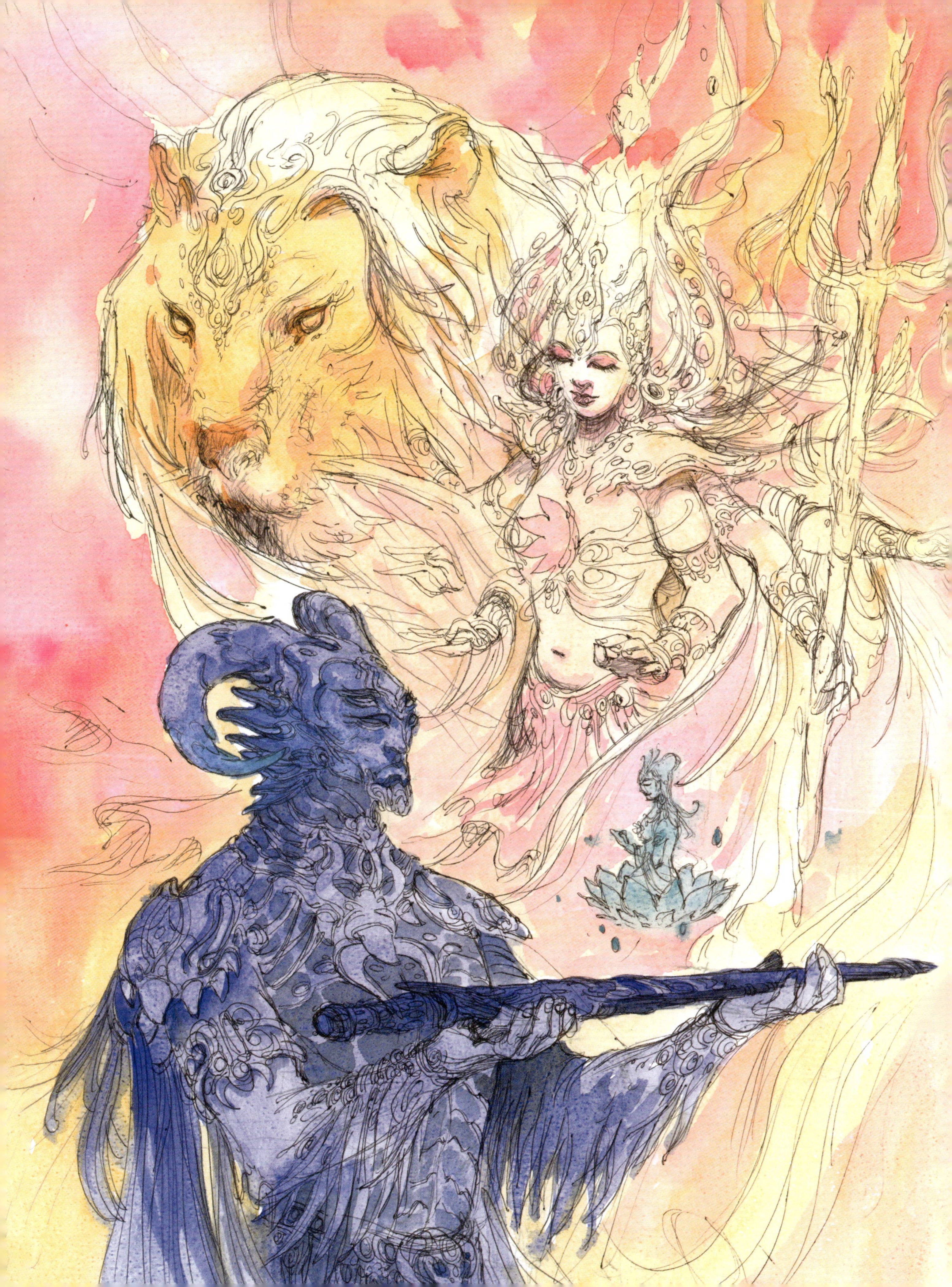

Devi looked at Mahisha and laughed hysterically, slowly changed her aura to a vision in which all the goddesses moved around her.

"Does the wind which assails the greatest mountains have a form, does fire, or the water which shapes the world of matter, limited by shape, O ignorant fool, the greatest of forces don't work through form, they take whatever shape they desire."

The Devi looked like a manifestation of all elemental forces, fierce and calm all at the same time, her vibrations sent shockwaves across the battlefield.

The ferocious sounds sent shudders down the bones of the asuras, rupturing their ears, blood dripping down their noses by it's velocity but to the ears of Rudra and Hari, who were watching the battle unfold from their mind's eye, the sounds sounded sweet, as if gently the universe was breathing in and out, coming out of its suffocation.

Mahisha, still puffed with pride, made a loud sound, which made cracks on earth, and said:
"I see beauty, but not in these visions of death, for they instill fear, how can someone see love and beauty in death?"
Devi, who was Durga, the guardian of the fortress of the mind, spoke fiercely.

"O lost one, try to move past your fixation of outer vanity and sense the being within, who is in shambles, burdened by this excessive sensory fixations. Try to be like the Earth, whose harmonic cycles don't privilege birth and beauty over decay and death, for her, every and all aspects are equal. Understand this profound alignment and you'd sense that the need to possess more than what you require, should be curtailed.

Once you comprehend that there is no divide between you and the universal spirit, you will not see yourself as separate, but part of the greater whole, you'd realize the state of equanimity, which makes one sense an intrinsic bond between all things, sharing life, decay and death.
Then you would yearn instead of ruling the heavens, to become that song, which moves through all things, immortal, unhindered, calming all in its path."

"O son of Rambha, forged in fire, if you would have followed that path, your burns and scars would have been purged, healing the places where love couldn't reach in time. You would not have divulged from your integrity or chased meaningless goals, be it the heavens or immortality. You could have gone where no Indra has gone before, but instead you lost your way."

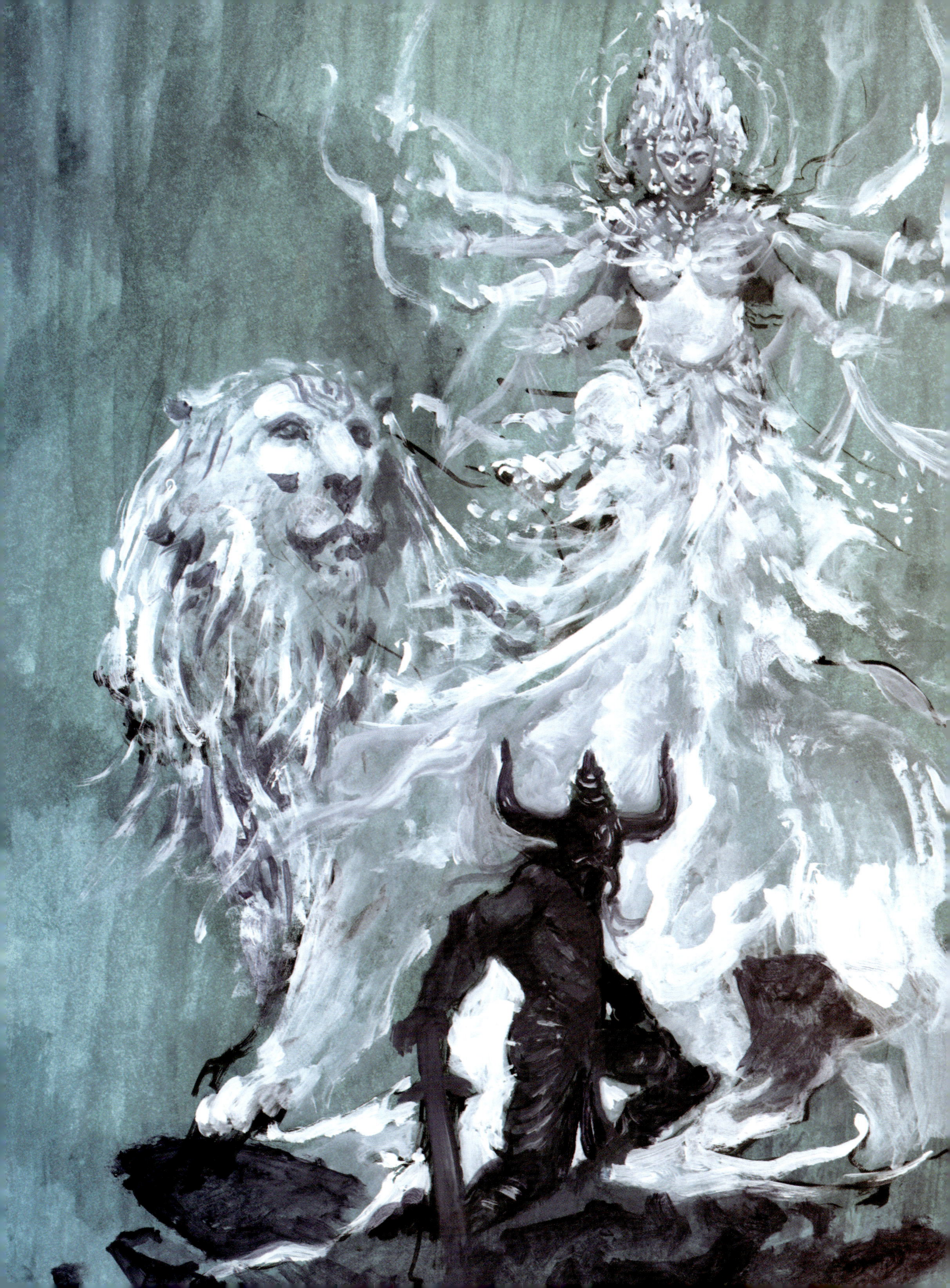

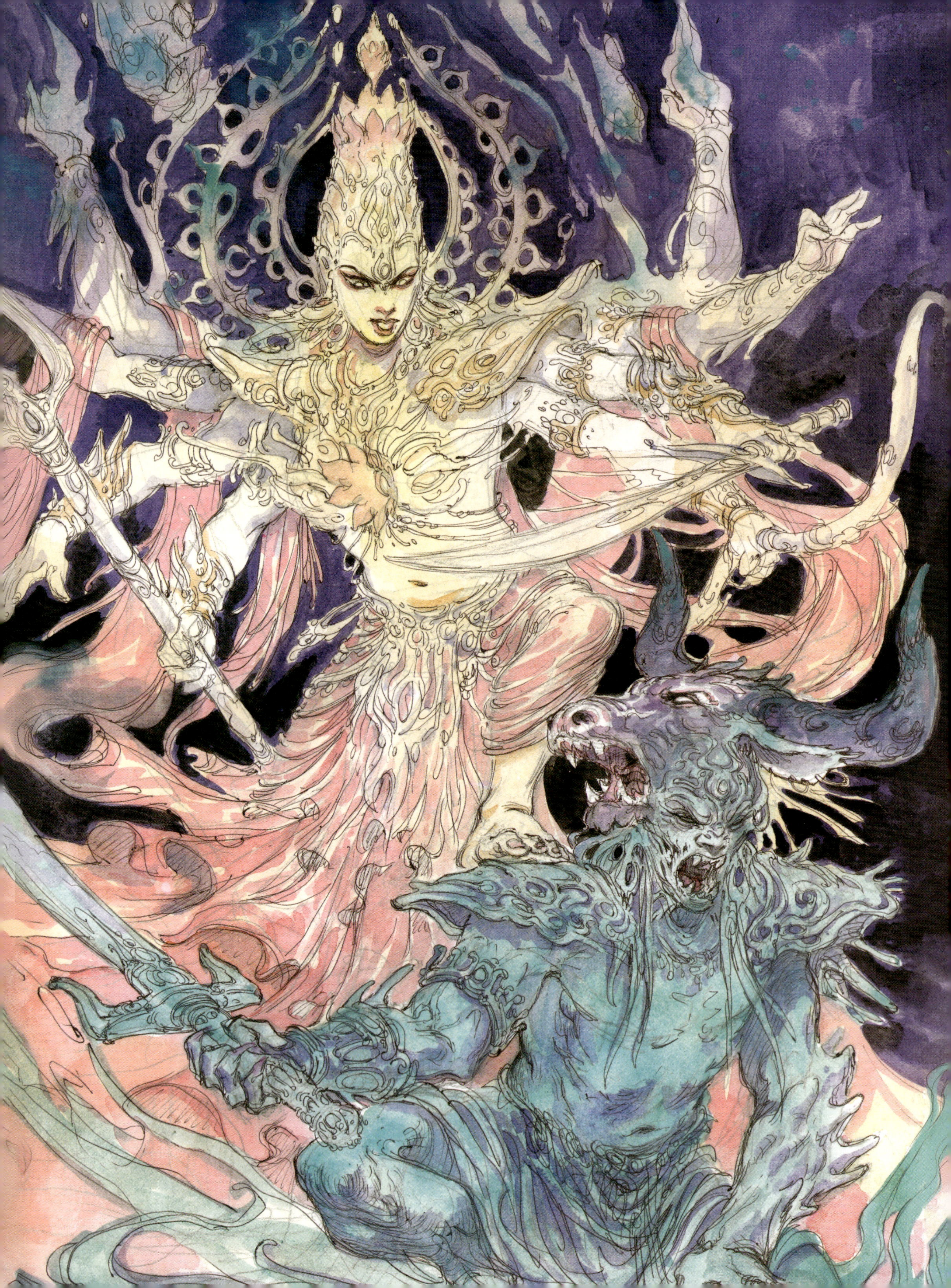

"O burnt by one's own fires of ego, only if you could have known that you are already immortal because you are not your body or mind, but the universal essence within, that you are Purnam, complete in oneself, you would have been in bliss. Then the respect you'd have given the body, the mind and the spirit would have been a harmonious pursuit."

Listening to this Mahisha felt that he stood at the precipice of his own demise, he had asked Brahma that let death come to him by the hands of a woman, and this was that moment, but knowing this and his impending fate, he hurled himself at her, for one last fight, the last slivers of ego were still weighing on him or perhaps, he had lived like a warrior and he must honor her to the best of his ability before he was vanquished.

The gods bore witness to the most dreadful duel, which ensued between Mahisha and the Goddess.

On the battlefield, Mahisha was already exhausted trying to change forms and attacking the Devi, as she remained unscathed by any of his attempts or illusions. Finally he turned into a bull and charged with full force at her, but the Devi remained still, like the most ancient trees, unhindered by the great winds and summoned her trident, the destroyer of illusions and pierced it through the heart of Mahisha, slaying him on behalf of all eternity.

A huge bolt of light, jostled into Mahisha, putting a stop to all the thousand illusionary forms he had taken, all the excess energy he had adulterated in doing so, gushed out from his severed bust, like a rainbow being freed, and all the life force, which he held inside of him unaccountably, was finally offered back to the currents of the world.

The gods could sense how the war had taken place on multiple levels, on the physical plane level the Devi fought Mahisha but at the psychological, spiritual plane she dispelled the ego and darkness which tainted the hearts of all beings, who had distorted their egos, even the gods and released them from all the prejudices they had accumulated within.

To acknowledge how Mahisha was manifested by them, and that the slaying of Mahisha's form was also erasing the one which existed formless inside of them, as sense tendencies, not the ego, Aham, but the dissonance Kara which manipulates it, which seeded Ahamkara, the manifestation of arrogance, an expert in deception, feeding on their insecurities and hubris but just as rain washes away the stones inside a pond, preparing them for new life, similarly the Devi had rejuvenated their spirits.

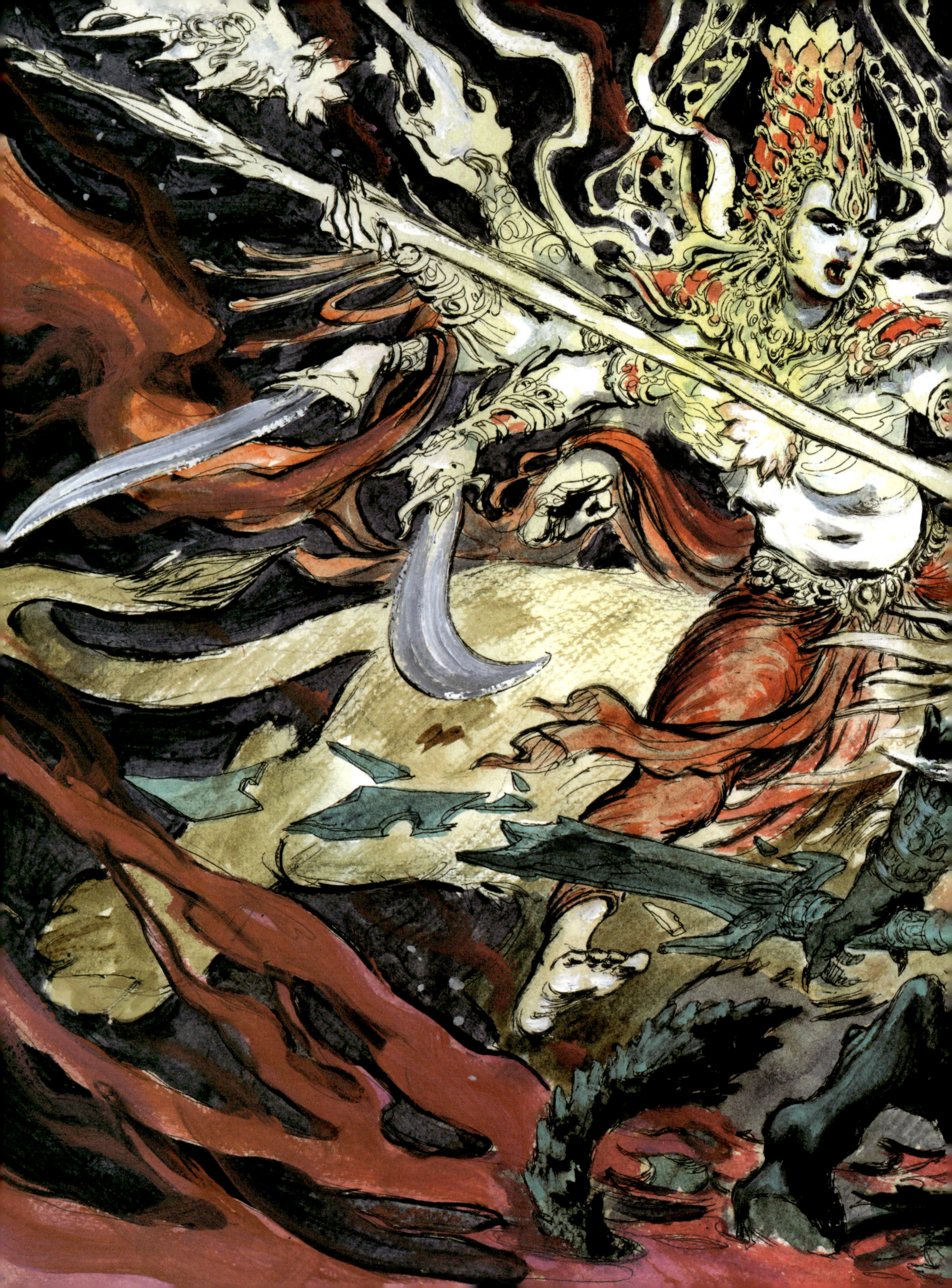

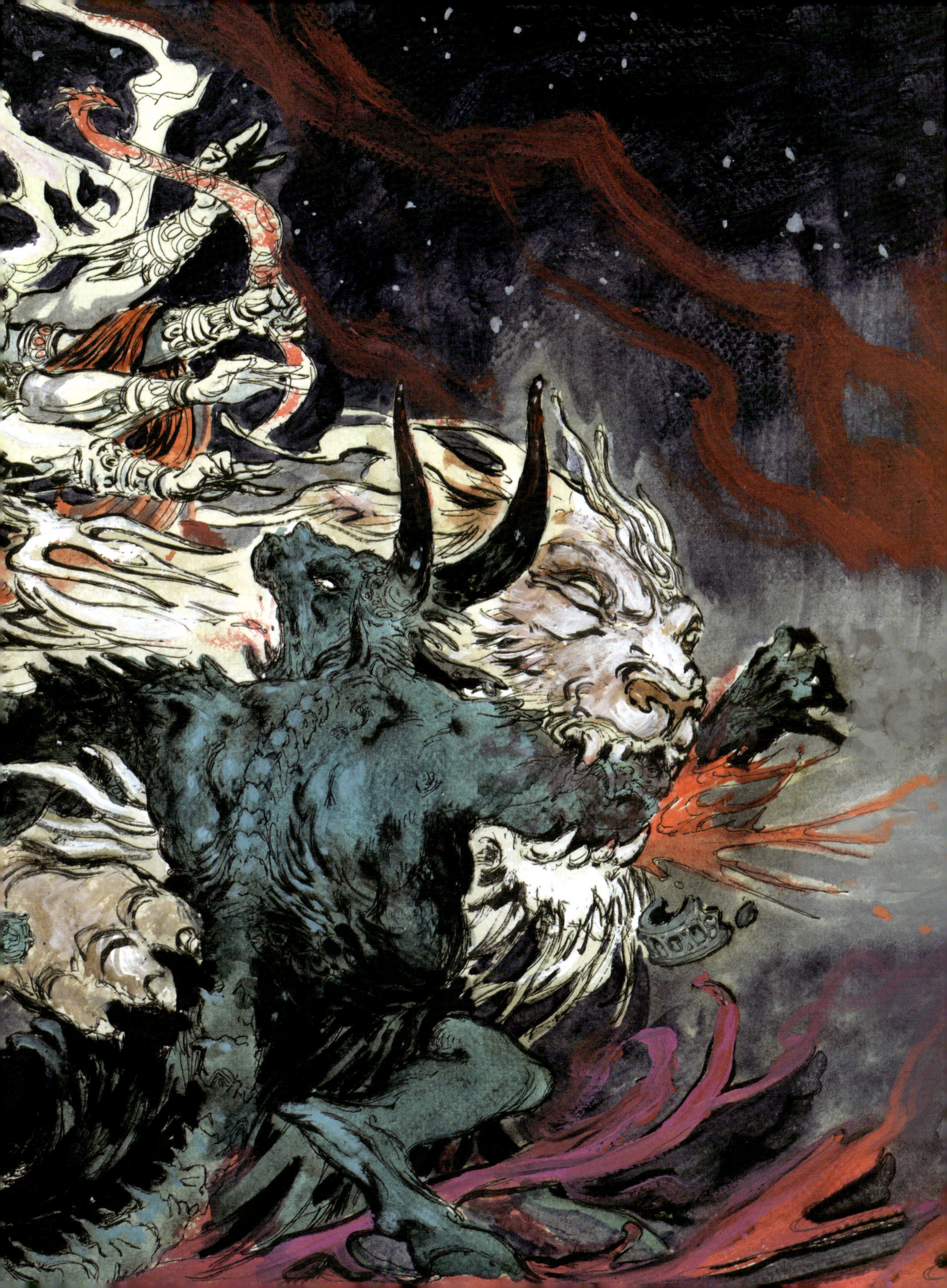

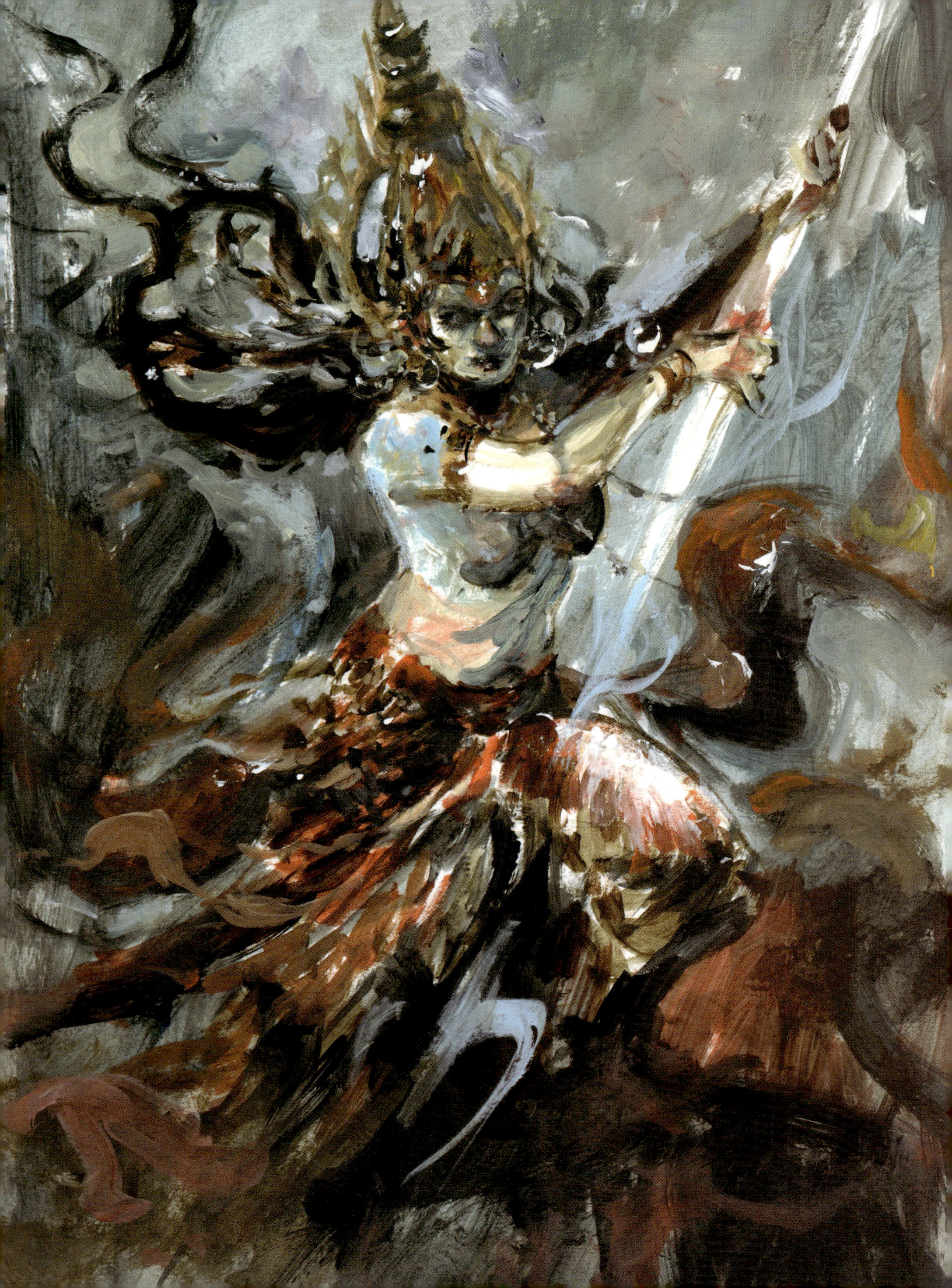

Mahisha's death was reckoning for the gods, through which their wounded wisdom was healed. This Vadh, was not a killing but instead a cessation of the ego, diluting its presence over the shrine of the mind, body and spirit, and reinstating the all mother, the Devi, serenity, in its place.

To the gods it felt like an intense meditation. A war within, which they had confronted, persevered and triumphed in because of the grace of the Devi.
She had been their united strength against the nefarious forces, and through her they had resolutely conquered back the heavens, re-establishing the lost balance.

As the Devi returned and channeled back the powers to the gods, they spoke with reverence and curiosity.

Gods: "O, all Mother, we remember the moment when you answered our calling, the invocation, where we all gave our energies but witnessing your marvels, we saw, that the way you used our powers was so much more than the way we use it, reveal to us this mystery?"

Devi, smiled and said lovingly...

“There is no mystery, in my space, all of your powers were together, aligned, and moved, with no friction, as one energy.”

The gods reminisced how depleted their strengths were while invoking her and in this contemplative moment, it dawned on them that not only had she won back the heavens, but when they had submitted their powers to her, she had kept them safely and had guarded their strengths all this while. Just as a seeker is rejuvenated by beautiful nature around himself, their powers were now cleansed and pulsated with even more pranic effulgence.

They felt a calming energy wash over them, and felt like parched Earth finally receiving its promised ordained rain. They took their places back as the guardians of elements and other phenomena, seats in myriad realms and started to repair back the broken energy cycles, thanking the Devi in their hearts. The Devi too in return opened her mind’s eye and welcomed both the suras and the asuras, as her children. She infused them back into the one spirit they were and then like starlight, blended herself back into everything as the great essence, moving beyond time and space.

As her form started to amalgamate back into nothingness, the gods, one last time asked her,
“Where will we find you, in our time of need?”

A breeze caressed everyone’s heart, taking away the last bit of restlessness, the Devi’s voice echoed in their hearts, where the sun washed itself into the ocean, preparing for a new morning.

“You’d find me in love and kindness.”

The three great Omni’s who had witnessed the entire spectacle returned to their realms, for they knew the future was embroiled in mystery that only the Devi understood. They will have to open the portals again to bring her back and for that they must too, become her.

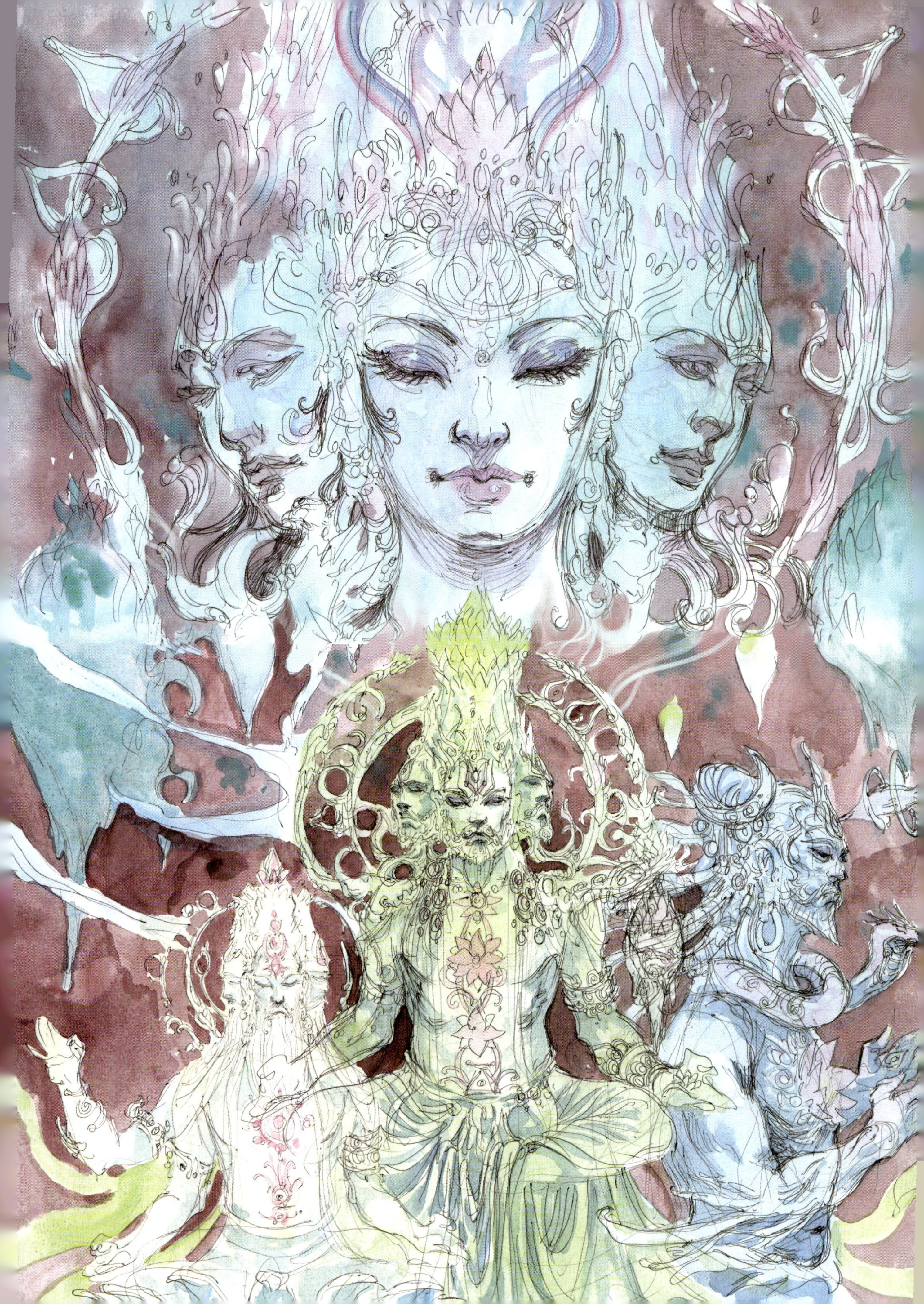

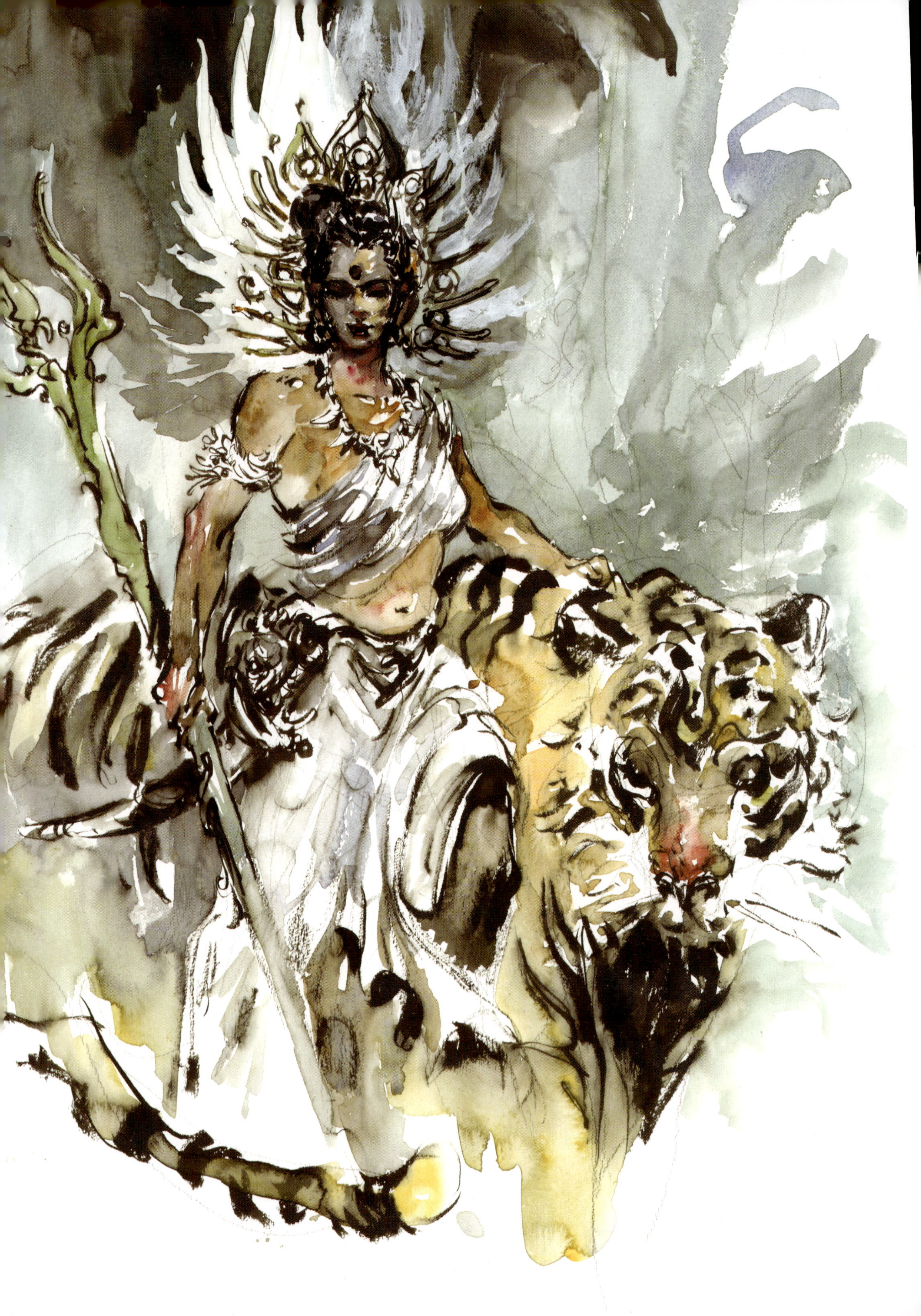

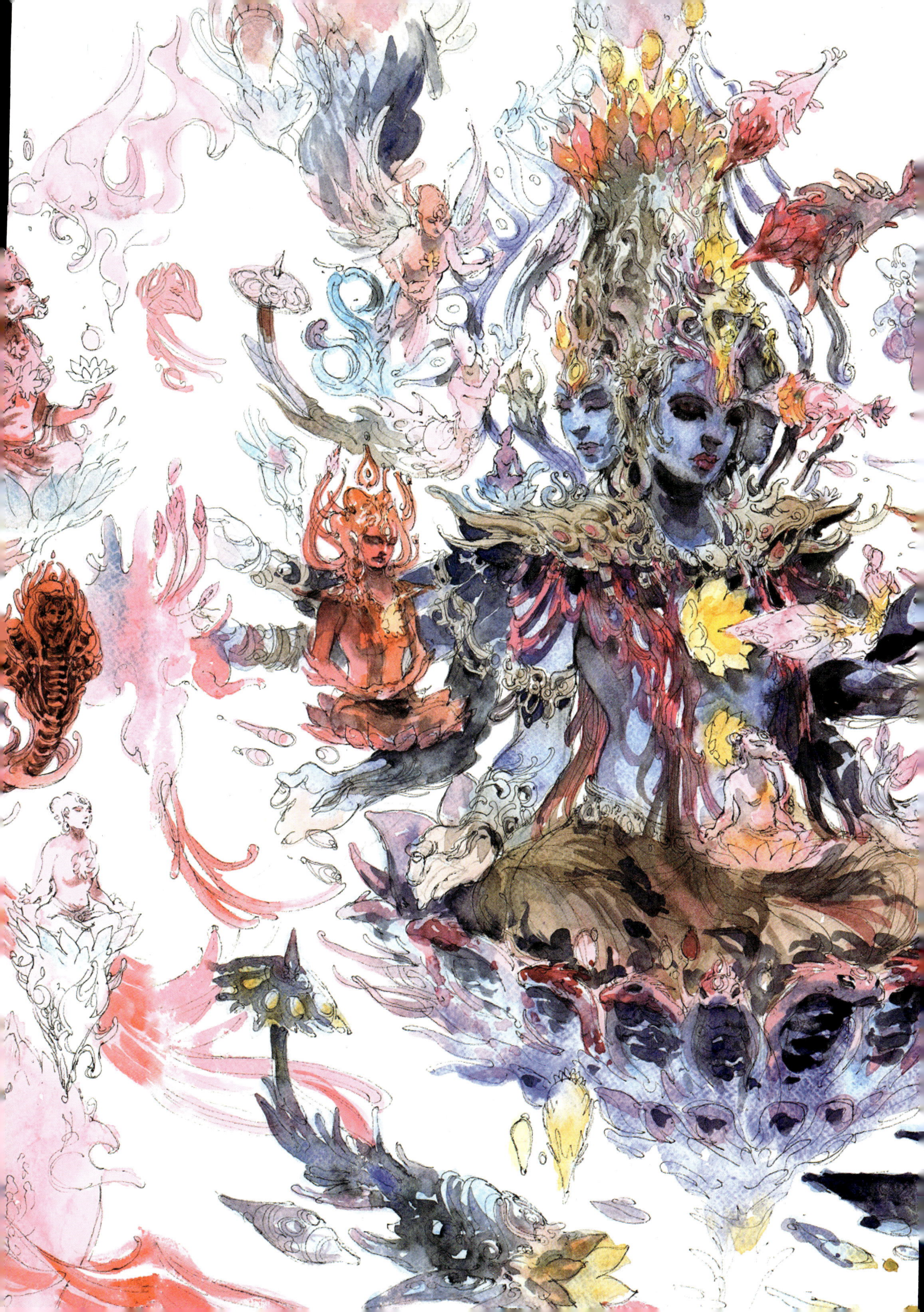

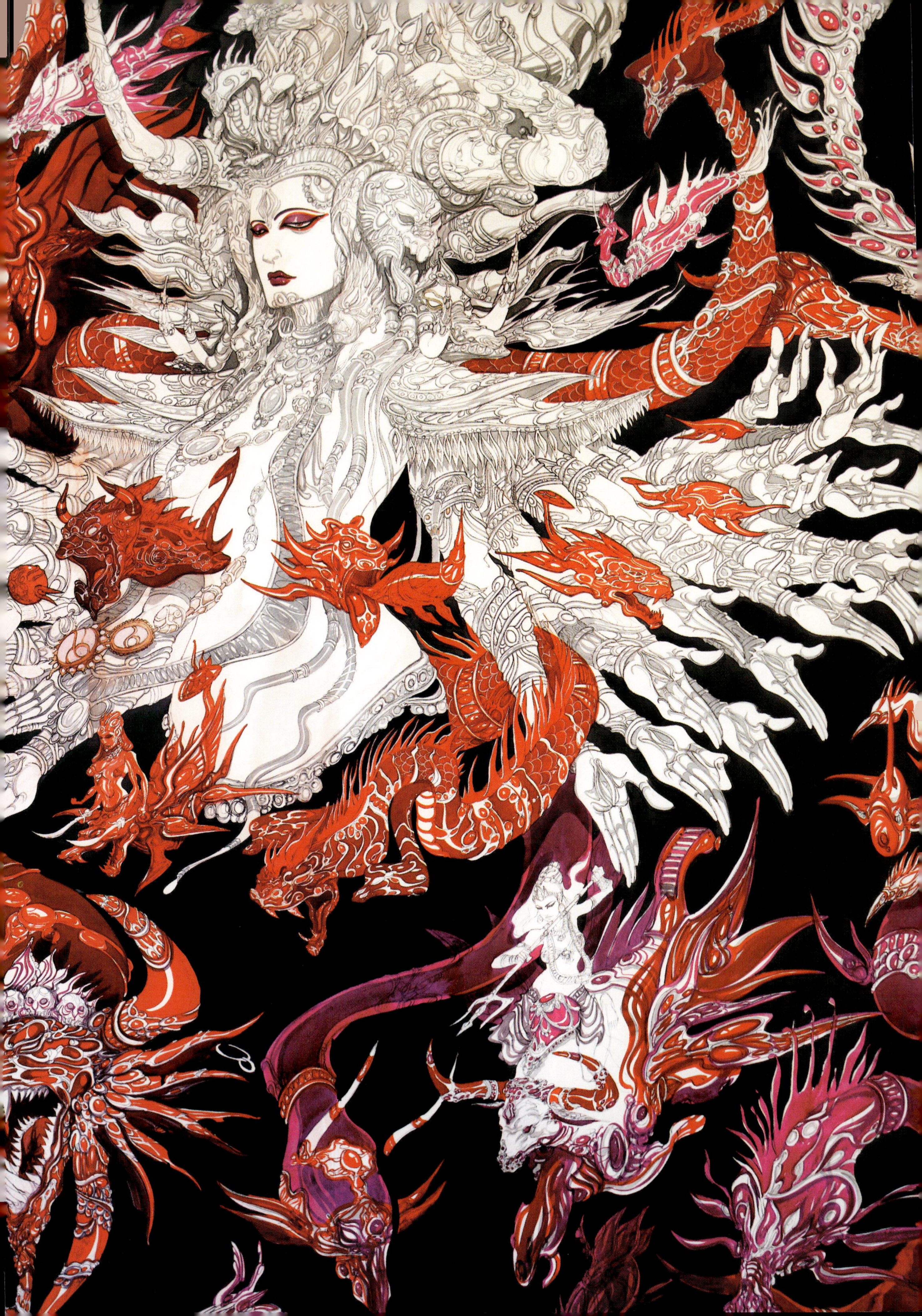

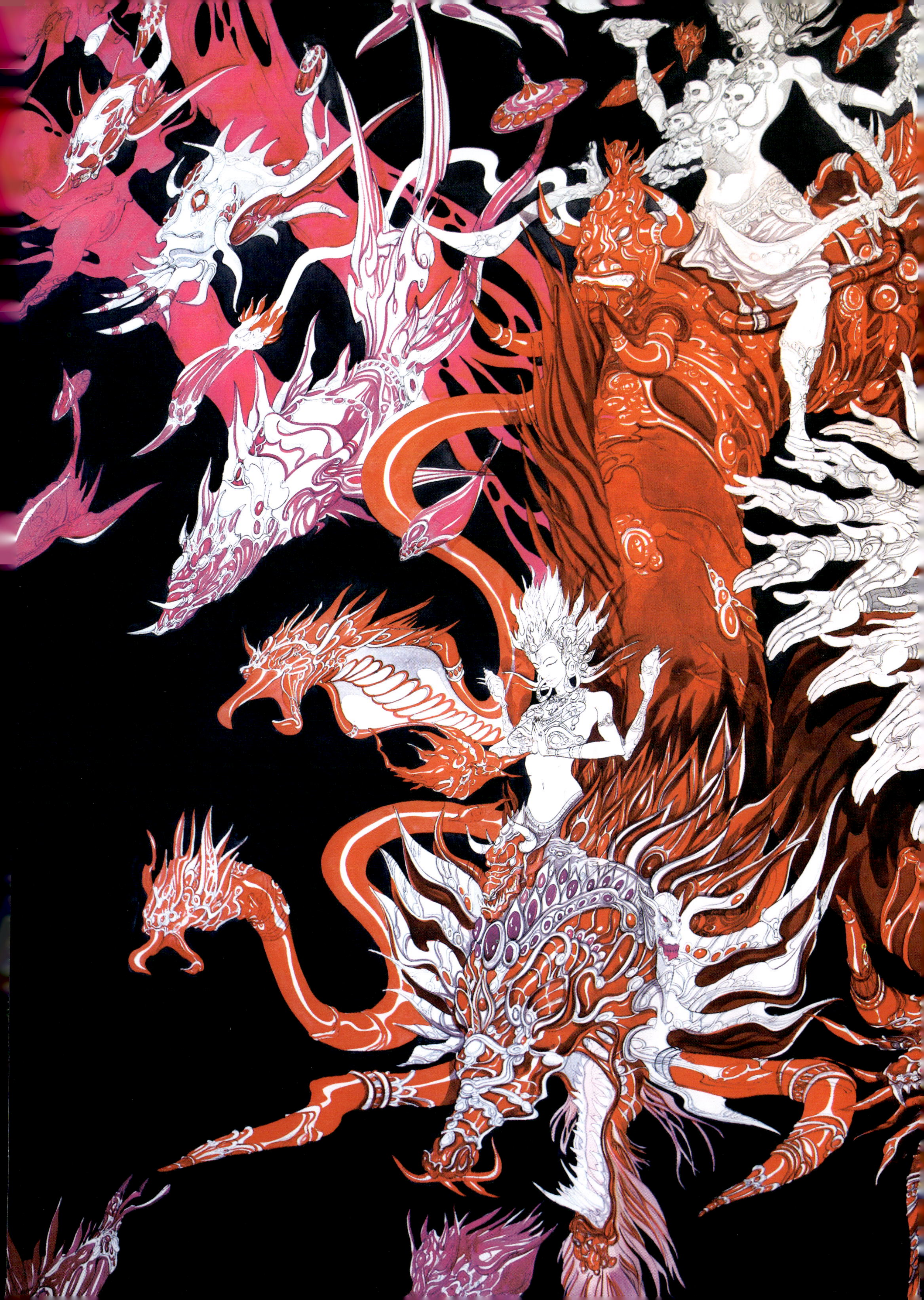

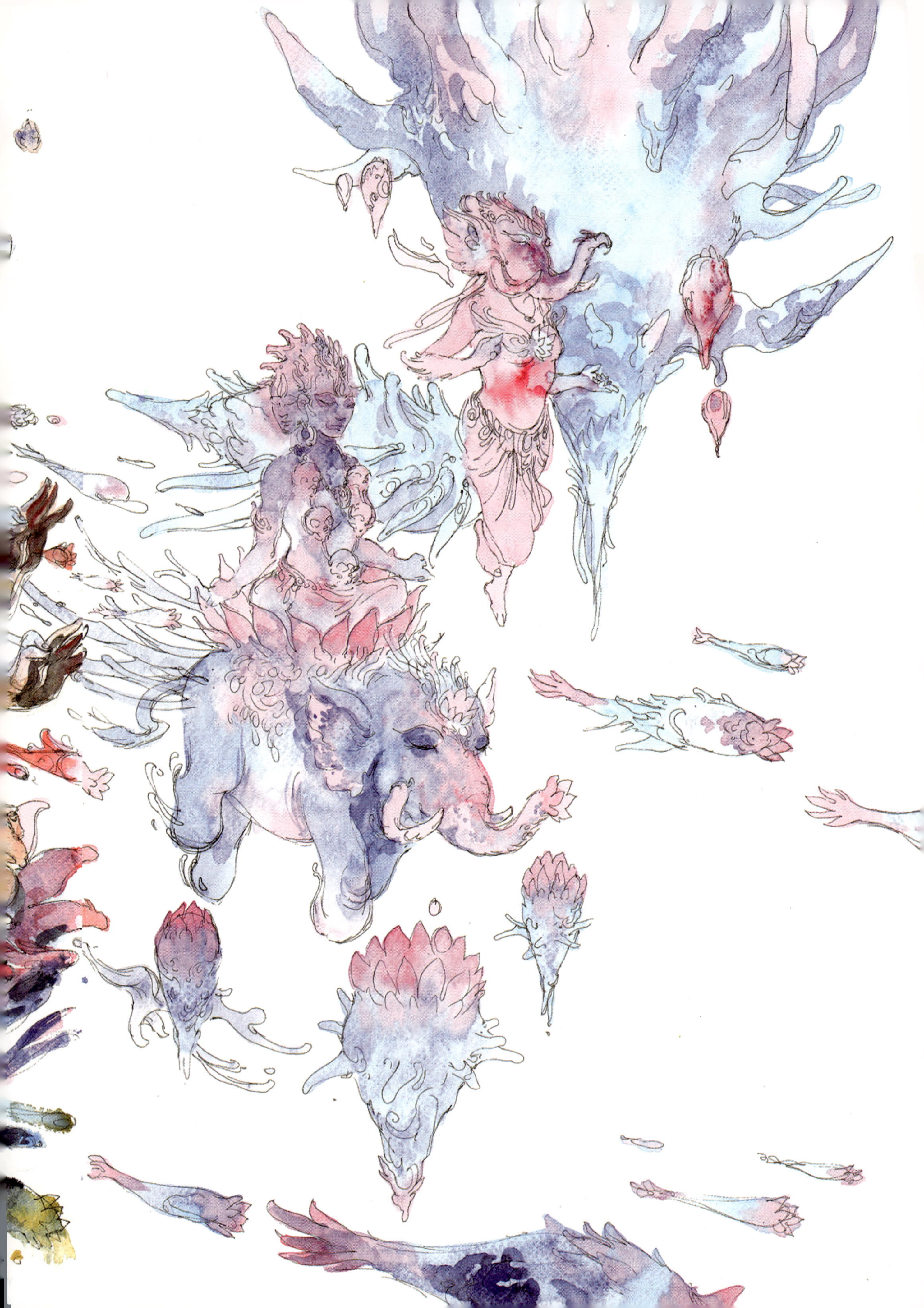

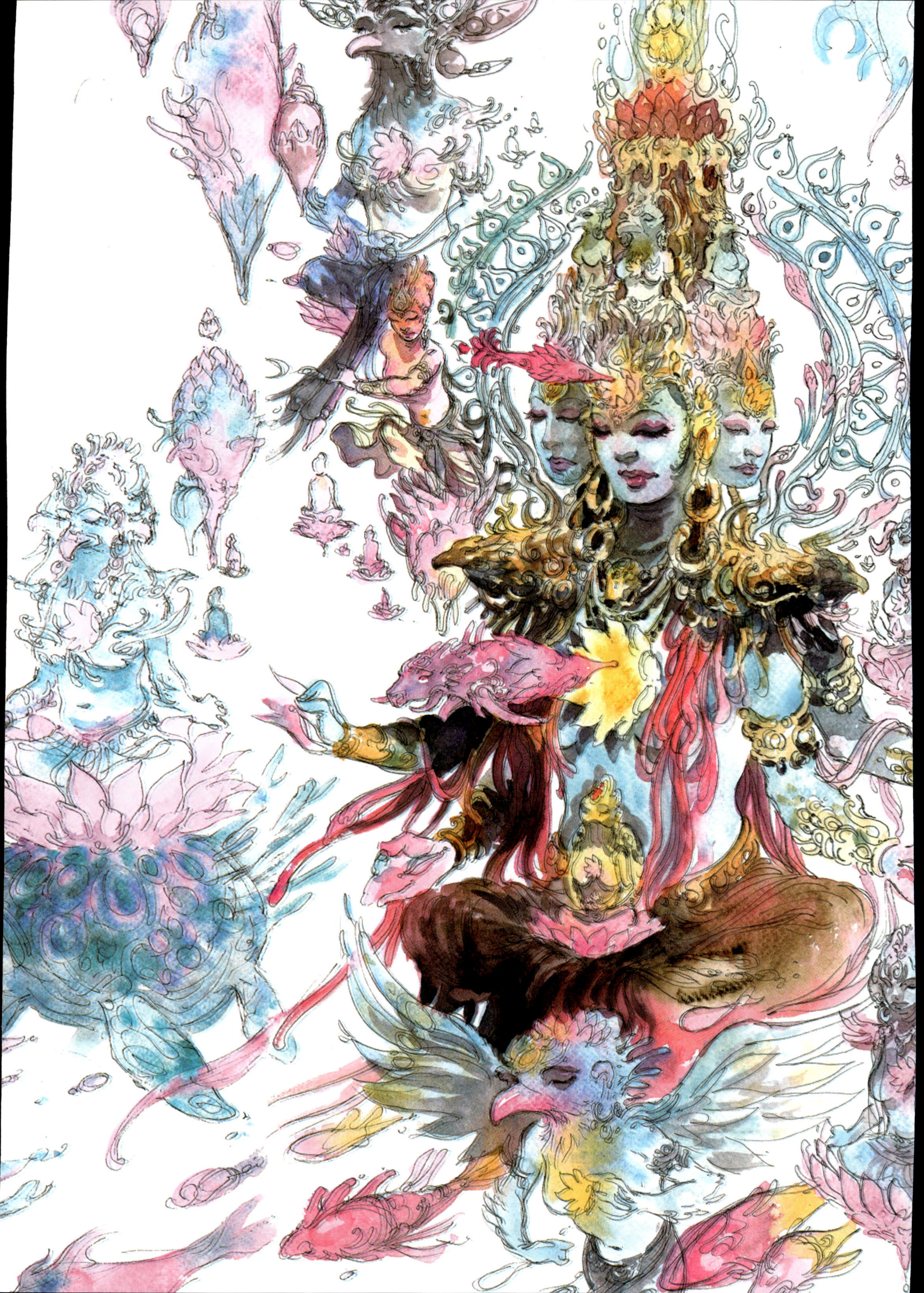

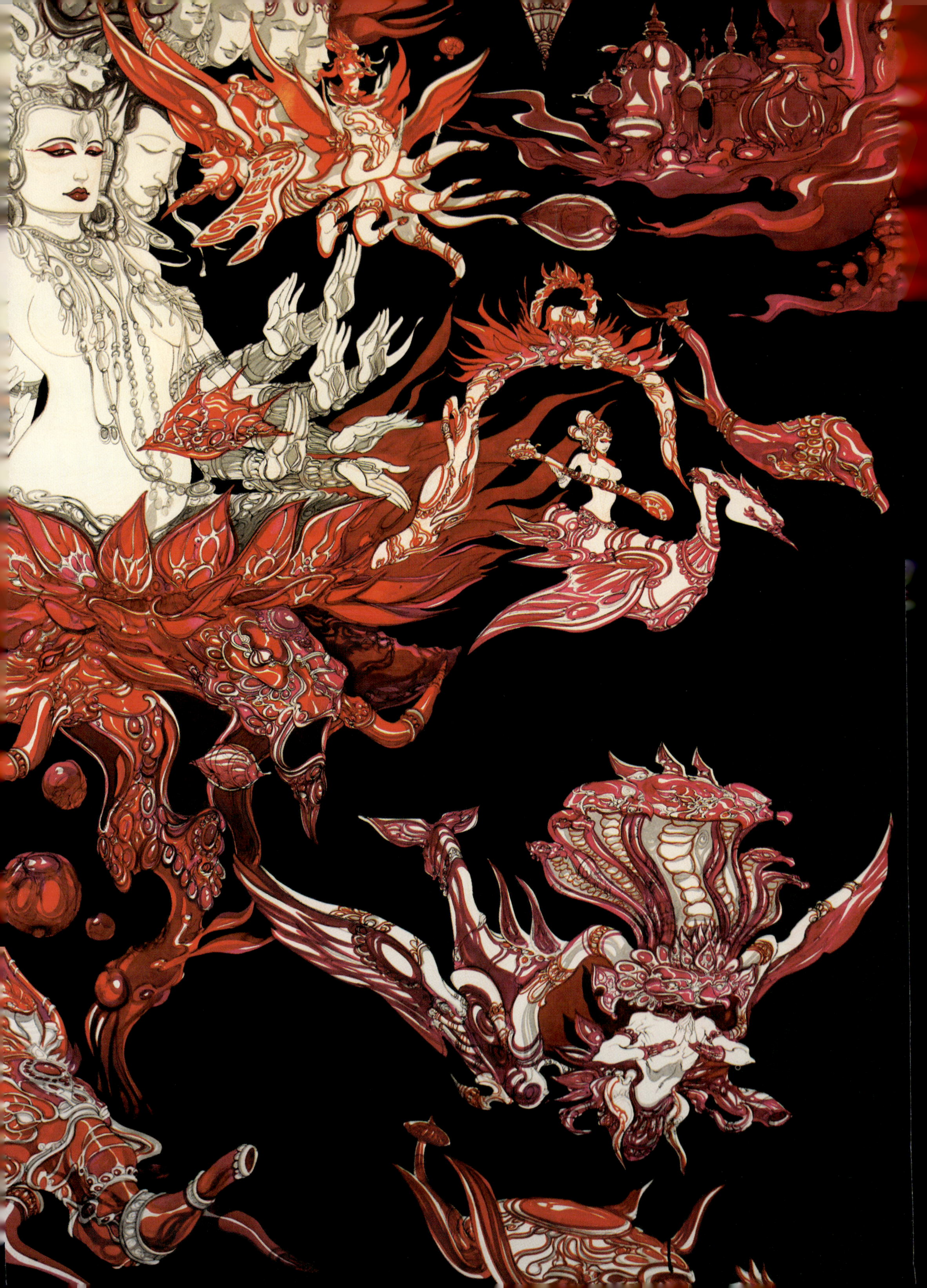

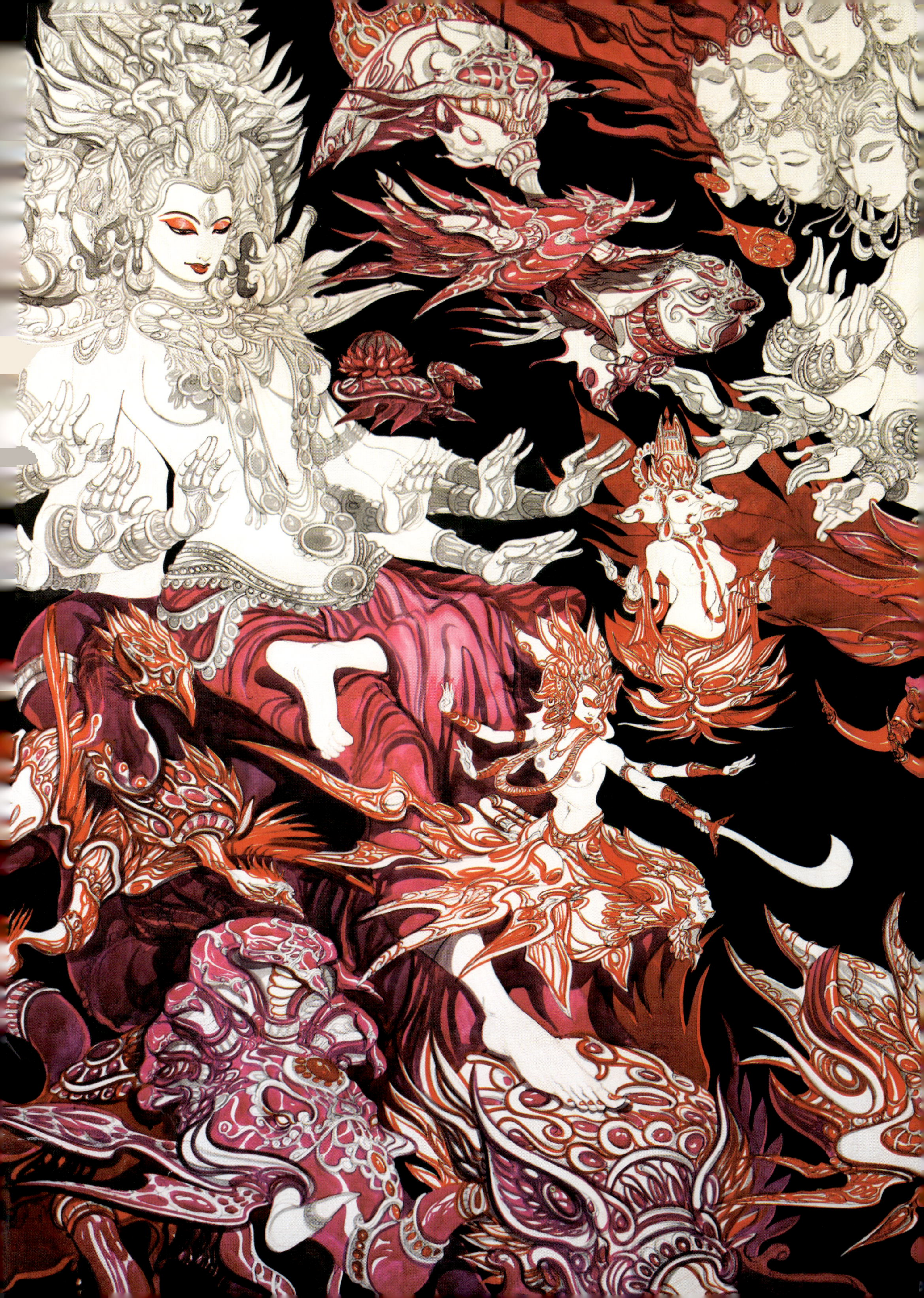

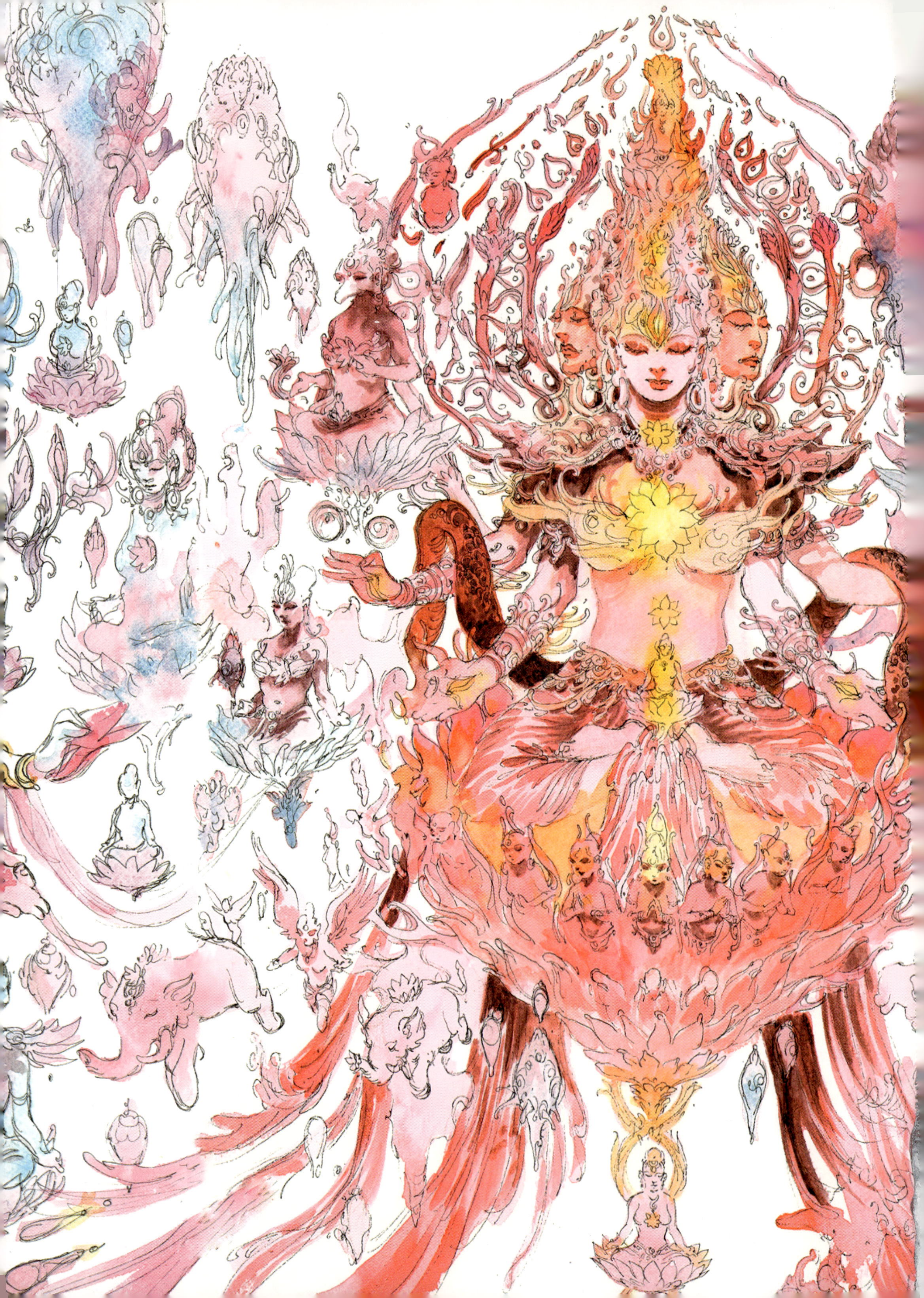

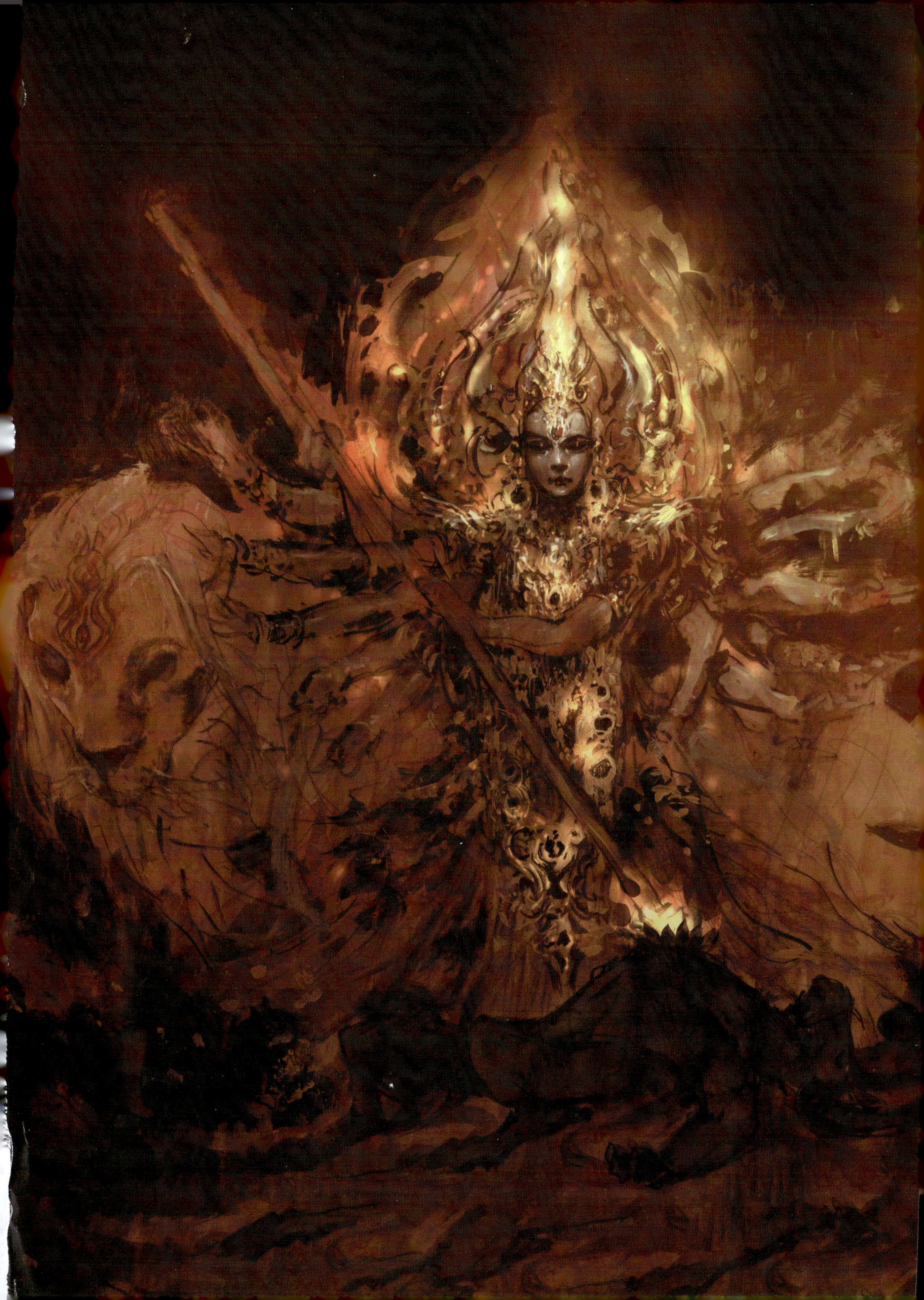

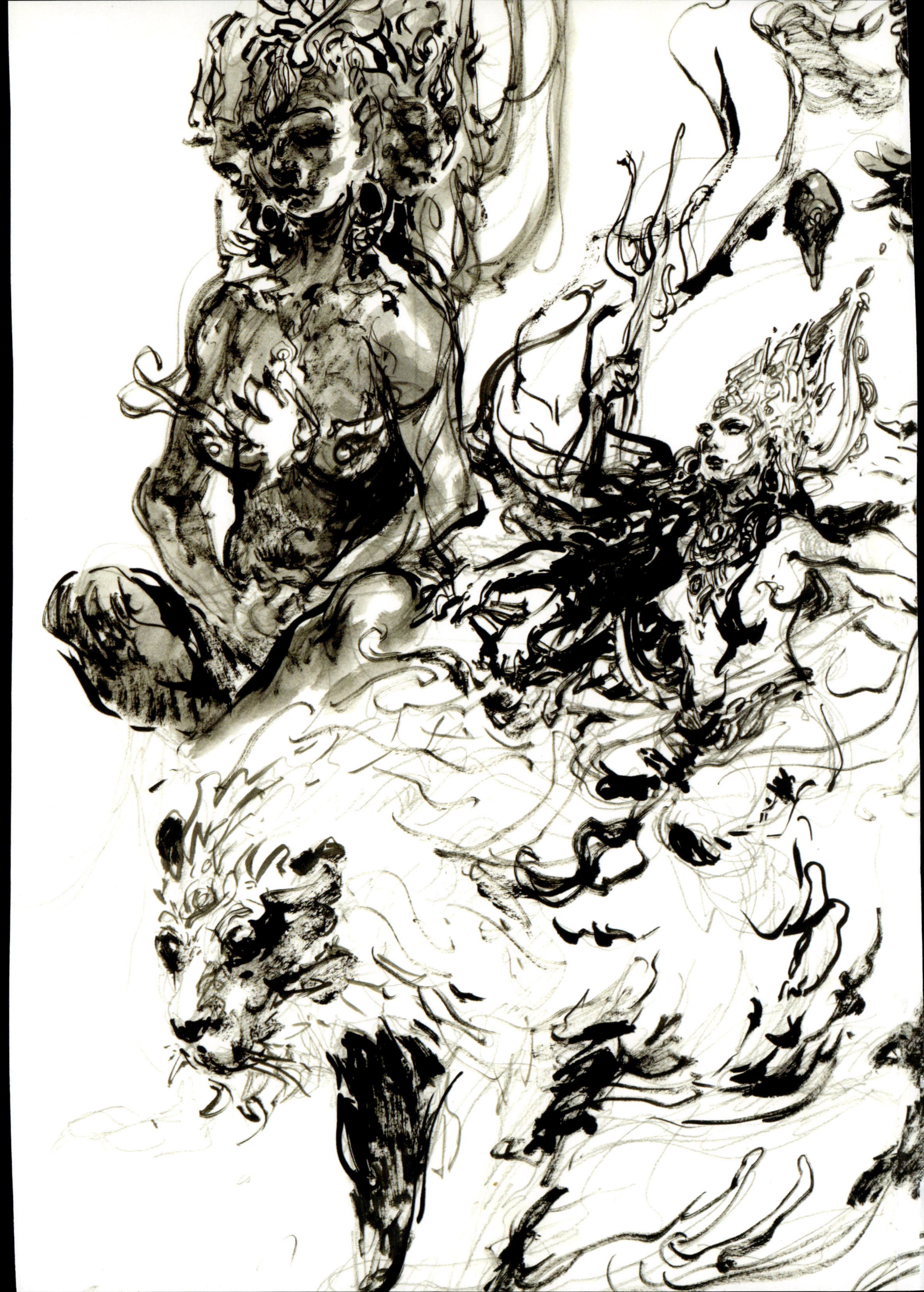

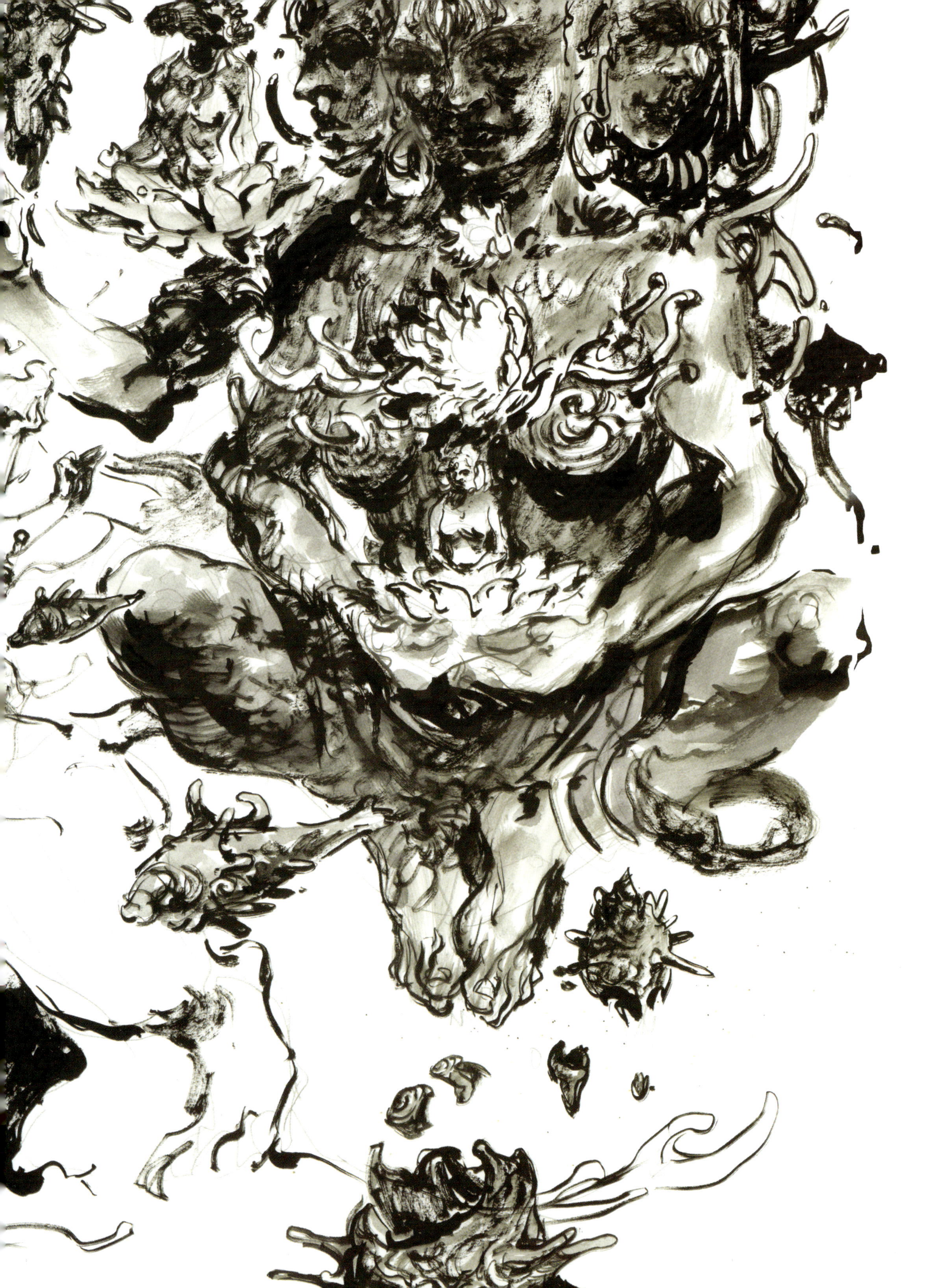

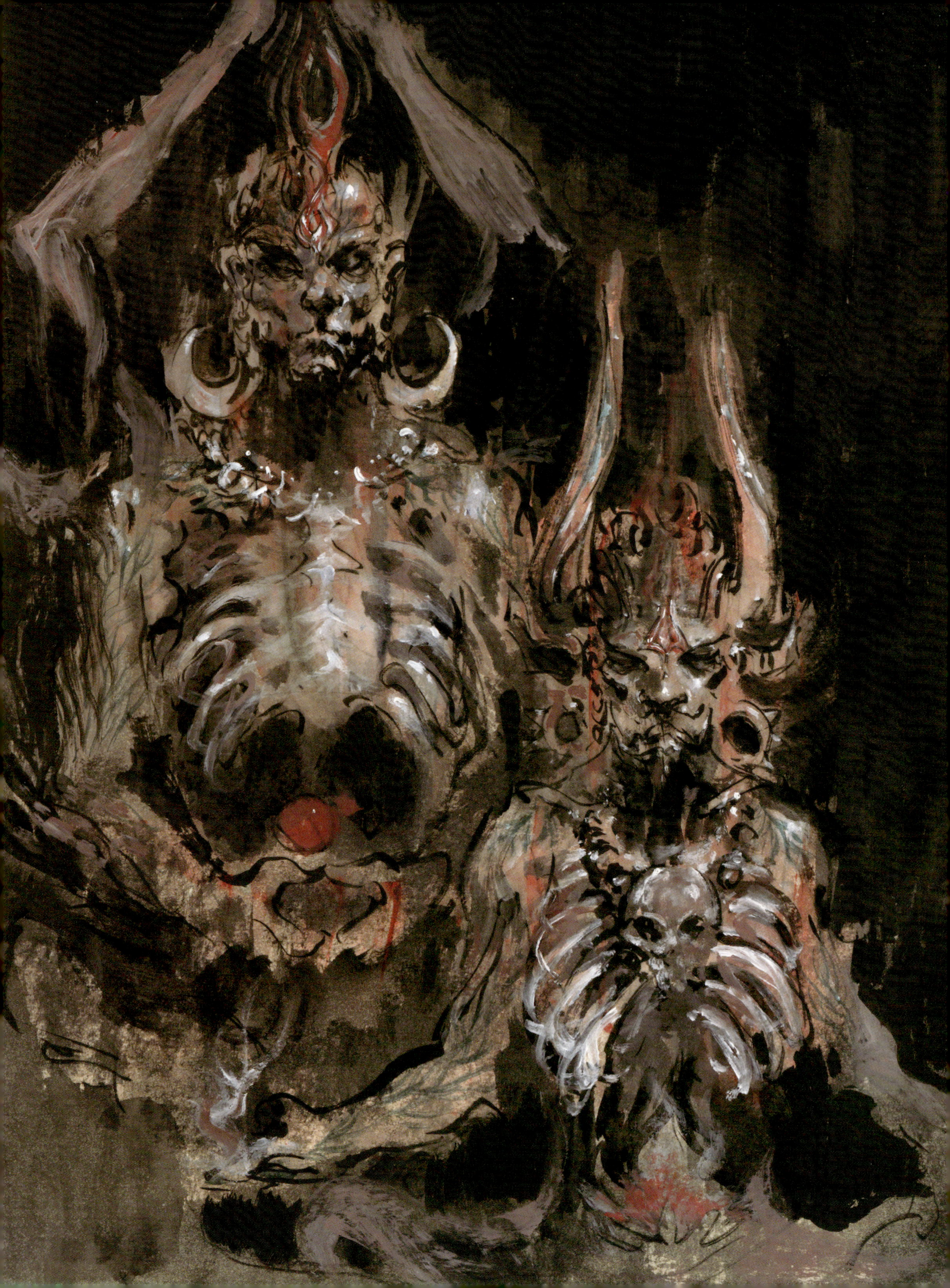

THE DEVI REAWAKENS

Cycles of evil repeat, Boon is an illusion, Heaven is lost, Army of Asuras, Chandika's scourge, Kali's vision and end of Shumbha

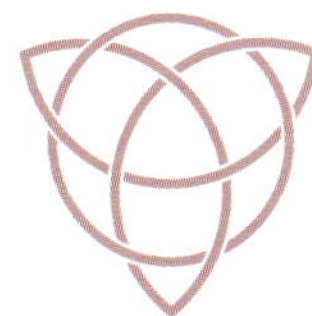

The intense penance of the two asura brothers, had already dwindled the sun, shriveled the fires of the stars and had sent reverberations shaking the many realms.

They had been immersed for thousands of years in this astute tapasya, hoping to appease the creator god, so they could ask him for the most unattainable boon.

Eventually, acknowledging their worthy prayer, the creator God Brahma, decided to descend, as he knew all too well what was to conspire.

Upon seeing the resplendent one, the two asuras kin, Shumbha, the invincible who was the eldest, and Nishumbha, mighty and youngest, spoke with venerated calm, wishing an impossible demand.

"We desire to live beyond the clutches of time. We want to be above its controls, for it inflicts decay and death. Immortality, is what we seek, O, lord of the worlds."

Brahma's energy had already healed their dilapidated bodies and had rejuvenated them through his aura, he spoke wisely as one should to insistent souls.

"Children of Dhanu, time flows differently for various beings, longer or shorter is just relative.

Even the sun, moon, everything in the universe abides by time.

No one can slow time or make it go fast or bend its will.

All life-forms approach their ends, in that moment the lived time seems like a dream, returning back to its ephemeral state, in that way, there is no death, only a transition from matter to non-materiality."

"Yet, on different planes and realms, like a river, it flows differently, based on the terrains over which it has to endure its course. The mind, body and spirit, experience time differently, and hence, to find an alignment becomes important, without that balance, turbulence may be felt across these worlds."

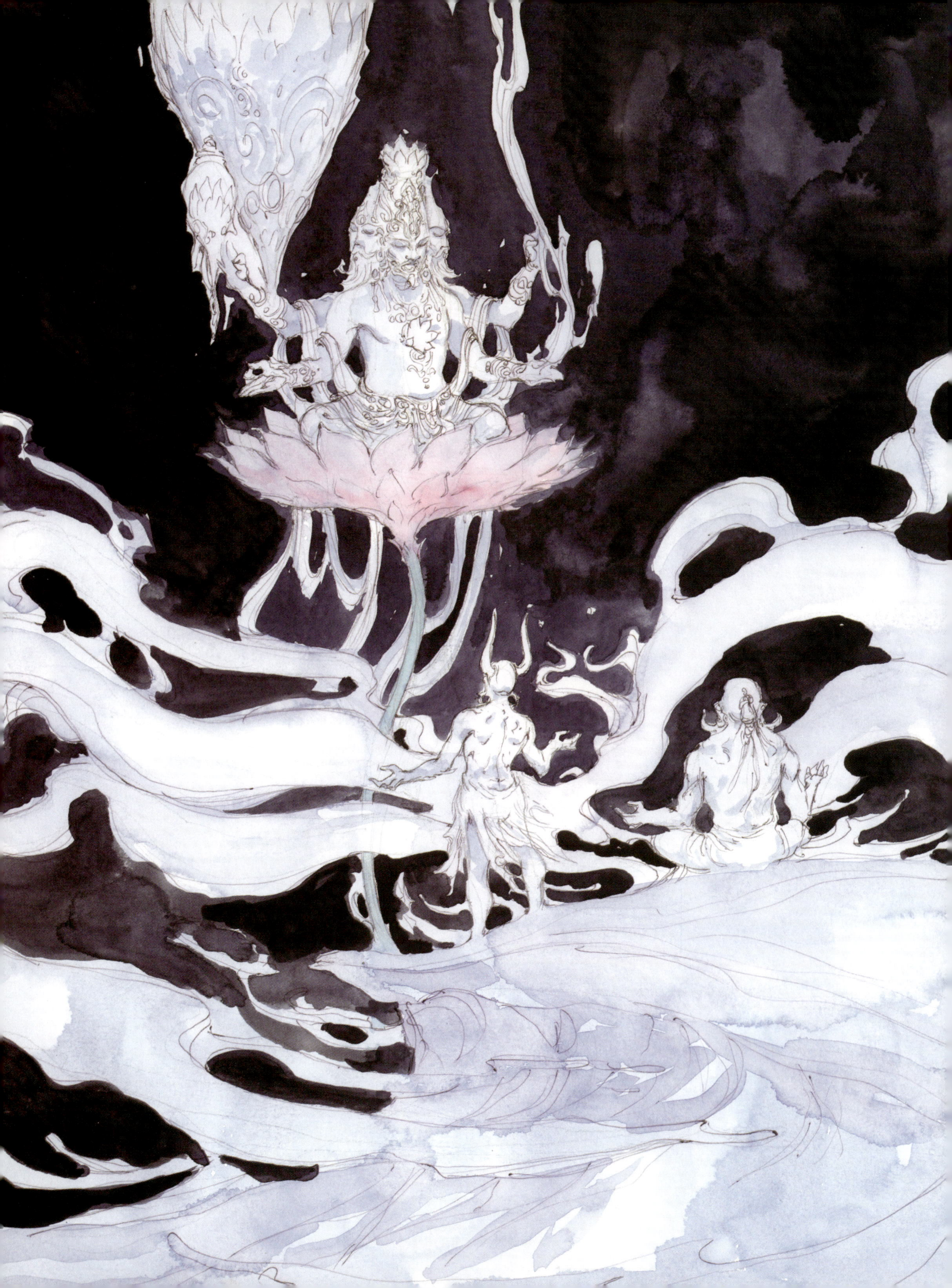

"The energy which pervades these kinetic reverberating worlds of waking, dream and deep-sleep, should not be obstructed or blocked. The wise thing for the powerful is to always let this flow maintain its course, that's the dharma of the worthy. Hence ask for anything but not that which is impossible." The two without contemplating the words Brahma had spoken, expressed back in entitlement.

"You are the creator of cosmic frames within which time works, why can't you give us liberty beyond those closed gates? We've prayed unhindered for thousand of years, performed severe austerities, we deserve this, give us what we seek."

Brahma kept silent, he knew words would only prod their desperation further.

He calmly said again, "All the memories drift and go back to where they have come from, only the essence is immortal. Ask me anything else."

This further curdled their desperation and their tone started to transform, flaring up the deep seated avarice. Surprising that even long years of austerities and prayer can sometimes fall short in front of insatiable greed.

Hence, evading all good-sense they asked for a peculiar boon, drenched in ignorance.

"Then grant us that no-one can kill us except a woman."

"So be it," said the stoic Brahma.

As he was about to vanish in the etheric clouds from where he had emerged, the two asuras asked him another question.

"Lord of Ether, Is there no one beyond the fences of time?"

Brahma said nothing and smiled gently.

As he disappeared back into his nebulous realm, he ruminated, that how even his being was not above that rule, being the appointed creator, he was simply an expansion of the cosmic cycles and even though he lived much longer than most, eventually he must too, perish like every other temporal being.

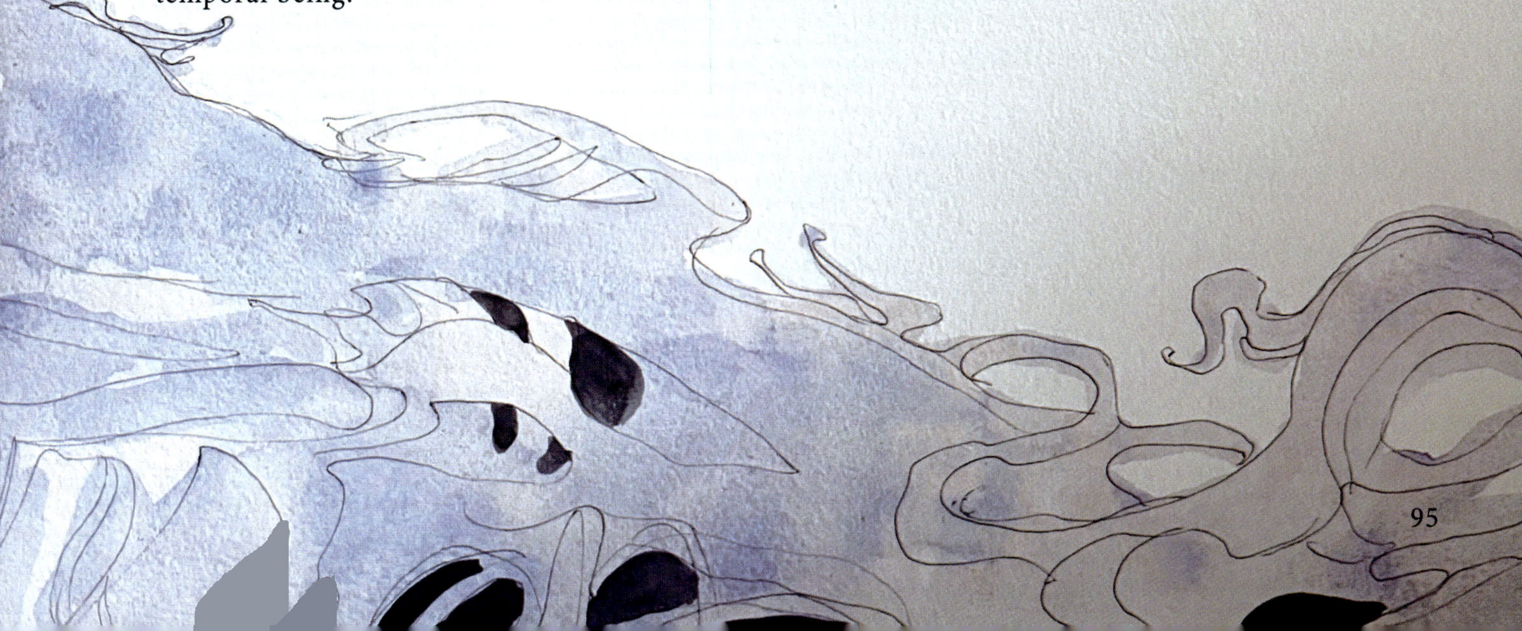

Then he contemplated about the only one who was beyond death.
The one through whom all facets of birth, life, decay and death are radiated as wisdom. The one who was there before creation, and the one who will be there cradling the ends. He thought that how no one except her has seen what exists or doesn't beyond the walls of time or death and that soon the two dissonant asuras will meet her and will reach their ordained fates.
Every boon for immortality was simply an illusion waiting to blend back into its ultimate end.

As he entered his formless state, the vision of Maha-Kali, the great one who controlled time itself, enveloped him and like a fleck of light he gave himself to that blissful darkness.

The Invocation:
The Devi elevated over the glinting rocks with her pranic energies. Multiple stars were being rekindled through her embrace.
If not for the darkness around, one could not look at her directly. She was equally present in the surrounding emptiness, inhaling and exhaling like the universe as much she was there in the calming illumination.

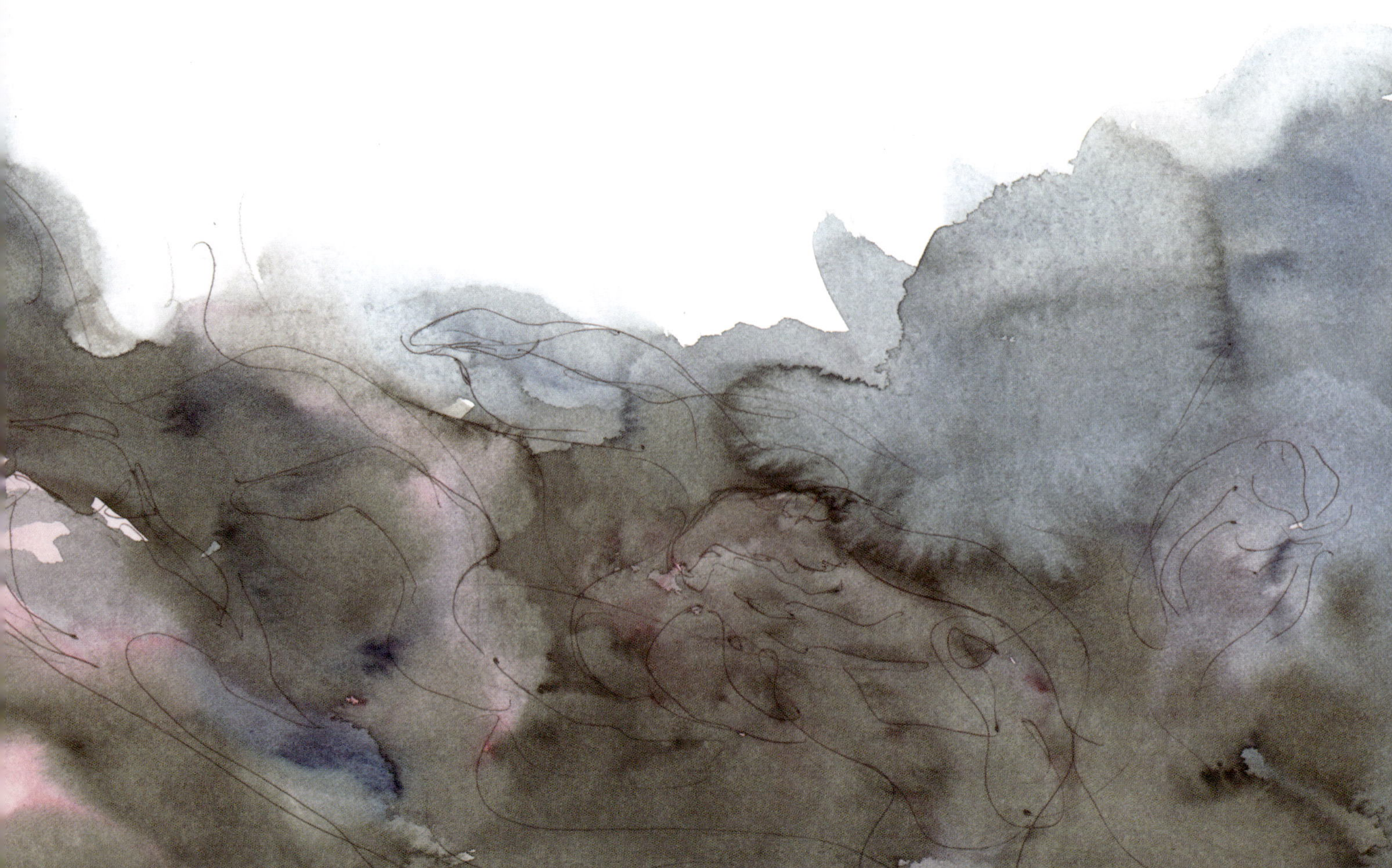

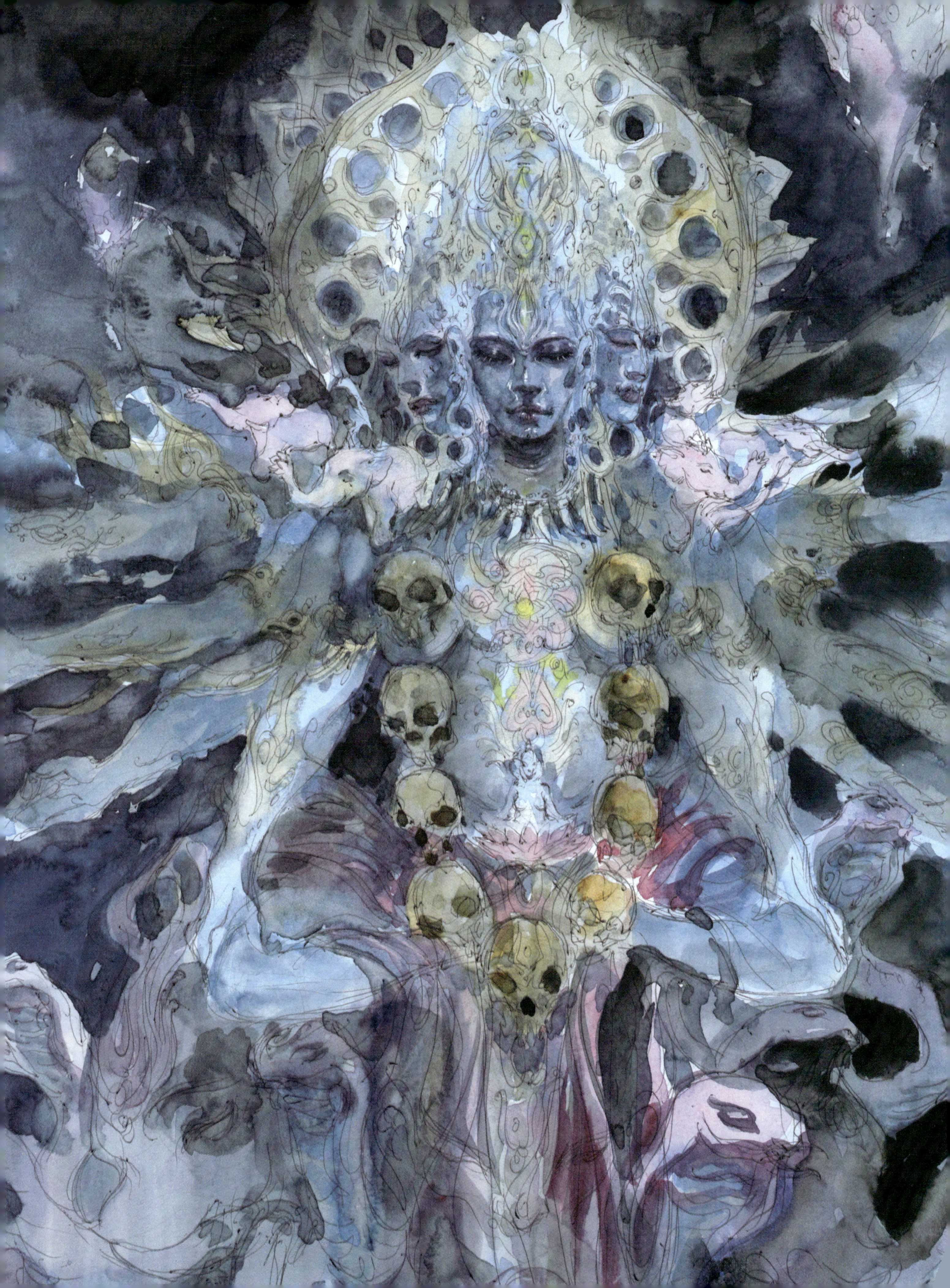

In her immersed state, devoid of the passing of time, she had been in her eternal formlessness, away from the clamor of the waking world but now cracks in time were letting sounds of sorrow pass through. The world was in disarray and was calling to her; the plea of the forlorn gods was coming through.

The yearning of the gods started to percolate in her realm:
"Adi-shakti, the most ancient of all, we call upon you, we pray to you, to rescue us from another calamity, as fate and fortune have abandoned us yet again."

She was unmoved, as she knew that this has happened many a times, the suras have lost heavens to the asuras again.

As cycles of time turn, the forces—both resonant and dissonant—which oscillate inside the mind, remain in perpetual conflict with each other. Fighting over the reigns of the etheric kingdom of the mind, as whoever controls it drives the entire empire of the self.

In her world no gods could enter, let alone their waning pleading voices. No one was allowed in this world of the Devi, except one.

Suddenly an ethereal voice called to her, this one didn't belong to the gods, but to someone beyond time like her, it was of Mahadeva Shiva, who benevolently spoke.

He had many names for her, as he loved her like he loved the Earth in all its myriad forms, Uma, his beloved, Gauri, the dazzling one, Shakti, the primeval one, and thousand others. Yet the one which came out of his heart, was... Parvati, the one who birthed the mountains, and in the mortal realms was birthed by them.
"Devi Parvati, the cycles of energy are again tormented, the Earth suffers and the fire of greed burns the oceans once again. The guardians of nature gods have been displaced. Hubris has again belittled their wisdom; resulting in a great defeat and now they roam in exile, realizing their mistakes, seeking absolution.

The asuras, Shumbha and Nishumbha, who wanted immortality, now rule over heavens. Unafraid of death or any consequences as no man or god can kill them, they have become tyrannical and have gone beyond the necessary threshold. Only you can restore this balance, so energy can move freely again.

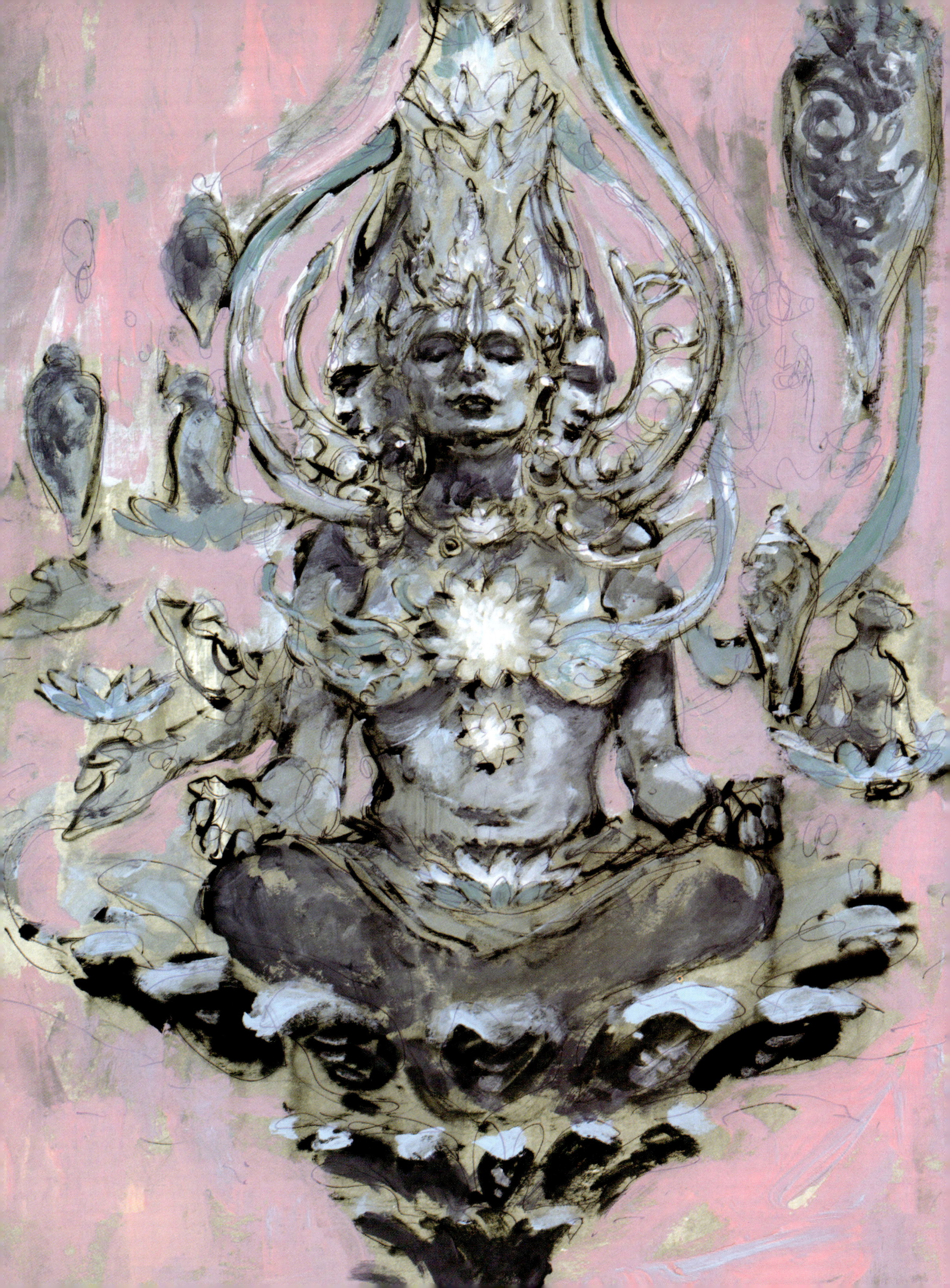

Parvati opened her eyes lovingly to glimpse at the Mahadeva, who with his five heads, enshrined the darkness, sharing every pore of her world inextricably."

Her words took shape, for him alone, like the first forms of life being born after thousand nebulas had aged. "O blissful one, Shankar, the suras and asuras are equal in our eyes, they both are our children in this play of time. Why must the Devas always rule? Perhaps its wise to give asuras an opportunity this time."
She paused, as Shankar, showed her through a vision how heavens endured under the asura reigns.

Parvati said, "I sense through your words, that the devas cannot themselves claim the throne because of the boon bestowed upon the asura brothers, that only a goddess may vanquish them. I also see how instead of being better leaders, they have slipped into a vortex of decadence, ignoring their duties towards the beings of nether and earthly realms. To be in charge of the heavens is to take care of all beings as one and they are neglecting this tenet.

Yet, if they can restore this lack, I would want to give them a fair chance to rule over the heavens. Would you be so kind to be the messenger of this, O Bhuteswar, the one who loves the Earth?"

Ripples ensued from the stars in Parvati's embrace and started to move closer to Shiva. His aura merged with her essence, taking the form of a woman, a messenger named, Shivaduti, a combination of both of them.

Her mind's eye opened a portal and she traversed with the speed of light, straight towards the place where the asura brothers were holding their court.

The vision arrived and startled everyone, all asuras looked at this messenger who seemed like Shiva in the form of a goddess, they were equally mesmerized and bewildered by her presence. She spoke to Shumbha, the eldest, with words full of unwavering wisdom.

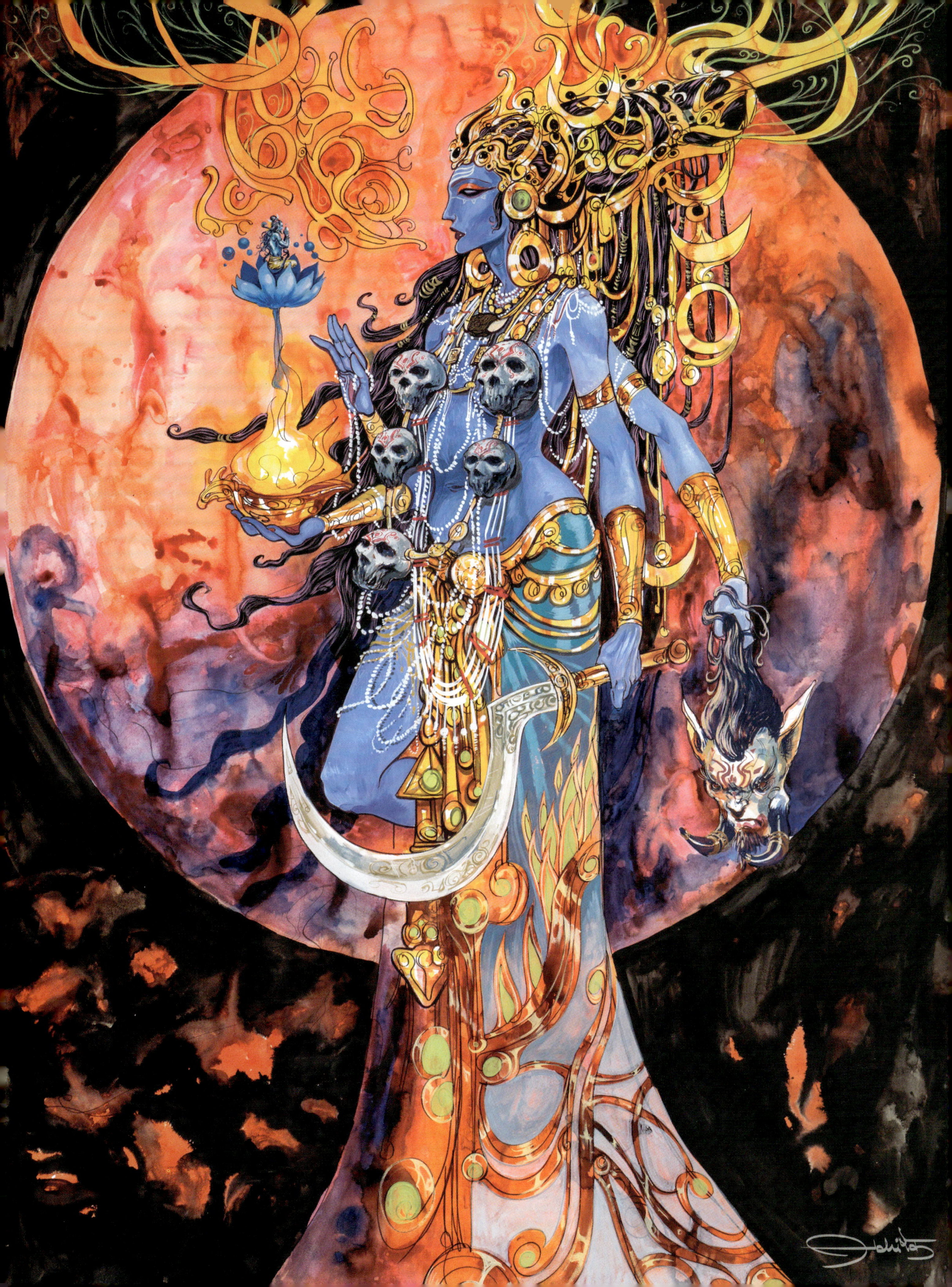

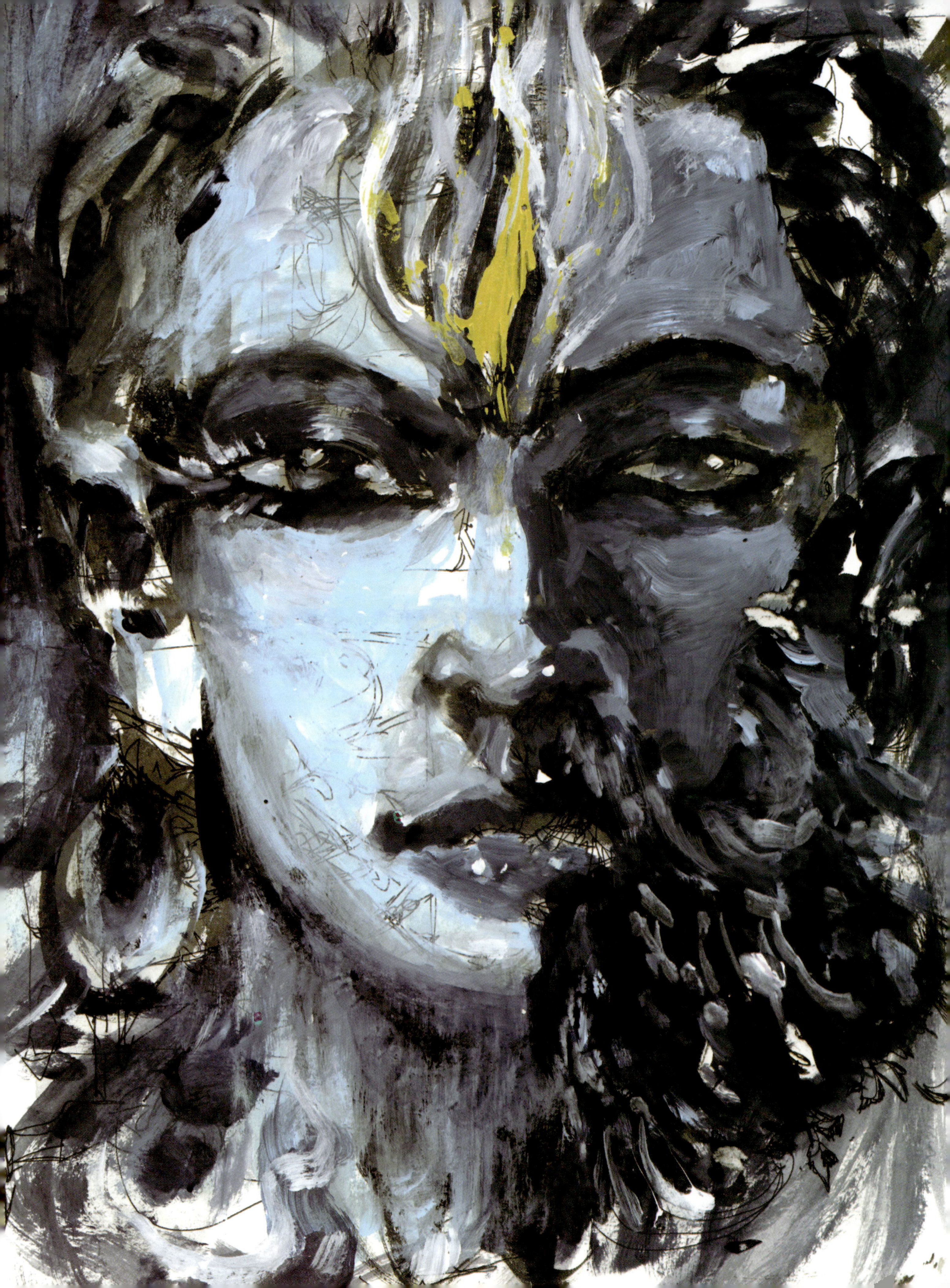

"True glory comes with responsibility, O King of asuras. To take over the heavens, means that you must comply with all the responsibilities, which come with it. Instead you are swayed by your own rhetoric and enjoyments. Send your brother Nishumbha to Patala and rule all places like there's heaven everywhere."

Without discerning the message, Shumbha spoke with rage, born out of sudden confrontation. "Are you an enchantress? Don't you know that I am invincible, I have earned this place through power which is beyond the comprehension of the gods, I don't fear anyone..."

Before he could finish his sentence, he realized that it was a message sent by a far away entity, and that the messenger was a projection of a primal power, beyond his grasps. Without warning, Shivaduti, evaporated like mist in the wandering clouds, leaving the brothers and everyone at the court shocked, about the prophecy of their impending doom.

The messenger Shivaduti, like a rain cloud seeking the sky, returned to Devi Parvati and merged with her aura.

Knowing that the confrontation with the asuras was inevitable, Parvati went into a deep pranic state. She channeled her Prana, the vital force of creation and manifested a goddess radiant like light and deep as the oceans, the great Mother Goddess Ambika, who appeared piercing the darkness of ignorance, healing the deserted minds.

While Shiva felt the presence of Adi-parashakti, the primeval creator of the universe, Brahma, through his mind's eye, sensed Maha-saraswati, the great goddess of knowledge, because the goddess was created from Parvati's energy sheath, Kosha, she was also called, Kaushiki, supreme of the Mahavidyas, the guardians of wisdom, having a deep blue hue.

Gods felt a sense of echoing in their heart chakras too. They saw numerous indescribable incarnations, which had descended in various timelines before, they felt how every strand of the universe and their being had become a goddess. They recalled how each time when the suras were in disarray, she had helped them like a Mother, reinstating order back into the rhythms of the universe. Some whose memory had witnessed the previous cosmic wars , remembered her as Durga, the protector, and could see the great Matrikas, Mothers present in her spirit.

They called her by multiple names, as one may attempt to call the spirit or love, yet never containing all of what it means in a word. All they could think of was a touch of love which had finally descended to show them the way.

Soon Devi Parvati and Shiva vanished into their etheric states, and instead of them hovered in the star-lit sky, the dazzling Goddess Ambika, who contained all other goddesses within her infinite being.

The radiant Devi then took a long breath, inhaling all the prana, being poured down from all the sacred constellations and elements, and decided to traverse from her realm to the battlefield close to the doors of heavens, where the asuras waited, unaware of the looming trepidation.

As Devi Ambika descended into the battlefield, the stars which she had cradled in her being, erupted outward, with fiery fumes sending tremors, ensuing a maddening laughter from afar, shaking and trembling the asuras, who were still baffled by the previous vision.

Shumbha, asked his minister to go and seek out the source of these tremors, he wondered, "Who in the three worlds could send tremors by their breathing alone?"

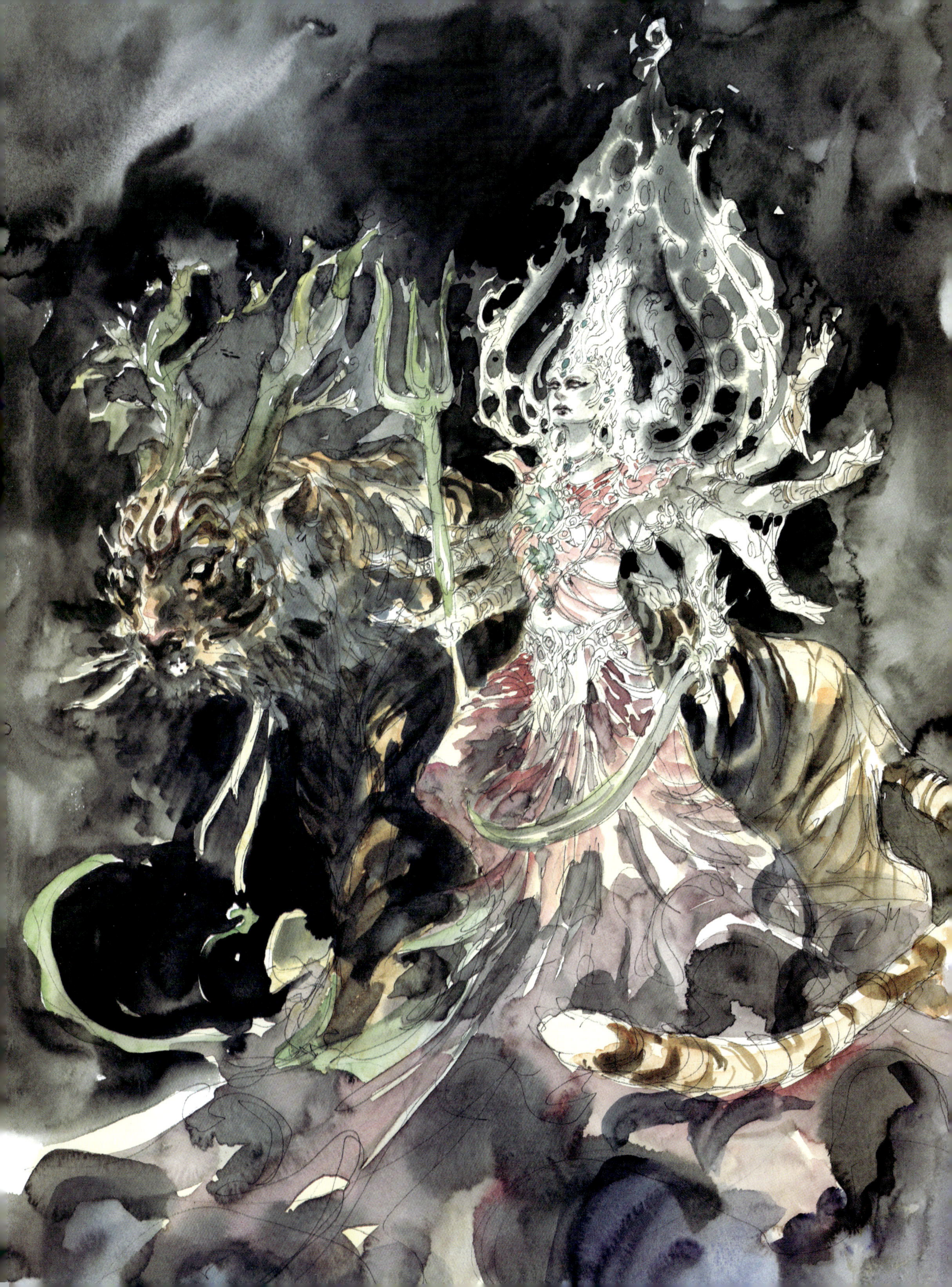

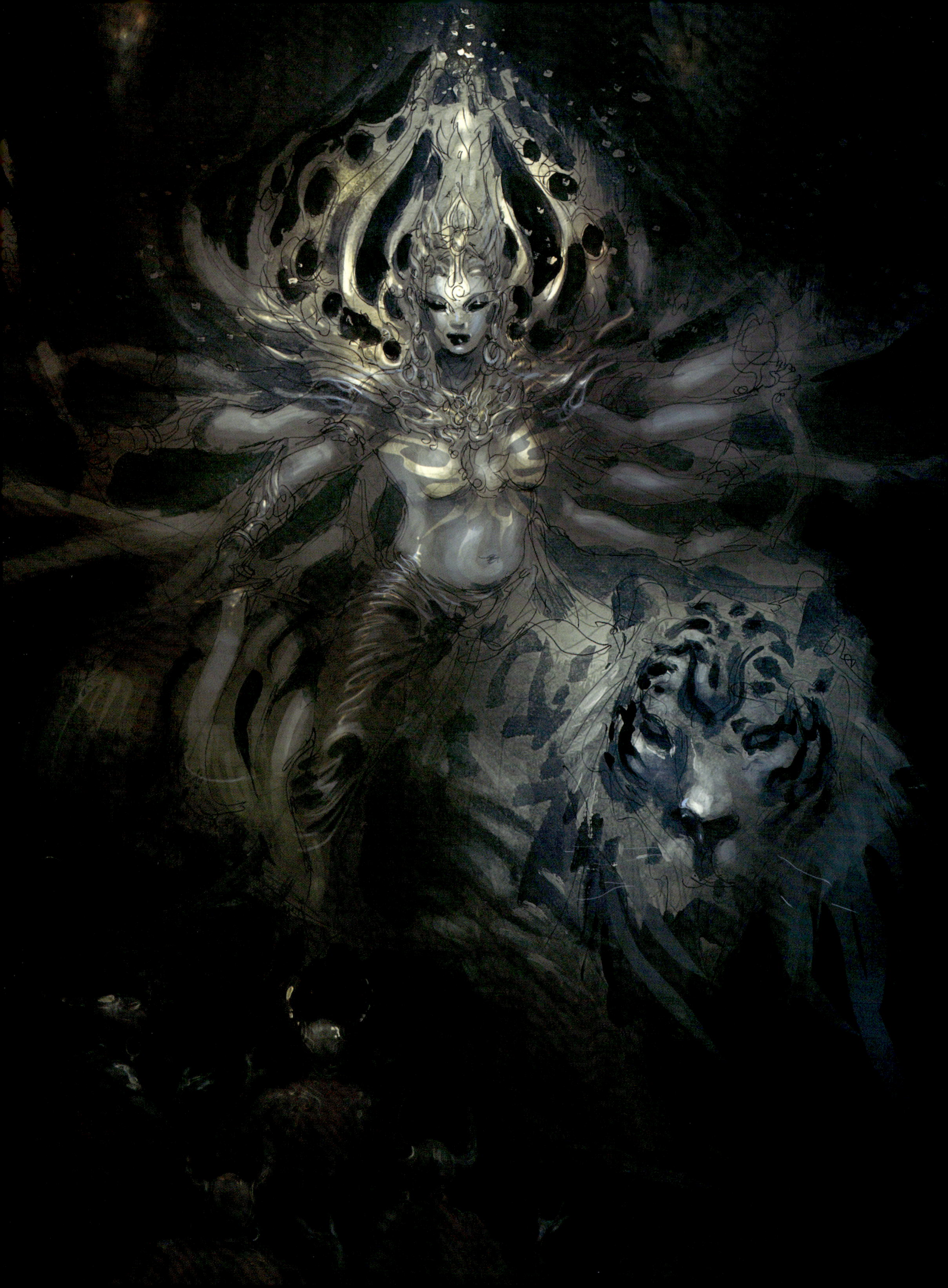

The curious asuras followed the orders and went in the direction from where the tremors were echoing. On reaching the battlefield, they saw the vision of the Devi emanating ominous rays, bemused by it, they for a second forgot their purpose. While her splendor enthralled them, the intense light radiating from her burnt them lightly, like how fire announces its power over a thicket of wood, but she was not just fire, she was also the rain which extinguishes it, so some felt a calming relief, and the ones closest to her, asked her in astonishment.
"O beautiful radiant one, who are you? How are such fiery tremors emerging out of you? Were you the same vision which appeared in the court?
Are you even real or a mirage sent by the gods to deceive us?"

The Devi smiled and exhaled a little, multiple hands came out of her, wielding multiple weapons, she had come to the battlefield with her lion, Kesri, who stood by her, exuding utmost stillness. She already knew that no further arbitrating will help and that the evil oppression of asuras must come to an end, so, Devi Ambika spoke vigilantly back to the asura army.
"I've said what I needed to in your court, adhere to good sense. Go and ask your king to give what he wrongfully possesses or confront me in battle."
The ministers scurried back with their egos curtailed, and upon reaching the court, described the resplendent Devi to King Shumbha, who besides feeling angry, also imploded with deep amorous desires for her.

With his good sense waning, he spoke,
"I should feel concerned by this challenge, but instead I feel infatuated by her description. Her fierceness eludes me; a woman of such brilliance must become my queen. This wish floods my heart."
Sedated by his ego, he called upon his warrior generals, and ordered,
"Dhumra-lochana, the resolute one, go and bring her to me. Convince her that I'm the most suited for her in all the three worlds, unequal and an indomitable force amongst the asuras."

"I will abide by your wish," said, Dhumra-lochana, and left to meet the Devi.
He saw her exuberantly glowing, as if the sun itself had descended down, mesmerized by her beauty, he said,
I bring you a proposal, coveted in all the realms. My king has grown desirous of you, his heart lurches to take you as his wife. You'd be lucky and well taken care of, under his protection, as his queen. He wishes you to grace his abode, I request you to come along with me.

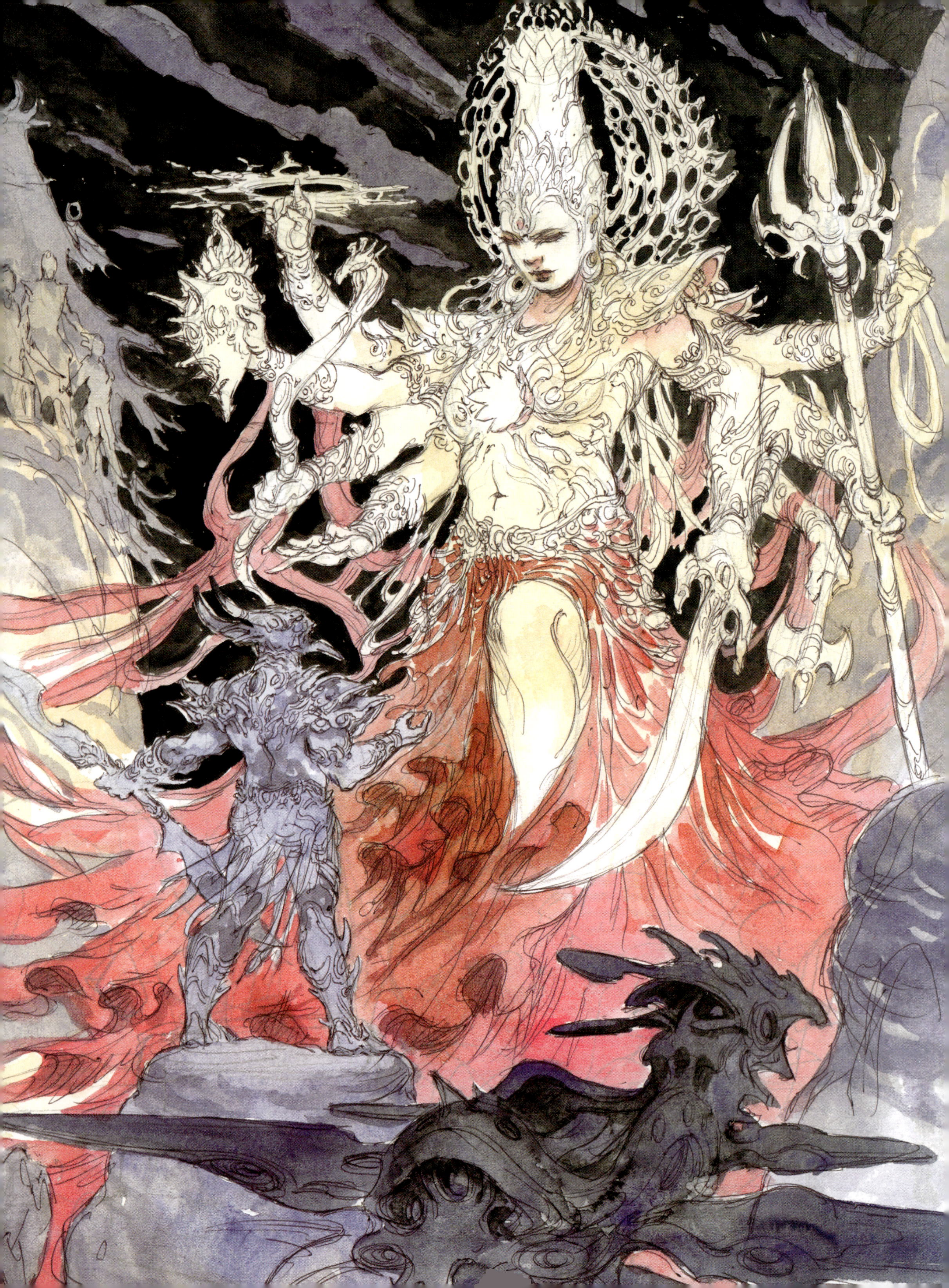

Ambika smiled upon hearing this,
Devi: "Why isn't your king here in person? What is he afraid of, that he sends along a massive army, led by his acolyte, who speaks in arrogance about love, ironic as that is, you should retreat to your king or this senselessness will led to your demise."

Dhumra-lochana became infuriated and hissed at the Devi, and losing all control attacked her. First by shooting arrows, which she plucked out from thin air like adrift flowers, and then by running towards her angrily with his heavily ornate sword.
Ambika, the one who looked iridescent against the deep black sky moved her hands in gestures, which catalyzed the pranic fires, and speared them towards the frantically approaching Dhumra-lochana and like a ray from the sun, incinerated him, in a moments blink. He was gone, just like his futile words, his being sprayed over the swirling dust, which now consecrated the ground the Devi stood on, transforming the colors.
Witnessing Dhumra-lochana evaporate like a falling dew drop in the expanse of time, made the rest of the asura army realize that the Devi was no ordinary force and they scrambled away, fearing for their lives, back to their king.

Shumbha's anger raged as he summoned two of his most superior warriors, Chanda, the fierce and Munda, the cunning skull, to go and fetch the Devi. This time he wanted her at all costs.

"Get her, by request any means necessary, or by abduction, or force, just bring her to me, I am the lord who commands all and she must be taught a lesson."

An army of asuras greater than the one which had defeated the gods, came towards her. The Devi remained unwavered by the approaching horde, and concentrated all her pranic activity, reinvigorating the many goddesses within her. She inhaled abundant cosmic energy to invoke the Matrikas, the great Mothers and retained her breath in a way where her entire aura, sparkled with colors beyond sensory perception. How inert matter is put into motion by energy, she exhaled and issued from her pranic state, many other guardian goddesses.

Ambika, the golden one, exuded immense stillness absorbing toxins, while Bhagwati endowed with the auspicious signs consecrated the space, Indrani, decked with light, wielded powerful thunderbolts and was accompanied by the celestial elephant, Airavata who moved around in the sky healing its clouds, Brahmani, was mounted on a swan and chanted the hymns which soothed

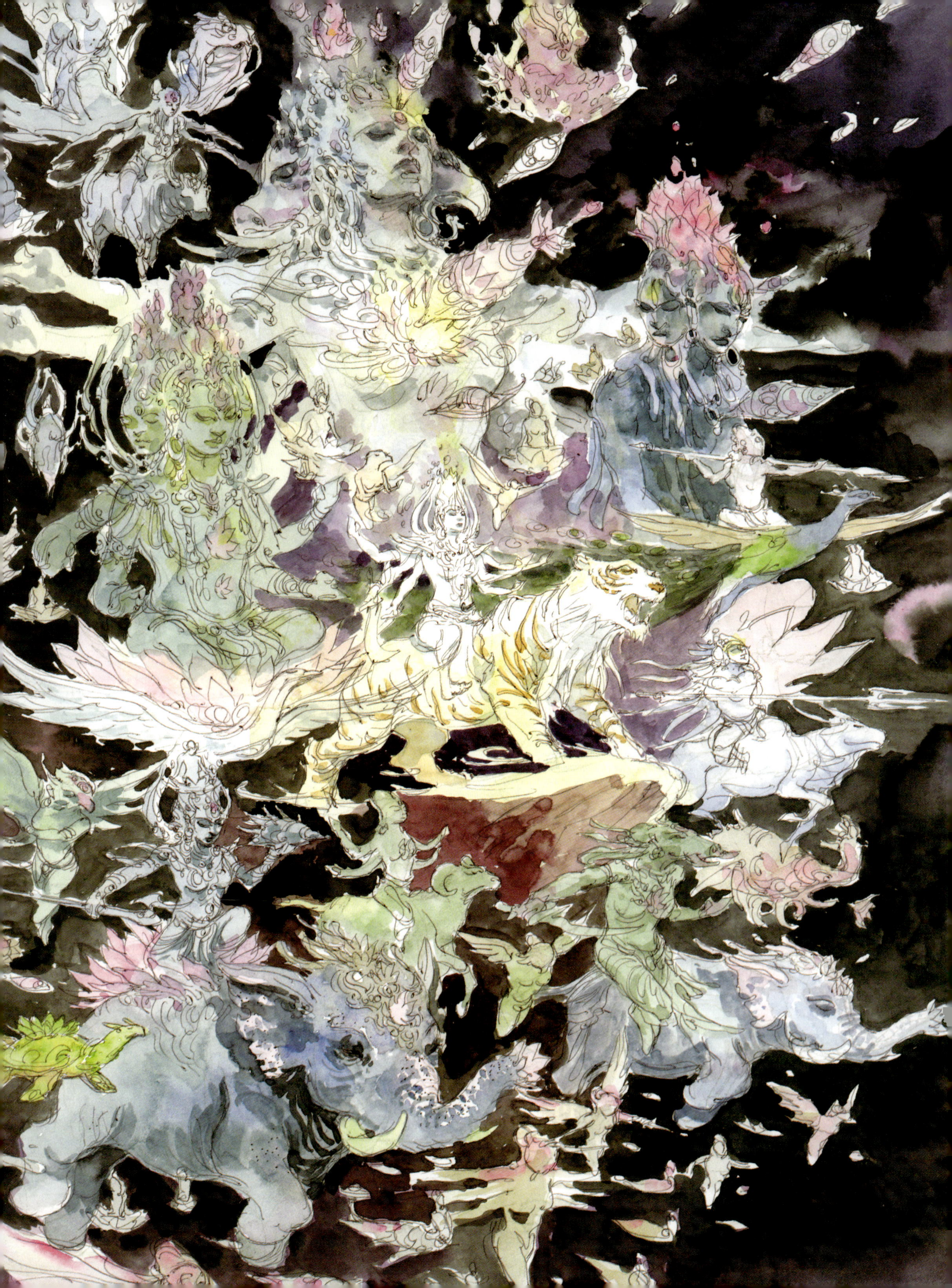

the souls, holding rosary beads and the most pristine waters in a kamandala vessel she carried. Vaishnavi adorned with yellow robes, like camphor flowers adorning the verdant earth, rode the most majestic, Garuda, king of all eagles, holding a lotus, mace and chakra (discuss) in her four hands, while her conch echoed soothing sounds everywhere.

Rudrani, came riding on the back of the bull with her trident, with unheard music reverberating all around her, becoming the eyes of the goddesses everywhere.

Varahi Devi came on an elevated seat of preta, ghosts, who only listened to her, she held the staff, which changed shapes and sang hymns to her. Narsimhi, half lion and half woman, and the merger of realities, started piercing through the illusionary web.
Yami came mounted on a buffalo, with a staff in her hand, controlling the noose, which represented time. Kaumari Devi came on a peacock, with spear and strength of many suns, and led the way to confront the asuras. Kuverini, came with gold, to absorb radiation, issuing from the weapons, Varuni, bought along healing, like an ocean, bustling with both mysteries and power.

Some saw the Pleiades star cluster morph into the seven goddesses, other gods watching saw eight and the yogis amongst them, saw sixty-four great goddesses, Brahma, saw even more. Agni saw, Agnimayi, fire goddesses becoming part of this alignment, the Rudras, Vasus, Adityas and Maruts, all elemental phenomena's, saw themselves becoming part of this pantheon of the goddesses. Likewise, Vishnu and Shiva, who witnessed the glorious expansion of the Goddess, from their spiritual being, saw the entire universe becoming an expansion of her radiance, everything in the universe in that moment had become a goddess.

The many goddesses had come together to cradle the energy back to its ordained place by quelling this blockage.

Chanda-Munda, witnessed how her effulgence dwarfed the sun and were stunned by the outwardly formation of goddesses who had collected around Ambika but their hubris soon cracked into the sanctity of the grand moment and they spoke with unchained arrogance to the Devi about Shumbha's proposal, ignoring in plain sight the power they had just witnessed.

"Your beauty surpasses all, of that there is no doubt but why are you being adamant? Our king can forgive your recklessness and take that as a test of your worthiness to him, if you agree to come with us. He owns the three worlds and thus, he is your rightful owner too."

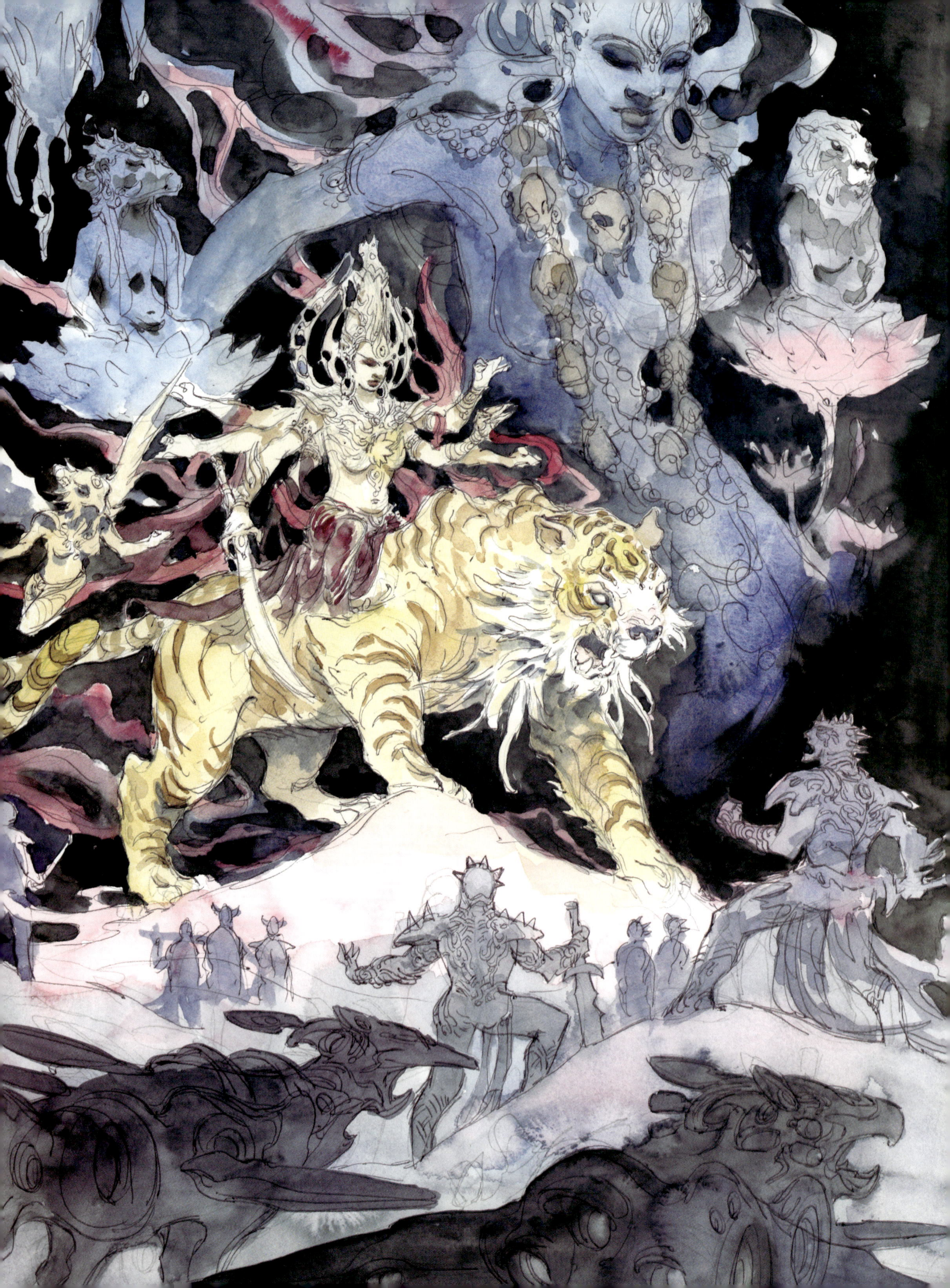

This time, the Devi laughed even more fiercely, the dark one Kaalratri, the great guardian of night, Varahi, the one upon whose tusk the entire earth rested, Vaisnavi, the one absorbing the pain of all beings, and several other emanations, added to the reverberations, cracking the ground underneath the asura army.

Devi: "Not even the body owns the soul, neither, the soul claims the body.
Man or woman can't be owned by each other, they chose to be together in this ocean of life. Its man's arrogance that he projects such claims. He owns no animals, plants, or beings of Earth, let alone his own fate."

"No one owns anyone in this world, we are at best, simply aligned in this great synchronicity and one must strive to realize this truth.

"Go, tell your king that he proves himself the greatest fool, the pasha (noose) of time is around everyone's neck, and those who think they have a way out of that, are senseless Pashus, governed by excessive avidya, nescience. The rope tightens with each of his regressive acts."

Chanda-Munda, decked with the most sophisticated weapons, conceded that there was no point in further convincing the Devi to come along with them and that they should now use all force to subdue her, so they brandished their weapons and with arrogant might, they viciously attacked her.

Devi, along with her emanations, cleaved through the asura army, like light evaporating the precipitating dewdrops. The mayhem peaked as Chanda-Munda started to retaliate even more nefariously against the many goddesses, waning at their patience.

Kaalratri went close to Ambika and said: "When a person gives into arrogance, he gives into inevitable death of his inner being, the body suffers, and corruption dictates the mind, Vadh, the cessation of ego must take place. The energy must leave these bodies, the matter should blend back with the elements."

Ambika Devi, who heard this in her heart, simply nodded her head in permission.
Kaalratri, went straight to Chanda-Munda and roared a war cry which broke not just their weapons but shredded through the entire army, wilting their bones.

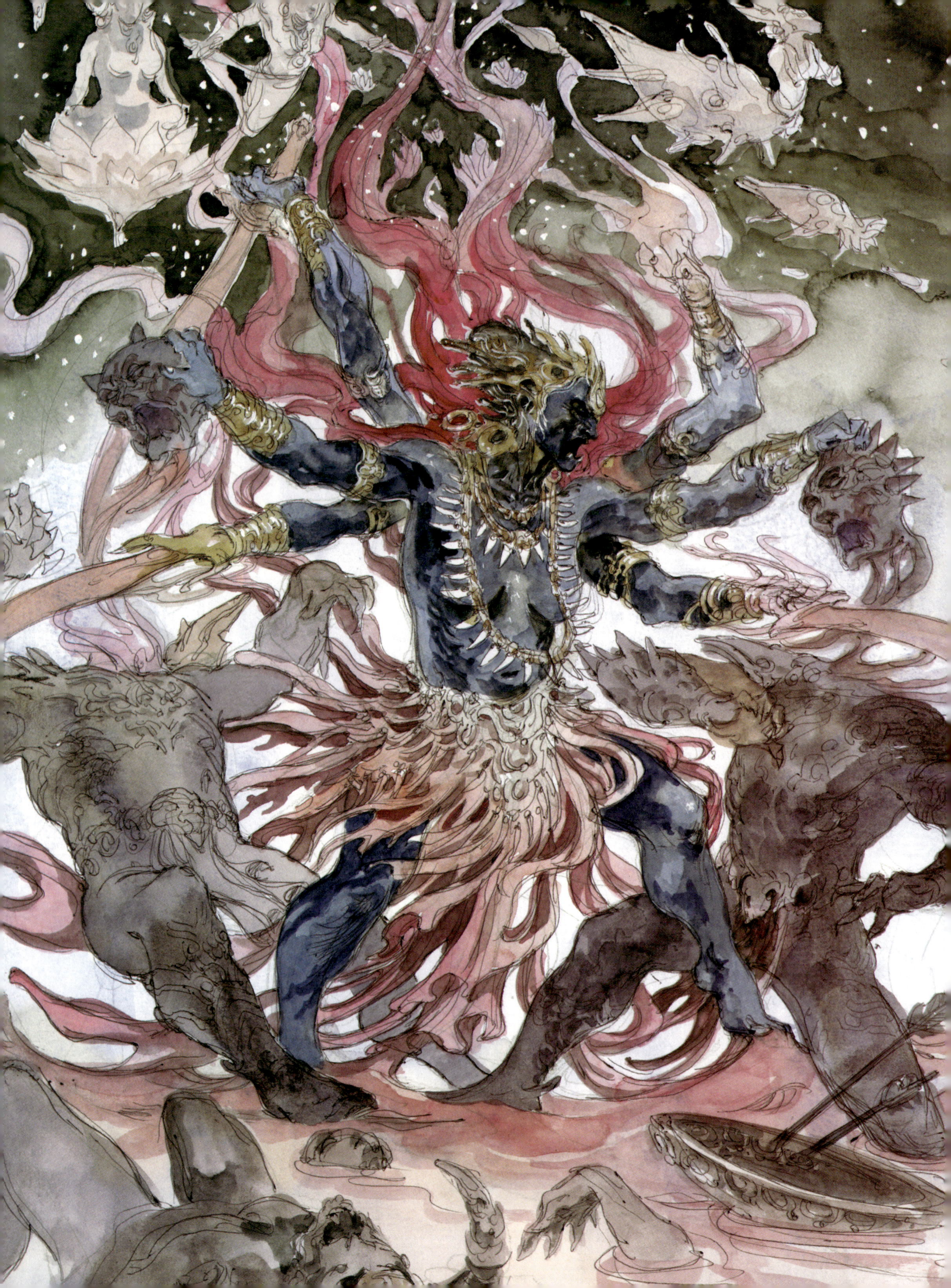

Along with the other Devi's, she rendered all attempts of the asuras useless and without flinching, confronted the two asuras Chanda-Munda, who tried every bit of their power over her to no avail and hurled the most illusionary weapons at her, which she absorbed like a vortex of energy, inhaling light. Never having witnessed this form of unthinkable raw power, their hearts were petrified, the abysmal vision shared their arrogance and the great dark one, the crucible of energy, swiftly, uprooted their heads, like time devours existence.

All the goddesses circled her in a helical formation, which seemed like a torus field, from where the fountain of life sprouts. Devi Ambika along with all the goddesses joined in the sonorous hymns, blooming out of the moment, hailing her as Chamunda, the one who had vanquished avarice and arrogance.

Hearing the account of their death Shumbha's anger aggravated to new extremes, his best warriors who had once made the gods quiver and shake, had not just failed but were deftly slain by the Devi, like fleeting torrents undone by the mighty ocean. How can it be? The disbelief tortured him.

He exploded dismissing his own rising nervousness and summoned the most invincible and deadly of all asuras, the mighty Raktveej, whose each drop of blood could create multiple others like him. He also was Mahisha's father in another form, carrying the fragmented memories of that past and had since, awaited an opportunity to confront the one who had vanquished his son.

Even though his vengeance ruled his senses, he was an ancient spirit and had retained some sliver of wisdom. He spoke in his coarse aged voice.

"Let me go and avert this crisis for you, I've known her, she's no ordinary being, she's the source of life itself, she's the illusions and the light which pierces it too. In her are both death and life, just as the Ocean and Earth know all its living creatures within them, all fates are intertwined in her being.
I will march towards her and put up my most valiant effort, irrespective of results, I know it'll be a mountain to climb, but I am no ordinary asura either, my blood will spawn a force unimaginable to any foe."

As Raktveej descended into the battlefield, blood red clouds swirled around him, and against the veneer of the ebony sky, darkened by the deep hues of the goddesses, they seemed like illusionary snakes, slithering and hissing at her many forms.

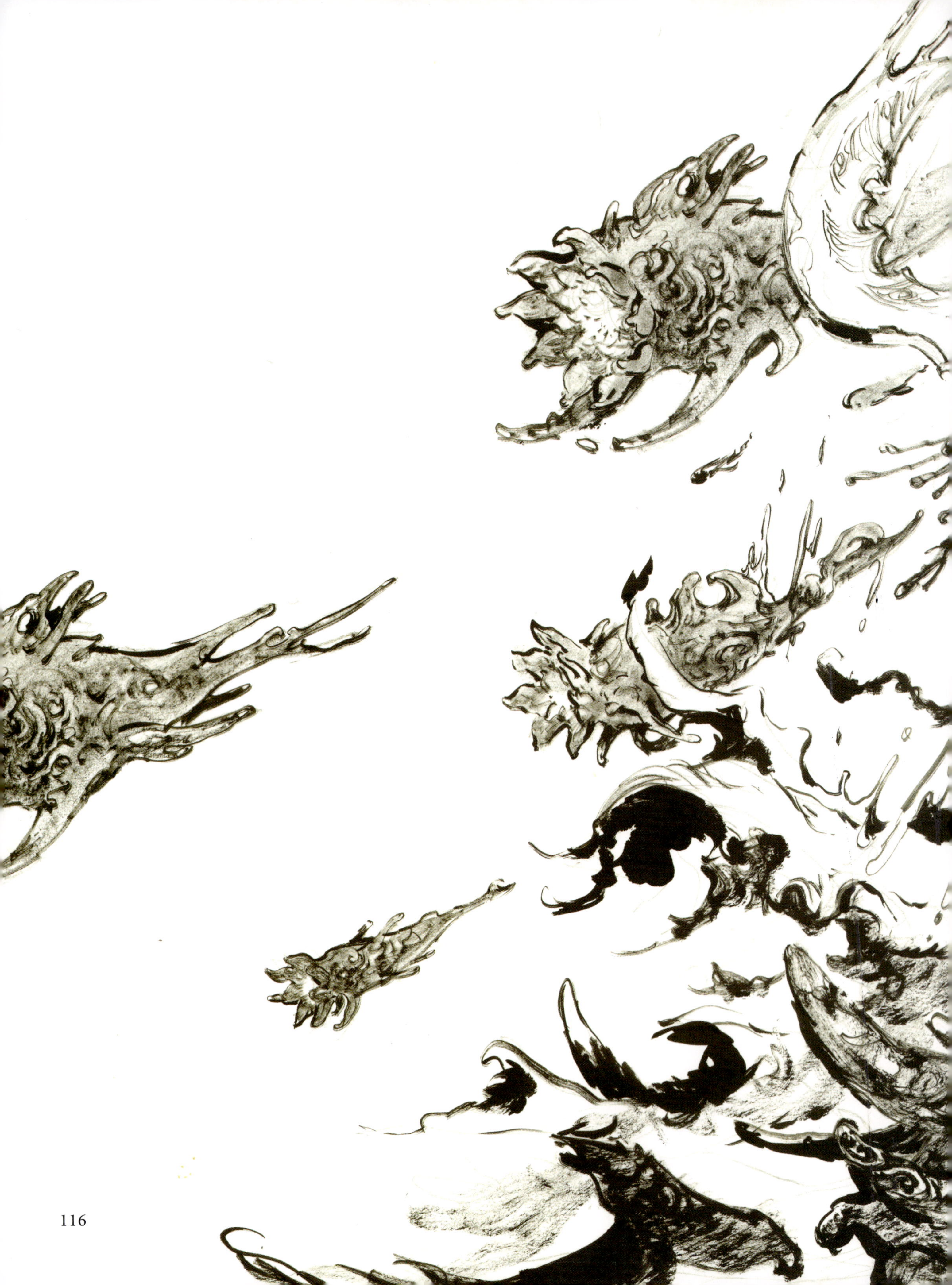

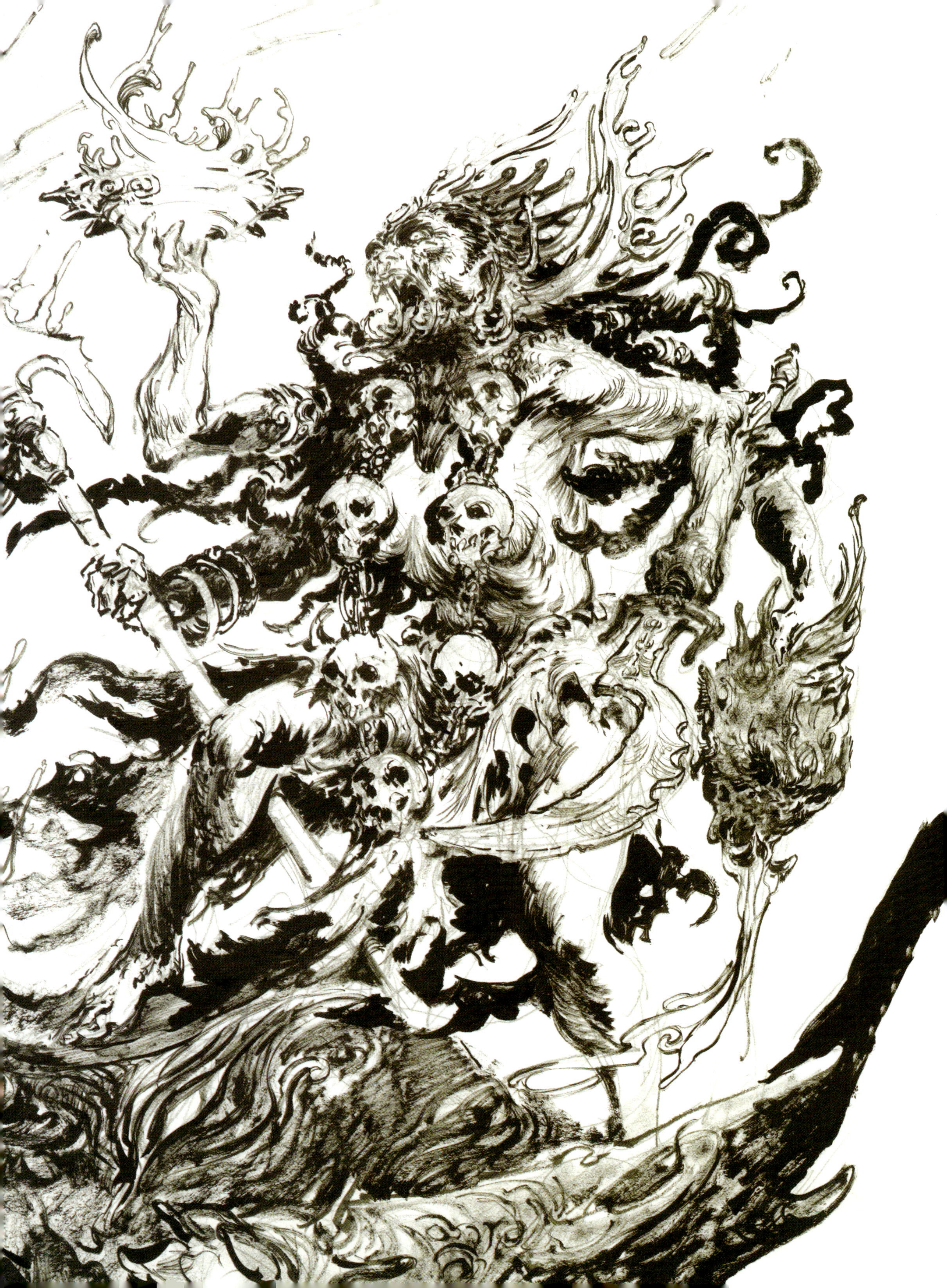

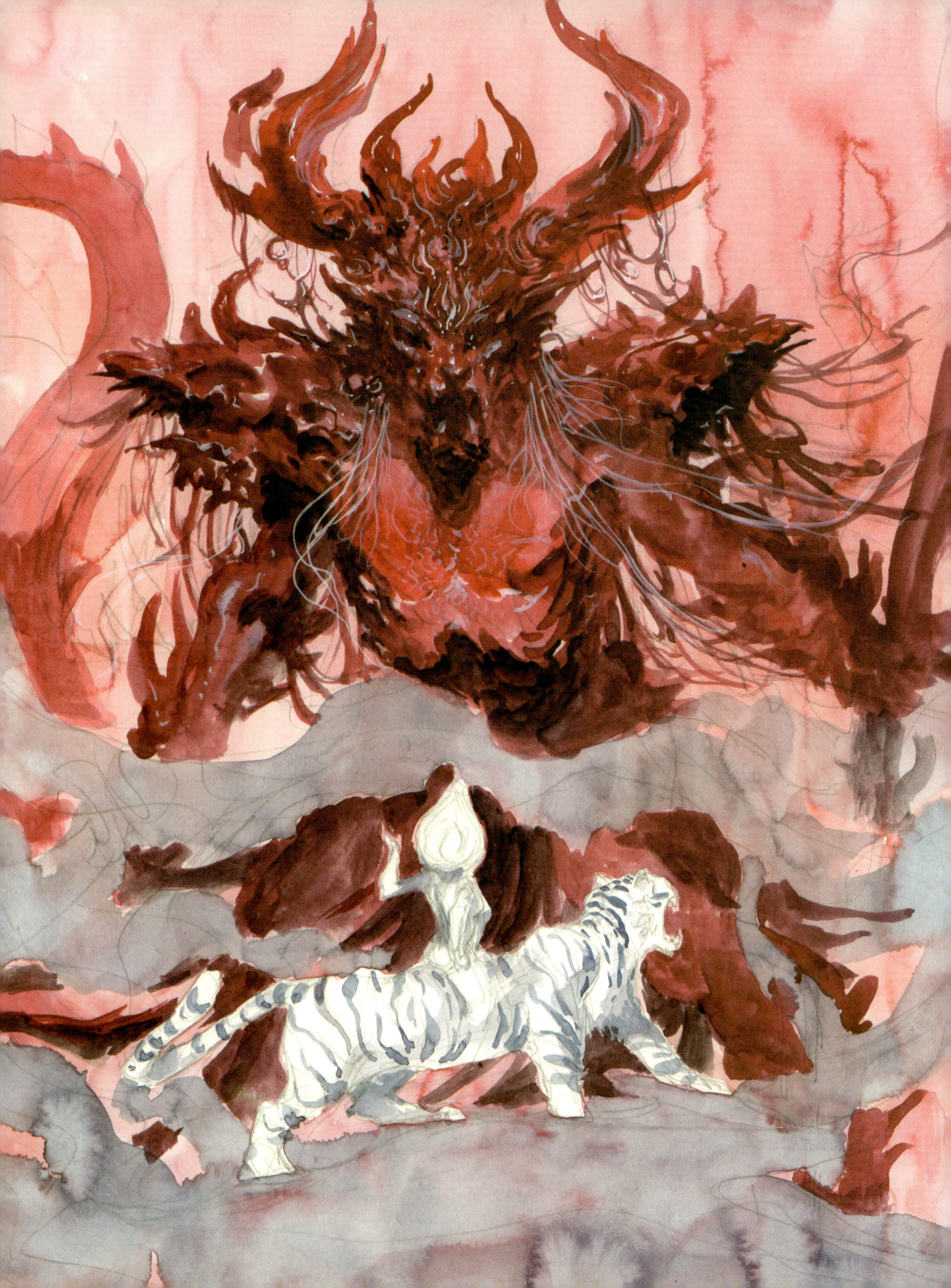

Unmoved by these illusions produced by the senses, the darkness around her took the form of another snake, multiple-headed one, blue and golden in its aura, swallowing the angry red serpents, marking the beginning of a relentless battle between the goddesses and Raktveej.

The looming redness in the sky was still visible, like a wound it hovered over Goddess Ambika, who emitted a golden aura and absorbed all the radiation the toxins were emitting. Amidst the snaring chaos, she seemed like the primal golden embryo from where all life had sprung forth. Everyone who witnessed this marvel was moved by its beauty, yet in contrast to this candescent vision, equally terrifying was the magnanimity of the eruptive power of Raktveej, who inflicted with each of his attacks, a snaring blow heavier than the last.

The sun would have come crumbling down; such was the destruction, which the Devi persisted on the asura. The ambience was bathed in streaks of gold and red, like comets contesting each other in space, a show of primal powers.

As Raktveej and Devi faced each other, every little noise receded, a long eerie silence devoured the clamor of the celestial display of powers, and suddenly like a sleeping volcano erupting and dismantling everything in its course, Raktveej, viciously hurled all his seismic power towards the Devi, no other warrior had channeled such devastating fury against her. He was indeed an ancient one, a primal tremor set in the fabric of time, finally conceding its path, not resisting and throwing himself entirely into his attacks. The Devi felt a tinge of sincerity in the undercurrents of his efforts and she acknowledged it back, by expanding her breath, permeating the violent onslaught, there was a sense of retribution to his madness, a wild fire yearning to be doused by rain, but for now their battle raged like none other.

He hurled many weapons at Devi Ambika, causing multiple lacerations to her lion Kesri, who protected her at all costs, like a wall. He sent multiple arrows and flying daggers, which changed shapes and paths, at the other devis with force a god would possess and valor which surpassed all previous asuras who had attacked them.

The Devi too, intercepted his every move deftly inflicting several cuts on him, severing his limbs, letting fountains of blood profusely erupt from the wounds, gushing out like rivers desperate to flood the cratered battlefield.

The army witnessed something miraculous then, from each drop of Raktveej's blood, another one manifested, rapidly multiplying to thousands, each drop created other clones and with each division, his own sanity reduced and wisdom compromised, all that filled the clones was pure malicious intent, steeped in evil. Like a sea of malignant beings in great number they spawned and charged at the goddess, like a virulent deluge, let loose.

The Devi, defended the incessant incursion of the clone army, slicing through thousands of them like the wind and decimating them, but to no end, as from each drop, millions other were produced. Soon the sky and land seethed red with Raktveejs everywhere. How malignant cells take over a body, encroaching everywhere where the nerves are weaker, hurting tissues which can no longer hold it together, the clones swarmed at the Devi in waves after waves.

Sensing this ceaseless phenomenon, the Devi inhaled a long breath and contracted all her energies in her mind's eye and became the Yogini Parvati, the meditating one and went deep into her pranic state, where one small moment was eternity, she conjured up a vision in which all time and death, creation and dissolution fused as one grand vision.

From death comes life, and in death, all life should merge.
From the beautiful looking Devi sitting in padmasana and brimming with all the fire of stars through her chakras, she transformed into the furnace which birthed them, and became the source from where cycles of time emerge and dissolve. She turned into the dark cosmos, laden with multiple universes dying and being born again.

As Parvati had manifested Devi Ambika from the light of her energy, she conjured up from the darkness of her aura, a transcendental vision, ferocious and terrifying, beyond and infinite. It felt as if the dark energy had descended wearing skulls made of supernovas.

Maha-Kali, the great goddess of time appeared onto to the battlefield and the sky, which seemed smeared by the crimson blood now started to feel a fleck of hope, not just by taking refuge inside of her but turning into the fiery massive tongue and burning red eyes.

The great dark one was death incarnate, wearing a garland of severed heads, which represented the demolished ego state, winding around her waist were uprooted hands of tyrannical men, in one hand she held the mighty Khadag, a sword synced to the cycles of time, pruning through the army and in the other, she gently held a lotus, representing reemergence. Blood swirled around her like falling flowers and souls of the dying encircled her, yearning redemption.

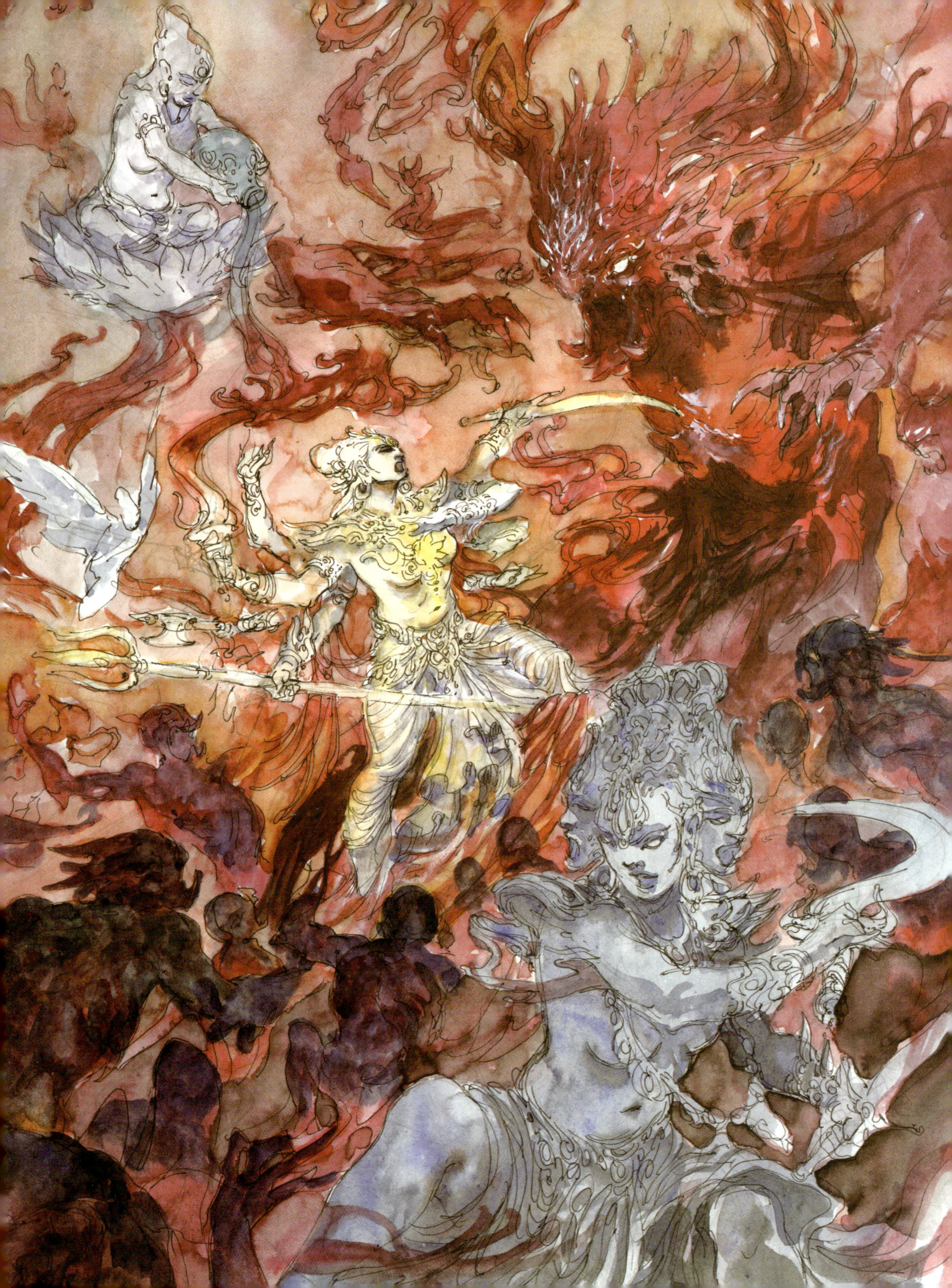

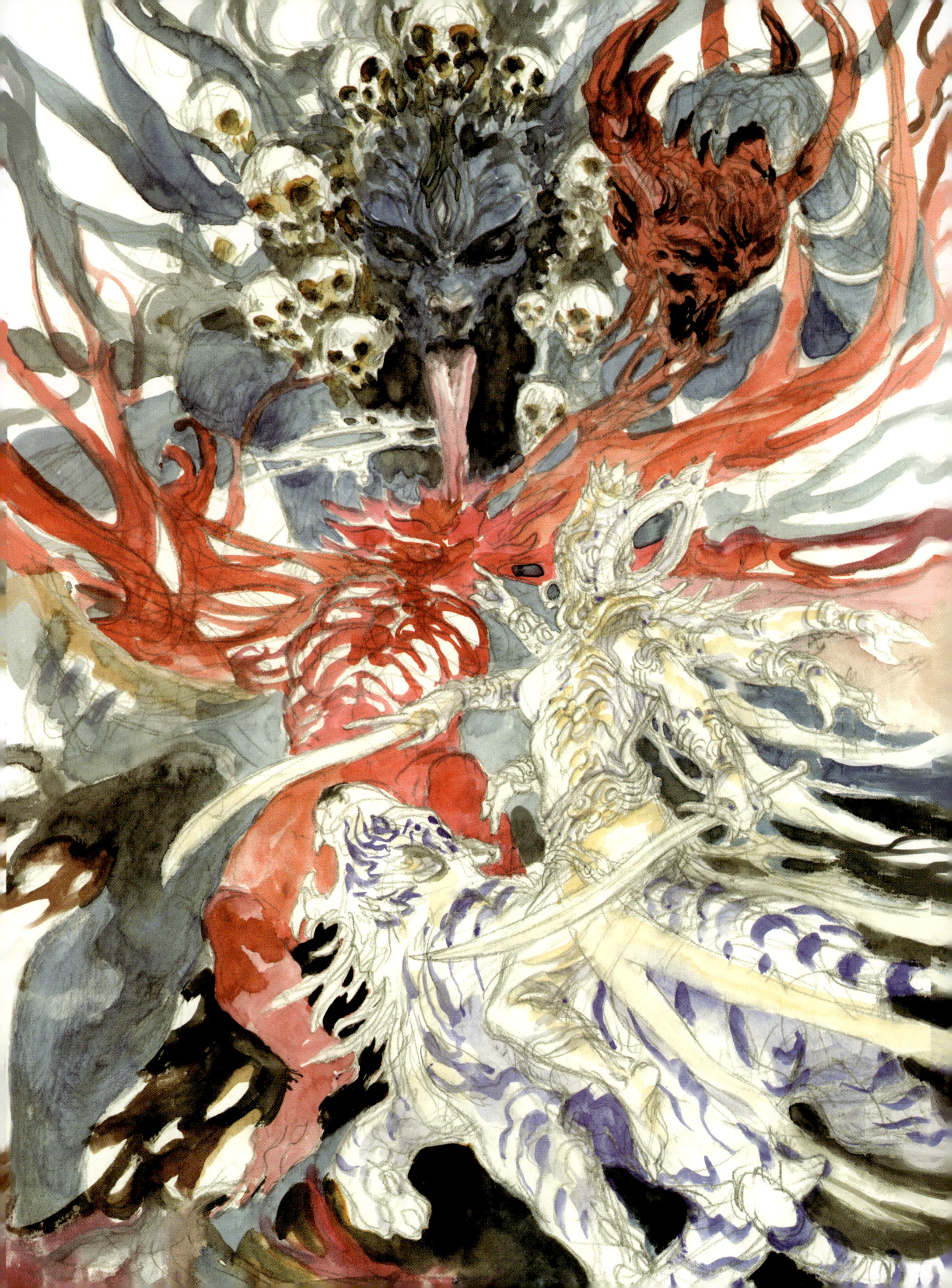

Her presence shook the asuras and most lost their senses just by seeing her terrible form. She leaped in the air, ensuing haunting sounds, which speared through the bodies of anyone in their path. It was, as if death had descended on them, in its primeval form, unknowable and dreadful but to the astute Devas, she looked like an all mother, who had come to absolve them.

Ambika along with other goddesses, without delay, cleaved through the many clones and before any blood could fall on the ground, this time, Kali began to drink it, like an ocean, consuming the incoming red rivers and fountains of blood spurting through the open wounds. She opened her mouths like a vortex in the cosmos, guzzling down the multitudes of red drafts, into a void, nullifying all possibility for the blood drops to create any more clones.

Raktveej knew that his time has come, a relief enveloped his fiery heart, his body was completely wounded, drained of not just blood but bereft of any desire to fight any further, he had offered all his energy to the all Mother of time, and she had put it where it belonged, reinvigorating the cycles of life.

Beholding Kali's aura, he went back to a state where everything ceased to exist, no identities, and no roles, no asuras or suras, just the substance which births life, a purity of thought washed over him. The last fountain of blood which contained much agony, was calmed as it entered the portal opened by Kali's mouth, going to a place which was brimming with the wisdom of death.

Devi Ambika summoned the sudarshan chakra, the energy disk, which was made from the remains of the sun itself and hurled it towards Raktveej, the rays of which, touched him from a distance, like a song from a faraway world, taking over the noise, severing his head, and moving him into the beautiful darkness, where he would forever rest in the peaceful nothingness, a proper retribution to his tormented soul.

As his lifeless body fell to the ground, Kali seemed like a water bearing luminous sky, framed by the effulgence of the many goddesses around her. The blood which swirled in the bowl of fire, created new life and her garlands of skulls swayed with the wind, letting the lost souls enter through the sockets and being cleansed by the invisible fires. Her deft hand held the heavy long sword and the multiple strewn bodies embellished her, like unmade matter, inert in peaceful formlessness.

Her eyes were still glinting with rage, and there was something profound in her aura.
Those who saw her with humility in their hearts, saw that, her hands gestured the Abhaya Mudra—state of forgiveness and fearlessness. She was the all Mother, treating both her children, life and death equally, nothing was hidden in her demeanor, all facets, negative or positive, calm or cruel, radiant or dark, animalistic or imaginary, temporal or transcendental, expressed themselves without bias.

Brahma was looking through his portal, and was reminded when Kali, had gone berserk, in her rage after killing another asura in a different Yuga, called Daruka, perhaps to teach a lesson, for losing their self to indulgence. When Kali had pruned through anyone who stood in her path, she seemed like a tsunami, treating everyone with the same indifference with which they treated nature. He thought, how most fainted seeing her ferocious appearance and only a handful who unwillingly stood their ground, turned numb in fear, getting decimated in the process.

Time and death are the two truths. Gods too had abused their role and power, and yet, this ability to realize their mistake and correct the course of their actions, made them gods.
Brahma, had understood the underlying meaning of her anger and remembered how she was finally calmed.

In her unstoppable carnage Kali was stopped by a vision of the calming blue one. Shiva himself lay down in her path, unlike others who were either terrified or fearing for their lives, he simply embraced his non-being, and was under her feet.
Without her, even he was 'Shava' without life, for she was energy incarnate, which instills life into everything.
As Brahma reminisced this, he made the sky shower myriad flowers over Goddess Kali for saving them from what seemed an impossible predicament.

Now remained the last confrontation with the two asura brothers, among them Nishumbha had already arrived at the battlefield.

He knew all too well looking at the unblemished Devi, who had slain all valiant asuras so far, that his tryst with fate was about to reach its end.

With his last bit of resilience he would fight to serve his brother.

Nishumbha spoke coaxed by the remnants of his blind arrogance,

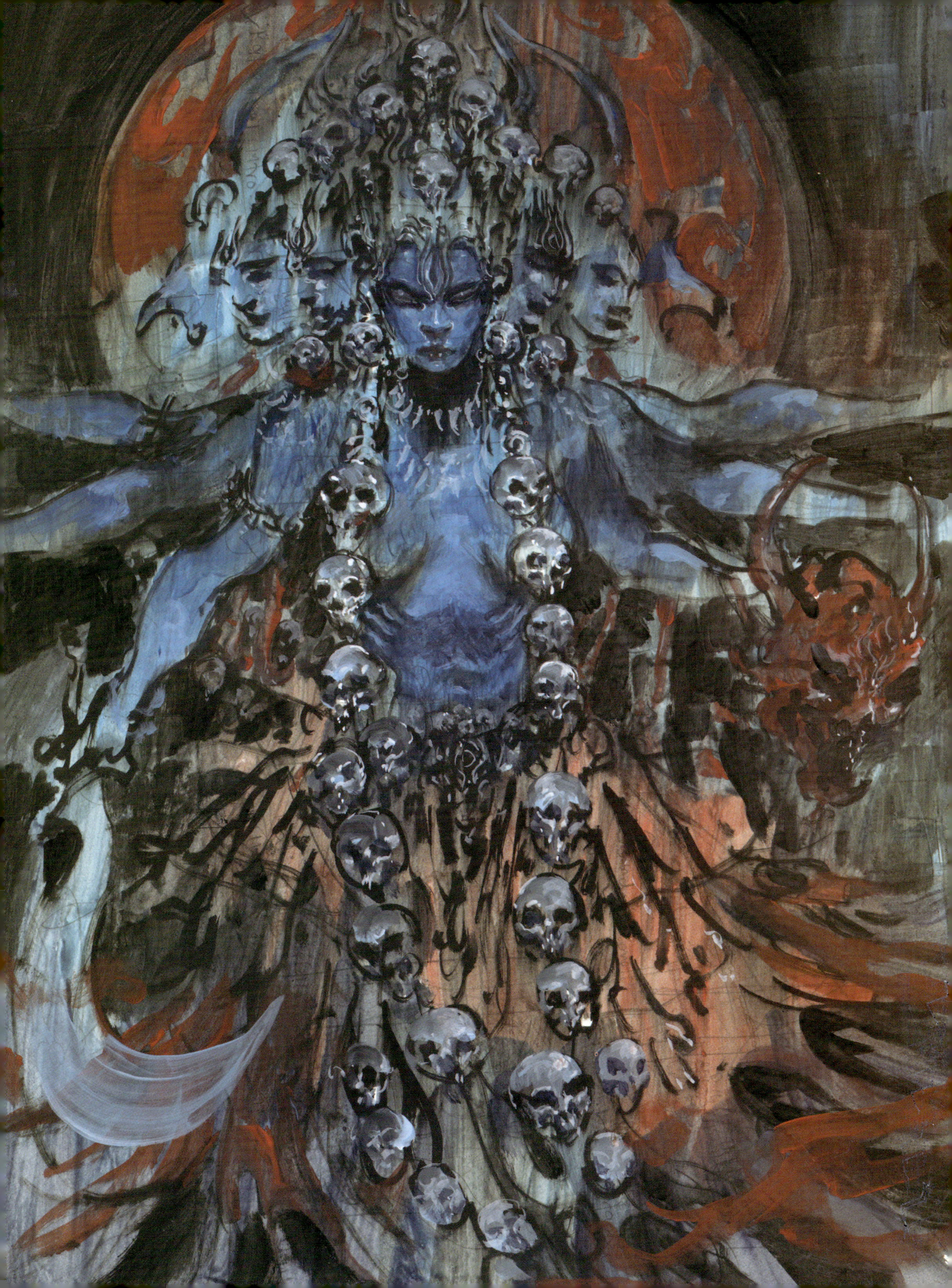

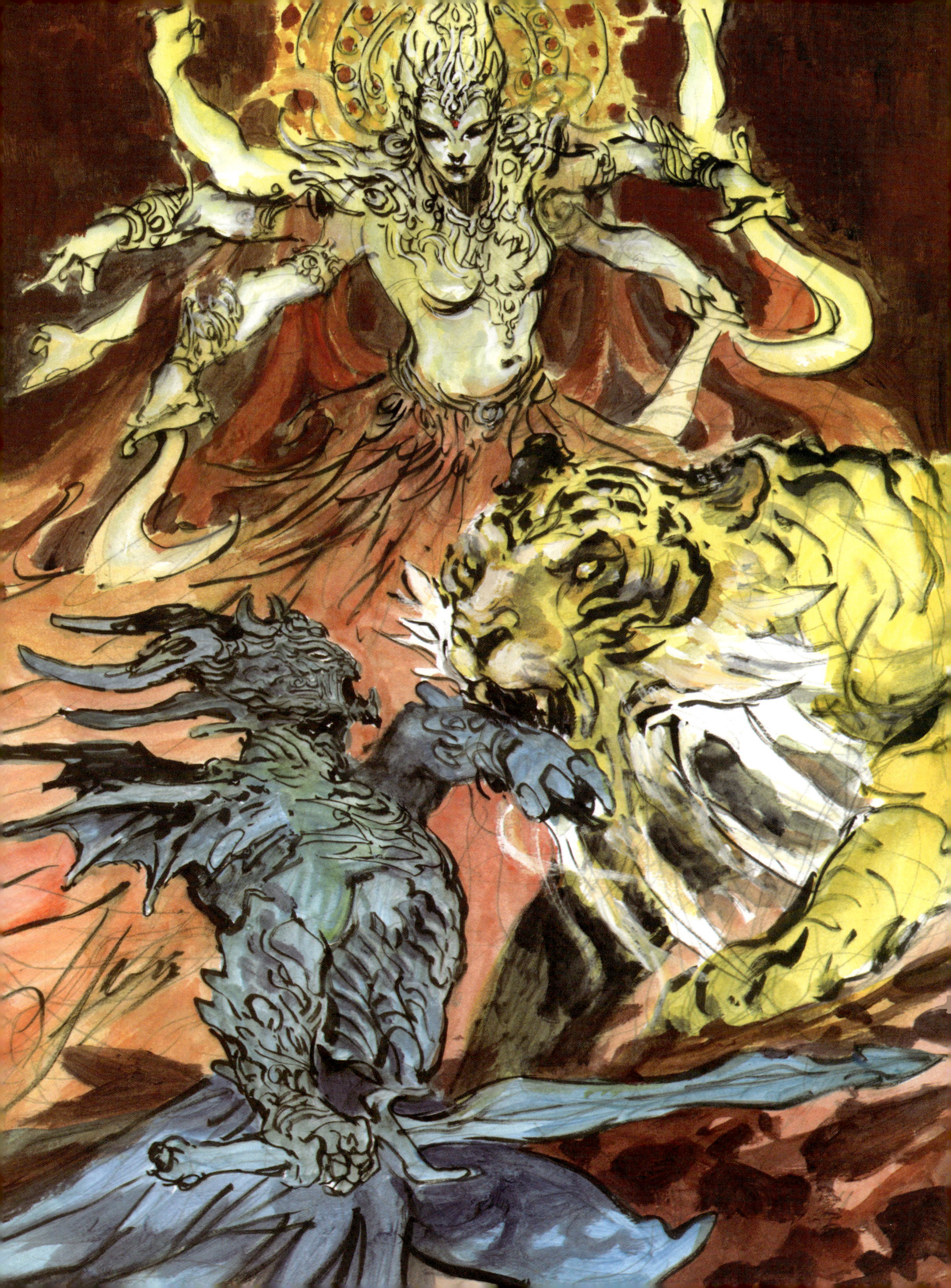

"O you terrible one, your illusions can fool all but not me. I've slain thousands of devas like I have felled many trees and I've killed many tigers like the one you ride, for mere entertainment. With my chariot, which moves at the speed of light. First, I will tear through the heart of your tiger and then the rest of you."

The Devi said nothing, as words didn't matter at this juncture, she remained stoic in her presence, like depths of the great ocean which remain unwavered by the fluctuation of the waves. This irritated Nishumbha further and he launched an unprecedented attack on the Devi.

The entire army swarmed at the Devi, blaring the conches into a cacophony, which was infused by their growing nervousness and mindlessly shooting spears and arrows at her, which was no different than hurling meaningless words, but the Devi remained calm and her breath itself, deflected all incoming weapons.

She touched the forehead of Kesri, who had fought valiantly in the battle alongside her, healed his wounds and unleashed him in the name of all the animals killed, trees chopped and scars the Earth had endured because of asuric tendencies, of impunity, greed and ego. The tiger Kesri, stood like a mountain in the way of the approaching asura, deflecting all arrows, fast beyond lightning, destroying Nishumbha's chariot into pieces and before its fragments could even fall on the ground Kesri's teeth pierced through the asura's heart, ripping him to pieces, Nishumbha too, with his last bit of life, understood his mistakes, and asked, to be amalgamated back into the cycles of nature.

The Devi, to a seeking heart had always given absolution, and so in the dream of his death, she made him, become part of the many trees and animals Nishumbha had damaged and killed, he swam back into the innocence, from where life seemed abundant, nothing to win, and no glory to achieve, just immense bliss of listening to the Earth's songs again.

The war was reaching its ordained end, the tired asura army had exhausted their energies, they were startled to see, how the Devi out of benevolence was conducting the energy of the slain asuras, back into the natural cycles.

Shumbha's voice heaving with anger, who had just witnessed the death of his loving brother from a distance, interrupted this transformative spectacle. Arriving in his shrieking chariot, decked with several illusionary armaments, which had beguiled and defeated the gods, he roared, savagely at the goddess.

"I did all of this, to get your love, am I not worthy of it? I have defeated mightiest gods and I rule the heavens. I lack nothing, yet you find faults in me? I wanted you at all costs, isn't that proof of my passion towards you? I've conquered all, but you remain aloof to that, why?"

Devi echoed her mind, and spoke with a voice which went reverberating across realms,
"You may have conquered the heavens, but you couldn't conquer your senses.
Your inner being is in shambles, how can you then understand love?

I don't dwell in the never-ending desires, I live in the intents, in the acts of kindness.
I'm not in the love which can be possessed, but in the one which abounds all, freely and lovingly.
Neither I'm the body you see, nor the beauty, yet I am, all of what matter makes."

"The beauty, which radiates through the body is not of the body alone, it comes from the heart and mind. You couldn't see past this physical self, to be able to perceive the inner beauty, which is what brings true contentment."

"To fall in love with me is to fall in love with life, with the earth, with nature. Love is not to possess, not to own, not to prove a point, but to cease proving anything, reigning back the ego, to go on a journey, to know courage, will, and faith. O king of asuras, hearts cannot be won by force, they cannot be imprisoned like the body, true love cannot be bought and be made a personal indulgence. Once you know it, there will be no other way you'd treat anyone with, no seat of heaven is bigger than that, all those conquests will not matter to such a one."

Shumbha: ... but I was truly in awe of your demeanor, there is no woman equal to you. Tell me, is there any who can equal you in any form or shape?

Devi, smiled and said...
"I'm All the Women. Which one am I not? They are all me and I'm them, from us has come this world, this entire existence, everything born is a woman in spirit. Everything through which the prana moves is me, what is not me, all of it, has my presence, for those who love, I'm in everything."

Shumbha, upon hearing the words of Devi, saw her differently now, his ego was absolved, and his entire existence started to sink into a sea of realizations. He saw in her vision, his long years of penance, where he had loved living simply alongside the beings who meditated with him,

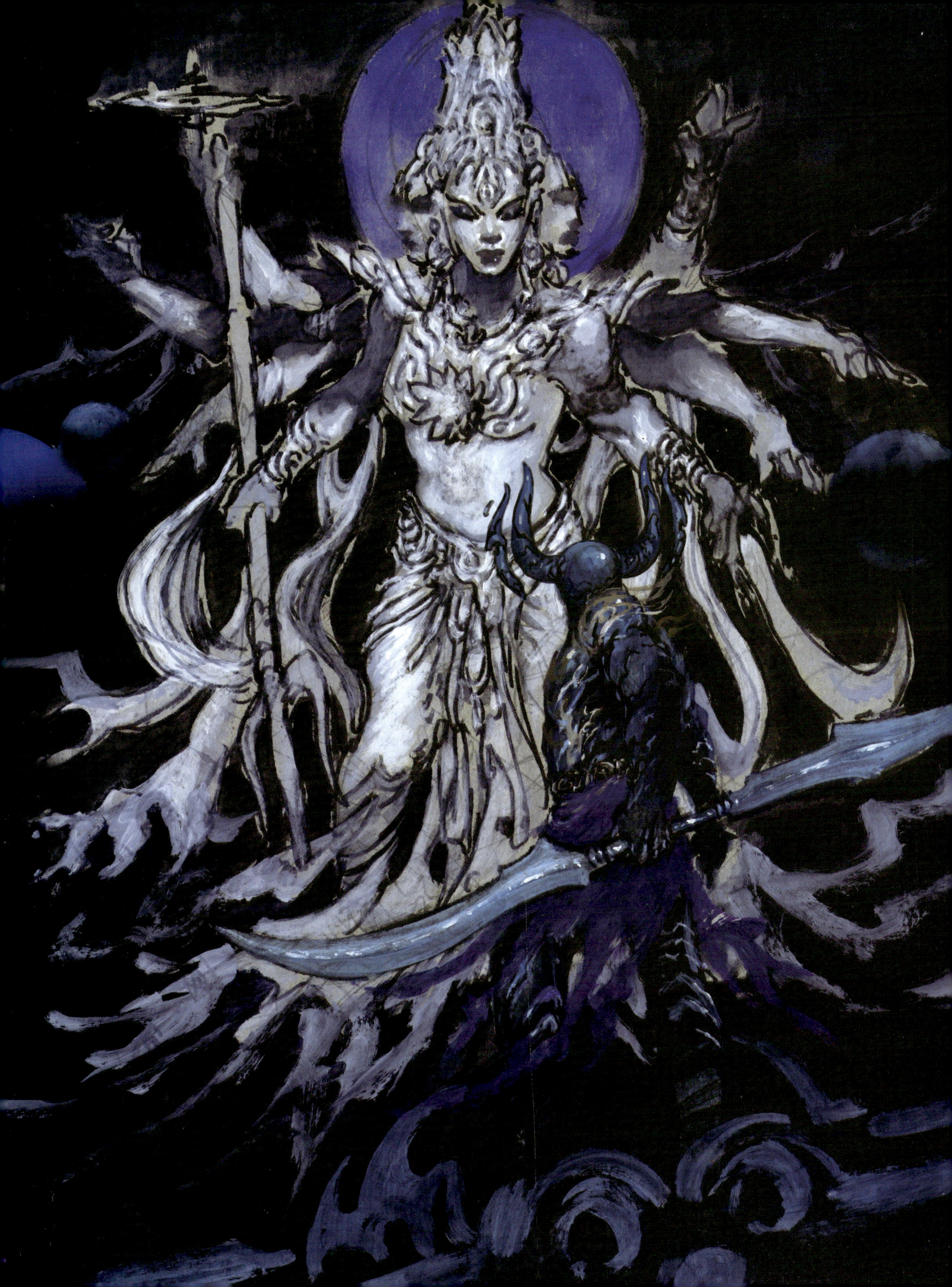

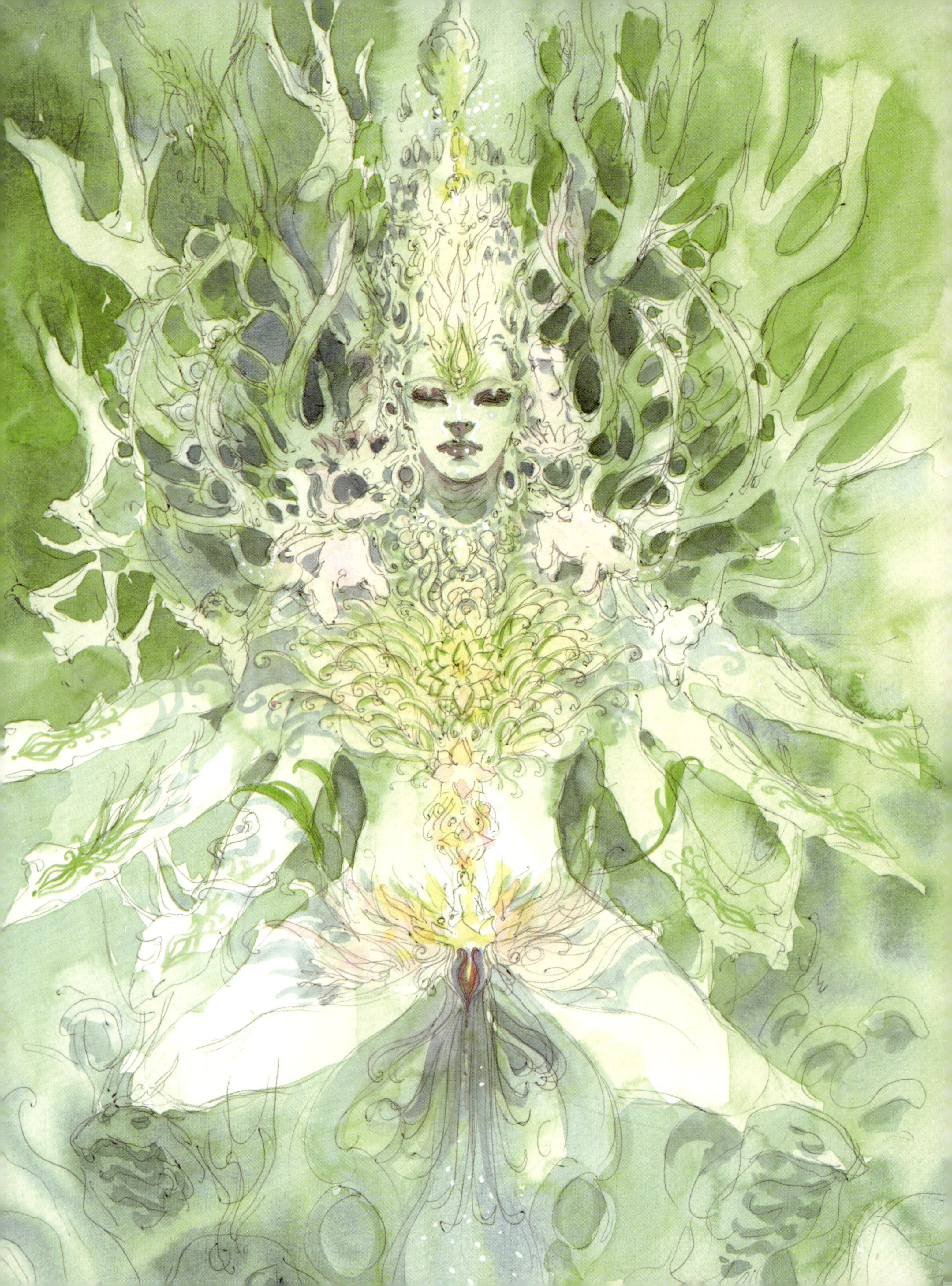

the joy he had felt, and the beauty which had touched him, in front of which all his lust for power and vanity seemed frivolous, meaningless. The birds began chirping again in his heart, the leaves blossomed again, the winters coursed through his bones, giving it the strength to keep going, and all of this which he began feeling, was because of her. Instead of weapons, he saw her many arms made of life giving trees, protecting the most ancient rivers and balancing many worlds through cosmic strings, there was no war, no weapons, a cyclic dream presented itself in her form, where everything moved in harmony with each other.

Finally, he understood what immortality was, it was to celebrate life in all its ways, to identify with nothing and know that, it is all what we can observe and experience, and be, is the essence which pervades, moving through this transient existence, not to win or conquer but to become love itself.

All the goddesses looked like a tree of life, each of her manifestation had amalgamated together to form this majestic vision.

The pandering asura army stood with their hearts open, hands in reverence. The, devas too, for a moment forgot the victory, and both like brothers, blended into a harmonious space, surrounding the great vision. There was no separation, no division.

She returned to her meditative state, invisible, smiling through all spores of existence, as the world reconnected back with its music through her.

REMAINED

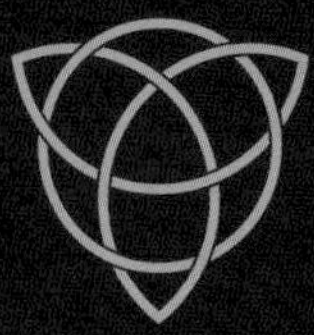

She sat, in that dread, unafraid, and became the forest.
In a place where fire did not show the way, and the water couldn't move,
Where the rain hung like a wound above,
yearning for that touch of life,
This land, this grotesque being,
Who shall be its healing embrace?
A drop fell from the bruised cloud,
The lamenting one gave it away,
The lungs started to wheeze,
Faintly remembering their travels,
a resilience stirred up the spirit again,
Drawing on that forgotten strength.
Through her, an effulgence for the first time entered this wretched land,
For she was unafraid and unwavering,
Like a cloud wiping the rust off the river stones, and filling the ponds with loving bliss,
A life renewed the cadaver of the forest yet again,
She stood her ground,
The last of anger slashed at her, but she made that into flowers, and took all the wounds upon herself,
The fire lit the paths again to those astray,
She returned the water to the clouds, healing their bruises,
The gift must be shared with all, she said.
In a place where no one dared step,
She sat, in that dread, unafraid,
And she remained.

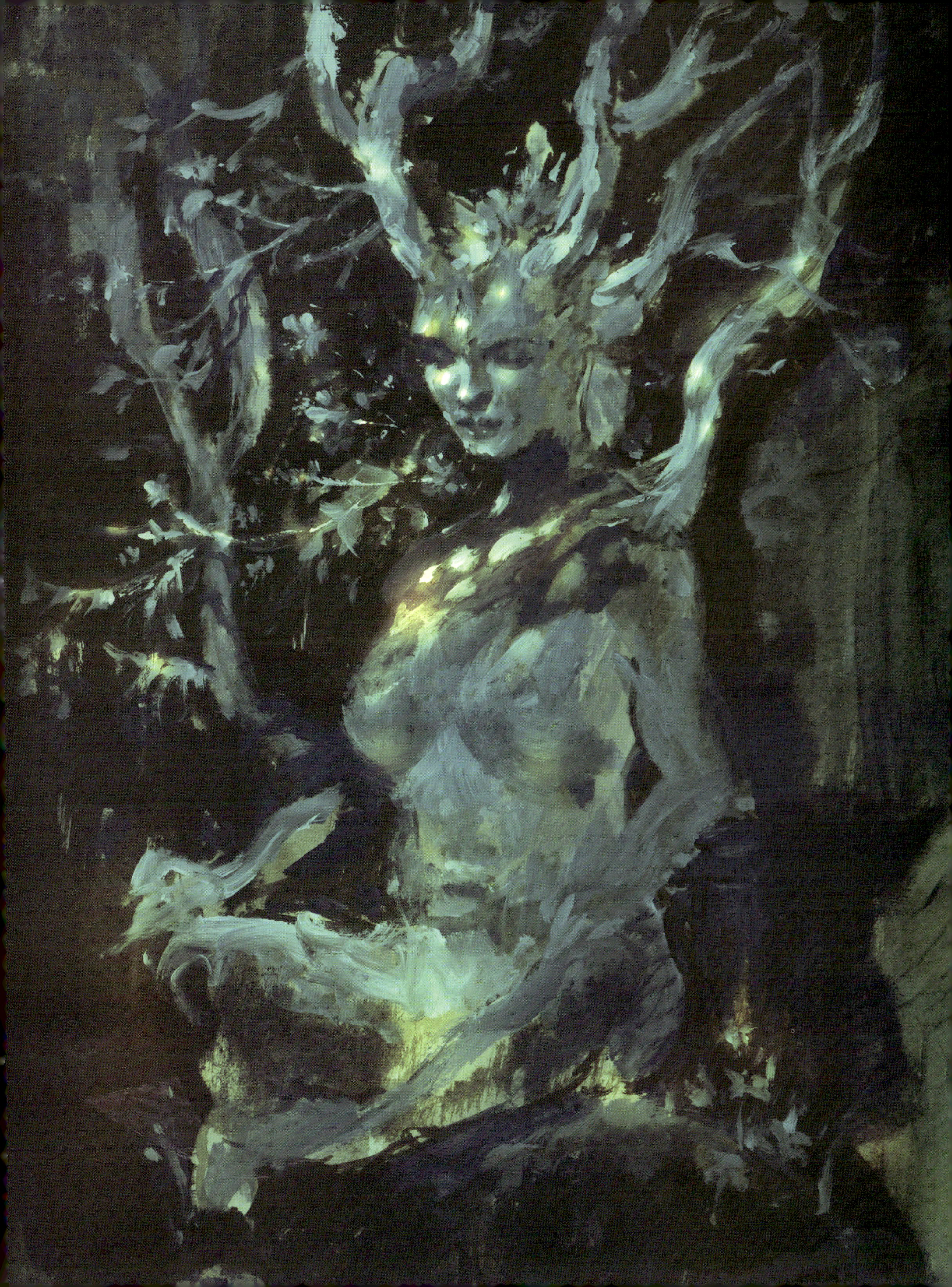

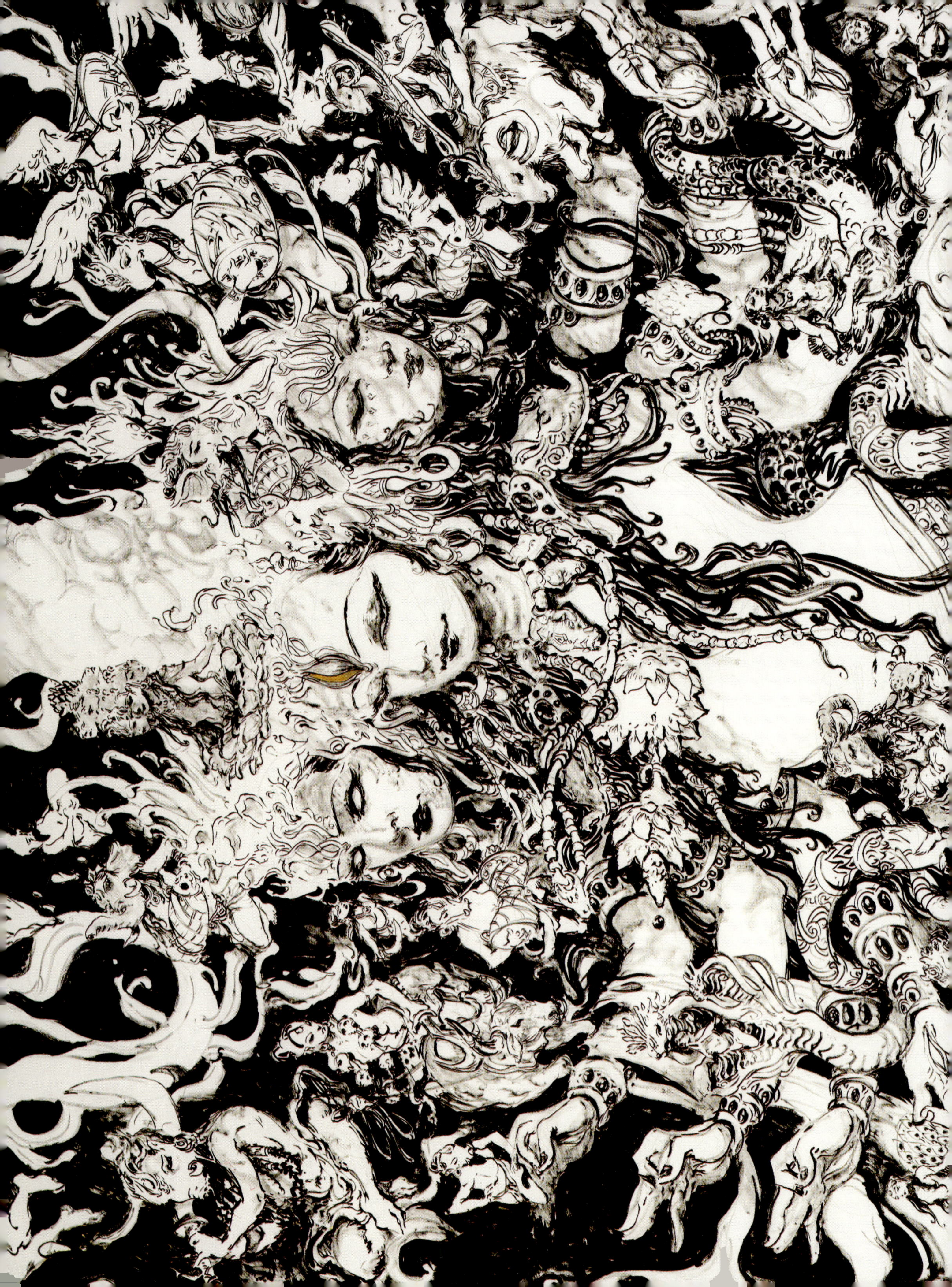

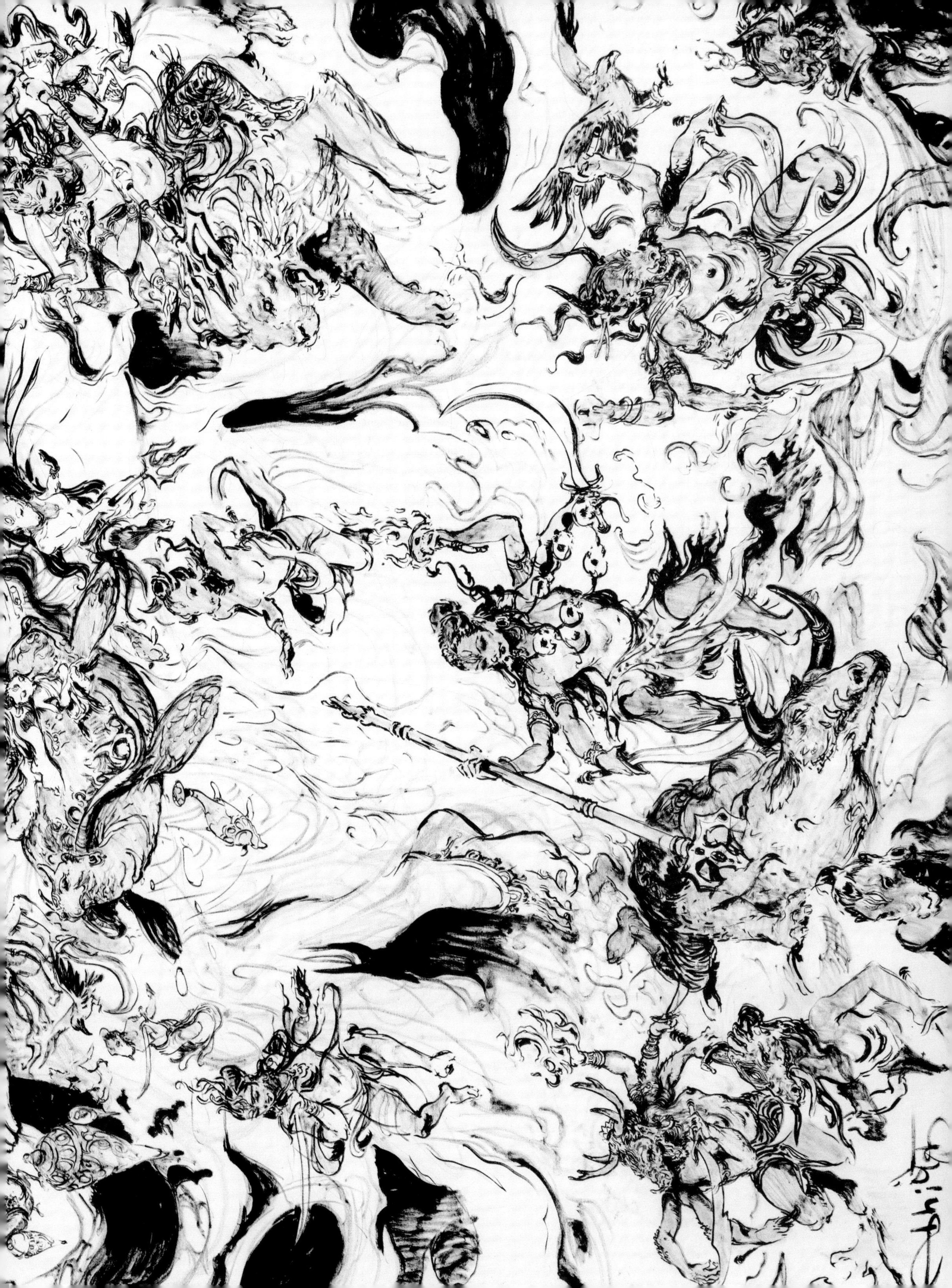

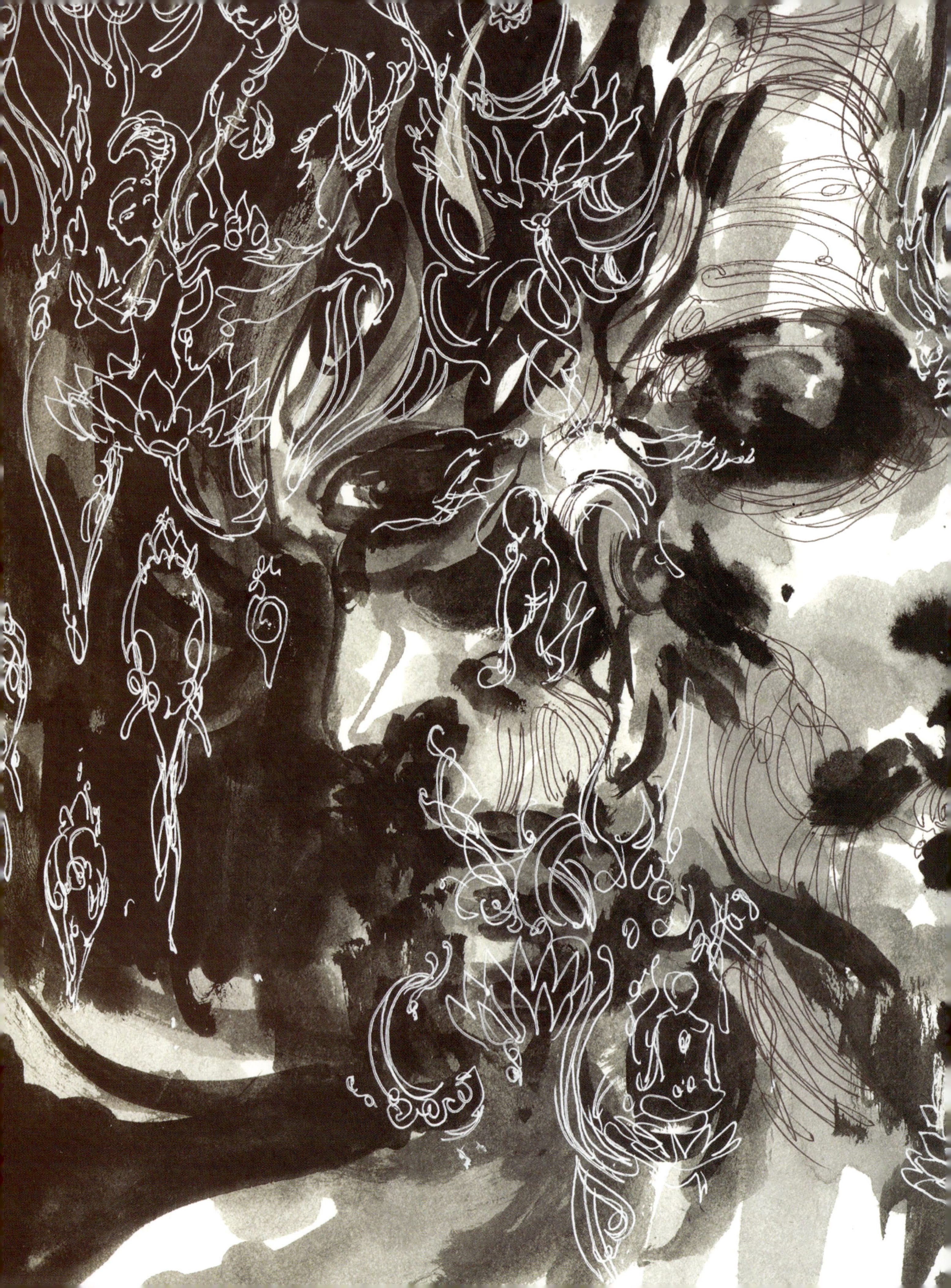

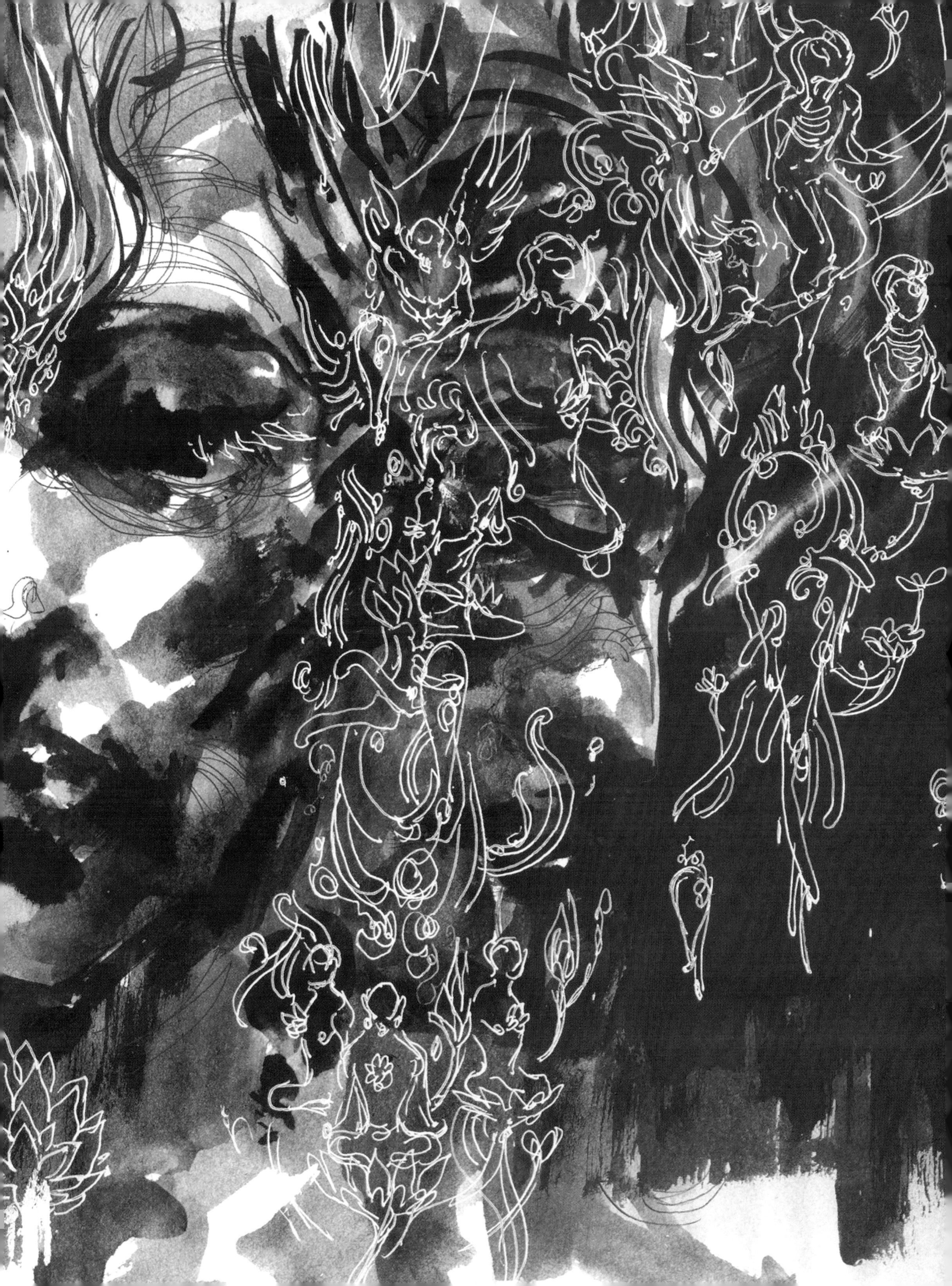

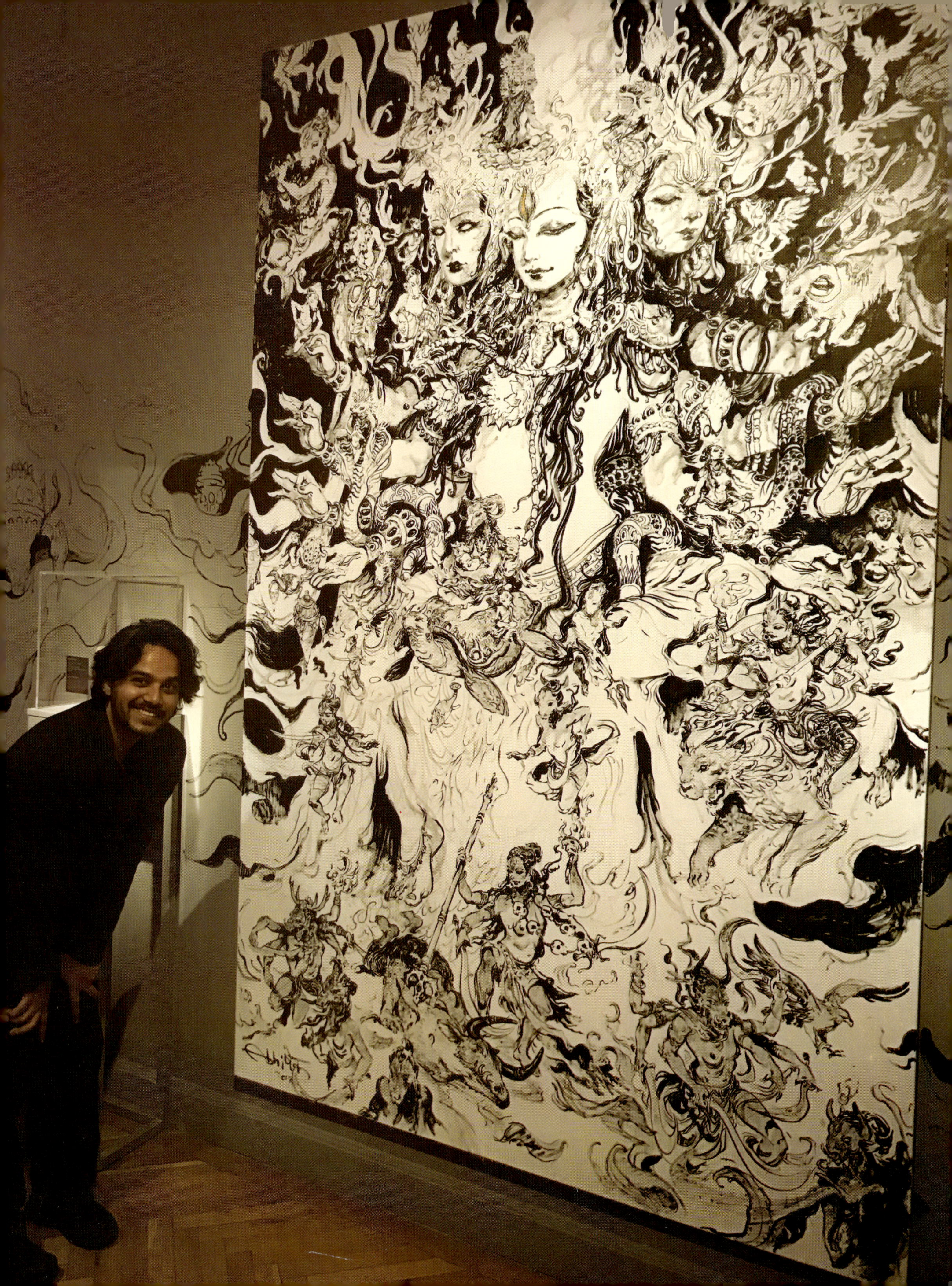

AFTERWORD

If you're reading this, you have my Gratitude!!!

The literature on the Goddess is both immense and esoteric, not that it is hard to grasp but without a sense of service or entering the ecological spirit, it cannot be internalized. Just like the many streams that make up an ocean, this book is cultivated from myriad literary and experiential influences. The venerated story of the Goddess from Devi-Bhagwatam purana, provided a foundation to unravel and celebrate Vedantic, tantric, folk, ecological, scientific and meditative ideas, with the hope that they can open a portal for further discovery.

Though I began working on this book about three years ago, certain moments of questioning and unlearning, became my true beginnings; one such strand which really made me ponder about the spirit of the story was, that I've not inherited the biological or social struggles of a woman or that large portions of their histories are not written by them, all of these conscious realizations, allowed me to dismantle a lot of my own presumptions and dispositions (as much as I could) and helped me realign, unlearn and rebuild my perception, starting from the resounding yearning of the earth to the most recent women reformative movements, my connection with my own grandmothers, with the animals and nature all contributed to this exploration and that's the story.

While there are some large-scale paintings in this book, still a lot of art has been made to compliment the long narrative, and that put us in a tough spot with time, moving back and forth between the writing and art before putting it all together. Most of this art is created in the traditional manner, something earthy, a prayer.

To, Gaurav & Prashant and the Wonder House team, you have my gratitude for being the most patient and best partner on this journey. Thank you to all and everyone who has supported my work and path, to all in whom the feminine divine thrives, to you, I dedicate this book.

The next book *Sarvam*, the last of this trilogy, will conclude our love letter to the ancient Indian wisdom. A different realm that will be!

As the river summons, we follow our path to the shoreless ocean.

Love & Light
Abhi

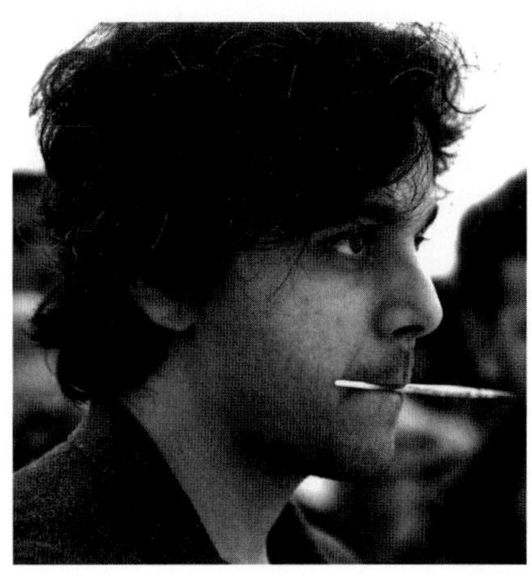

ABOUT

Abhishek Singh's work is acclaimed around the world for its unique style and storytelling. His books, Krishna – a journey within and Namaha – in the land of Gods & Goddesses, have been praised and cherished for their presentation of ancient wisdom literature.

His work has been exhibited in various prestigious museums & places like LACMA, Asia Society and Burning Man and he has performed various live drawings across the globe, blending social themes with stories of the Earth, myths and philosophy, like Shiva in Varanasi, Message from the Trees–Ojas Art, India, Goddess story–Ferenc Hopp Museum, Budapest, Elephant Rain–Michael C. Carlos Museum, Atlanta, Yugas–Guadalajara, Mexico, Dialogue with Death–JLF, Jaipur & various others.

Abhishek volunteers with the elephants, animal shelters & whenever possible retreats for a meditation trek in the Himalayas.

Initial Book Design - Rachita Rakyan
Photo on left - Vicky Roy
Afterword - Thank you to Wonder House Team

Picture Credits

Thank you Ferenc Hopp Museum of Asiatic Arts, Budapest, Hungary, for providing us with the image of the big scale painting: Trilokeshwari- Realms of the goddess.

Ojas Art, Delhi, India, Thank you for the continued support. Anubhav much gratitude for your incredible friendship & Contribution. To all who welcomed the work, commissioned paintings and supported me on my path.

Immense gratitude.

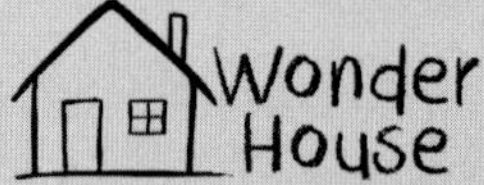

(An imprint of Prakash Books)

contact@wonderhousebooks.com

©Abhishek Singh

All rights reserved. No part of this book may be reproduced or transmitted in any form by any means, electronic or mechanical, including photocopying and recording, or by any information storage and retrieval system except as may be expressly permitted in writing by the publisher.

ISBN : 9789354406911

Printed 2025